THE CLANDESTINE COUNTESS

CLOAKS AND COUNTESSES BOOK TWO

JUDITH LYNNE

JUDITH LYNNE

BOOKS BY JUDITH LYNNE

<u>Lords and Undefeated Ladies</u>

Not Like a Lady

The Countess Invention

What a Duchess Does

Crown of Hearts

He Stole the Lady

No Titled Lady

<u>Maids Done Waiting</u>

The Lord Trap

The Lady Escape (Forthcoming)

<u>Cloaks and Countesses</u>

The Caped Countess

The Clandestine Countess

The Castaway Countess (Forthcoming)

<u>Ladies' Own Bakery</u>

The Regency romance comedy serial

GENTLE WARNINGS AND DISCLAIMERS

The Clandestine Countess contains mentions of violence, orphaning, child neglect, attempted or contemplated sexual assault, and substance abuse and addiction, as well as killing animals for food. Like all Judith Lynne books, it has a happily ever after; we mention these things, which are only parts of the story, so that if they are not your cup of tea today you may peacefully pass them by.

Historical notes at the end refer to real historical facts and persons who inspired parts of the story, but this is a work of fiction and all names, characters, places and incidents either are products of the author's imagination or are used fictiously, with no intended resemblance to actual events or locales or persons, living or dead.

PREFACE

My dear readers,

Followers of *The Caped Count* have seen Lady Winpole's villainy revealed. She has allies, and plans. Perhaps they can only be foiled by a similarly cold heart.

Dan Fox has waited a lifetime to be different. He has dreams of his own, and a young woman for whom he dreams them.

A young woman of many talents, whose heart you may judge for yourself.

Your obedient servant,
Judith Lynne

PROLOGUE

*L*ondon, 1802

A lady did not like to admit that she'd been startled into attacking.

But everyone had limits. When her ancient husband wheezed, "I can't help myself, Belly," he sealed his fate.

Lady Winpole never looked twice at the fleeing, sobbing maid. Only at him, his fragile shoulders bent in over his swollen middle.

He could have persuaded her to abandon her resolution. He could have moved her to pity him for spending his last strength overpowering one more maid. He might have even tried to laugh away the nickname he knew she hated. She might have dismissed it as one more stupid comment on having a short, stout wife.

But then he said, "You should retire to Bristol," and everything she had not let herself feel for seventeen years rushed through her.

This was her house. Her name was Arabella, not Belly. And she was not going to spend her remaining years shuffling cards alone in Bristol.

"Lord Winpole." It only acknowledged his existence as she went to the window to look out as if she were thinking, as if there were anything left to think about.

Then she moved back to his side, put the stopper back in his crystal bottle of port, and looked down at his shining head with its last wisps of hair.

Should she mention how she'd always deferred to him, showed him the respect he demanded when he gave none?

He was looking after the maid who had fled, not listening to her.

So she didn't bother.

Once she pulled the pillow tight around his head, stuffing it into his mouth and nose with her other hand, there was nothing left to discuss.

Even less once he went limp.

She dropped the pillow to the floor as she crossed to the door. Someone would pick it up.

"George," she calmly called to a footman. "Lord Winpole has had a fit. Fetch the physician."

Alone in the apartments—alive, her husband had barely counted as company; he certainly didn't count dead—Lady Winpole sailed through his dressing room into hers.

A sea of possibilities lay at her feet.

She closed the door to her dressing room, settling into her silver-damasked settee.

The blue Turkish tile table held a Pandora doll even shorter than she was, fifteen porcelain inches tall. It had come from France before the revolution, wearing a *robe Anglaise* Lady Winpole adored, all posy embroidery and lace.

Most Pandoras traveled back and forth between drapers and ladies, demonstrating the latest fashions. Lady Winpole kept hers in gowns of the old style, the gowns she herself still wore, viewing the graceful, long-necked doll as a preferable sort of mirror.

She liked the old styles of wide wire skirts and tiers of ruffles. They built a woman from the ground up. New girls clamored for shapeless, girlish Empire gowns, and soon even women her age would wear them.

So would Lady Winpole. She did what others expected... in public.

"Pandora," she addressed the doll on her linens chest as if they faced each other over breakfast, "the new Lord Winpole will sail for India." Her son hadn't been home in years; armed with Winpole money, he would no doubt go to the other side of the earth. "The revolution is fading. With slavery back in the islands, sugar competition will be fierce. I wonder what else will sell for high prices."

She knew her husband's will very well. He had only left her a widow's portion.

If she wished to do anything with her remaining years other than shuffle those cards in Bristol, she must increase her fortune drastically.

"It's obvious," she told the doll, "we're going to need a lot more."

CHAPTER ONE

*L*ondon, *1813*

Stop offering me everything I want.

Years of painful climbing, scrabbling, *clawing* for what he needed, and now Fitz offered to put all Dan's dreams within reach.

Rich puppets like him could do things like that, and that only made Dan hate them more.

"Lady Winpole kills people who cross her. And I can't afford to be killed." He gave Fitz his off-center scowl, puckered by an old scar over the side of his lip and an oft-broken nose. Under his sharp black brows, it usually shut people up.

He suspected it had no effect on Lord Henry Fitzwilliam, seated across from him in a sticky corner of the Bottle and Bird, for two reasons. One was Fitz' notorious good nature, preferring to conquer everyone around him with smiles and questions.

The other was that Fitz was a known friend of the Caped Count, and for that reason alone no one dared touch him.

He was offensively cheery. "Yes? Is there a Mrs. Dan after all? Baby Dans? A Dan dog? You know I'm dying to hear."

Dan remained packed defensively in his chair, back to the wall, watching the room. He'd been raised a cautious thief, and Fitz wrote for the papers. Anything Dan told him would wind up in *Bridle's Gazette.* Dan wouldn't explain his obligations even if he could, but that never stopped Fitz trying; Dan ignored it. "I've seen men hanged for thieving, while she does what she likes. She *offends* me. But I'm through."

Fitz scoffed.

Dan had to make him understand. "No one swears complaints against her. Not the blackmailed Treasury man, not the bribed shipping clerks, and *definitely* not the maid who left the night her husband died. Her I rode the back of a mail carriage to bloody Sussex to see. Said *Lady Winpole* to her face; she almost fainted. Hell of a time with her husband, he tried to throw me out. Winpole doesn't fight her enemies, she *destroys* them. And I can't afford that."

He couldn't afford to wait much longer to wait his fortune. Five long years he'd tried to make money the honest way. He was honest, no longer a thief; he was also poor.

And poor wouldn't do for righting the wrongs he had to right.

He could reach across this table and strangle the smile off this bastard; but that wouldn't accomplish anything, wouldn't be any pleasure. He'd never enjoyed hurting anyone. He'd only done it to protect the light in his life.

She needed more, much more, than for him to give in to the momentary pleasure of releasing his frustration.

Fitz stretched his long legs under the sticky table. "Records are everything. You must see her ledger."

"Mate..." Dan hunched forward. "You think it'll say *illegal permits, thirty pounds? Murder, twenty?*"

His scowl's failure to repel Fitz was annoying, and a bit worrying. It usually sent people scurrying, even in the orphanage. He'd got the scar that pulled his lip up into the hint of a sneer as a child. But he'd been born with the scowl.

But Fitz just grinned. "Aw, are we mates, Dan? That's the nicest thing you've ever said to me. Someday you'll tell me what *you're* hiding."

"Nothing."

Fitz made a big fake nod, eyes sweeping over all of Dan. "Worn clothes, chasing thieves, trading secrets, with a clergyman's accent. Parish boy at Harrow?"

Typical for Fitz to think someone had given Dan charity. "Could be."

"Well, parish boy," Fitz went on after a big swig of ale, "you remember Mr. Storey, her bookkeeper. He's going east, and he never parts with his books. I can put you in the same house with that ledger."

"I don't want to *be* in the same house with that ledger."

"Show me another sneak who can read ledgers, and I'll leave you to glower in peace."

He even took the pleasure out of glowering.

Fitz peered over his ale. "For all your money-grubbing, you helped save my life. You didn't get paid for that. You've got noble charity in you; how do I enlist its help?"

Dan's heart thumped. His instinct was to fade farther back in the shadows of the Bottle and Bird.

He'd joined the Caped Count's rescue of Fitz that night because of the street women caught up in it. Helping them was pure habit. The last thing he needed was for anyone to discover why.

The next-to-last thing was for anyone to discover he had a heart.

He muttered, "Haven't you ever atoned for your sins?"

Fitz' tankard slammed down.

He gave Dan a silent stare, which Dan gave right back.

Dan was better at it.

"Of course I have." Fitz' smile was gone and his voice rough. "I've been to war. What have *you* done that needs atonement?"

Things I can never put right.

That, Dan didn't say.

Instead he said, "King and country can go hang. They'd put me in Bridewell for stealing bread, but they'll never touch Lady Winpole, even with evidence. She's one of their own."

"So you know Bridewell from inside?" When Dan scowled again, Fitz pulled his own reins. "Sorry. Habit." He leaned in; Dan didn't move.

Fitz' words were low and urgent. "It's dangerous chess, but the ledger's just one move. Just tell me what you find. You'll be well paid; you don't have to play the game through."

Dan had to remind his stuttering heart that money was everyone's weakness. Fitz didn't know. No one alive knew why Dan needed money.

Dan's every waking moment, ever since he could remember, had been devoted to protecting one person. And *protection* meant *money*.

After five grueling years, he was nowhere close to having enough.

Fitz' offer would put him there, if he survived.

For five years his life had been locked in ice. Fitz' money would melt everything. Dan couldn't finish his plan—give her a wealthy life, a *safe* life, and keep his damn distance—without seeing her again.

Because for this, he'd need her help.

Damn it all, Lady Winpole was going to cut him in half like a deck of cards. "I'll do it for five hundred pounds plus any expenses."

The number made Fitz blink. "You're joking."

Dan gave him a look that said *you know damn well I don't joke about money.*

"Very well." Fitz gave in with a speed belying both his wealth and his generous impulse not to haggle with a man who might soon be dead. "You'll have to hop. Our beloved Mr. Storey leaves in five days, and you'll need a bit of training to take the position I've arranged."

"I won't be some fart-catching footman."

"Hell, no. That takes far too *much* training, and there's no time. You'll be a secretary." Point won, he lounged back and sipped his ale. "Think you can manage that?"

Dan could.

Theft was as easy for him as drinking ale for Fitz. It was reassuring to face Mr. Storey rather than Lady Winpole herself, but a lone thief was a dead thief. It was the first rule he'd ever learned.

He needed a partner. One with polish, or who could fake polish. Dan knew gutters, but drawing rooms were different.

He tried to tell himself that he wanted her help because she was the only person he knew with natural grace who could pretend to good manners as well as pick pockets. Loathed himself for even thinking of asking, for planning to put her in danger, when he wanted the money to buy her safety.

But the truth was Dan had lived much of his life on nothing but cold air. He knew when he was hungry.

He *wanted* this, to talk to her again. He was hungry for it. He was starving.

He was pathetic, that was what he was, and to top it off, they hadn't parted well. Her temper didn't cool. It started in ice and stayed there.

"I don't suppose you care I'll have to cross bridges I've already burned."

The geniality drained out of Fitz's face, showing its edges.

"I didn't fight the French Empire to make Lady Winpole rich. She and I have too much history, and I have all the scars. She and Storey both know my face; I can't get near her. So if you burned the bridges, unburn them."

CHAPTER TWO

She had the audience in her hand, in her pocket. That ought to be enough.

Slowly, Bess sank to her knees, hands falling gracefully open against the floorboards, fingers gently curling up. It took tremendous strength to hold her body there like a statue of a broken woman, half-collapsed in despair at the loss of her true love.

Everyone loved a broken woman.

The audience leaned toward her, motionless, breathless, a million-headed animal completely under her control.

She'd captured them during the mad picnic Dido held to celebrate her newfound love. Silly Dido.

Bess had given the queen a fiery energy, drawing on the power of crushed-pearl face paint, on black stockings and gloves that outlined her limbs and promised more but never delivered.

The audience had chattered and laughed at the picnic's beginning, but slowly they'd come under her spell, eyes on her, *hearts* on her as she'd given them the image of a woman, already emanating the power of her crown, discovering the power of desire as well.

She'd pulled out of them the haze of lust that hung in the air with the candle smoke, as easily as she could have picked their pockets.

For a second, it was enough.

Now she trembled on the floor, drawing from inside herself the last drops of all the abandonment, the hopelessness, on which she'd built this dance.

Her paste jewels glittered in the footlights, for one shining moment, the center of the world. She was the center of a globe of silence she'd made, seducing, convincing the audience it was for them. But it was for her.

Outside the theater walls, as if nature itself colluded in the staging, a roll of thunder, distant, muffled, punctuated her final collapse.

Riveted, everyone remained silent.

It should have been enough. It was the culmination of months, *years* of learning the *ballet,* training a body honed in more dangerous pursuits to look delicate, desirable, and when necessary, weak. Of learning to project the person she wanted them to see out into the audience, all the way to the rafters. Learning how to draw them in.

She told herself it *was* enough, because she refused to search the audience for his face one more time.

Finally the silence broke; some goat-kneed weakling clapped. A flood of noise followed as Bess rose, curtsied. They loved the part where they made noise, but Bess didn't need it. They truly adored her in their silence.

At least, the *her* they thought they knew.

The lead *ballerino* returned in a stately *pas de basque,* helped her rise. He was perfect for her purposes: good-natured, easily bored, and always waiting to disappear for a drink between scenes.

And generous. He didn't mind sharing the audience's attention. He paraded her off-stage like a delicate flower, a jewel.

The Tourmaline, the ballet's new favorite.

The power of it all thrummed through her veins. She'd *had* them. An entire audience in her pocket, in her *hand*. She concentrated on that, pushed the empty part of her down. She'd had them, they'd been *hers*.

Her legs trembled as she reached the ropes in the wings that held the scenery aloft, but it was normal to be a little light-headed after such a performance.

Preparing to begin another.

In the wings, where illusions went to collapse, she ducked between stained boards and ropes to the enormous baskets stacked there after the third act's wild picnic. Applause covered the sound of her whisper. "Dory."

The *corps* dancer popped out of a basket, already wearing the Tourmaline's signature black stockings and gloves. A little taller—everyone was—she had Bess' elfin chin and a passable copy of her smile.

Bess whipped off her jeweled veil, pulled a shroud from a basket, and transformed Dory into a half-mummified Queen Dido standing among the wreckage of her party.

Stupid Dido, to celebrate falling in love.

The applause died down, the *ballerino* wandered away. Bess heard shifting movements out in the audience, then the orchestra's dramatic *bah bahhhh*. "Go on."

Dory paused, trying to slow her panting breath so she could go out and die as Dido. "You're sure?"

She'd be the Dido on stage when the curtain fell. She'd mince off-stage and greet Bess' admirers as the Tourmaline. Steal their attention. When gathering admirers was half the business of *ballerinas*.

Bess didn't approve of fits of conscience, but she'd

prepared for Dory's. Though she could climb ropes to the rafters, Bess was tiny.

Nearly everyone thought *tiny* meant *helpless.*

And Bess was an even better actor than she was a dancer.

"I can't bear it," she whispered in a rush, as if overcome with delicate timidity. It was easy. Though she largely avoided thinking about the roiling pit in her gut from which she drew whatever it took to be this person or that one, it wasn't a stretch to go from abandoned queen to over-emotional *prima donna*, unable to bear the attentions of too many men at once.

Plus, it had the force of truth; Bess *wasn't* interested in their limp offerings, either of drooping glasshouse roses or what they had in their pants.

She'd never had to be, because of Dan's protection.

She told herself that was why her Dido was so good. Because Dan's attention had let her perfect the art of queenly disdain, even as a girl, practically as a baby. Not because Dan had abandoned her.

There was no similarity to the story, anyway. Aeneas had just been a soldier passing through. Dan had been all her days, her every minute for as long as she could remember.

Bess was above the kind of emotions that had brought Dido down. In fact, she pitied the queen for falling prey to seduction.

Dory still hesitated; the audience was wavering. Bess gave her the assurance she needed, and shuddered. "The way they crowd the wings. Waving their flowers and trying to touch me."

Reassured that Bess wouldn't begrudge the loss of her admirers, Dory circled the scenery and gracefully collapsed.

Well, it was Bess' own fault for cherishing her grudges. Perhaps she should have made less of a point to warn others away from her specially compounded face paint.

In retrospect, waving a knife had been excessive.

While the dying Dido held every eye, Bess stripped off her own black gloves to rummage in another basket.

Now she had her mirror, her clothes, everything. No one was watching; the stage-manager was off looking for the *ballerino*, like he did every night, and the ballet master was already downstairs, drunk.

A little cold cream on Bess' hot face melted away Madame Franck's unique face-paint with its finely crushed pearl.

In seconds she swept a ladylike yellow bibbed skirt up over her spangled, sweat-marked costume. Tucked a spotless scarf at her neck, covering her collar; added slippers, white gloves, and over it all, a usefully fashionable cardinal cloak.

Passing the stairs that led under the stage, she swept towards the door hidden behind the scenery, covered in red.

She was now a young lady like so many others in the theater house at that moment who wore exactly the same cloak. Overexcited, perhaps, she imagined herself now. A red-faced girl made restless by the passionate display.

Someone who snuck out of the theater both ashamed of her feelings and indulging them too.

In the cobblestone yard, snow was falling.

Lightning struck somewhere ahead, up in the sky, never touching the ground, its thunder muffled by the low clouds and the snow.

On the stage, she'd felt wrapped in the thunder's sound, limitless, exultant. Now the sky's violence felt dangerously impersonal, just more of this bitterly cold autumn. Had she felt fear, she would fear the winter.

The cold slapped her face, making Bess wobble. Bess never wobbled.

Perhaps she had a fever. Hot from dancing, she couldn't tell. Plenty of Covent Garden women fell ill; but like most troubles, their diseases came from men, and those Bess avoided. How could she be ill?

Never mind. Right now she was a girl so alarmed by bodies' vigorous motion on stage that she'd had to go outside unchaperoned to breathe. She crossed the cobblestone yard.

The usher at the side door smirked as if he thought her a lord's daughter stealing a few minutes of freedom. Perhaps a quick encounter with someone forbidden.

He did not recognize her.

She rounded the corner.

A handful of men in dark coats scuffled past, their laughter drowning out the stage. One leered at Bess and scratched his expensive wool crotch. "Looking for a rooster, little chick?"

She almost swerved to follow him. He wore a large square diamond on that scratching hand, and Bess loved sparkle.

And he'd insulted her in her own house. She'd spent forever here pushing her body to do what the dance required. She knew every crack in its plaster walls. It might be shabby, but it was hers, not his.

Her fingers clutched her neck-scarf. The snowy linen was impossible to break. It made an excellent garrote if someone needed to be strangled.

During all the years alone, Bess grew a little colder each year. This was the coldest she, or London, had ever been.

But she had plans tonight, and told herself that it wasn't conscience that made her dismiss the idea of teaching the man a lesson and availing herself of his diamond once it had no more owner. Dan had been her conscience, and he was long gone.

The brute defiling her theater expected a blushing virgin, so she gave him one. Turning her red face to the wall, Bess gasped with fake horror.

Did this count as performance number four?

The men didn't stop, just guffawed as Bess crept silently the other way. She still had a lot to do.

But a few seconds to wait till she could do what she liked best. If she mastered this, there'd be no more chasing the feeling she hadn't found on stage.

She paused in an alcove next to the gallery; the distinctive rustle of silk skirts made her turn to identify the source. Men moved like cattle, but women were stealthier, and the last thing she needed right now was to be discovered.

There, the sounds were coming from the gallery stairs just opposite. She could hear the whisper of a young woman, panting, desperate.

"Oh Charles, I shouldn't let you but I can't help myself!"

Bess rolled her eyes. The stupidest lie fine ladies told. Of course they could help themselves; they had all the means. They didn't *choose* to help themselves, that was their problem.

Whoever Charles was, he only had a lot of rubbish to tell her in return. *Desperate to see her,* mumblety mumblety mump, *no other woman so lovely,* wah wah wah... All among motion so vigorous it made the walls creak.

The creaking piqued Bess' curiosity. She peered into the shadows.

Light caught the silk of the lady's skirt—chiffon, Bess noted, very fine. The skirt was tossed up around the lady's waist to hide whatever complications tangled her together with the lover whose black coat covered his motion. Both had such a white-knuckled grip on each other it was no wonder the wall behind them had creaked.

"We shouldn't do this." A near-silent whisper.

Bess restrained her snort.

They both shifted, and faint light fell on one side of the man's face. This Charles, whoever he was, had his eyes closed, thick eyelashes against his cheek, with darkly flushed lips, presumably from whatever he had just done to the lady's neck.

He looked hungry, and blind to anyone stealing past. Bess could have had an orchestra behind her and he wouldn't have noticed.

Bess didn't know this Charles and didn't want to. But the look on his face was raw. It tugged at her. Made her hungry, not in her stomach, but under her skin.

Made her wonder what it would feel like to act like that.

Bess didn't feel awkward watching; *they* had put themselves on display. But she was a little curious.

If men had any charms, she counted herself immune. She suspected they didn't.

The stair-man offered a glimpse of something she'd be better off not knowing. The heat and hunger of him were obvious, and they had an appeal.

She'd felt hints of it in the past; after all, even though she didn't know her birthdate, she was years older than twenty. And her body was her instrument; she knew so, and tuned it well.

That heat, with someone else? Dangerous. On the one hand, she knew to keep her distance from rakes like that one; on the other, when Bess wanted something, she took it.

Bess enjoyed a lick of danger every now and then, but perhaps not that kind.

She had the feeling that someday, she'd find that heat sparkly, irresistible, and she didn't want to be as ruthless as Charles about getting it.

Or as stupid as Lady Chiffon-skirt about giving it.

Bess could tell from the shifting, chattering audience noises that floated down the hallway that Aeneas had marched away from Dido's tomb to follow the cruel dictates of fate. Applause flooded the place, peaked, flowed away.

And people began to leave.

The itch under her skin stayed and irritated her as she escaped her alcove to walk on into the silly herd. First came the poor people, chattering and pointing and grinning at each other. For them, this was the highlight of the year.

Bess had stopped searching their faces for Dan years ago.

He might have been there. He could have hidden right in the footlights, with his worn coat and black-swan hair. True to their shared profession, he reflected no light.

But she'd have seen the space around him.

People used to keep their distance because of his scowl.

Now they'd have to leave room for his terribly large morals.

Regardless. He wasn't here. Her neck often prickled like he was watching, but that meant nothing. A habit. Those days were gone; he wasn't.

And if he were, he wouldn't be in this next wave of people trickling down from above, weighed down by jewels and petticoats and the desperate need to be seen.

All of them thought themselves fine, flawless, unable, apparently, to see themselves in a mirror no matter how often they looked.

There went Lady Villeneuve, patroness of second-rate virgins. She'd spent decades sheltering girls with money but no friends and ruthlessly finding them husbands. Like half of London, Bess wondered what she earned for her efforts.

Lady Villeneuve always went straight to her coach, always at the same door. Her charges trickled after, seeing and being seen and even talking while under Lady Villeneuve's supposedly iron grip.

Among them was Bess' target. A dark-haired girl in blue sarcenet gown. *Pretty,* Bess noted with professional detachment.

She was Bess' cue.

Time for *awe-struck clod-girl.*

"Wasn't it lovely? Wasn't Aeneas just a *dream?* I *wish* it weren't over." Hands waving everywhere, she stumbled into the girl in blue. "I do beg your pardon!"

She steadied the girl with a two-handed squeeze, then looked as if she recognized someone else over her target's shoulder. "Oh! Elizabeth!"

It was a safe ruse; half the girls in the room were named Elizabeth.

Unless the blue-gowned girl had an uncanny knack for faces, she would not associate this red-faced stumbler with the pearl-dusted, black-gloved Tourmaline.

As an awkward stumbler, Bess surged past, with only the briefest impression of the girl's face...

...and two rings from her gloved hand.

As good an actor as Bess was, she was an even better thief.

Five performances in ten minutes. Probably her fastest changes ever. It was only habit that made Bess check behind her for Dan's face. The smile reserved for her. His approval.

A habit that was pointless. He wasn't there.

After five years she should know to stay afloat in her feat, in the pleasure of achieving it, not sink into the empty place where Dan had always been.

He was dead by now, surely. Had he lived, he'd have come back.

Waving as if to friends, Bess drifted slightly across the crowd to land back in the side gallery. It was empty now, only a few new smudges on its whitewashed walls.

She hadn't eaten her usual dinner, that was all. That was why her stomach complained and the world was bleak.

She didn't need his approval. That Dido had been perfect, she'd had that audience in her hand, as well as the usher, the ruffians, and now the two rings in her pocket. She had everything she wanted. It was all easy to take if one knew how.

It should be enough.

And if it wasn't?

Well, one ring had been requested by a certain gentleman, and soon she'd be dining with *him*. His approval wasn't the same as Dan's, but it was approval, and any meal would do when one was hungry.

Bess cared little for his games; but she needed something to win, so she was willing to play.

Both stomach and head were in danger of spinning out of control as she silently approached the side door. Its usher was gone.

Just a few steps through the courtyard and she'd be back among the players, hot and laughing. Scattering for the rest of the night.

But the second she opened the door, she froze.

Blue lightning in the sky did nothing to illuminate the dark shape in front of her. His hand reached toward her.

No thought. Only reaction.

With the tiny, focused strength of a *ballerina* she grabbed that hand and pulled it closer to pinch in a very particular place above the elbow.

When it bent with inescapable pain, she lifted it backwards and drove a hard knuckle, just as precisely aimed, into the pit below his arm; then as he fell back, once more, over his liver.

It was all so quick and smooth that an observer might have thought the shadowy man had simply groaned and collapsed at her feet. If anything, she might have appeared to help him down amidst terrible pain.

He *was* in pain. Now. For her touches were terribly painful.

"Hello, Bess," he managed to say, with an all-too-familiar, teeth-gritting acceptance of pain. Rolled on the flagstones at her feet till she could see his face.

It was the face she'd been missing. Every happy memory she had, and all her saddest ones, were cut through with shadows of that face.

Tears, hot blood, *something* flooded through her, remnants of all the times in five years she'd turned to tell him something, and he wasn't there.

He'd been alive all this time? While she'd wondered night after night where he'd gone, what she'd done? Wondered what could possibly have taken him away from her side when he'd been there every single moment of her life?

How could he have been gone so long and still be whole, alive, here, now, simply appearing at her theater door?

She'd kill him herself.

No performances for Dan. He'd get the real Bess, the one he'd made. The one underneath all the bits and pieces from which she built her performances. The one that was pure ice.

"Dan," said Bess. "Whatever it is, I don't care."

CHAPTER THREE

$\mathcal{D}$ an had expected the night to be painful, but not like this. He was choking on pain. His elbow, his chest, the whole side of his body throbbed with it. "Where did you learn to do *that?*"

He knew better than to expect things to go his way, but this pain barely left him able to discern her face under the hood of her cloak. He could just see her disapproving frown, an upside-down U over her chin, and it instantly reminded him of a thousand moments of little-girl sulk.

Only reminded, because the little girl was gone. Little Bess had been sunny, always looking for fun; this one had bitter eyes expressing just how much she hated him.

Her fragile features were still the same, with just enough imperfection to save her from being too memorable. No artist would have painted the particular slope of her nose, the point of her chin; they wouldn't have bothered, unless they had the skill to capture the way the bow of her upper lip perfectly fit the lower, or how it all went together to convey captivating emotion.

When she chose.

Ice wasn't the same as emotion.

"So," said Dan, trying to conduct a normal conversation despite his position on the ground, "you *are* still angry I left you with Madame Franck."

"No insult intended to Madame Franck," said Bess, lifting her skirts as if to keep them clean as she stepped over his body and walked on.

"Bess, I'm here because I had no choice." He had to make her stop.

She turned. Tendrils of her hair crackled and clung to the edge of her red hood.

"Charming." She sounded as hard and cold as the paving stones. "What *forced* you into this unwelcome visit?"

He knew Bess. He had perhaps three more seconds of her attention.

"Help me up." The pain was incredible. He truly could not make a fist, rocking on the icy ground in the shredded remnants of his pride.

"No."

"We can't talk like this."

"Good."

But she looked back at him, and even in the gloom he could see her eyes.

Her admirers probably wrote sonnets about her emerald eyes. Obvious men who assumed the obvious. But Dan knew better.

* * *

"The lady of this house owns several cut-steel pieces that are rather good, two gold chains—mind you're not fooled by the brass ones—and a Ceylonese tourmaline. Exquisite blue-green."

"Oh!" squealed Bess. "Can I keep the tur-ma-leen?"

The Grand H looked over his copper-rimmed spectacles. "Do you wish to eat?"

"Yes!" She was still tiny enough to interpret this as an offer. "I want an apple!"

"Don't worry, sir." By this age, Dan's speech had lost its street tang. His words had a ballroom shape, like those of the Grand H. "Bess knows the rules. I'll remind her."

"Good. Off you go."

And Bess had slipped through the kitchen window, the only one of them small enough to squeeze between the bars.

Dan had faith in her. She would find her way to the window of the lady's dressing room. She always did.

He slipped off his shoes, freeing his toes to climb the wall despite the chilly London night. He'd be at that window when Bess opened it.

She'd be confused if he wasn't there to meet her.

* * *

He'd spent five years trying to earn enough money to make sure she never had to do those things again. All the things the Grand H. had required of them both, mechanical monkeys plucking jewels to feed the man's endless thirst.

All the things he'd taught her.

"I need your help," was all he could say. The rest of his breath and strength went into getting a foot under him, and staggering up.

Her arms folded hard. "We few? We happy few? We band of brothers?"

He winced at the sharp sound of her voice. "Never your brother. You know that."

Bess had been the one person who never looked at him like this. Suspicious. Repulsed.

Uncaring.

"I need your help." He had seconds left to persuade her. "I don't want to die."

"A lone thief is a dead thief," she murmured. She knew it as well as he did; they'd been practically her first words. "Well, goodbye, Dan. You've done poorly with your life."

Then turned so all he could see was her back.

* * *

THE NIGHT WATCHMAN'S grip on Dan's collar was turning him blue. "I've been watching you. I don't like your looks."

"No one does," gasped Dan, knowing that when he went out, he'd fall, and hoping the watchman lost his grip when that happened. Otherwise Dan could break his neck.

No sense anticipating the hangman's noose.

"Lady Withers lost two silver spoons an' a tablecloth. Lucky for you 'at's less than forty shillings, or you'd swing."

"I don't suppose it interests you that I didn't steal them."

Confused that Dan sounded like gentry, the constable's grip loosened. Then tightened again. "You're the type what does."

Black spots crept across what Dan could see.

Still, in the shimmering black he saw a bright white kerchief flap before the constable's eyes, confusing him, then settling neatly round his neck.

One of the man's torn fingernails ripped Dan's skin as he let go, but that was fine with Dan.

The staggering constable seemed confused that something small and heavy was on his back. He clawed behind him, then dropped to his knees.

Then on to his face.

"Sorry to be so slow," whispered Bess, still hanging on to the kerchief round the constable's throat. "It's so hard to get the knots in just the right place. It would be easier if I were taller."

Gasping for air as quietly as he could, Dan made no complaint.

She hadn't grown very tall, though she was still several years shy of twenty by anyone's reckoning. Pretty enough no one noticed the muscles in her arms till it was too late.

"Loosen up on him," rasped Dan. "You don't want him to sleep forever."

She shook the constable's neck a little, loosening her makeshift garrote. The dark twinkle in her eye these days replaced her younger sparkle. "What if I kill him just a little?"

"He wanted to hang me for some spoons." Dan rubbed his throat. "Just think what he'd do with a reason."

Bess released her scarf from the constable's throat, then kicked at his button-covered chest with a tiny foot.

"Lucky for him I have you to worry about." She pulled at Dan's sleeve. "Come on, some rich baker died and left money for dresses. I'm going to get one."

As they wound their way through narrow alleys, Dan listened to make sure the constable didn't follow. He hoped the man woke quick. If anyone stole his trousers while he was down, he'd be after Dan for that. "Dresses?"

"For poor women. So they won't feel ashamed to go to church." In the deep dark he couldn't see her in her black cloak, but he heard her snort.

"I don't think he meant you."

* * *

EVERYTHING about her felt as comfortable as warm bread in the winter. The turn of her neck, the way her hands moved.

He almost smiled. Seeing her was like breathing again after years of drowning.

Dan leaned against the door-jamb. Bess knew he was there. All those years of silent conversations, and loud ones, not to mention carefully marking each other's every move when knives came out. All that didn't just disappear.

Though it might be buried under miles of ice, and, he now realized, the rest of the history she'd accumulated while he'd kept his distance. Someone had taught her more about inflicting pain than Dan had ever known.

She didn't say anything, just kept her back to him and slipped off her cloak. Untied the tapes at her shoulders that held up her bibbed dress.

His shadow of a smile faded away. He wondered exactly what he'd avoided wondering for five long years.

Wondered if she'd learned anything about pleasure.

The efficient way she flipped off her cloak and slippers flicked him in a raw place. There was nothing in them of younger Bess.

Though of course there was. Younger Bess hadn't been shy either. He was the one who'd built her a closet out of old boards and nails when *he'd* grown an uneasy sense that her undressing was something he shouldn't see.

Convincing her to humor his flights of whimsical morality was always tough. Clearly the theater had rubbed that nonsense away.

Well, what of it? He didn't care. She was his responsibility. His *reason*. That hadn't changed.

Then everything Dan had ever feared happened in an instant.

She untied the tapes of the dress' bib and pushed it away. Underneath was her costume. But Dan's blood hadn't known it was there.

It had leaped, hot, eager, anticipating. Pounded in his veins in a way subtly different from anything it had ever done before.

Watching her simple act of untying, pushing the fabric away, had wakened something he *did not* want.

Something he'd left five years ago to prevent.

Not through any fault of hers. It was Dan's fault, the

legacy of whatever devil gave him this face. He'd always wondered if he'd come from hell, or was destined to go there.

Now he knew. He might have come from the devil, but hell was still in his future.

He ought to ask about *her*. Ask what game she was playing, putting all that over a stage costume. But the golden rainbows of her hair distracted him, clung to her shoulders, floated down her back. He reached out to touch one, stopped himself.

If he touched one, it would be the worst shock of his life.

The voice nature had given him was rough. "You always wear your hair that way when you dance?"

"No," she said calmly, folding her arms to face him, tapping one toe. "Sometimes I set it on fire."

There was a lot of fake blood flying across London stages, even water for naval battles with tiny cannons; but Dan had yet to hear of a *ballerina* on fire. "Well, given constant fires, it's remarkably long. I knew that death scene wasn't you. I went looking for you."

He'd expected her to tumble out of the below-stage with the players so he could talk to her in the courtyard. Expected to see her alone.

He'd also thought she might let him talk.

Only Bess could be angry as hell and ignore him at the same time. She was doing it now. And up to something.

She pulled some shoes from a basket, sat on the floorboards to swap them for her slippers. When she hauled up the short dancing dress, he saw her black-clad leg from toe to thigh.

Dan did look away then, though the picture stayed with him. Likely would forever.

That damn dance teacher had promised she'd learn ballet, not to be *demi-monde*. So why the disguise? "This isn't how I wanted us to meet again."

She still said nothing. She put a lot into her silence.

He couldn't apologize for leaving. He'd had to; the way it felt to see her again proved it. But he could give her an honest apology. "I'm sorry I startled you."

"You didn't startle me." Her eyes flew at him like darts. "If you'd startled me, you'd be dead."

* * *

"IF YOU HAD A WEAPON," Dan said, still leaning back against the door, "which you don't." His eyes darted to the neck kerchief she'd dropped on the floor and he revised himself. "If you wanted to kill me, which you don't."

How *dare* he be unscathed? Unchanged? She wanted him cautious. She wanted him *hurt.*

Just the sight of him—black eyes, hellish confidence, and apparently an icy heart she'd never guessed at as a child— roiled up nameless emotions she didn't currently need, and Bess hated those.

Worry. He'd been there every day of her life, then just gone. *Worry* didn't begin to describe the feeling. It had verged on *terror.* And a nagging sense of something she might call shame if she didn't know better. He'd just *gone*, claiming it had nothing to do with her.

And now he stood there, wearing that secret soft almost-smile that had always been just for her. After cutting her out of his every waking moment like it didn't make him bleed.

How could she have thought him so perfect, all those years ago? *Children were stupid*, she told herself, without inwardly admitting she had once been a child.

"I suppose you don't interest me enough to kill you," she shrugged with one shoulder.

She could have forgiven him for dying. But five years

gone, when he was *alive?* Standing here now as if nothing had happened?

Except time. He was taller, thicker somehow. The steel-hard muscle of his arm when she'd bent it had felt familiar enough. How could that be, when he'd made such extravagant claims of giving up a thief's life?

What was he doing with all that muscle, without her?

He pushed himself upright and his confidence faded. He looked tired, and sad, and somehow desperate.

That was a look she remembered, too. Her fingers stilled on the buckles of her shoes.

"I'm not here to be proud. Hate me if you like, but give me your help. I won't let you wrap a scarf round my neck, but you can smash tomatoes on my head."

She would not let him make her smile.

She almost asked him. Why he was here, what he needed. She'd never *tell* him anything. She'd done too much, and he didn't deserve to know. But she could listen.

A voice called from the stage. "Bess? They're locking the doors. Are you out here?"

Bess pushed herself to her feet. "Yes, Madame Franck. I'm just coming."

That didn't keep Madame at bay.

"What are you doing back here—*You!*"

Dan slumped back again, eyes falling shut. Bess smiled after all, just a little. She'd enjoy this.

Like Bess, Madame did not hesitate to attack. "You pusillanimous worm-eating wart-toad! How dare you accost Bess in the theater! The theater is a *special* place, a *sacred* place! With filthy, toothless men fondling themselves in the front row. You dropped her here, you venomous turd, you dropped this sweet little princess here to do the best she can—"

"I left her with *you*, Madame Franck." All his secret softness was gone; his black eyes gave Madame the kind of warning that scared away big men.

It had no effect.

Madame Franck always seemed to be wearing three or four dresses to make herself seem larger. Silk scarves fluttered everywhere she went. Above the dark glow of her skin, her hair teetered in high black waves, topped with a towering peacock feather. It all rustled when she moved, and now she moved toward him.

Bess lived by the street rule: to anyone who asked questions, she was born yesterday. She told no one what she knew.

But in five years, she'd told Madame Franck a few things, and Madame loved a chance to take center stage.

The *swoosh* of her peacock feather was threatening. "You dropped her here, you bollocky dog-tongue, like a gold ring in the dirt, and then you have the *gall*, the *audacity*, to come back and accost this sweet child while she earns her daily bread with the only skill she has?"

"Not her only skill." Dan's scowl was in full effect. "She's just been claiming she can cut a man's throat."

"No one should work in the theater who can't cut a man's throat. Bess. Come away right now from that nasty man."

Bess raised one eyebrow. "Madame Franck is right. You *are* a nasty man. And a liar. You said I'd never see you again."

Dan looked past her at the scarred pillar behind her. He didn't want to meet her eyes.

Onstage, the last of the footlights guttered. Shadows danced against the black stubble on his face.

They used to be able to speak just by looking at each other. He'd always had secrets, but now they were from her. And what right did he have to keep secrets after five years of silence and *reappearing*?

She wanted apologies—detailed regrets, maybe tears.

Anything to roll back time to the minute he'd said she'd never see him again.

There was none of that. He only said, "I need your help. To steal something so we'll never have to steal again. I mean it."

Bess made a rude noise. "*Stealing is wrong, Bess. You don't really want to do this anymore.* I suppose that wore off, Mr. Saint?"

He winced. "We're not going to keep it."

She felt her face do things she couldn't stop. Felt the horror show in her lips pulling back with disgust, the collapse of her skin.

"You want my help to steal something we won't keep." The last thing, the very last thing she expected him to say.

He wasn't Dan. Not her Dan, anyway.

"Now Bess, send him away." Madame Franck waved her hands and her peacock feather. "You haven't time for this."

Dan's scowl deepened. The slight permanent sneer pulled back farther and showed his teeth. "Why, do you have an appointment? This time of night?" The roughness in his voice got rougher. "You have a *protector*?"

Madame Franck opened her mouth, but Bess answered quicker. "Yes. And the gentleman is waiting. You can't afford my time."

Those glittering black eyes stayed trained on Madame Franck. "I sent you money to ensure Bess never had to seek a protector."

He'd sent Madame Franck money? That was news to Bess. She turned on Madame Franck. "You told me we lived on our earnings."

Her teacher had a catalog of sounds she employed as needed on stage. Bess thought the blustering, sputtering noises she made now were number four. The outraged mother.

"Mr. Fox. You tasked me with seeing to Bess' care and reputation. I thought they mattered to you. When neither of us has seen you in five years, and you suggest something like this, naturally I suspect your motives!"

A bit much, but Bess tried not to correct a performance in progress.

Dan hissed. "God damn you to hell. My money should have reassured you my instructions had not changed with time."

Bess whirled on him. "Did the money ever come with a note?"

For the first time since he'd reappeared, his eyes fixed directly on hers. And the rest of the world fell away.

Back in the ramshackle alleys, other girls had sighed, half fearful, half swooning, when they talked about Dan. They shivered even as they raved about his strength, his eyes. *So cold*, they said. *So calculating.*

They'd been too right.

Danger was only exciting when you knew you could escape. How had she never seen it before? His black diamond eyes were the real kind of dangerous. They looked beautiful, but they were hard and they cut.

* * *

"Bess, name your price. Money, and a lady's wardrobe." He was losing her. Her attention, at least; the rest of her he'd never get back.

Madame Franck clutched her hands with an excited gasp; Dan shot her a look. "Not for you."

He'd decide how to deal with the teacher when he had a better grip on himself. It was slipping now. He couldn't tell what would happen if he lost it.

The truth was, he'd been too slow. He wanted to blame

Fitz, but it was his fault he hadn't been faster. He should have given Bess everything she really deserved. Lifted her high enough to find a respectable husband, live a decent life.

With someone, anyone, who wasn't him.

That was everything he wanted for her that he couldn't steal. A clean life. A kind one. One no one could take from her, not the gaoler or the hangman, and definitely not Dan himself.

He was no saint. He'd practically prayed every night, not to any heavenly ears, but to her. *Stop risking getting caught. Stay safe. Fall in love. Marry someone. Stay far from me.*

Instead, she'd fallen for some protector's trap, and Dan hated his own desperate urge to pick her up and carry her away from here, from all the dangers he'd been too young and poor to stop.

He looked at Bess, a little granite statue hating him, and felt his face soften. He had plenty of time to hate himself and settle accounts with Madame Franck. But none of it was Bess' fault. He'd never once blamed Bess, and that hadn't changed. It never would.

* * *

"NEVER CLAIM to be his sister. Your coloring says you're not." By then, they knew that tone meant the Grand H. expected them to follow a rule.

The old man was older, his back stooped, and he no longer brushed the ashes from his shoes after a walk.

Bess, somewhere around eight years old and watching people pass by the end of the alley where they huddled, saw the logic of this rule and had logical questions. "So then what do we say if someone sees us together?"

"Perhaps he's abducted you from your nanny."

Bess looked up at Dan, likely twelve and stringy, leaning

against a door-frame and eating the last of their bread. She bounced on her toes with excitement. "That will be fun! You grab me round the middle, and I'll scream."

Daniel dropped the last crumbs of bread in his mouth. "We don't want to attract attention. The story's only if someone sees me. But they won't. I'll stay out of sight."

"Dan!" She'd stomped her foot. "That's no fun."

Dan, old enough to know that there was no pleasant reason for a stranger like him to be following a girl like Bess through a crowd, looked sad and serious, too much for his age. "If someone sees us together, just look frightened. Everyone expects a pretty little girl to look frightened."

"But I'm not frightened of you!"

"It's just for show, Bess."

The little girl nodded.

"Then for today." The Grand H. handed her the sharp little folding knife, and she slipped it in her pocket.

"Fine," said Bess. "When I see a rich one, I'll start to cry and get them to hug me. Once I've got the purse, I'll run away."

"From them," the black-haired boy clarified, as Bess could be all too literal.

"Yes, from them. Not you."

* * *

Feeling like she was handling a bare knife, Bess still felt moved to offer Dan help. It was a lifelong habit, too ingrained to give up in an instant. "I suppose you asked old Lucius."

"Dead." After a second Dan added, "They hung Melinda."

That did make Bess' stomach drop. "You didn't go see?" No matter what his eyes looked like, Dan was too tender to watch a hanging.

"No. Nor did that husband of hers. He threatened to beat

her all to hell and robbed her employer. That's why they hung her. They didn't believe her when she said it was him."

Well. Dan didn't have to remind her how thieves turned on their partners. If he wanted her out of the business, he had an odd way of showing it.

He'd just use someone else. With a pang of another nameless, useless emotion, Bess ventured, "Emily?"

He just shook his head *no,* not mentioning what they both knew: Emily worked in the same brothel where she'd been born. Fleetingly Bess wondered if Dan saw her professionally. Not his profession, hers.

She didn't ask that. For some reason, she didn't want to know. "Jack and Jackie?"

Now a ghost of his soft smile threatened to surface again. "I'm trying *not* to get arrested. This isn't what you think, Bess. I need your help, but we're not going to keep what we steal."

That put an end to any inclination Bess might have had to relent.

She said tightly, "We never kept any of it. It was for the old man. We never got to *keep* anything. All I had was you."

That wiped away his last trace of a smile.

When he spoke again, Bess knew he was keeping a tight grip on himself. Not strictly temper; Dan didn't have much of a temper. The force of him came from his determination, the way he never gave up.

He was holding it all back as he said, "Is that why you found yourself a protector? You wanted things to keep? What? Clothes? Money?"

"Not for money!"

Her outburst set him back on his heels without touching him.

She felt better, having landed a blow.

But only for a second. The rings she'd just stolen lay

against her skin under the virginal white gloves she still wore. She hadn't taken them for herself; well, she'd only taken one for herself. Dan made that seem foolish when Bess wasn't foolish. The Grand H. was dead; she might steal for someone else, but not for him. Not any more.

And not for Dan.

He'd always acted like he was her snake in the garden, explaining the nature of evil. The truth was, like that snake, even after he'd cast her out, he'd marked the location of home.

For five years all she'd wanted was to go home.

Now he was back—for her ability to steal. Not for her.

She said, "You were all I had, and you left me."

Then she turned her back on him one last time and floated out the stage door as cold as the snow.

ou were all I had. Bess' words burrowed into Dan's brain, his gut, the veins in his skin.

Wasn't that the twisted truth?

If she knew that, she knew why Dan had put space between them. Every second of his life watching her, and her watching him. That was beyond peculiar, and she deserved so much better.

At the rate they'd been going, they'd have been hanged from the same noose.

"I'll settle accounts with you later," he managed to get out. Madame Franck said nothing; he didn't look at her. Let her follow Bess.

If Dan did it, he and Bess would go back to dancing around the same fixed point, pretending they lived in a world where only they mattered. Without any of the innocence he could no longer claim.

Not that he'd ever had any.

In childhood, everything had been so much simpler. With only three simple rules.

Lurk.

Hit.

Watch Bess.

The Grand H. hadn't dictated those rules; Dan had derived them for himself. Underneath it all, from the day Bess entered his life, those were his orders. He'd kept them to himself.

Staying quiet had been easier then; he'd had little to say.

Now he needed words but didn't have the knack.

Dan's room was near his custom, both for snooping and keeping books. Close enough to reach Bess if she needed him, far enough she wouldn't see him by accident. It wasn't smart to walk heedlessly there, through parts of London where bodies and their safety were things to buy and sell. This late, it was plain foolishness. But walk blindly he did, staring into the past.

* * *

"HEY, little girl. If you come with us, you can have all the apples you want."

Bess looked up from the one she was eating, attention torn from the passing billowing skirts and flashing trouser legs. People stayed burrowed in their own little lives on the street; they never looked hard enough to notice Bess.

Apples were her favorite, and she was born knowing that if one apple was good, two were better.

She looked over her shoulder to Dan in the brick shadows. He shook his head no.

Dan's no *was all she needed; she went back to her work. Her task was to stand at the end of the alley and watch for cullies. People with purses to cut. Within the shelter of the crooked stone wall, she could see everyone at just the right height to see who was feeling their pockets, and stay out of the flying muck of the muddy street, churned as it was by hooves and carriage wheels.*

40

There were three of them, old enough to be on the Continent fighting the French; older than Dan, who counted himself fourteen. Dan moved a little so his scowl would be out of shadow.

Sometimes knowing they were watched was enough to send such rats on their way.

Not these three. There was a taller one, who had done the talking; a squatter one beside him, with the most unpleasant eyes; and a scrawny one out to prove something by sticking with such bad company.

The boys circled her, blocking her from Dan. "Hey. I'm talking to you, stupid."

"I know," Bess answered the tall one, swallowing her bite of apple. "I'm ignoring you, stupid."

Snarling, Tall tried to backhand her across the face. It was always straight from talking to hitting with that kind.

They never considered how fast Dan could move.

Dan caught the hand before it landed, jerking it so Tall fell forward, letting Dan knee him in the jaw as hard as he could.

He stepped past the falling body to bring his own head up under the chin of Squat, who was shorter than Tall, but taller than Dan. Teeth snapped shut, with a squall. Hopefully, the bastard had bitten his tongue.

Scrawny wasn't used to alley fighting, fast and unfair. He'd had time to put up his fists, but his heart wasn't in it; it showed in his eyes. Dan swept his leg out from under him, kicked him in the chest as he fell. He joined Tall on the ground.

Bess' cool gaze never wavered. "Now you've met us," she told them, two writhing on the ground and one holding his face, blood between his fingers. "We don't need to meet again. Got it?"

It bothered Dan for Bess to see that. Bothered him more that she barely blinked. It shook the hell out of Dan; he felt himself trembling, and none of them had landed a single hit.

As they walked away from the three predators, giving them a chance for a retreat, she whispered, "What did they want? My apple?"

"No." He knew what they wanted; so would Bess, since her friend Emily lived at the brothel. But he couldn't bring himself to make it clear. Bess might be hard as nails, but she was still so little, with such an open look. "Ask Emily."

"She wasn't even there!"

"She'll know."

* * *

FIGHTING, Dan learned at the orphanage. Fists and clawing hands pulling at whatever thing they needed.

Ferocity had come from protecting Bess.

In Dan's world, the ranking originally started at a God who had it in for him, then button-men who could nick you and put you in jail, then Bess. Over the years Bess rose to number two, then easily to number one.

You were all I had. She must know the same was true for him.

That was exactly why they had to stay apart. As a child, she'd needed him. Dan had done the best he could and still failed her completely. He couldn't keep her tied to him, even though he'd be tied to her forever.

Partly by the weight of his conscience and partly by choice.

He'd been glad the day the Grand H. paid his apprentice fee and led Dan out of the orphanage. The old man had been a thin tie to existence, but one with a vested interest in keeping Dan out of the clink or off the gallows. Dan had still been more like a spoon than a person to him, easy to put in one's pocket, easy to toss away.

No matter what else happened, he'd make sure Bess *never* felt like that.

He was just trash not worth keeping. He remembered his mother, dimly, not by face but by feeling, and remembered how she brushed off her skirts the day she'd sent him crying into that orphanage. As if free of him. As if clean.

Small Dan had accepted that his fate was to be owned, moved and dropped at will, but Bess? Never.

* * *

"Don't look at her like that, boy."

"Like what?" True, Dan didn't need to stare. Bess knew to eat every smidgen of her oat porridge, and the door was barred for the night against anyone who might try to do her harm.

She was smaller than Dan had been at her age, and so strong.

Dan was too, plenty strong enough to climb any garden wall in London. But he found himself wondering if pound for pound, Bess might be stronger.

Or if she was just more ruthless.

The Grand H. scoffed, soft jowls shaking in the smoky lamp-light. "The worst danger you have to protect her from, boy, is you."

It was proof the old man was crazed. Dan would never hurt Bess; that was true the way it was true that the sun came up every day. More true, since there were plenty of days the sun couldn't make it past the murk of coal smoke and clouds.

It gave Dan enough guts to contradict the old man to his face. "You're crazy."

The old man's slow contemplation made Dan's insides shake. He'd never hit Dan, not with a fist. Just made clear their dinner depended on Dan taking whatever he told Dan to take. So Dan did.

Bess did the same, but someday she'd be free, Dan would see to that. And he'd never, ever hurt her.

"Women have to belong to someone," sighed the Grand H., as if he regretted it somehow. "But not a bastard like you."

* * *

IT WAS the first time Dan had felt how that word hit different when a person meant it. The Grand H. was only being exact, same as he was with maps of houses and lists of jewels. He meant Dan was less than other people. Different. Worse.

The funny thing about the Grand H. had been that, by his own odd code of morals, he kept to the right of things. That included telling Dan what was what. Gaolers who took bribes? Proved prisons were about money. Bubbers who stole tankards from taverns? Couldn't see past today to tomorrow. Fine men in wool, who cheated their coachmen and whores? They only proved a mirror was the wrong place to see the right thing to do.

Dan could wish the old man had kept his assessment of Dan to himself. But no matter how he sliced it, the truth came home to roost. The Grand H. hadn't thought himself evil; neither had Dan, till he was so informed.

Who ever really saw the evil in themselves?

Bess was different from such things; she sparkled. A golden-haloed doll-child grown up impish and smart.

She was beyond anyone's reach... except Dan's.

Those weeks after the Grand H. had died, Dan had felt like a tiger, pacing back and forth in a cage with his dinner. It felt awful. It felt *wrong*.

He'd been grown, long past sleeping in the room or even across the threshold, with some of his nights spent dabbling in the kind of fun one found outside opium dens or at the bottom of a bottle.

Then one night, she'd accidentally locked him out.

* * *

BANG. Bang. Bang. *Dan's knuckles cut on the rough planks of the door, but he wanted in.*

Why, he wasn't sure. He was used to sleeping on the street, had been for years. Doors kept Bess safe; that luxury wasn't for him.

But the ale had been strong, and it tilted something in his head. That was his place. Bess was his. "Open the door!"

A rat skittered away from the refuse blown against the alley wall by the cold wind.

A vision of light opened the door.

She tried to speak. "Good—"

Dan pointed a finger. He felt dangerous. "Don't swear."

Bess didn't notice. "Mercy Bennett," she said, rolling her eyes to show how she indulged him. "One knock does perfectly fine. I bathed while you were out. I just needed a minute to dress."

Dan staggered in. He caught himself against the chair by the door. The way it stood askew told Dan she'd just been using it. Maybe to hold her clean dress. Maybe to balance a foot while she rolled up her stockings.

He knew those stockings. She'd stolen them last week.

He blinked. He knew those legs, too. She balanced on his shoulders every day before diving off to tumble over the back of a horse at Hughes' circus. It was steady work, with good pay, as long as Bess kept her hair short and bound her chest to fit into a boy's acrobat costume.

With steadier food, she was putting on weight, and that ruse wouldn't work much longer.

Balancing upright with one hand on the rungs of the chair, Dan looked around. It was the same little room where the Grand H. had breathed his last. It smelled of the printing press ink upstairs, the rendering tallow of the candlemaker next door. It was rank and dim and all he had. This room, and Bess.

He looked at her hair, softly curling from the bath, and idly wondered how it would feel, that soft skin on the back of her neck.

Instantly horrified that he could imagine, even for a moment, treating her the way he treated the barmaids who'd smiled at him, the way the shopkeepers treated their exhausted wives, the way the men with carriages treated the women at the brothel.

Horrified that the Grand H. was no longer here, but still right.

* * *

DAN NEVER TOUCHED LIQUOR AGAIN, and the next day he'd started looking for a new life for Bess.

The theater wasn't the Queen's house, but it would do. Bess could learn a new trade and get away from him.

What if he'd said something? What if he'd *touched* her? If she hadn't wanted him, where would she have gone? What could she have done?

That hadn't been freedom.

As he walked, a clutching hand reached out of the shadows. It wasn't just to cut his purse. Dan knew he looked too shabby for that.

One snarl was all it took to set the man back, shoving himself against the brick behind him. He made a little noise of fear.

Whatever he wanted, he would not get it. Dan didn't give him another thought.

Little Bess had loved the glamor of opera girls, loved to dance. If she played it right, she could live clean, without stealing. He hadn't intended to see her again, not without a dowry in his hand so she could find a proper husband.

Well, he *had* seen her; she was no child any more, and the worst had happened. He'd *wanted* her. Wanted her now, so badly his hands were shaking with it. He wanted to bury his face in that hair, wrap her in his arms and never let go. An evil prophecy come true.

If the Grand H. had a grave, Dan would spit on it. This twisted life of raising Bess, protecting Bess, and ultimately wanting Bess was that bastard's fault. Dan's boots felt heavy. It was the small hours, and he still had work to do. Bess' hate was surprisingly hard to carry.

Then brutal honesty forced Dan to admit there was nothing else the old man could have done. At least he'd warned Dan about his own nature.

He shouldn't have been so picky about how he made his money; the honest stuff was too slow. Where did this *protector* live? How deep was his purse? What did he intend for Bess? Did he have a wife? Did he have diseases? Did he know what a treasure he had?

The blood-red questions pounded along with his heavy steps till he realized he was home. His rough-cut door, the broken stone in his pavement. Well, paid for by the week.

His customer. A big-bellied baker named Mr. Stewart.

And next to him, damn the man to hell, was Fitz, jabbering as always.

Oblivious to the dusty knuckler picking his pocket.

Dan sighed.

The creeping man's dirt-stained fingers slowly slid the purse out of Fitz' coat pocket while Fitz talked on with the baker, never shutting his jaw.

Dan's arm snaked around Fitz and grabbed the bony wrist.

Twisted it backwards so the man would go to his knees, drop Fitz' embroidered purse. He did.

Where had Bess learned how to pinch him like she had? His elbow still throbbed. Dan's way was brutish, but it worked. "This street is mine. Go to hell."

"Bugger!" The knuckler, never standing upright, mumbled apologies and lurched away into the night.

Reminding Dan so painfully of all the people he'd grown up with that he felt truly sick to his stomach that he hadn't handled the man more gently.

He pointed at Fitz. "You go to hell too. Mr. Stewart, our appointment."

The big flour-dusted man gave a quick nod, crowding Dan as he unlocked his door, he was so eager to follow instructions.

"I have questions." Fitz swooped up his purse and followed.

"If he'd recognized you, he'd never have picked your pocket. Everyone knows who you are. Get away from here."

Fitz's famously close association with the Caped Count was his armor anywhere. No one bothered him, precisely because of the lanky man's distinctive appearance. And of course it helped that he'd somehow managed to marry a duke's daughter, making him a shining example of the society he'd once told Dan he hated.

Society Dan wasn't too fond of either.

Society Dan planned to beat at their own game. *For Bess.* Society that hated people like them.

And the pickpocket he'd just sent scuttling.

Growling at himself, Dan left them at his door and ran after the pickpocket.

He hadn't gone far; he was either genuinely lame, or too tired. When he heard Dan's shoe leather on the paving stones, his fast look back flamed into fright and he hobbled faster.

"Stop, I'm not chasing you. I am, but—Just wait." Dan grabbed his arm.

Seeing that there was no escape, the man gave in and stopped, hunched head clearly expecting a beating. Inwardly Dan sighed. "You know not to come back here, right? Not to pick pockets. You won't like what I'll do."

"Yes, sir. I've got it. I've got it." A bit garbled due to lack of teeth, the pickpocket tried to pull away. Which Dan didn't mind—he smelled awful—but Dan didn't want to chase him again.

Dan fought the urge to shake him. "I'm nobody's *sir*." This had to have been the fifth time this happened. How did they know to pick his street? "Can you do anything besides steal?"

The man gaped, genuinely astonished, showing how many teeth he lacked.

"I was a stableman, s—." He stopped before he said the offending word again.

Sure he was. Tons of horses in Spitalfields. No matter; lies didn't bother Dan. After all, Bess loved lies.

And there went what was left of Dan's good humor. And there hadn't been much.

Dan pulled tuppence out of his pocket. "See Mr. Stewart in the morning, and he'll find you some bread. If you've drunk the coin by then, don't bother, you won't get the bread. If you're sober when you see him, you'll get another tuppence for a bath and maybe a bed. And a chance at some honest work. Do you see where this goes?"

"Yes sir, sir, I will, sir, yes, sir."

He wouldn't; he was stuck in the habit of being someone's slave, saying *sir* to everyone he thought his better. He hadn't even asked Mr. Stewart's direction.

Well, most hatted nobs would beat him if he didn't say it, and at least Dan had temporarily salved the crushing weight of his conscience.

Profoundly grateful he'd avoided becoming a slave to drink himself, Dan stalked back to his door, taking deep breaths. He must attend his customer. He wouldn't earn any money scolding himself.

Not that he could stop. Why hadn't he *told* Bess to wait till he could provide for her?

Because she's better off with no part of your life.

Still bleak and feeling sticky, he climbed the uneven steps to his room.

"Fitz. Take leave. Mr. Stewart, let's have your ledger." He didn't want Fitz here, in the monkish room where he plied his trade. Fitz would see too much. Dan would look too soft.

"Oh, I don't mind Mr. Fitz staying." Fantastic. He'd fallen to Fitz' charm.

"It's just Fitz," grinned his inconvenient guest.

It's Lord Henry, actually, and he's a pain in my arse, but Dan didn't say it. Mr. Stewart was a gentle soul.

Finally at his desk, Dan threaded the wire temples of spectacles over his ears. Conscious of how they dimmed his glare, he pointed a quelling finger at Fitz. "Stay there. Don't touch anything. Why are you here?"

Fitz raised both hands in fake capitulation, then dropped one, leaving the spread fingers of the other. *Five days?* "We don't have much time."

Silently swearing, Dan tried to devote his attention to the baker while Fitz peered intently at every inch of the room.

* * *

"Mr. Stewart, that is not how addition works."

Dan found numbers beautifully simple. No one ever hit a seven; a nine never starved to death. They were clean and eternal.

The fat baker leaned over Dan's table. He never visited till the morning's small hours when his apprentices were well at work. He didn't find numbers so simple.

Dan's eyes were starting to cross.

"Ye're daft." The baker set his thick fingertip against the ledger, both liberally smudged with flour. "I spent these shillings for some silk. Mrs. Stewart's birthday, and well worth it too!"

"I'm not questioning the value of your wife or her birthday. I'm saying you cannot subtract the shillings here, then add them back because you earned more shillings the next day."

"But we did!"

Mathematical abstraction was nearly too much for the baker, but Dan couldn't give up. Mr. Stewart was a good man. He was also in debt.

And Mr. Stewart had six children, four of them daughters.

"Mr. Stewart." Dan removed his spectacles and rubbed his nose. "You do know that if you can't pay your debt, you'll be arrested? Are you so eager to see inside Marshalsea? Your family will live with you—and three other debtors—in a room ten feet wide. Navy prisoners, chained to their floors, will be set free every afternoon to mix with your children. What good will a silk dress do your wife then?"

Mr. Stewart's face went red, then white.

Dan tapped the book.

"*Here* are your total earnings for last month. The shillings you spent on the gift are here. They're an *expense*. All the shillings you earned this month are here. You cannot just erase an expense because you made more money, but you can see what you earned once you total *everything,* expenses *and* income. You need to see a bigger picture than any one day. Understand?"

"I think so," said the baker, scratching his head and leaving flour in the roots of his hair. "I'm thick, but I believe I do understand it, sir."

"Good. By the way, in Marshalsea prison? It's five shillings sixpence per bed. They only let you buy one." Dan sighed as he stood. "So *please* don't spend more than this amount—" his pencil softly hissed against the paper, circling the number, "before I see you again. That's all you have, even when it feels like more coins have come in the door."

"I'll do just as you say, Mr. Fox, I will."

And then the enthusiastic man stopped by Fitz on his way out. "Mr. Fox can help you if anyone can. Just you do as he says."

"I'll try," said Fitz, bowing.

In a deft move that recalled his days juggling pick-locks and purses, Dan snagged Fitz' coat with one hand, pulling him closer in, while with the other he pushed the baker out the door. "Good night."

He wished he'd kept his thoughts about Marshalsea to himself. He'd only spent a quick turn there once, when he and the Grand H. had a bit of bad luck; it had been before Bess.

He'd done anything and everything to avoid it since, swearing Bess would never see the inside of the place.

"So." Fitz cocked his head under a ceiling so low he had to duck. The baker's footsteps faded away. "Since we spoke last, I've met two milliners, a governess, and a squadron of dairy maids who say *you* kept them out of debtors' jail. Our mutual friend Gerry says you find things out for a fee. So what *don't* you do, sir? Rescue kittens?"

Dan hated journalists. "I don't cross swords with Lady Winpole. Till now."

Fitz' eyes got sharp. "Will you? By yourself?"

Dan shrugged.

He'd spent years on this plan to get enough money for Bess' dowry; there wasn't time for another. Bess might have a man, but that didn't make her safe.

Damn Fitz and his story-hunting eyes. "I've seen all kinds of men doing all kinds of things. Yesterday you had a spark. Now it's out."

It would be a relief to tell someone what Dan was trying to do. It would be such a relief to have a friend.

But his last friend would rather walk over his body in the street than help him, and Fitz wrote stories for a living. Dan held his tongue.

Dan put aside the haunting thought that he was trying to find another man to take his own place. That was the point; it wasn't his place. He refused to admit, even to himself, even the possibility that he might stop worrying about Bess, looking after Bess; he never had, and he never would.

He could haul her back to live with him; but that meant a prison she'd never escape, because if he gave in to his own demons, he'd never let her go.

Escape meant money. Time had run out.

"Whose secretary will I be?"

CHAPTER FIVE

$\mathcal{B}$ess had never felt such an itching, tearing urge to escape their little rooms at the players' boarding house. Her bed was a whirlwind of things she shouldn't have and shouldn't wear, and she picked through them fast, dying to leave, leave, leave.

"I don't believe you have a protector." Madame Franck stood in the middle of the cramped room, hands clasped at her tiny waist, an obstacle to Bess' whirling.

Bess snatched up a tight ribboned spencer. "That's fine by me. I don't believe you set such store by lizard poetry, yet here we are."

"And foxes," said the actress, referring both to her ancient Tamil poetry and to Dan's last name.

Bess ignored this bait and swept up two tins of rouge. A quick change kept her from thinking, and she did *not* want to think right now.

Her approach to feelings was the same as her approach to turds in the street. Give them a wide berth, pretend they weren't there.

Madame Franck did not relent. "I don't believe you have a

protector. If you did, you wouldn't meet him disguised as a poxy whore."

"As peculiar tastes go, I've seen worse." She stood on one foot, pulling on a sturdy shoe. "So what did you do with Dan's money?"

"It's safe."

The Grand H. had often said that. About money safely converted to liquor and safely stored in his belly.

Bess snorted and switched to the other foot. "All your lectures about the guidance of poetry and letting go of things, and you're just as crooked as everyone else."

Madame Franck looked pained. "So lucky you know how to look striking, child. It makes up for your lack of charm."

"No blame intended. I might have done the same." Not that Bess had ever had the chance. "I'm still grateful for your teaching. Dan surprised me in the dark, and I had him on the ground before he knew it."

Madame Franck's fingers fussed with each other, betraying her agitation. "Thank you. You're a poor student."

That shocked Bess into stillness, standing on both feet.

Madame Franck's peacock feather *swooshed* as she nodded. "You like fighting, but not the healing part of *varma kalai*. And will you know which to choose when you don't know where you are?"

Bess swept one arm overhead, a truncated fourth position, and dropped it. "I'm right here."

"So distressingly literal." Madame Franck perched on the edge of her bed. "I know. My first husband was British. It's a national fault."

"Please. No poetry lectures." These moments of Madame Franck's also reminded Bess of the Grand H., and not pleasantly. "My—"

She'd never known what to call the old man. Certainly

not father, or grandfather. Madame had taught her enough French that *directeur* seemed the likeliest word.

Bess dropped the whole quest for the right word. "I knew an old man who talked about philosophy too. Apparently, it leads to being drunk."

"It's nice that after five years, you've at least grasped that *akam* is philosophy and poetry too. A map, child. To the world out here—" she moved one arm through a balletic second position more graceful than Bess', "and in here." She put her hand on her heart. "You are so lost in the world. Suffering. I can see it. But facing him lit a fire in you I have not seen in months. He might be waiting in the forest while you dance with fury on the beach."

"He's not in any forest." All this time she'd wondered if he'd ever come back. She thought he might be in prison. She thought he might have been *hanged.* He could have written one note. Even one. "Obviously, he just does as he pleases."

"Child!" Madame slapped her hands together, loud, like she did on stage to get everyone's attention. Bess' head jerked up. "Stop and listen to yourself. You were angry he was gone, and now angry he has returned. You are *angry. That* is what it means to be stuck."

"I'm not *stuck.* My Dido tonight was *perfect.*" All in a moment, Bess felt that wobble again. That made her angry too. She wouldn't show the wobble, she wouldn't show the anger, she wouldn't show anything she did not wish. She was an actress with *perfect* control. "I *had* them. They were in my hand. *London* was in my hand. I had *everything.*"

Madame's little brown hand shot out and grabbed Bess' wrist.

"That's not what I meant and you know it. I don't know where you go so late at night, but what worries me is how urgent you are. *Why* must you go?"

Frozen, Bess blinked.

Up close, under the waving feather and piled hair, Madame's eyes were searching.

"Why, child? I *don't* believe you have a protector. Still you go, in the middle of the night, more and more, and nothing else matters. You haven't bathed, you haven't *eaten*. What *drives* you so?"

Bess tried to yank loose her hand. "You're nothing if not dramatic, aren't you? Turns out, you've been paid. I don't owe you anything."

Madame Franck's hand let go.

Bess' skin itched, the sensation pulling her toward the door. She *had* to go. And she wouldn't explain. Not to Madame, or Dan, or anyone.

The older woman's voice was quiet. "You will come back?"

There was no way to hide her comings and goings from Madame Franck, not in their tiny rooms beside the stairs.

"Never fear, Madame Franck. I doubt Dan will come back. If I disappear, his money will keep coming."

Bess shut the door behind her.

Madame Franck just sighed and laid out Bess' stage gloves to air. "That's not why I asked, silly girl."

* * *

Bess' shoes crunched quietly on the snow-frosted pavement. With her hair under a coarse blue scarf and the tightly buttoned spencer framing her small but mighty assets, she looked exactly like the sort of woman men expected to meet on the street late at night.

Thanks to the tins of rouge, she had red lips and a copper-penny rash before she'd gone ten steps from the door.

Poxy trollops had an interesting kind of freedom.

The thunder and lighting had moved on, leaving the streets foggy and silent. Bess wished them back. Her feet went north, the route familiar. She didn't feel for the rings in her skirt pocket; that was how cutpurses knew where to cut.

She knew they were there.

All that tied her to Dan was their past. If that hadn't been enough for him to send word, one word, all those years, it was nothing.

He was the one who'd explained how the Grand H. used them both. Used their stealing to buy the liquor that filled his veins. It was Dan who'd harped on about *freedom.* How it could cure all their ills.

Guess he was over that now.

Come to think of it, he'd sounded a lot like Madame Franck wittering on about philosophy. Well, he'd picked her, after all.

He was so much bigger. Could he still climb a wall?

She'd forgotten how his shoulders curved in like a cat's. It was plain now, why those girls back in the alleys had sighed at his silent approach. Danger was fun when one knew one could escape, and they'd known at least a little about his gentleness with Bess. The breath of danger that followed him everywhere had only been like salt, making him delicious.

Odd how clear that was now. She'd never seen it back then.

How dare he be whole and well? How dare he reappear, and on the night of what should have been her triumph? She'd fooled everyone she had to fool, and had not one, but two rings in her pocket. Then in strolls Dan, not dead at all.

How dare he?

She was so lost in fury that he wasn't shipwrecked, slaughtered, or otherwise dead, she didn't see the shadow move.

The arm from behind latched onto hers, yanking her sideways.

Her attacker didn't see what he had coming either.

She let herself fall, let the arc of her weight at such an odd angle break his grip. He kicked at her but missed as she tumbled on the ground over one shoulder and got her feet under her, stood up with a powerful push of those ballerina's legs.

In close, she pinched his above-the-elbow spot; the pain brought him to his knees, below her height. Quick as the passing lightning, her grip shifted to the back of his neck and squeezed as Bess pictured herself interrupting the flow of his body, his very breath. He collapsed at her feet.

Her kick rolled his body to lie face-down before he could move. She could use her kerchief to strangle him further, but she had other business tonight.

She knelt in the small of his back and pulled one of his arms backward in a way it didn't go. That wasn't *varma kalai*; that was an old trick she'd learned from Dan.

"Aghh! Leggo! I didn't hit ya!"

"So? You tried. I should let you try again?"

Sensing his logic had not been persuasive, he went limp. "Have a heart for a poor man!"

She was in no mood for yet another man to ask her for something. "No."

Quite deliberately, she twisted the arm a little farther than it could bend, giving him a sprain to remember her by.

By the time he struggled up, cursing and holding his arm close, she was gone.

* * *

ON A WARMER NIGHT, she might have shed her shoes and stockings at the edge of the grass at Lincoln's Inn Fields. It was her favorite square, the last place in London one needn't have money to enjoy a bit of green.

Too chilly tonight. She didn't pause.

Under one of the trees, in cold air so dark she could barely see, a flash of movement caught her eye. Black, with a faint tinge of red. A little triangular face peeked out behind the tree trunk. Bess shivered. It was a fox.

* * *

"CATCH IT. Some trapper in the market must've lost it, they'll pay to have it back. Should be twelve shillings." The Grand H. studied the scraggly beast; no one else in the square had noticed it yet. "Maybe ten."

"No."

Jowls flapping with astonishment, the Grand H. whirled on Dan, who stood guard by the tree while Bess wiggled her toes in the grass.

He glared at Dan's feet. "You've got shoes on. Catch it."

"No." Dan watched the little animal recover. It had panicked at the sight of them, and froze; now it dashed away, trotting, then lolloping out of sight. No one else saw it.

"Idiot. This is London. Someone will catch it, then they'll have the ten shillings instead of you."

"Yes, sir. I know." Dan stayed where he was, eyes following where the little animal had disappeared. "Everyone in London is trying to catch and kill everyone else. Why not get mine, my ten shillings in exchange for a little murder? Not me, sir. Not today."

The Grand H. grunted, their possible prey lost. He laid back against the tree, his old bones creaking in the sun. "Of all the things I suspected of you, I never suspected you were soft."

"I know," said Dan, staring into the distance as if he could still see the fox.

* * *

SOMEONE WOULD CATCH THIS FOX, too, and sell him again at market. Perhaps for the third or fourth time. Someone's twelve shillings, or maybe ten, would change hands in exchange for his freedom.

Shaking off the chill, Bess moved on.

A man in a rumpled shirt and greatcoat stopped in the shallow snow on the pavement, fumbling with the ribbon tied round the neck of his small dog.

"What was it?" he fretted as Bess crossed the street. Sufficiently alarmed to speak to someone like her.

"A bear," she told him without pausing, and rounded the corner.

Bess had never felt like a fox, bought and sold, chased for a rich man's pleasure. Not once, not even the day Dan said the Grand H.'s death had changed their lives too.

* * *

"WHY?" Her fists were so tight, she wanted to hit something. Dan hadn't moved. "Nothing has changed! I can still cut a purse as well as ever. We could go farther north—"

"We can't keep playing this game. It was his game, and he's dead." He'd looked down, hiding his face, shoulders hunched forward. "We're not children anymore. You need a life."

"This is my life!" Her outflung arms took in their threadbare rugs and empty stove. They were the sole inheritors of the Grand H.'s chipped teacups and two plates, which were plenty now.

"You've never belonged here."

* * *

THAT HAD FELT like the end of something. Then he'd left her at the theater, left her with some woman she didn't even know. That had felt like—

When she was little, Dan's compassion for the fox had confused her, tugging at something she felt but couldn't say, something cloudy and far away against the practical acquisition of money.

Now she understood better. She'd seen enough children snatched away, fists thrown, sickness caught. She was the fox —all three of them had been foxes.

Dan had said he'd wanted something else for her.

Good thing she didn't believe that anymore.

Still steaming inside, Bess passed one drunken group of gentlemen with a wave and a "Ten pence for a pull?"

"Aye, ye're a tasty little bushel," said one, leering at her chest.

Once they drew close enough to see her face, though, one swore aloud, and they scurried away, which cheered her up. They saw what she wanted them to see.

What had Dan seen? Did theft show on her face?

He'd never blamed her for stealing before.

Shunted it aside, yes. Slowly over the years, as the Grand H. had grown weaker, stiller. That was how they'd wound up at the circus, somersaulting and juggling, vaulting over horses.

Anything they could do together that would avoid the fates written for them on the streets.

Dan hadn't just been determined she wouldn't wind up in a brothel like so many other girls. He'd disallowed the possibility. It no more existed in his world than purple snow. Bess' conviction that would *not* be her life had come from him.

And her suspicion of the men who cajoled, begged, demanded and took what they wanted from women, willing or unwilling.

That Charles tonight in the stairwell. As far as Bess was concerned, he was the worst type of all. Because he'd convinced the woman that she wanted to yield to him when he gave her nothing in return. Attention? Praise? Had she really yielded herself to him for such paltry things?

Had that been freedom?

Bess doubted it. The man had looked lost in her, yes. But for himself. He'd taken his pleasure and Bess very much doubted he'd given anything in return. What kind of freedom was that? The freedom to be swindled?

She crossed another street, keeping watch for herself as her shoes slid on the packed earth coated in frosty snow. The black tracks of carriage wheels wove in and out of each other, showing where horses had pulled them all in the same direction, rich and poor, heavy and light.

The muddle in her head was Dan's fault too. He didn't keep things simple. Take what you needed, what you wanted; Bess felt that was simple. Dan couldn't keep things easy like that. Morals, and price. He concerned himself with way too many things Bess could do without.

If she'd ever seen a man she wanted like that, she'd have had him. But she hadn't. They were like the stairwell man, takers. She was too smart to fall for that, and too quick.

Her freedom would only be in danger if the man was different, and they weren't.

Suddenly she had a flash of what Dan would look like bent that way over a woman's shoulder. It hit harder than the man who'd tried to drag her into the shadows; it made her stumble. She put a hand out and braced against the wall.

Dan *wouldn't* take. Dan always gave. Her day's bread. Carrots. Apples. The occasional taste of roast beef. A lamp, and oil, so she didn't have to sit in the dark. A friend on the streets. A job at the circus.

And always, always, arms to catch her if she fell.

Dan gave everything. At least to her. If she felt that way about *him*—

If. The picture of it exploded behind her eyes. Dan's black hair under her fingers. Dan's half-sneered smile against her mouth. Dan's shoulders under her arms, Dan's body against her—

She had to stop. Those pictures turned the world upside-down. What defined Dan was his difference from the men who did those things, took those things. Dan would never take. He gave.

But he'd never even hinted at giving her that.

Bess shook herself. A dusting of snow scattered off her skirts. She hadn't even seen it falling again.

She'd caught some cold. That was why she was hot and shivering at the same time, a little dizzy, a little short of breath. She remembered the wobbling at the theater, and straightened.

She might still be at the theater where Dan left her, but she'd stolen her freedom back. That was what she was doing right now, going where she liked, to see whomever she liked.

In this case, a man who definitely was not like all the rest.

The things he gave, she wanted. And the things he took, she gave.

Dan didn't matter. Bess had already found the perfect partnership, and if she kept atop her feet, she'd see him soon.

* * *

BY THE TIME Bess reached the tall house on Portpool Lane, her mood was truly foul.

The locked door made it worse.

What made the gentleman play games like this? It was icy cold and dawn was still far off. She wanted a refuge, not a challenge. And definitely not even the appearance of a trap.

Dan never let her swear aloud, but she was no damned fox.

Despite her annoyance, and the sensation that she was indeed putting a foot into a trap, Bess studied the house from below. Three windows showed faint light.

Clearly, he wanted her to choose.

Madame Franck's questions rang in the back of her head. *Why* was this such an urgent game? Why did it even matter? Why had she mentioned the man to Dan at all?

She'd had no reason to mention him. Just like she had no reason now to search for a way into the house. Still, she had, and she was.

And when it came to getting into the house, she would.

The lit window belowstairs was likely a cook, stirring pots, sorting beans. The light under the eaves must be a ruse; no one in servant's quarters willingly burned candles all night. They couldn't afford it.

The flickering light in the southwest corner, above the wing enclosing the courtyard. That was her target.

She pulled the back of her skirt forward between her legs and tucked it in at her waist, making an odd kind of trousers. Then sat on the cold cobblestones to unfasten her shoes and stockings. So much on and off of shoes tonight. Why weren't they easier?

She rolled the stockings into the shoes and hid them in the stone well of the kitchen window.

Barefoot to the cold, Bess circled the building's edge.

* * *

The Grand H. didn't attend the thefts anymore, but he paid a farthing for news if it was good, and this house was largely empty.

Its maids were asleep, its footmen feasting on a jug of cider Dan gave them. Bess could hear them laughing in the kitchen below.

"Don't worry." Bess said it so often she thought maybe Dan couldn't hear it anymore. "No one can climb better than me." She was already six feet in the air, but felt that Dan, hovering on the pavement below her, was the one who needed calming.

"No, they can't." His confidence in her was always better than a rope. It held her up. "And no matter how high you climb, if you fall I'll catch you."

* * *

No, he wouldn't, Bess thought bitterly, fingertips searching the wall for seams between stones.

Dan had been the one who told her never to look down. Dan had showed her how to find tiny spots her fingertips could catch and hold, not to rely on strength. Dan had showed her how to hug the brick and look for the next ledge, how to sag against the stones so friction caught her clothes. Dan had taught her to place her toes carefully so they bore all her weight.

Rather like ballet.

Everything she'd believed about him was suspect. He might have done all those things then, but he was someone she didn't know now. Maybe that whisper of danger was real.

And more importantly, he no longer knew *her*. Bess no longer hid what she could do. She'd showed it to all of London tonight, and they'd adored her for it.

She could do so much more than he'd ever suspected.

And the gentleman waiting for her didn't moralize; he praised her for it.

With a running hop she found purchase on the annex wall, two feet up, then climbed from there. Many ballerinas suffered as they learned to dance and their feet hardened with callus and marks. Bess' feet, toughened by years of running and climbing across cobblestones without shoes, only looked dainty on stage because she was so small. Her skin didn't tear as she scaled the wall to the low roof and crawled up its shingles.

The ridgepole was firm under Bess' feet as she tiptoed across. Half-fearing she'd have one of those wobbles, she breathed silent relief when she reached the wall. Then edged out into the brick, hanging from her fingers till she could brace her toes and push up.

Finally, Bess hooked her fingers over the sill to the candlelit window. It was a casement window and swung in like a door; and it was unlatched.

She pushed it, and pulling up smoothly on strong arms, vaulted into the room.

CHAPTER SIX

"*V*oilà!" Bess shook out her hiked skirts as if she'd arrived on stage.

Which she had, in a way, as the man in the low leather chair had become her most important audience.

He sat so the candle shed its light across the book balanced on his knee. He had a little desk beside him bearing a glass pen and inkwell. As always, a cut sheet of paper lay there; as always, it was blank.

She could just see the glint of silver in his hair and his faint smile.

It spoiled the pleasure of her arrival that his smile was a cold echo of Dan's.

He nodded toward the corner. "There's your prize, but it may have grown cold."

The tub, a deep oaken cup big as four barrels and more, lay beyond a glittering lacquered screen. A polished board lay across its brim offering dark wine in a crystal chalice, slices of cold beef and cheese, and Bess' favorite, a cut apple that bled the scent of honey.

All for her. Her reward. Not payment; *indulgence*.

In a second that soft water would melt away her roiling emotions, *all* her emotions, soak her in peace and leave her blissfully empty.

This shadowy man never lunged at her; he stayed still. Nor did he disappear. At least, not without leaving her clues where to find him.

In his chair his head was lower than hers, but she managed to look down and smile through her lashes. She'd experimented with seductive looks; they were tests. He passed them with his lack of response.

Slowly she unwound the scarf, letting linen and hair fall free.

He never asked for it. She did it partly because he *didn't* ask, proving to herself that he wasn't like the groping men in the theater. He was more than twice her size, and if he had, it could have been ugly.

But he stayed delightfully still.

Everything she'd told Dory was true, as true things made the best lies. Bess despised her admirers and didn't deign to meet them... as she'd already acquainted herself with the one who was exceptional.

He showed no signs of even ogling her. If anything, it made her bolder to try and catch his attention. She dropped her spencer.

His lack of response was both needling and reassuring. On the one hand, she felt safe enough to cross the room to the tub.

On the other, it made her wonder if her ability to sense danger had failed completely.

One step at a time, she crossed the room, untying the ribbons of her overdress, letting it fall and stepping out.

He didn't move.

His silence and stillness felt like a cue. Bess could go on as she liked and he wouldn't interfere. Once sheltered behind the lacquered screen, Bess untied the rest of her tapes so she could drop her chemise and then her last petticoat, letting them puddle on the floor. She climbed into the water with a deep, honest sigh.

He always said it was cold, but it was still silky warm, enveloping, buoying her up with soft aromas of frankincense and lilies.

The very peculiarity of this performance reassured her. She had built up each step, each flourish, over months, with him as her partner in the scene. As long as she kept returning to him, he would give her all this, and the most delightful words.

Baths were the ultimate luxury. Impossible to steal and their pleasure went bone-deep.

Her annoyance sparked higher as Dan's reappearance shook loose memories. Washing behind a screen Dan made of scraps of wood and linen stolen, not for the Grand H., but for her.

That sense of utter safety that other people would probably call *home*.

Was that why she'd chosen this scene? Memories she'd forgotten? Feelings she didn't realize she chased?

Now she tried to let the water rinse away her prickly feelings and popped a bite of apple into her mouth.

"I'd given you up tonight." Cool words in his deep, velvety voice.

"I had to attend to a matter of business." That line came from one of the first plays Bess ever saw. She thought it wonderfully off-putting.

She couldn't see him past the screen, but his voice rose and betrayed something—disdain? "If it was another admirer, greed is hardly seemly."

The wine was both bitter and sweet, and went down smoothly. Bess sent a creamy bite of cheese after it. Perhaps she ought to offer him some sweet words for once. "I have no admirers. You and I are more than that."

"Ah." He stayed quiet, perhaps listening, as she swung her hair outside the tub's edge and sank into the water with faint sloshing sounds. "You do have some regard for your Silver Duke."

He sounded gratified. Bess relaxed. He loved that name; he'd signed his cards that way, long before they ever met.

He would have been surprised, perhaps, that among the handful of trash the Grand H. had left behind when he died had been a fat little copy of Debrett's *New Peerage.* Bess knew perfectly well there was no Silver Duke.

But he was here and had been for months, and Bess needed that.

He liked to change his game, like locking the door, but that was only a minor confusion compared to the resulting bliss. Generally, Bess liked surprises. That was one reason she came.

"You must be tired. Rest."

That line was no surprise; he said the same thing every time. Bess adored both the line and the soothing repetition.

"You must be hungry." Another familiar line, but he was right. "Eat."

The crackling of the fire and the sloshing of the water competed for her attention, capturing it, letting it drift. The beef was cut in bite-sized pieces; she ate it with her fingers.

"Was the Dido taxing?" The sound of a turning page.

And that she loved the most. He knew what she was doing, what mattered to her, and shared that he knew, but kept his distance. He didn't fawn or shout; he always asked about the opera.

The audience there drooled, while the dancers sneered at the audience. Bess loved talking to someone for whom it was neither drudgery nor mystery.

Because the little world inside the opera house was enthralling. Pretty people living pretty lives interested her. Ever since she'd been small, crawling into their bedrooms and touching their things, she'd been curious about such shiny lives.

From stage she saw them all.

And as they adored her, she learned about *them.*

"The Talbourne box was almost empty. Lady Hadleigh and Lady Fawcett were there."

"Well, we know Lady Hadleigh hates to miss an entertainment."

That *we* was soothing. After Dan had disappeared, making Madame Franck a genuine friend in his place had seemed too great a risk. She had only herself.

No, she didn't. Dan was back.

She pushed that thought away.

"The Duke of Gravenshire was there, alone. Oakland was too, though he had a party with him. Not his wife." In the sweet warmth of the bath and the wine, time, memory, and words got tangled. But she was very sure she'd seen the elderly Duke. She'd seen him before.

Early on, she'd asked everyone in the wings. *Who was that pretty lady in green? Why did everyone look when he came in?* Now she could identify the opera's patrons by sight.

"Was he?" His voice was even as always, but clearly interested in Oakland. "Are you sure?"

"Quite. He's so old. His box sits on my left. I saw him well." The chandeliers lit the audience through every performance, so they could judge one another by their clothes and company.

"Who was in Oakland's party?"

"A man I didn't recognize, a gentleman. He... seemed related. From the shape of his eyes, and his mouth." He'd been handsome and had clearly felt awkward. "Half the people in the audience spent the first two acts watching *him.*"

That stung. Bess despised Dido's weakness, but it was an excellent performance.

Her host's perfect answer melted her annoyance away, "Even people who never clap see you dance. It melts into their hearts like water in dry sand, present even when invisible. It could change their lives. Who knows?"

There it was. The sweet words that fed her more surely than the wine and cheese.

Other admirers had written stupid hypocrisies that she could just tell they'd written a hundred times. The Silver Duke's admiration had always been original. Sweeping in scope.

He often told her she was the best dancer, not just in London, but probably in Europe. He admired not just her black stockings, but her strength. He spoke in terms of revolutions, not performances.

And he convinced her that her dancing had great effects, caused changes she'd never see. "Yes. That's true." It was true; her dancing had introduced her to him. She rested her head against the edge of the tub. "Do you think some other admirer will ever send carnations, night after night, until I agree to meet?"

"No." Final. "There is only one you, and only one me. Who else would send you the coronation flower?"

On other nights she would have enjoyed that, imagined herself a secret princess admired by a duke. Tonight it felt flat. "Oh, yes." She let her sour amusement show. "The Tourmaline and the Silver Duke. A child's story."

The silence stretched. For a moment Bess wondered if she had finally said something wrong. She sipped again at her wine.

One tremendous appeal to these visits was that she could

do no wrong. That made them comforting. Five years of wondering what she'd done to drive Dan away, where he'd gone, why he didn't come back, and she had learned to love a certain kind of certainty.

Now she wondered if she'd destroyed it all with a careless word. It made her heart pound, but in the warm water her limbs stayed limp as ribbons.

Finally he said, "I signed myself the Silver Duke for my own reasons. If you don't like that name, pick another."

Of course she could. She could do anything. He often told her so.

Relieved, she laughed. "You chose your name; how could I do better?"

It sounded like he smiled too. "Any other theater-goers of note?"

Dan flashed into her mind, and only the habit of not giving Dan's presence away kept her from blurting it out.

She cupped her fingers over the edge of the tub, as if she were climbing it. Rested her cheek on that hand.

She'd only seen him, spoken to him for a few minutes, and yet she felt different. All this felt different.

As though she'd stood on a gray empty stage, and Dan's reappearance had lit the footlights, illuminating how the trees in the scenery were false.

She'd chosen this. Not all at once, but word by word, over months of the Silver Duke's persuasion. He'd offered her choices, and she'd picked. A quiet room instead of a party; a bath instead of dresses; always the very best apples. If she finished this one, he would likely give her another.

She'd built herself a refuge like her childhood, but with all the luxuries it had lacked.

Complete with an old man in the corner she could safely ignore, as long as she brought him things. She smiled into her fingers.

"Oh!" The water slapped from her sudden movement. Had she drifted to sleep? Memory startled her awake. "Lord Ayles! He sat with the treasury secretary. You described his suit perfectly, and his wart." The wart belonged to the treasury secretary, not Lord Ayles; his lordship was a comely man of middle years, likely never troubled with warts.

"Lord Ayles. Did he?" Her host sounded pleased.

Shoving to her feet, she stood for a moment, reaching over to her skirt pocket, heedless of the water dripping from the tips of her breasts. She took out the rings.

"The ring was just where you said." She left the signet on the bathing stool but slipped on the sapphire. Her fingers were tiny; it was too large to stay on her fourth finger, but fit the one in the middle.

"And you found another ring to keep." He didn't reach for the signet, just stayed behind his screen.

The Bess raised on the streets was suspicious of strangers, and strangers were everyone not Dan or the Grand H. That Bess would have noticed him mentioning the sapphire. That Bess would have realized the screen between them was a stage property.

This sleepy Bess did not.

"She had it atop the signet. Maybe to keep it on. It's pretty."

"Of course it is."

"I'd like it. Perhaps a matching brooch."

"Would you? They'd suit you. A match for your lovely eyes."

Bess' head felt heavy in a way she could easily blame on the wine, warm water, and long, long night. She blamed his mistake on the same things. Lots of men decided her eyes were blue; she didn't care, that only made her more difficult for the law to chase. "I can take anything I want."

"Yes, you can," he agreed, smooth and calm as ever.

"You're such a *marvelous* thief, Bess. What other crimes do you like?"

Bess' mind flooded with the image of Charles and the lady in the chiffon gown, crashed uncaring against the wall. Then a flash of the way Dan's shoulders moved in his coat. What kind of crime did the Silver Duke imagine?

She must have made a noise, she thought, because he chuckled. "What crossed your mind *then?*"

"Why so obsessed with my past?" He loved hearing about her crimes, when Bess couldn't even remember why she'd originally told him she'd been a thief.

"You're an *artist*, Bess. You are grand, in everything you do." She heard him turn a page. "Perhaps I'm impressed by such grand ambition in such a tiny package."

That made Bess snort.

She tried to stay ladylike in front of the Silver Duke, but now she was warm, clean, fed, and it was hard to keep up the appearance.

He said, "You could change the world with the smallest push of your finger. What have you toppled, Bess? Taken? Burned?"

She'd always seen in Dan's eyes a kind of proud amazement at what she could do. She'd seen it tonight, after she'd put him on the ground. It was still there.

It weighed about the same as the breathless attention of an entire theater audience entranced by her every move.

She squeezed the sapphire ring on her finger.

She *had* given up stealing. Spent whole years focusing on the dance, the language, the transformation of natural grace into something organized and perfect.

In fact, hadn't she started again at the suggestion of the Silver Duke?

His voice had grown darker, like the room. Was Bess falling asleep? The sound swung like a hammock, like a hanging-rope. "Have you sunk treasure in the Thames where only you could find it? What have you *destroyed*? Whom have you *killed*?"

"I haven't." *She wouldn't*, she wanted to say, but the words inside her had melted like her bones in the heat. The wine wrapped over her head and her eyes closed. She still felt it in her fingers.

"Aren't there people who deserve it?" Even in the dark his voice followed her, threading through the wine, the water, the warmth until she couldn't object.

There *were* people who deserved it, she knew that for a fact. She'd seen many.

"You could kill a man to change the world, couldn't you, Bess?" His voice hissed around the edge of her fast-fading consciousness.

"Oh yes," she said, so confident she surprised herself, just as she fell asleep.

* * *

LATER, outside the heated room, Lord Julius Avery, Marquess of Vellot, smiled at the way the girl called him *the Silver Duke*.

It was a child's game; the girl was right about that. But children dreamed big dreams. He, for instance, had dreamed in his nursery of a dukedom, and soon his dream would come true.

Regaining his own oak-lined chamber, he splashed cool water on his face, then dried it with linen so snowy it looked frozen. It was the work of a moment to don his hat and swirl his cloak about his shoulders as he left.

Outside, sleet iced the road. He climbed into his waiting carriage.

Street beggars did not approach the featureless black carriage, nor did it swerve for them.

Falling ice streamed from the hat-brims of driver and footman till the coach rolled to a stop before a great house, ancient gables also hissing with sleet in the night.

An old London residence for a very old duke.

Vellot leaped out. "Wait here," he told his footman.

"Sir."

But once his black cloak had swept past, the house's footman ventured down the steps with a broad waxed umbrella.

"You won't step in?" he asked his counterpart clinging to the back of the coach.

The Vellot footman looked longingly at the dry perch only yards away. Melting ice had soaked through his coat and dripped from his sleeves. "It's not worth it," was all he said, and stayed where his master bid him.

* * *

"Your Grace." Vellot swept into the Duke of Oakland's drawing room. His cloak swayed, still dripping freezing water.

The old Duke, receiving in his dressing gown, gave the dripping cloak a disapproving glance, but only moved to lift a crystal decanter. "Devil of a night. Brandy?"

Vellot took the fragile glass, then stood waiting. An awkward pause stretched. Finally, the gray-haired Duke realized his visitor would not drink till he saw his host drink from the same bottle.

With obvious distaste, the Duke poured a splash for himself. He sipped the liquor and watched his guest taste his own glass. "You can't have news already."

"Some, and not to trust any other way. Our eyes and ears will serve as hands too."

The Duke's eyebrows climbed. "All in one person?"

"One remarkably well-suited person. Strong, angry, and untethered from false faith in king or country."

"He brought you proof?"

"As I've so often told you, Oakland," said the visiting Marquess, taking a liberty his host clearly did not like, "no one can bring me proof. I must extract it from them, or what good is it?"

His Grace scowled again. "And you have. Extracted it."

"Quite. Tell-tales are useless to me, while an unwitting witness is everything. For instance, you were in your box at the opera with a young gentleman tonight. Or, I beg your pardon," said Vellot with an exaggerated flourish toward the clock, "last night, I suppose we must say at this hour."

Oakland's shaggy white brows pulled tight together. The frown was the only sign he'd heard.

"Not particularly notable, you may say," Vellot allowed, "but something you can confirm."

The old man's hand was steady as he swung his glass to the table. "Nothing noteworthy. Any young man might have visited my box; I have many friends with sons and grand-sons, of course, as well as the cousin who is my heir."

"Odd that your mind went toward family connections. But I quite understand. The gentleman might have been anyone. But he's someone dear to you. Is he not?"

The old Duke scowled again. "See here, Vellot, I didn't trade my support for your insolence. Any number of people saw me at the ballet; I have no reason to hide that I was there."

"Quite. Just as I've always said, knowledge is not enough. We must have its context. I have ears everywhere—"

"Spies, you mean."

Vellot only raised his own eyebrows in surprise. His impeccably brushed hair ignored fashion; its silver temples were held immobile by pomade, and perhaps the same habit of fearful obedience that drove his footmen.

Instead of acknowledging His Grace's accusation, he only said, "Context. For instance, I told you I would not be at the theater, as I was promised to another of Lady Woolacre's interminable musicales."

"A virgin parade," snorted the Duke. "Shopping for a wife?"

Vellot ignored his jibe. "You took someone to the theater you preferred I not see."

The Duke only shrugged one thin shoulder. His frame was frail under the evening coat. "There are many in Britain who don't deserve your company."

The words might have implied Vellot was above them; the tone implied he was below.

Vellot's tiny smile faded. "Surely I'm fit to meet your bastard grandson. Or should I await your invitation? Will Lady Oakland be hosting a reception?"

The old Duke drew himself tall. "Her Grace is beyond your threats. I already know you don't have the mercy not to pester a bedridden woman fighting for her last few breaths. You must have the *context* that she has long been aware of my son, and grandson."

"Does she? Touching. Silent about it, of course. I suppose she even knows your bastard son was got on her best friend. Women are susceptible to guilt. She must have felt guilty she never bore you a child."

Now the old Duke's eyes were snapping hot, and measured the distance to a sword hanging on the wall; Vellot saw it. The Duke spit his words. "Get out."

Lord Vellot only sipped his brandy and stood his ground, dripping water on the richly woven carpet. The drops left tiny coal-colored streaks.

"Your Grace, I'm only congratulating a family that

contains so much honesty!"

Oakland moved as if to force him out, then paused. Perhaps wondering who in his house was a Vellot spy. A footman? One of his wife's nurses? Were they also ready to be, not just eyes and ears, but hands?

Vellot continued. "Of course your wife knows all that. What I wonder is if she knows about the other young lady at the theater tonight. Your far more recent daughter."

At that, the Duke's face grew red, then mottled. The color seemed congealed by his forced silence; whatever would escape his lips if he spoke now would cause him more trouble than he wanted.

It was just what Vellot wanted to see.

"Your daughter is *much* younger, isn't she? Younger even than your splendid grandson. But you didn't provide handsomely for her at all. *Now* she circulates among the *ton* under Lady Villeneuve's protection, wears your family ring..."

Here he twisted the gold circle on his smallest finger, showing that the Oakland crest was now in his possession. His proof.

"But before, wasn't she employed?" He drew out the word *employed*, implying many things with it. "Why, she was listed in Mr. Harris' guide, was she not?"

His reference to the famous list of brothels made the Duke practically purple with rage. One gnarled old fists rose in the air; Vellot only observed with interest.

Then the Duke pulled a bell rope.

"I see," said Vellot, as if he'd been answered. "So your wife does *not* know of that. And you wish to preserve her good opinion of you, or whatever's left. I wonder, can one carry hate into the next life?" He looked pensive. "Or perhaps contempt? What do you think?"

"Show him out," said the Duke to the arriving footman.

That young lad, alarmed by impending apoplexy in the

Duke and eager to get a dripping man off His Grace's carpets, rushed to the far door and opened it, awaiting Vellot's exit.

That was fine. He had made his point. No family secrets were safe from his methods, and he would not hesitate to put them to use.

The convoluted trials of Oakland's family did not interest him except for this. The old man was difficult to bring to heel; but heel he would.

"Pout if you like," Vellot said softly, pitched to reach only the Duke's ears, "but it is *all* good news. Nothing in London can happen without my knowledge, and these eyes and ears have hands that will serve."

"To kill a man? He has that strength?"

"Strength, and a moral emptiness that will make a beautiful weapon."

"Watch the sun rise somewhere else." The Duke of Oakland didn't want any more *good news*.

But good news it was. "Soon," was all Vellot said.

Oakland knew what that meant. Soon they would lose a few troublesome upstarts in the House of Lords. Soon the British public could be persuaded to tire of the wars, the soaring price of bread, the bitter cold. Soon all of Britain would turn to new ministers, who would steer the Prince Regent in a new direction.

Soon there would be peace with France, because Britain would be part of Napoleon's empire.

CHAPTER SEVEN

"*I* know how to use a fucking napkin."

"Do you?" Fitz waggled the one in his hand. "How do you know?"

Dan stared at the printed rags covering the table: flattened, unsold numbers of *Bridle's Gazette*. Fitz had slapped on circles and ovals of cheap yellow paint to represent serving dishes on an elegant table.

Dan was waiting for Fitz to notice this wouldn't work. Dan's language ought to be the final clue. But Fitz just kept offering him another fork and talking about mollusks.

When Dan didn't answer, Fitz dropped the napkin at Dan's elbow. "My grandfather used to wipe his fingers on the tablecloth. Called it good manners. My parents thought it disgusting."

"How about licking your fingers? How did they feel about that?" Dan had the urge to wrap that napkin around Fitz' neck.

He wanted to see Bess again, hated himself for it. He had safeguards in place long ago, knew she was safe; but having broken his own rule, now he craved more, and the idea of these dinners was a poor distraction. How like the rich to make a game of eating their rich, pretty food in rich, pretty dishes. With sparkling silver all around.

They'd never been hungry.

* * *

Dan had never seen a room packed so full.

Full of tables, golden chairs, candlesticks, and yellow light; full of women, in clouds of skirts and hair; full of silver in their hands, jewels at their throats, shining dishes in front of them holding mountains of food of every kind.

Roast birds, a piglet, diced fish topped with butter; a tomato salad like rubies spilled across a plate. Nuts wrapped in sparkling sugar; plates of cream on ice. The smells were rich, unctuous, so thick Dan almost tasted them on his tongue.

He stood gaping until a footman slapped his head. "What are you doing? Move!"

Dan scurried back to the kitchen, down a long corridor and two staircases, where he'd been commandeered to carry a heavy tureen to the dining hall. His return prompted a kitchen maid to set him to scrubbing pots.

Those sparkling beings at the table hadn't eaten more than a few bites of any one dish. But the plates he saw were bare. The footmen, he realized, finished their suppers on that long walk back.

Looking around to make sure no one was watching, Dan touched his tongue to the foamy edge of a pot waiting to be washed.

Just potato starch, sticky, with a little salt.

He could not imagine the wealth of sitting before all that food, the chance of actually eating it.

As Dan trudged back to the Grand H.'s cellar from the house where he'd served as a kitchen boy for a month, secretly spying out its weaknesses—because wise thieves didn't steal where they lived— he tried to imagine it. What would it feel like? Those soft linens against his skin? Those luscious tastes on his tongue? The feeling of not being hungry?

They were a different kind of person, Dan decided. They simply couldn't be the same sort of animal. He would have reached over plates to get to the last bites; he could never be full. He'd been hungry every day of his life.

As he reached the low door, Bess threw it open.

"Dan! Let's run to the green to see if there's fireworks!"

Funnily enough, Dan had forgotten it was Guy Fawkes' Day.

Like waking from a dream, he realized the fire in the alley wasn't some new random violence. There were more bonfires up the road, threatening all their shelters if a spark reached the old over-hanging stories.

Most of all he noticed the orange-gold glow on Bess' face, so excited, so happy. She flew past like a bird bent on escape.

She was one of those people. She could have sat in a rich room, plucking at bites of guinea hen. She glittered. A completely different kind of animal.

He intended to follow her once he made sure the Grand H. didn't want him. The old man was troubled by coughing these days.

But he didn't have to rise to see Dan's face.

"Why do you look like that?" he snapped, more brusque than usual, then coughed. Dan couldn't see his own face, but he was used to accounting for it.

"Bess went to the green to see fireworks," was all Dan said.

"See she gets back safe," croaked the old man between coughs, confirming what Dan knew. Bess was the sort of person who glittered; Dan was the sort who made sure she could shine.

* * *

DAN SCOWLED AT THE NEWSPRINT. "When they serve food *à la française,* you can help yourself to whatever you like. Footmen might pass dishes, or guests, but you're expected to eat what's near. If the table's long enough, you'll likely never try what's at the other end. If some peculiar hostess wants to serve *à l'anglaise*, she serves soup, then her husband cuts the meat. When she's done, the course is done."

"Now how did you know all that?" Fitz murmured, largely to himself as he knew Dan wouldn't answer. "And what about wine?"

"What *about* wine? People drink it." In truth, Dan only drank wine or ale if someone else bought it. It was an unnecessary expense.

In fact, he'd once bought Fitz an ale, and look where that got him.

"Guests only drink when there's a toast, so the gentlemen make toasts. All night. If you dine with your host, you must be prepared to toast."

"Jesus Christ." Dan ought to explain he wasn't this sort of person. But what good would that do? He had committed. "What the fuck do I say?"

"I have a book."

Not soothing. "People won't notice I've memorized toasts out of a book?"

"Don't be daft. Half of them have done the same. As long as you look sufficiently genteel, they won't question it."

"I won't look *that* genteel."

"You won't?" That perked Fitz up. "How shall you look?"

"Not like me," grumbled Dan. His life might be paltry, but when this was over, he wanted it back. He didn't have Bess' knack for disguise, but he'd make an effort.

Fitz knew what it was like to have his enemy know his face. "I'm sorry you're going alone after all. One doesn't go into battle with just one weapon."

"I'm not a fucking weapon, Fitz. I'm a bookkeeper. I have to come back."

He might not be the kind of person who deserved to eat

at glittering tables, but he intended to live. At least long enough to do this job. This was his best chance to make his dream happen.

Bess might want him dead, but as long as he got paid, he'd leave her the chance to climb his bones out of the gutter.

* * *

Bess woke slowly, far slower than usual. Daylight was a shock. She felt over-warm.

Where was she? Dan wasn't watching... Madame Franck wasn't watching, she corrected herself blearily. Some button-man could be sneaking up right now to snatch her away to jail.

Blinking in the light, she dragged her body upright, clutching the linens. She was naked and wanted to vomit.

She hadn't drunk that much wine. Perhaps she was too small to drink any. The Grand H. had always warned her against drinking games.

Surely she'd tasted every gut-rotting, home-made spirit in London. Something last night left her stomach churning. It couldn't have been the Silver Duke's wine.

Where were her clothes? And a comb? She desperately needed one, she dimly realized, touching her head. When she lowered her hand, the wink of the sapphire caught her eye.

Well, she still had that.

Above her, a vast canopy of ivory lace threw textured shadows on the carved bedposts.

She'd never been in this room.

Wrapping herself in the sheet, she gingerly swung her feet to the floor. Her clothes lay almost in arm's reach, over the back of a chair.

Despite the horrifying situation, she felt calmer than yesterday, and that made *no* sense. This situation did not call for calm. Nothing hurt, except toes and fingertips she'd rubbed raw in the climb. But was that any assurance of what she'd done—or what had been done to her?

The door knob clicked.

A heavy bronze frame on the table was the only possible weapon. She snatched it up and hid it among the folds of the sheet she wore.

The Silver Duke walked in.

In the daylight, he looked older. Grayer. Frantic laughter tried to bubble up into her throat; she shoved it back down.

It felt stupid not to have another name for him, stupid to be standing in his house wrapped in a sheet with a sick stomach and no idea where to find her shoes.

"Ah, you're awake," he said, as though *ballerinas* fell into various rooms of his house every day.

"I suppose I forgot to tell you when to wake me."

He ignored her regal attitude, ignored *her*. He seemed to be looking for something small, on the tables, on the windowsill. At one point, he picked up her clothes and dropped them again.

That small motion felt invasive, as if he'd dropped a lock of her hair. And dangerous. As though Bess didn't own those clothes, or her hair, or any of herself.

And the way he kept searching past her, like she was the same as the furniture—not pertinent to his task. That felt dangerous too.

A disoriented thief was a dead thief, and this was more disoriented than Bess had ever felt before in her life. She twisted the sheet tight around her chest. The picture frame dug into her fingers.

Back at the door, he paused. Turned to finally look at her.

The daylight showed his slight wrinkles, his slight self-indulgent pout. The way he filled the door frame reminded her of the difference in their sizes. "You'll have to hurry. The hackney will take you back to your rooms, and then on to your hostess. You must get there before he does."

From her earliest memories, Bess had been taught to behave in the middle of a crime the way others expected.

This felt like the middle of a crime.

Bess had many questions about *there* and *he,* but started with *hostess.* "How shall I address her?"

His smile crinkled only one eye. "Lady Dunsby's very affable, and won't mind any address; but you told me you knew how to behave in society. Surely you wouldn't lie to *me.*"

"Never," she said, silently resolving never to tell him another true thing for as long as she lived. "I'm only surprised. I didn't realize you meant to begin today."

His head turned to glance over his shoulder, as if he didn't wish to be overheard saying anything incriminating. "Lady Dunsby has a daughter about your age; you can act as her companion. It will be the perfect disguise. The man in question won't expect danger from a demure little virgin."

He'd said that to provoke her; Bess returned fire. "Demure little virgins can be as deadly as anyone."

His slow smile said he knew he'd ruffled her. "*Are* you a virgin, Bess? I never guessed that. You know my appreciation of your talents is less carnal than intellectual."

Then why did he look like some dog-creature starving for meat?

"Stay watchful; when the time is right, you'll know." His faint smile faded away. "Unless you lied to me about what you can do."

She remembered his question *very* clearly. He'd asked if she could kill someone, and she'd told him *yes.* In fact, it was the last thing she did remember.

Her stomach sank. Then further, and when she thought it couldn't go further, further still.

What had she said? What had he assumed she meant?

She'd come all this way to prove she was no fox and no saint either, but what did he think that meant?

He filled the door, blocking Bess' escape. The window was latched, and she wore no clothes. No one shy survived in the theater, but to her embarrassment, Bess found she cringed at the idea of climbing down the outside of the house completely bare.

This was a trap. The teeth closed; she felt them in her skin.

He knew where she danced on the stage. No, she realized; he knew where she *lived*. She'd given her direction the night he'd returned her from a sumptuous dinner at Jacquier's Hotel. He hadn't asked her to come to his rooms, and she hadn't asked why. Some quirk of him, the kind of thing that made him sign himself the Silver Duke. Interesting, but distant, and safe.

As often as she thought others foolish, here she was, the biggest fool she knew.

It was not reassuring that he showed himself clearly, in daylight. He was not a duke, but he had title and wealth, and he wanted her to know that. To know that she was less than a knick-knack on his mantelpiece.

Here was one feeling Bess hadn't summoned for a role. Loathing. For herself.

This Silver Duke had distracted her with wine and apples, and she'd let him pick her pocket.

She'd been so many people just in the last day: a heart-broken queen, a breathless girl, a thief, a whore, a pampered spy. Because she knew her reports were payment for the bath, the candlelight, the wine. Nothing was free.

But none of those people would get her out of this room.

Well, icy and uncharming were her strengths; they'd have to do. "Aren't you always saying I can do anything?" She couldn't believe she stood here reassuring him she could kill.

But she'd have said worse to get free.

"Yes. I believe you can." In the daylight, she could see how he watched her lips.

That shook her iron control, started a quake in Bess' stomach that threatened to surge to the surface.

He leaned his forearm against the door and spoke just above a whisper. "Killing can be a mercy, you know. It's power, and revenge. But it can just be... an accomplishment. You like to do what's difficult, right? Like dancing as Dido. Like climbing my walls."

In her clenched left fist, the hard sapphire ring nearly cut her finger. Too much bragging about purses cut, homes invaded. He thought she was that cold.

She recalled how firmly she'd answered him. Her blood slowed. She *could* be cold.

But not for money. And not for him.

Her stomach twisted; she could not stay still. With nowhere to go, she dropped to her knees.

Then acted as though she wanted to be there.

"I'll dress and be on my way." She peered under the stool. "I don't suppose you know where my shoes are?"

"Her ladyship will give you new ones," he said, as if expecting her to get in the hackney barefoot.

With that he left, closing the door behind him.

Bess clutched her waist, hair hiding her face, willing away the shivers. All her childhood instincts fought to surface. She wanted to hide under the bed, to climb to the roof, to leap out the window, to *scream for Dan.*

It was a childish urge of the Bess who'd been a child. Dan had been her compass, her snake in the garden of good and evil; cut loose of his tether, she'd found another. She could see that now.

But compared to this snake, Dan had been an angel of charity. Compared to *anyone.* Dan's core was pure kindness; she might be the only person in the world who knew how true that was. Maybe he had given up on morals, but somewhere in him was still the Dan she knew. She had seen, once or twice, the ghost of her old Dan, his only-for-her smile.

She could blame her fever the night before for how suspicious she'd been, how cutting. But what could she blame for having let down her guard so disastrously? For thinking a man who didn't bite had no teeth?

She knew how actions mattered, how masks worked. It helped Dan to have scars that made him look heartless; he'd used that to protect her, never hurt her. This cursed Silver Duke had looked rich, distant, like a ruby on a shelf, and tempted her with food and wine and the most glorious baths. He never sat too close, only challenged *her* to come closer. So did bawds.

And spiders.

Silently she whispered in her head to her memories of Dan, *what do I do now?*

And he whispered back, *Keep moving.*

That brought the reality home. *Dan was back.* If the Silver Duke exacted any punishment, it could splash back on Madame Franck, and that wasn't fair.

But it would be far worse if the Silver Duke found out about Dan, used him for leverage.

She hadn't wanted to give Dan the satisfaction of her dropping everything in her life to help him steal again. But she couldn't bear it if something happened to him because of her.

As she loosened her grip on the heavy bronze frame in her hand, it left grooves in her palm. Of course. It framed the Silver Duke's miniature.

She'd take it. Stealing a bit of his vanity didn't balance the scales, but it appealed to her sense of rightness.

Then she caught sight of her shoes, tossed in a corner. Brown leather, beaten and worn.

Like he assumed Bess must be, after such a show of control.

But Bess was not.

She stood and dropped the sheet, quickly donning her costume from the night before. He'd better have paid the driver of the waiting cab. She must get home, work out what to tell Madame Franck, and send some sort of message to the opera house. One way or another, the Tourmaline wouldn't be on stage tonight.

This wasn't over. She didn't run. He wanted her to feel like she had no escape. He'd failed to realize that closing Bess in a trap was far more dangerous for him than for her.

"Go ahead, corner me," she muttered as she rolled on her black stockings.

* * *

"Vellot. Get your feet off my embroidery."

Lady Winpole paraded into her parlor in a rustle of gray bombazine skirts. Behind her came a footman carrying her tea.

Men never failed to disappoint.

The Marquess swung his boots to the carpet. "Some courtesy, madame, at least."

She ignored his requirement of courtesy when he gave none; his petty wants weren't as important as her cushions.

Once the footman placed her tea and left, she spoke.

"Give me the note."

Vellot's aquiline features couldn't decide whether to

scowl or laugh. "It's in code, Lady Winpole. Really, one could take your lack of faith as an insult."

"Take as much insult as you like. The paper."

Shrugging one shoulder, Vellot drew the folded packet from inside his coat.

Lady Winpole went three steps to the fireplace and laid the note in the fire herself.

The heavy cotton paper caught slowly; then a burst of flame consumed the wax seal.

"I ask my correspondents to burn my notes; they fail me. So dissatisfying. I hope you have made progress; it's been a distressing day."

Why was it so much to ask that a man simply acknowledge what she needed? Money did not come from thin air, and she required money. Vellot was like all of them, like her husband. Assuming that if her wallet ran dry, she'd simply rusticate, survive on cucumber sandwiches.

She would not.

And he was in an appallingly good mood. "On the contrary, Lady Winpole. I've found the day utterly charming." Leaning back in his chair and letting his legs sprawl in front of him, Vellot laced his hands behind his head and grinned. His dark wool coat creaked with the stretch.

"Well, out with it." She picked up her saucer and tea. "I despise you making me prompt you."

"The ladder is all but built; all the rungs are in place. Talbourne journeys next week, and *our* surprise will await him."

Even her cough sounded disappointed. "It is more important for it to be clean, Vellot, than surprising. Surprise *me* by making it untraceable to our association."

"You might admire such efficient achievement of so many goals. Britain will join the Empire's fold diplomatically and help both sides out of a long and weary war."

Lady Winpole did not care. His assumption that she did annoyed her. He *was* like her husband, blithely assuming the right to demand her attention.

That made it entertaining to needle him. "Why would the ministers give up imminent victory?"

"They worry over Napoleon's faithful armies. Or another purge, if they execute him; too many of Europe's crowns now have come from him. They will leap at the chance of peace with the Continent that will look like a victory, because Napoleon will grant their every wish." He rocked upright, hands clasped in visible excitement. "Britain's vapid prince and lunatic king will no longer be a problem. Napoleon will appoint a new British crown as he did in Naples and Spain and Holland, and name them second only to himself. There will be peace, the price of bread will go down, the screaming populace will calm, and I? I will be rewarded with a dukedom."

"No one cares about your dukedom." Lady Winpole's speech was precise and crisp. "With *enormous* effort, I've gathered stores of copper in Connecticut and New Spain; they wait for shipment. Cotton and wheat in the southern colonies, and fur in the north. Everything I need waits while Wellesley and Napoleon waltz. You told me you could make it stop. Make it stop."

"Politics is delicate business, my lady. But never fear. One delightful side effect of my doctoring the ills of state is that your merchanting will proceed at an accelerated pace. Be of good cheer, Lady Winpole, if you can."

CHAPTER EIGHT

The Thames was a silver ribbon in the weak autumn sun, musty scents of river water and barnacles mixing with rain. Everything shone silver and wet.

The rattle of cab wheels and cobblestone accompanied every rocking bump as Bess and Madame Franck wound out of the densely packed old streets toward more open roads in Greenwich, on the river's south shore.

Bess was eager to see all of it and put aside for a moment questions of what to do about the Silver Duke. She could not simply track him down and murder him. That was a sure route to the noose. Rich people did not simply up and die without the law taking notice, though it happened to poor people all the time.

Neither did she want to think about Dan, whose judgment she also wished to avoid.

Madame Franck in her turn was distressed by the weather, the need to rush out of their home, and the necessity of putting away her peacock feathers.

And her suspicions of Bess.

"We have no idea what this lady expects. How can I prepare a role when I've no idea what she expects?"

"You're a *duenna,* I suppose. A governess. Like Juliet's nurse in that tragic play." Bess never turned away from the window. Here everything seemed to be about the water. As the cab climbed, the view improved and Bess could see ships bobbing like toys in the river.

"That woman was loose." Madame Franck pointed a thin finger. Without her peacock feather, she needed something to make a dramatic gesture.

"Juliet, or the nurse?" Bess wasn't really listening.

It felt oddly easy to push aside the shocks of yesterday and sink into the revelations of today. She was away from the Silver Duke, at any rate, and away from him, it was easier to breathe. Easier to contemplate what to do about the looming threat of him. Easier to look Madame Franck in the eye and pretend she knew what she was doing.

Some back part of her brain, something kicked awake by Dan's appearance, whispered that it shouldn't have been easier; but it was.

The house came into view, blotting out all the other warehouses, side houses, and alehouses. It was vast, with white-arched windows taking up every wall. Several of them had little wrought-iron balconies like cake baskets.

Bess had never seen a house like it.

The garden in front led overtop the hill and trailed down, giving a spectacular view. Anyone walking among its roses would feel like a king.

Why the sight affected her so, Bess wasn't sure. She'd seen the inside of many a London townhouse, at night in the dark; grand ones, with ironwork over their low kitchen stairs and tiny gates.

But this was different. Perched up here in the open air, all the Thames and London spread out at its feet, it was like a castle made of glass. Something fragile, for a princess.

"Bess, I'm frightened."

Startled into attention, Bess turned and grasped Madame Franck's small hand in her own. Their hands contrasted in color, but in all other ways were so alike.

Bess felt so much more cheerful today, despite the Silver Duke's shadow hanging over her, and couldn't explain it. Not even embarking on a new adventure could explain it. But then, Bess often couldn't explain how she felt; it was easier putting on someone else's feelings by consulting a script.

Madame Franck turned over their hands and looked at the sapphire ring. Bess hadn't mentioned it; so the Madame didn't either. But they both knew she saw it, and knew Bess had gotten it somewhere, somehow.

"I think you're lost in the wilderness, child. And I'm worried you like it."

Bess didn't answer. Her morning had bled into an afternoon of Madame Franck muttering about wilderness, foxes, and shallow graves. Bess *was* lost, she *didn't* like it, but the only way out was forward, surely.

Now Madame Franck whispered, "Should I be frightened of you?"

There was only a second for Bess to frown and shake her head *no* before the carriage rolled to a stop and the door was instantly thrown open.

A girl stood on the alabaster steps, soft dress whipping in the wind. "You've *come!*"

Bess was drawn out by a little hand, this one wearing a gold chain bracelet topped with a green jewel. *Emerald, small, bit clouded, nice color* went through Bess' mind before she managed to focus on the girl.

"Hello." Bess put on her sweetest smile. Her hair blew across her eyes, and she almost reared like a horse.

She'd forgotten it was brown.

When she'd returned to their rooms with the simple information that she had to leave, *now*, Madame Franck had been worried, but calm. "Do you need money?"

Bess didn't know what it helped to ask that when no one ever had any. "I must go on a visit."

The Madame had sent a boy to the theater with a short message—*The Tourmaline has fallen ill, no idea when she can dance again*—and started packing immediately.

For both of them.

Asking quietly, "You are playing a part?"

"Yes," Bess had answered without thinking. She was always playing a part.

No one took make-up more seriously than Madame Franck. She pulled an iron pot from under the bed, one holding the slurry of ground walnut shells and water Madame used to darken her own hair.

Knowing nothing about the part Bess intended to play, she urged Bess onto the bed, hanging her head over its edge, and darkened Bess' gold-streaked hair, wrapping it in linens and then smoothing it with an iron heated in the fire.

"I must be different too!" she decided aloud as Bess lay upside-down watching her sort feathers and spangles into one trunk and respectable chemises into another.

Theater *accoutrements* safely stashed upstairs with Madge the milliner, Madame Franck had rinsed and combed Bess' hair dry before venturing out to the street.

They found their cab driver in a tavern, deep in his third cup. A couple of shillings stopped his grumbling.

So in less than two hours Bess became a demure maiden with ash-brown hair, accompanied by a *duenna* soberly dressed in beige, even the scarves at her waist and neck. Madame Franck had turned a gown inside-out and pretended its seams were stripes.

Now, as Madame stepped from the swaying cab looking uncharacteristically subdued, she didn't need any acting skill to look worried.

Bess had no more chance to reassure her; the girl who had captured her hand was pulling her forward and talking breathlessly.

"I'm *so* glad you've come! I have counted every moment since my mother told me of your visit. I'm Lady Agatha, of course; do greet my mother. I must show you everything. Lady Dunsby, here's Elizabeth Page."

"Please call me Bess," said Bess, ignoring a sudden new last name she hadn't picked.

"Miss Page. We're so pleased to have you." Lady Dunsby, a round figure encased in glorious wool damask, balanced on the steps with two canes. Bess hadn't even noticed her in the rush of everything else to see.

She had the kind of face that came from a lifetime of smiles, full cheeks and a round chin. She didn't look the sort to insist on formality, even though she'd just dispensed it; and she seemed immensely pleased.

Bess tried to seem pleased in return. "I'm so delighted to meet you, Lady Dunsby, and thank you. Your hospitality is very generous." She curtsied.

The sensation of playing a part with no script at all was extremely unpleasant, like walking a sharpened tightrope.

But Bess could do that.

"Not at all, not at all, we are *so* glad of your visit. Agatha ought to be more in London, but my gout has held us back. It's our good luck Lord Vellot has no wife to help you into society. Helping him, and you, is our way of helping ourselves."

Bess smiled even though the name temporarily blinded her with confusion.

Lord Vellot? Was he her Silver Duke? And what sort of

game was he playing that he never told her so, yet let Lady Dunsby toss his name about freely? Was it *meant* to confuse?

If so, it worked.

But in the next moment, Bess was drawn forward again by Agatha. "We'll be just inside, madame."

Bess waved toward Madame Franck as Agatha pulled her away. "Yes—ah—Mrs. Frank, my governess—" Her introduction drifted away into the wind, but over her shoulder she saw Madame Franck drop a curtsey to her ladyship, and saw Lady Dunsby's silver curls bob back, beckoning this visitor, too, toward the house.

Most people mispronounced Madame's last name, anyway. She wouldn't find it hard to be Mrs. Frank. Number two, *concerned aunt,* would do just fine.

"What instruments do you play?" Agatha was still talking, in her mad dash showing finely embroidered slippers as well as a good bit of stocking. Bess gave up worrying about how to walk right. "We've a fine *pianoforte* and harpsichord too but I can't make heads or tails of them. I do all right with the flute. I don't suppose you play violin?"

Bess had spent a lifetime squirming through one small space after another in London's dark wood-beamed alleys with the rest of the struggling poor, looking for another day's survival.

Walking into Lady Dunsby's soaring entryway, with its glowing wood staircase climbing one side and marble-topped tables on the other, was like walking into a slice of heaven spiraling upward.

But her hostess didn't stop there. She kept pulling Bess forward, pausing only when she reached the music room. "It's really this light I like best," she said shyly, finally dropping Bess' hand as if realizing she's been dragging Bess along.

"Mercy Bennett." That was all Bess could say as she took in the view.

It was a *cathedral* of glass, the high arched windows looking out over roofs and trees to a sky full of seething, swirling clouds, every shade of ash-white, pewter, and gray, its churning mass of colors reaching all the way down to the dark horizon slashed with the silver ribbon of the Thames.

"I can play the guitar," Bess managed to say, faced with a view she'd never imagined of an unchained sky she'd never seen.

With a view like this, Bess could learn to love the daytime.

"*Can* you? That's *perfect*. Let's—do you mind, I mean, if I show you the rest of the house?"

"The rest?" Who could possibly need more than this room?

But Bess invisibly shook herself to concentrate on Agatha, a column of chagrin and sugar-white skin in spotless linen. Her curls were a pale gold, several shades lighter than Bess' usual hair, and she ought to have looked fragile, but didn't.

Only lonely, and eager.

"Yes," Bess said with conviction. "Show me everything you like. I am completely at your disposal."

That had been a line in a play Bess thought pretty bad, but apparently it captured the right spirit. Agatha's face lit up. "That's *perfect*. We shan't have time for many amusements, as Lady Dunsby has a whole plan to fit you with wardrobe, dance steps, anything a country cousin might need. I believe she secretly intends to get me more into society by launching you, but all I want is to have a bit more fun. I am quite resigned that you will outshine me, so you needn't worry I'll feel jealous. I don't do that sort of thing."

This gave Bess so much more to work with: that she was playing a country cousin, whom Lady Dunsby had agreed to help into society, likely to look for a well-heeled husband.

Also that Lady Agatha was entirely too sweet for her own good and possibly had poor eyesight. Bess wasn't likely to outshine this girlish column of light, especially not in darkened hair and country manners.

Searching her mind for performances of country manners, Bess said, "There's no chance I'll outshine you, Lady Agatha."

"Of course you will," Agatha said, already dragging Bess on to other rooms so Bess couldn't see her face.

* * *

"The clothes fit, at least," Fitz murmured under his breath as he escorted Dan into his house off Grosvenor Square.

"Except in the sense that I wouldn't be caught dead in them," Dan muttered back.

It wasn't Dan's first time in the house, but it was his first time dressed like this. Either Fitz' butler was admirably close-mouthed, accepting Fitz's offer of Dan's new name as if he'd never seen Dan before, or Dan was unrecognizable dressed like this.

Dan suspected both.

"Don't scratch. You're only meeting my wife, Lady Donatella, and her friend Lady Wendover. I just want to make sure you can pass muster with ladies."

"Simple answer. I can't. Why does one get called by her first name and the other her last? Or does it only sound that way?"

Fitz looked surprised even as he offered Dan a silver snuff box; Dan just shook his head.

"Lady Donatella is the daughter of a duke. By marrying a lowly third son, namely me, she dropped down considerably in the precedence of peers, but by courtesy keeps the title she had when unmarried. Lady Wendover's title is courtesy of her husband."

"It's a lot of courtesy to keep straight. Do they know what I'm doing?"

"No." Fitz' warning shake told Dan not to say more. "I told the ladies I'd found you a position as a secretary, and let them help pick your clothes."

"Both blind, then." Because never in a million years would Dan have chosen these green trousers, nor this pale blue waistcoat, nor this navy coat. He felt like a mallard.

"One has to choose's one's jokes for the right room, sir." The lady who sailed in was the tallest woman he'd ever met. Her deep blue Grecian tunic draped elegantly from her shoulders, tied at the sides, and her gloves disappeared into its sleeves. "The Duchess of Talbourne is a friend of mine, and both blind and impeccably dressed."

Dan was spinning trying to remember what to do first—greet her? Answer the remark? Look chagrined? But Fitz was there to smooth the waves. "Lady Donnatella, may I present Mr. Burton? He's an interesting fellow I met in the course of my work."

"Mr. Burton." She nodded.

Dan recalled Fitz' instruction that gentlemen were always introduced to ladies, not the other way round.

This felt like crossing a sea of rocks.

"My apologies, Lady Donnatella. I'm not accustomed to colorful clothes." Dan hadn't ever been the best liar. Especially around new people, it was easiest *not* to lie. And he'd never have picked these clothes.

"Truthfully," she said, "I wouldn't have chosen that combination."

The way her eyes measured his clothes wasn't provocative, but it wasn't simple either. Dan had the feeling she was measuring *him.*

"Julia, can you explain yourself?" Her ladyship looked over her shoulder.

Another woman came forward then, from the table where Dan could see she'd been arranging flowers. She was rounder, shorter, and, at least based on her expression, sweeter. "Lord Henry gave me to understand that Mr. Burton prefers not to be noticed. In my experience, the louder one's clothes, the less noise one is expected to make."

Her curtsey felt peculiar to get.

Fitz said with good humor, "And who am I to argue? Lady Wendover, this is Mr. Burton."

Belatedly, Dan bowed back.

He wished Bess were here. Not only to keep an eye on her. He'd made peace years ago with the fact that he couldn't keep eyes on her every minute. But Bess had always been good at pretending to be something she wasn't, and Dan could use some help.

The lady moved on to her friend. "And you *did* help choose those clothes, Tella. Don't you remember? We went shopping last week?"

"Did we? Last week is a blur. And men's clothes are so boring."

On that note, the ladies preceded them to the table, and Dan tried to breathe.

They weren't even in the large formal dining room where Dan had practiced recognizing forks. A small table had been set in a parlor, probably, Dan thought with a suppressed scowl, for his benefit.

Well, a face like his was out of place in any room this shiny. If he couldn't manage to dine at the small table, he wouldn't manage a big one.

Through the first remove, he limited himself to stupid remarks about the weather and trying not to yell at every new taste.

A brace of silver trout at one end of the table was matched by a roasted leg of lamb on the other, with carrots, spinach, fresh butter, a tangy sauce, and a dish of lemon pudding in the middle. While the ladies discussed the possibility of traveling to Bath this year, Dan restrained himself from shoveling it all into his mouth. He was accustomed to bread, stew, and pease porridge, and here was luscious dish after luscious dish, nearly all within his reach.

He was the glittering person at the table.

It was beyond bizarre; he felt like he'd fallen through the center of the earth and emerged on the other side into a world where everything ran the wrong way. This was never supposed to be him.

Fitz kicked him under the table.

Remembering his task, Dan lifted his glass. Fitz had already toasted king and kingdom; Dan could safely toast his hosts.

"To your health, Lord Henry, Lady Donnatella." He tried not to drink too deeply; wine hit harder than ale.

It didn't taste quite as pleasant as it smelled, but Dan could have smelled it all day. It was a fantasy land in liquid form: tart grapes, lush plums, even a bite of pepper and the sweet rare smell of vanilla.

Dan had stolen some vanilla pods once, so he knew.

He didn't feel like an imposter; he *was* an imposter. Not only as a secretary, but in this place, in this life. This wasn't for him.

But what if he could get this life for Bess?

He could do anything, *be* anything, for that.

The food held him so rapt that, until the second tablecloth was laid and more dishes displayed, he almost forgot to listen to the conversation.

"We ought to visit Talbourne House more often," Lady

Donnatella was saying, "but the drive is so long, and the card players far too good."

Lady Wendover laughed. "You mean you don't always win."

"Quite. Lady Winpole won back nearly all she owed me, even with Lady Dunsby as a game partner."

Dan felt some sensation sharpen in his fingertips at the name *Winpole,* but said nothing.

Fitz tried to take good-natured arms in defense of Lady Dunsby. "Is that fair to Lady Dunsby? You sound like she's a weight around the neck."

"She is a decent player, but *decent* isn't really a compliment," said the lady of the house with an elegant shrug. "What about you, Mr. Burton, do you play cards?"

Dan could play and he could cheat, but since he wasn't the best in London at either, he demurred. "When it won't hurt my partner."

"The partner is all," Lady Donnatella agreed. "I should try playing with—what's the fellow's name? He played at Lady Winpole's party last spring. Mr. Storey, that was it. He must not win much; he's always wearing the same green coat."

Dan's life often depended on knowing when he was seen and when he was unseen. Nothing about Lady Donnatella had changed; she had not turned so much as an eyelash.

Yet Dan knew for certain that her attention was sharply, wholly on him, as intent as if he were a card dealer about to turn over the next card.

Storey was Lady Winpole's bookkeeper in her illicit affairs, and maybe Fitz' wife didn't know that. But she knew something.

Dan stayed silent.

Lady Donnatella might be waiting for Dan to speak, but it was Lady Wendover who answered. "Perhaps Mr. Storey has other priorities, Tella. Not every man indulges himself at every opportunity. There are other responsibilities that may take precedence over a new coat." She smiled with a pretty little dimple. "Not for *you*, of course."

A sick wave of horror settled into his gut. Was he about to jail a man with a family of his own? A sweetheart? Dreams? What if Storey had a Bess to provide for?

Then he pulled himself together. No, Dan's questioning had been thorough; Storey had no one. The man's only care was pleasing his employer, and these days, that was Lady Winpole. Dan had uncovered that secret; if there were others, like a wife and family, Dan would know.

He couldn't start thinking that Storey was anything like him. Thieving meant knowing absolutely everything about the target without giving them an ounce of sympathy.

But this isn't thieving, a little voice reminded him. *It's spying.*

Even spying, Dan suspected, took knowing that he was himself, and Storey was Storey, and though they might look similar on the surface—two men reaching above their station to rub elbows in London's titled society—they were completely different.

For one thing, Dan never had people killed.

That was a difference between him and Mr. Storey he'd do well to remember.

At least, if he intended to earn his money *and* survive. He'd need to be alive to finish his plan and have the means to provide a good life for Bess, even a dowry so she could marry someone decent enough for her. He'd do what he was put in this life to do.

Protect Bess at all costs.

CHAPTER NINE

*R*iding a horse was *excellent* fun. Bess even considered smiling.

"All right, Miss Page, come on back," called the groom, and for a moment Bess felt tempted to see if her gleaming gray horse could jump the fence and keep on to the coast.

Why stop there? Perhaps the horse could swim.

For a little while, hair whipping in the cold wind, tiny Bess was tall. Powerful. A leap into the saddle and *poof*, she was a giant.

She and Dan had been tumblers at Hughes' circus; she'd vaulted over many a saddle. But this was her first chance to just ride.

To be a giant, fast as the wind.

Slowing a little, she leaned forward to pat the sleek muscle of the horse's neck. Its power under her fingertips felt familiar. She forgot all the characters she was supposed to be and remembered what it felt like to be herself.

She looked over her shoulder.

Of course, Dan wasn't there.

Of course he isn't there, she told herself, smile fading. That Dan had disappeared years ago, the way she never thought he could.

Bess had to watch her own back, and she should be watching for the Silver Duke. He was a problem who couldn't be escaped or ignored; he required a solution. She was going to have to solve him.

There was no reason for Dan to come to mind.

"Miss Page?"

"Of course, Sam," she said, a little breathless as she rode the horse back. This kind of luxury was hard to steal.

Even for men made of muscle with cold black eyes, she told herself as she slowed the horse to a walk, letting him stroll.

Greenwich might be far from the middle of London, but it still had scant space for horses; somehow Lady Dunsby managed to have a small, tidy paddock behind her glass castle. From Bess' first moment in the saddle, she'd have swapped even the music room for this.

It felt wrong to enjoy it so much when she was really only lying in wait for the Silver Duke. But it was her only option. What else could she do, tie Lady Dunsby to a chair and interrogate her? Even Bess couldn't imagine that.

Though she did watch Lady Dunsby warily. The woman was a fountain of generosity, and even before the Silver Duke had poisoned that well, Bess found inexplicable generosity suspect.

The key to an unexpected attack was surprising direction. She ought to be searching the house for a way to come at the Silver Duke he wouldn't suspect. But the thoughts that kept coming back to her were of Dan, the old Dan she knew and the new one she didn't.

And besides, for the first time in a long time, she felt a little... happy.

The house was delightfully free of horrible men, and Bess was determined to enjoy all its pleasures.

Slowly her horse approached the mounting block, standing in the grass beside the hoof-chewed ground of the paddock. Pretending to struggle a little to loosen her knee from its sidesaddle position, Bess silently vowed to find some trousers and steal this horse.

"We should have good riding in the country." Agatha clearly sensed how Bess loved it. She helped Bess down to the step; Bess pretended to need it. "I believe Road's End has some nice horses."

Riding in the country. Nothing could sound more grand. And in this riding habit, too. It was fine soft wool, though it barely touched her skin given its long-sleeved chemise, another gift in her *trousseau.*

Bess had learned some French in the theater, most of it to do with dance positions. This was a delightful new word that meant *chest of clothes to take with you when you get married,* or in Lady Dunsby's case, *when you are launched in London society to look for a husband.*

There was a very real danger Bess would begin to adore her.

You'll need this was Lady Dunsby's favorite phrase as, from the comfort of her settee, she picked laces for chemises, a velvet stole with a fringe, even an evening gown beaded with crystals. All Bess had to do was work out how to stuff it all in her pocket.

She couldn't possibly know the Silver Duke's intentions. The lady was all fluff.

Bess doubted she would even grasp something as unkind as murder.

Vellot must be using her for his own ends. Worrying for someone else was one of the most uncomfortable feelings

Bess had ever had; it was new, and it was deeply unpleasant. She'd never worried before; her world had been Dan, and he'd been invincible.

Now she had not only Madame Franck to worry about, whom she couldn't leave behind to face the Silver Duke alone; but also these two rich ladies with hair as bright as money. The thought that Lady Dunsby or Agatha might come to harm from sheltering Bess turned her stomach.

And then faintly, out of habit, she supposed, she did worry about Dan. She worried where he had lost his soul, and whether he might be following her despite the way they'd parted at the theater. She worried he would cross paths with the Silver Duke, somehow be drawn into the man's traps.

He might not be the Dan she remembered, but the very muscle and bone of him forced her to recognize how many millions of breaths she had taken, waiting through each one for his return.

She would not let the Silver Duke learn of Dan's existence. She owed him that.

But what if Dan learned about the Silver Duke?

Dan was poised on the edge of something dangerous. As confusing as their reunion had been, that had been clear. If he decided he had to protect Bess, he might fall. Truly fall into being someone too far from what he had been. Then the Dan she'd known would only exist in her memory.

Of course, if the Dan she'd known still existed at all, he wouldn't approve of her truly solving the problem of the Silver Duke.

Climbing the marble steps into the great glass-windowed house with Agatha, she found her ladyship once again sifting through trinkets.

Agatha drifted towards a polished brass toy she called a *telescope*, uninterested by baubles. The telescopes were everywhere in this crystal palace, and they let one see astonishingly far away in every direction, revealing the tiniest details. Agatha said nothing about them except that they'd been her father's.

Lady Dunsby called out, "Here, Miss Page, Madame Andre has finished some dresses; you must try them for fit."

The harried *modiste* had stashed three seamstresses in a drawing room, taking in clothing as fast as they could. Lady Dunsby wanted an entire wardrobe unreasonably quickly, and Bess was too small for anything on hand. They'd already altered the riding habit, three chemises, three linen petticoats and a woolen one, two walking dresses, two day dresses, and light and heavy night-rails.

Looking at the large stitches in one waist, Lady Dunsby clucked her tongue behind her teeth, but the *modiste* just shot her a quelling look.

So she fussed in the pile of notions. "This is too bad. I ought to have had more time to choose you a really complete wardrobe."

It seemed impossible that even a lady needed more clothing than this, but Bess knew when to stay quiet.

Not that Lady Dunsby wanted an answer. "Oh, I like this," she'd exclaimed, picking a gold-rimmed locket out of the pile of treasures.

It bore a posy of pink and red roses, formed from tiny shells cut into a mosaic.

"That's not suitable for a young girl!" The *modiste* tried to look shocked at the idea. Bess really wanted to ask what was unsuitable about pink and red roses.

How tiring rich people were with their *symbols* for this and *appropriate* for that. They had the time and money to complicate things, Bess supposed.

"Nonsense," Lady Dunsby told the *modiste*, "they're flowers, not lovers. Don't be silly. What do you think of it, Miss Page?"

Bess had to take the offered locket.

She'd held much finer jewels, but none had ever been simply handed to her. It was a new and peculiar experience. There was no thrill of accomplishment, but no terror of a tap on the shoulder, either. No question that keeping it might lead to the gallows.

It made her wonder how she might look in it. Not a character, *her*. Again she thought of Dan instead of the Silver Duke. What would he think of her, cold eyes and all, if he saw her wearing an honest jewel?

Even successful thieves lived in fear. What different lives these people led, where having a pretty necklace might not kill you.

"I think it's lovely, Lady Dunsby," the words came out before Bess had really decided to say them, "but too extravagant for a country beggar like me."

"Never say so!" Lady Dunsby's cheeks trembled with indignation. "You mustn't think that of yourself, Miss Page. Not ever. Surely you know how in fairy tales, princesses, and princes come to think of it, may be hidden everywhere. One knows their quality by their actions."

"Forgive me, my lady, I don't think I've read a fairy tale."

"What!" This clearly horrified the lady, who pressed her hand to her chest. "Agatha, go put one of Madame d'Aulnoy's books in my luggage. We should have some fairy stories on this trip."

Agatha drifted out.

"Madame Andre, you may take these to your seamstresses. Miss Page will be along."

The *modiste,* knowing a dismissal when she heard it, draped the new things over her arm and, with a curtsey, withdrew.

"Miss Page." Lady Dunsby's face settled into more serious lines. "I'm quite conscious that it is odd for a gentleman like Lord Vellot to seek my assistance in outfitting a young lady."

"Is it?" Surely it was all right for Miss Page to be as ignorant of the niceties of the gentry as Bess was.

"I should tell you I'm very sorry for the loss of your family, and glad to help you any way I can."

Bess expected the next line to be *but you must get out.*

Instead, Lady Dunsby said, "But I'm afraid Lord Vellot has some inappropriate intentions."

He definitely does. "Really?"

Lady Dunsby nodded firmly, hands atop one another in her lap. "I fear he does, and I can see it surprises you as it did me. He asked to call on you, and I have put him off; if you don't mind, I'll continue putting him off, as he seems to expect sole possession of your company. I doubt he should. He's so very much older than you. Do you have a *tendresse* for the gentleman?"

It was no effort to look puzzled.

"Tender feelings. Affection," she prompted. Bess must still have looked confused, because Lady Dunsby added, "I'm asking if you like him. Or perhaps love him."

"No!" Bess hid her surge of revulsion. "I mean, I haven't even met him. He sent a carriage for me." At least the last was true.

Lady Dunsby nodded again, with pursed lips, as if Bess only confirmed her suspicions.

"When you do meet him, you mustn't seem too grateful. Men sometimes think that doing a good deed gives them rights. Privileges, if you will." She studied Bess' face. "I'm a poor one to bring you into society, but I *will* do it. I think you might prove popular, and you ought to have choices."

This simple speech caused many unnameable feelings to

slosh around inside Bess, some swamping walls she thought unbreachable.

Bess hadn't suspected anyone with a title would balk if asked to hand over a country wench by another of their kind. And she certainly hadn't suspected one would want her to have choices.

"You're kind." Bess astonished herself by laying the beribboned pendant she still held back in Lady Dunsby's soft hand. "I am no secret princess."

Lady Dunsby made *fuff-fuff* noises, putting the pendant on the stack of things—fans, gloves, lace-edged kerchiefs—to take as part of her transaction with the dressmaker. "My daughter has all sorts of sparkling jewelry; this piece is perfectly appropriate for her companion."

The word *companion* knocked Bess' feelings into a falling spiral. Lady Dunsby's kindness was the sort one would show a servant. Bess was no servant. She had danced as a *queen.*

Bess braced her hands on the settee cushion on either side of her, the wave of feeling shocking her so much she had to hold herself still against her own inner revolt. She was playing a companion's part. Why be *angry* if Lady Dunsby addressed her that way?

Perhaps she had a recurring fever. She'd almost cried at lunch when she'd discovered there was no more mint jelly.

Well, the last time she'd felt this, it had passed. It would again too.

"Thank you," Bess said softly. Three days ago, if anyone had offered her the position of lady's companion over that of *a ballerina,* she'd have scoffed. Now, she saw it offered a softer, cleaner life. Raw feelings aside, she didn't scoff at any of that.

She could see now the appeal of what Dan had always told her to want. A life without watching over your shoulder. The easy calm of having enough money. Freedom.

Did he still want that? Had he found it?

It didn't concern her. She'd let herself be trapped in the Silver Duke's game; she had to play it through, both to stop him and to get him out of her life. It chilled her to the bone to know he wanted to see her.

Both Lady Dunsby and Lady Agatha were palpably lonely and bored in their glittering castle; so bored they would take in a girl they'd never met and shower her with gifts. Bess wouldn't enjoy a life like theirs.

Nor could she spend the rest of her days watching for the horrifying man over her shoulder.

But would she find freedom if she removed the problem of him completely?

If she set her mind to it, she might find herself in the hangman's hands after all, and avoiding that had been a life-long habit just as ingrained as looking to Dan for protection and help.

* * *

"ONE MOMENT. YOUR TRAIN, LADY WINPOLE."

The footman was being flattering; one could hardly accuse her gown of having a train. The skirt was simply caught on the carriage step. The days of truly exquisite gowns were gone, Lady Winpole mused as she waited for the footman to transfer his attention from her hems to Lackington's door.

The Temple of Books was an unforgivably long drive from her home, and Lady Winpole preferred comfort. Still, it served admirably as a place to meet people she did not want observed going in and out of her home.

The mountains of books inside it did not distract her from quickly mounting the stairs. Reading a book for oneself was no luxury. Her maid's voice was passably good, but not entrancing enough to make Lady Winpole spend her evenings agog over a book.

The book palace's vast dome sent light even into the lounging rooms above, and there she went into the third one from the left.

"Sir." She nodded at Mr. Storey, too cautious to use his name even where she was so unlikely to be overheard.

He rose immediately, as he should, his bottle-green coat immaculate as always. Every time they met, Lady Winpole expected to find him slovenly. The nature of beginnings like his would eventually show.

Fortunately, he had not yet given her reason to find fault with his person or his keeping of her books.

"My lady." His bow was rough, as he wasn't born to it, but it would do. "You wished to see me?"

"Only from necessity; paper records are so apt to go astray."

"My records, as you know, are quite safe from prying eyes."

"I've heard." Lady Winpole was unwilling to rest even these drab skirts in a public chair. But she was more unwilling to stand. Settling gingerly upon a wooden seat, she addressed him. "I hope this furniture does not house vermin. Please come sufficiently close that I may speak quietly, but do not breathe on my hair."

"Of course, madam." He came to what he judged was a suitable distance; she waved him back. A few inches farther away, she seemed satisfied.

"Put aside the legal businesses. The brothels, opium dens... Only for now. I know your affection for such things, but we must focus on less..." Her voice quieted even more. "Legitimate things."

"Just as you say." He did not take notes, and she liked that too, to the extent that she liked anything about him. She knew he would remember all her instructions, or they would have parted ways long ago.

There was a distinct pleasure, too, in holding his undivided attention. In the past he had served other masters, but she did not like her things touching other people's things, and that included Mr. Storey's attention.

"Obviously, we cannot rely on your taste in henchmen." That was all the reference she need make to his disastrous associate from that spring. The bumbler had given Lady Winpole an unnecessary enemy in the Caped Count, and failed to quickly kill his colleague, the flea-bitten journalist. It was a small complication, but Lady Winpole preferred to have none.

Mr. Storey acknowledged the rebuke with his silence.

She went on. "Attend to my shipments yourself. I expect them secure, with ships engaged to go anywhere immediately if they should receive such notice. No more landing on British shores till the treaties are settled. We'll soon be able to sell on the Continent again. But so will every other trader of any significance. You understand me?"

"I believe so, madame. Perfectly."

"Good." She stood and brushed off the rear of her skirts. "I don't want to have to meet again. I've arranged for a colleague to sponsor your travel. You may appear to be his man, or no one's; I don't care as long as you answer any summons I send instantly."

"Of course."

"Sir." She disliked showing him even that much deference. His plain face, beginning to groove on both sides of his mouth, bore no trace of smugness or glee, so she persevered. "The gentleman to whom I must connect you does not deserve an ounce of trust. The connection is *only* because he assures me of the earliest news when our ships may land in imperial ports. Should *anything* about him threaten our interests, I trust you will sever our ties in a very final way. With no loose ends leading to me."

"Madam." He bowed as if to reassure her. It put her teeth on edge; this was not the appropriate time for a bow. But he spoke, and she allowed it. "I assure you that even if my book fell into the wrong hands, it would be quite illegible to anyone but me. And if the gentleman fails to deliver on his promises, I will fulfill your wishes."

* * *

"*I hate spinach!*"

Bess' outburst at the supper table revealed to everyone that something was indeed very wrong. She hadn't meant to snap, certainly not at Agatha, and certainly not over spinach.

The dumbfounded look on Agatha's face just confirmed no one expected stewed spinach to cause such a reaction.

"I'm so sorry." Bess' sincerity was all real. She was fighting back tears for no reason. Even Madame Franck, on the other side of the table, looking very governess-like in a quiet blue dress, was clearly appalled. "I'm feeling a bit ill."

Agatha, who for three days had been just as angelic as she looked, nodded firmly. "Nerves. Travel is such a strain on them. This trip to Road's End is only a little one; you'll see. It will be so much easier to have your first social event outside London, with only a few eyes on you."

Lady Dunsby jumped in. "And then you'll be completely comfortable at musicales and such this winter. Never fear, Miss Page. We will look after you."

"Of course. I—" While part of Bess looked on with a horror usually reserved for prisons, the rest of her burst into sobs.

"All right." Madame Franck saw the need to move center-stage. "Let me take you to your room, Miss Page. You need rest."

Amid a volley of reassurances from Lady Dunsby and her daughter, Madame Franck hustled Bess away from the table.

"Are you ill?" Her whisper didn't carry as she walked side by side with Bess down the long gilt-decorated hallway. "Or is this some new game of yours? I like Lady Dunsby and her daughter. I'll tell you right now, whatever you plan to do to them, I don't like it."

Bess didn't answer till they reached her room. It was a confection, with rose-colored wallpaper, adorned with painted apple blossoms, and plaster reliefs of bouquets on every wall. Yet it felt like a box closing in.

Bess put out her hand to show Madame Franck how her hand was shaking.

"I'm a bit ill," she said, subdued. "Perhaps I need sleep. These days have been strange."

Madame bustled about, untying Bess' laces like a dressing maid, putting back the coverlets, laying the warming-pan near the fire. *She plays a governess very well*, thought Bess, a little dully. *Number six.*

Then something shifted, and she saw that the Madame wasn't doing any of those things to play the part of a governess. She was doing them for Bess.

The worry in her eyes as she came back to Bess looked real. "Once the warming-pan is hot, I'll put it in the bed. Sheets are so clammy in weather like this."

"No worry, Mrs. Frank." Bess never strayed from character on stage, and now her life was a stage. "The sheets will warm quick enough. Go eat with Lady Dunsby. I know you like her company."

Madame Franck made worried little noises and bent to unbutton Bess' new shoes. They were soft and fine, like everything in this house.

Bess just waved her off. "Really. I'll be fine."

Every second ticking by, watching Madame Franck's skirts rustle out the door, felt like a cat scratching at the underside of Bess' skin.

Once Bess heard the soft *click* of the door latch, she swung into action.

CHAPTER TEN

Fortunately, her riding gown buttoned in front. She moved fast, changing her shoes for her new little riding boots, wrapping herself in scarves and a woolen shawl to keep warm.

She really did feel ill.

In what seemed like only moments, she slid into the little stable. "Hello, Feather."

The sleek gray gelding shifted, and Bess smiled at the recognition in his eyes. He nosed at Bess' hand, and she realized he must expect a treat like the carrot Agatha had brought him *every time.*

Imagine, thought Bess as she swung his saddle from its peg. *Imagine having so much food you could feed it to horses.*

She'd closely watched the grooms and now she mimicked them, slipping the bit between Feather's teeth. It didn't feel odd, though she'd never been allowed to harness circus horses.

There was a moment of panic when she tried to push his ears through a strap and Feather shook his head, not letting her. He was much larger than she, but she was afraid she'd hurt him. Trembling, she saw she should have unbuckled the strap in the back.

She really had no idea what she was doing.

Still she did it, latching the girth underneath his belly with fingers already numb from the cold.

She didn't *want* to see the Silver Duke. She hadn't decided anything. She wasn't ready. Mere hours ago, she'd felt flooded with relief that Lady Dunsby had kept him away.

Still she felt a starving sadness, driven by a throbbing urge to *go, go, go*. And the feeling—no, the *knowledge*—that if she didn't go, she'd never be happy again.

She'd had that feeling before, of course, when she hadn't seen him for a while. She'd longed for that quiet room, her deep bath, the food, the wine.

The fake impression that she'd found freedom, and home.

Now the longing hurt.

Nor had she ever been so cold. Bess couldn't tell if she had a fever, or if London really was icier than it had ever been before. *Perhaps both*, she mused as she swung up and settled her knee in its ridiculous required position, in case she was spotted.

She was very good at finding west and north, even at night.

But as she rode Feather into the gloom, the long journey into the city seemed impossible. The stars were half-clouded. The saddle slid too much; afraid of hurting the horse, she hadn't sufficiently tightened the girth. Sidesaddle was awkward.

She was the Tourmaline. She was *Bess*. She should have been ready to vault to her feet and take a somersaulting dive off this horse. She and Dan had spent months at Hughes' circus. She'd get scrapes from the cobblestones, but she'd had worse.

Instead, she barely kept her balance as the horse quietly

clop-clopped its way to the end of the cobblestone drive, then onto the street's packed earth.

She didn't understand what she was doing or what was happening to her.

Then she was flooded with one more new revelation, a new discovery about the tumult of emotions inside that she tried to keep hidden. The past week had been full of them, but this one made her doubt herself the most.

This was fear she felt.

Her way grew rougher quickly. Where there was any land, it was marshy; and off to her right she could hear, past the humps of smaller buildings, the shouts of sailors of all kinds.

Few riders shared the road, and Bess couldn't decide if that was lucky or unfortunate.

Itching fury under her skin drove her on, even as she calculated over and over how long the entire ride would take. It was all guessing. This was England; nothing went in a straight line. She could end up wandering till morning.

Which would be unwise, she knew, as the laughing sailors grew louder.

Behind her came sounds of another horse's hooves, and wheels on packed earth.

She waited for the carriage to pass, but it didn't. As slow as she was, they stayed behind her.

Dizzy, fighting for balance, sweating into her fine new clothes, Bess felt her heart pounding harder and harder as she desperately tried to to calm it so she could hear who followed her.

It could be the Silver Duke. He could have set a watch on her. He liked being unpredictable, and he liked control even more. Their last interview proved he also liked her uncomfortable.

She wasn't uncomfortable. She was terrified.

A lone thief was a dead thief.

Confusion made it worse. Bess always made sense to herself; now she didn't. How could she be puzzled by her own actions? And why didn't she stop?

That horrible urge inside pulled her forward. It was no emotion, or perhaps it was all emotions. It was no thought. Only the reality that she *must* go on, she must get to the Silver Duke's house.

Those wheels behind her were really too close.

A man's heavy shoes hit the ground, and Bess saw someone reaching out of the gloom.

When ballerina Bess accidentally yanked on the reins, Feather reared back, and Bess felt herself falling.

* * *

"Sir, I must insist you keep your distance from the young lady."

Lord Vellot looked up with annoyance.

Lady Villeneuve, hard as an oak tree in corsets, had been a fixture of London society for years, shuffling girls from place to place looking for husbands. It wouldn't do to antagonize her.

"My lady," he said, restraining his irritation, "the power of the treatment derives from the magnetic force between my hands and Miss Buckley's body."

Lady Villeneuve's sharp eyes pinned him. "She doesn't need any more magnetic force."

In truth, the young lady didn't need any. She had begged for a display of Lord Vellot's command of animal magnetism, and though he agreed with tutors that such work should not be done in public, she was fresh and eager and Vellot could not resist.

His mistake, he realized as his hands dropped from

moving above her; a public display distressed him more than it did her. He could not fully enjoy his power over her, nor test her complete submission in waking sleep.

For she was asleep, that curious state of sleep induced by the application of his will and the gentle forces of invisible attraction between them as two objects in the universe.

"You may lift your hand, Miss Buckley," Lord Vellot continued, keeping his voice low, reassuring, quiet, yet insistent.

Her white hand lifted and remained in air.

"And you may drop it again."

The excitement he felt at his absolute control when she dropped her hand against the damask couch was visceral, an animal sensation in itself.

It had always been that way, from the first moment he'd seen one of the French government's pamphlets against Dr. Mesmer's new science.

Young Vellot, hungry to study the effects of magnetism in the body, had recklessly traveled through a France at war to find the Society of Harmony in Strasbourg. He'd been that desperate to gain access to another person's inner mind, the hidden part even they didn't know.

In Strasbourg, he found Lord Puységur, one of Dr. Mesmer's own students. The Marquis had given up the motions of his hands, considering them less vital than his voice in imprinting his will upon the subject.

Still, when asked to display his skill in public Lord Vellot enjoyed using his hands. He fancied he could feel the magnetic force between him and the supine girl, felt himself shaping it, pulling her. And the titillating threat of nearly touching one of Lady Villeneuve's virgins in public made him smile.

The Ayles party spilled out of every room, ladies in frothy gowns and gentlemen in dark coats laughing and talking everywhere, even the hallway to the edge of the stairs.

But this little drawing room was as quiet as it could be given the sounds of revelry coming through the closed door.

"Miss Buckley. What did you hope to gain from magnetic treatment?"

"For you to admire me."

Behind him, Lady Villeneuve smothered a gasp, and the girls with her made slight movements of shock as well. Such a bold admission would never come from one of her charges.

Vellot knew her ladyship couldn't see his smile.

"Very well. I admire you as a young lady who knows what she wants. How else may I help you?"

Half-anticipating that the girl's statement would be bold indeed, Lord Vellot began planning how to spirit her out of London to his country house, should Lady Villeneuve renounce all responsibility for such a secretly brazen creature.

The girl's delicate feet showed under the hem of her gown, which draped her curves. She was juicy as a plum. Lady Villeneuve had not permitted her to lie flat, though it would have been more comfortable for the girl. One round white arm dangled past the cushions toward the carpeted floor. Her lips were slightly parted, eyelashes dark on her cheek beside the tumble of shining curls.

She was sweet, helpless...

"Help me admit I've fallen in love with Lord Waresham."

And in love with a rake. Damn.

The whole attraction of a girl under his power was that she was thinking of nothing else, no one else. He'd had that opera dancer nearly there, but even magnetized, she'd been distracted. Someone had agitated her, though she wouldn't mention a name.

Vellot needed entire attention.

Behind him, Lady Villeneuve grabbed his sleeve. "This is unseemly, sir. Wake her at once."

"She is not truly asleep." Knowing the misconceptions of the uninitiated, Vellot began to revive his charge. "Miss Buckley, you are crossing this state like a river; you will meet me on the other side with calm nerves and a calm mind, feeling more peaceful than ever. You have crossed the river. You find that you are at the foot of the stairs in Lady Villeneuve's house, and you are going to climb all the way to the top. Mount each stair one at a time..."

He heard her ladyship hissing something to the young ladies with her and took the chance to lean unobserved toward the girl on the couch before him. "And think better of me with every step."

She smiled, and he knew she welcomed the suggestion.

"There you are... up and up... and now at the top, there is the door that leads to your room. Remember how pleasant it is?"

The girl still smiled. "I have dried flowers pinned all along one wall."

Christ. She was practically a dairymaid. The more fool her, pining for Lord Waresham; if she got close enough, he'd take her virginity and drop her like a stone.

He ought to suggest she give him up; but it was none of his affair.

The door opened. "Is all well?"

It was that damnable Jefferson Shale, always stealing Vellot's thunder. Shale had been to Strasbourg too, though he claimed it was out of his own interest, and not to dog Vellot's footsteps. He wore an amiable expression, but Vellot thought him sly as he took in the cluster of ladies, one reclining on the couch with Vellot bent over her.

Lord Harman, the host's son, peeked in over Shale's shoulder.

"Of course." Vellot suppressed his irritation at being interrupted, especially by men he couldn't ignore. "When you go through the door to your room, Miss Buckley, and hear it close behind you, you will be quite comfortable, able to say anything you like, and remember all we've discussed. Are you ready? Here you go, through the door, and it will close behind you in seconds. One." He gestured for Shale to shut the door. "Two. Three." The motion of his hand made it clear once again Shale should shut the door.

Shale did, while staying in the room.

Miss Buckley fluttered her eyes open. She still smiled. She was juicy and ripe, but in an unspoiled way; he'd like to have spoiled her, had she fallen into his power with more privacy. "Why, Lord Vellot! I feel so light and warm, just as if it were a day in spring."

Lady Villeneuve clapped her hands impatiently then held one out to help the girl rise. Miss Buckley rose, still smiling.

Her ladyship wasn't smiling. "Lord Waresham, Miss Buckley? Really? Has all my instruction been in vain?"

Shale looked interested. "Is something wrong with an interest in Lord Waresham?"

He was either the stupidest man in London, or accomplice to the rake's traps. Either way, Vellot had nothing to add.

Miss Buckley didn't blush, but she did cast her eyes down. "I've always dreamed of attracting the notice of someone like him. He's very charming, madame! And so handsome."

"Neither are necessary qualities in a husband," was Lady Villeneuve's clipped answer. "If you will excuse us, Lord Vellot."

He just bowed as the lady ushered her charges out of the room. Lord Harman followed them.

Still Shale stayed.

"When I studied there, the Society of Harmony did not

believe in magnetizing people as a form of public display." Shale's words were quiet but clear.

Brushing away his irritation at the young man's attempts to instruct him, Vellot shrugged. "I was merely educating the public regarding the power of the mind."

"Really? It looked more like a game." Shale didn't move or bend, the bulk of him that had moved aside for the ladies back to blocking the door. "And Miss Buckley agreed to be part of the game?"

"Education," hissed Vellot, "is no game."

"I suppose that depends on the teacher." Shale gestured back with his head. "A syllabub is being served in the front parlor; I didn't want Lady Villeneuve to miss it."

"Wise to stay in her good graces," said Vellot. It was difficult to shake his irritation at Shale's interruption, though whether it was because he was bereft of prey, or only interrupted in the flow of magnetic forces, he could not say.

He had far greater matters to attend. He needed to start within the day to be in the right place at the right time and ensure all his pawns were in order.

In future years, when they wrote of Napoleon's last battles, none would generate as much interest as Vellot's, fought over years in the delicate play of people's minds, with powers humanity had yet to fully understand. It was a new type of warfare, and his name would be associated with it in every treatise, every general's tent, from now till the end of time.

"Go on," he told the youth at the door, waiting as if Vellot were interested in something as pitifully small as a syllabub.

CHAPTER ELEVEN

*D*an intended to stay away from his own rented room till this Winpole disaster was over. The less anyone saw him going back and forth to the place, the better.

Then he got the message he couldn't ignore.

The scribbled marks on the scrap of paper came from thieves in his old streets, thieves and the people who helped them. Words were useless among illiterate people.

It said to come home and see Bess. Home was variable—he had to assume they meant the room he now rented—but *Bess* was always the meaning of the four-sided diamond.

Wisps of fog reached across the black road, trying to reach each other. A cab emerged from the mist, its thickly humped driver hunched against the weather.

It stopped at his door.

The heavy man swung down and his hump disappeared, revealing it had all been clothes and cold. Familiar. His old friend Jack, one of the few Dan still trusted.

He had a red and swelling eye.

"Where is she?"

Hooked a thumb at the cab. "In there."

Dan pushed past him before he could say anything else.

Bess lay slumped, still, on the seat. Dan felt his heart stop.

Jackie with his shining silver hair leaned out of the shadows behind her. Put out his hand. "She's not dead."

She was so still. *No, no, no, no, no...* Dan barely heard his own voice repeating it. The air made it quiet. In his head, it rang like a church bell.

He gathered Bess in his arms. She felt so light, so small. So limp he could barely hold her.

Her hair streamed over his arm like liquid glass full of light. He barely noticed it was brown.

"What have you done, Bess?" he murmured, trying to sound calm, but his arms spasmed, squeezing her tight.

"She's got a fever and won't wake. Fell from her horse right to the ground." Jackie's voice underlined his surprise at that. "She got to her feet, landed a wallop on Jack, then fell again, out like a light. But Dan—"

Dan didn't wait for more talk. Hitching her body close, he carried her to his door, fumbled it open with two fingers, and took his stairs two at a time.

Where could he find a physician at night? Such men didn't live on streets like his. A surgeon would bleed her. Dan never trusted them with himself, much less her.

She had always been so tiny. She was still so tiny. He sat down on his bed, still holding her in his arms and cursing the faintness of his only candle. He had to lift her close to his face to see hers.

She was pale and sweating, and shivering hard enough to feel.

"Wake up now, Bess, tell me what's happened." His voice held years of experience, practiced from a thousand little mishaps with a fearless little girl.

But the grip of his arms was something else.

He finally noticed Jack and Jackie were in the room. "She

needs a physician," he rasped, "No bloodletting hacks. If you ask—"

"Dan," Jack interrupted. "I've seen this before."

"Don't panic. *Guarda.*" Jackie, with his pompadour hair and his fine coat, pulled the quilt from the bed to wrap it around Dan and Bess. Gently, as if both of them were precious.

"Quiet. I'm not panicking. Jack. What is it?"

Jack squatted next to him, one thick finger reverently touching Bess' fine sleeve. "Opium," he said bluntly. "When you stop it."

"That's insane." Bess had sparkled on stage. She was the furthest thing from opium or its use.

But then, said a traitorous little inside voice, *is she the Bess you knew?* This Bess felt too heavy and too light at the same time. He knew her weight like the weight of a shilling; it was that common, and that dear.

No. Dan wouldn't believe that. "She's got an *ague* from the water."

Jack just shook his bald head back and forth slowly. "In that fine house? And no one else has it?"

Faced with Jack's horrible certainty and a lifetime of physicking their own ills, and not knowing where to find a physician this time of night who would come, Dan gave in. "What do I do?"

"She'll come out all right. Day or two of fever. Not long." Dan's desperate eyes pushed the man to add more details. "She won't want food, but give her some. She's so little."

Jackie shook his head and clucked his tongue. "She's going to be miserable, Daniel. I'm sorry for her. I'm sorry for *you.*"

"I pay you two so things like this don't happen." Dan rocked Bess a little, back and forth, hoping her shivering would ease. Inside, he blamed only himself. He had been too slow, he'd trusted her to others, and most of all, he'd wanted her back. Wanted to touch her again like the selfish brute he was.

But not like this.

"All right, let go that line." Jack had come from a fishing village in Tuscany to live among London sailors. "We kept an eye on her fine in Covent Garden. Then you appear and *brrrp,* she's out of sight."

"An *eye* on her?" Fear and fury in equal measures wrestled to get out of Dan; the fury was safer than fear. "You said this is when opium *stops.* So where has she been getting it? For how long?"

Jack had the grace to look abashed as he stood from his crouch and turned over his cap in his hands.

Jackie piped up. "That teacher lady is clean as a bone. But it's a *theater,* Daniel. We can't see inside. When she's in there, who knows what she does?"

Dan had done this. Just like he'd done everything else to ruin her life. He'd let someone poison his Bess.

No. He couldn't think of her as his, or he'd never let her go.

He'd spent a lifetime fighting to keep her free; he wouldn't lock her up himself. Having these two land pirates following her was as far as he could go.

"In that theater or out of it, someone's giving her this. Find out who. Double pay if you find out." He knew his anger would cool off, and when it did, he'd still need their help. "First, go to the Bird and Bottle, and get Glory. She owes me a favor. Get coal, and some water. Take my purse—"

"We don't need your purse, *tipo,*" Jack cut him off. Jackie shook his head too. "Back in a second."

Dan didn't watch them go.

Shaking himself, he laid his cheek against the top of Bess'

head. She'd gotten a very fine lawn gown somewhere. It didn't matter.

She was still Bess, the center of his existence, and she was ill. Somehow, somewhere along the way, he'd failed her.

* * *

IT WAS *the fourth time Bess had thrown her bread on the floor.*

The Grand H. just shook his head. "She's your responsibility, Dan. If you can't get her to eat, how are you going to keep her alive?"

He said it like Bess was a pet. A dog or a tame rat. An indulgence they couldn't afford.

But Dan knew, even as a small boy, that of the three of them, the only one worth anything was Bess.

"We need some cleaner milk for her." Dan had quickly learned to assess dairymaids and their cows with the intensity of a horse racer measuring horses. He didn't like the look of the milk in the square, and was determined to get Bess something better.

He just needed to steal it—or something that would pay for it.

The Grand H. shook his head, turning back to his open book. Stoic philosophy. By the time Dan was ten, he'd devised a dozen ways to steal and burn that book. Even at seven—maybe eight—he hated it.

The Grand H. quoted it a dozen times a day, and he did it again. "The ants and the spiders do their part every day building the little corner of the world they've been given, and so must you, Dan."

Dan picked up the crust of bread Bess had thrown and dusted it off. He'd eat it.

He went to the table and broke off a new clean piece for Bess.

She still didn't say much, only noises he couldn't understand. She was so little it was hard to judge her age, but she could walk, even run; in fact it was hard to keep her from climbing out the window. Judging by other children he knew, she should be able to talk. Perhaps she just needed to hear someone talk besides the Grand H.

"You eat this," he said slowly, placing the chewy hunk of bread in her pudgy little hands. "Eat it. Good."

She'd looked up at him with those big blue-green eyes. They were indignant, and disdainful. How could a tiny child hold so much disdain?

But she saw him bite the piece she'd thrown.

Sighing a little-girl sigh, Bess nibbled at the bread in her hand, clearly understanding that neither of them was getting anything better.

After a while, she seemed to tire of the hard chewing, or perhaps she was full. Dan suspected she simply wanted something better.

But she didn't throw it again.

"Dan," she said clearly, and held out the rest for him to take.

"WHAT HAPPENED, BESS?" he murmured into her hair, wondering if he only imagined that her shivering seemed to ease next to his heat.

It was so much like old times, and so different. The scent of her, like lilacs in the rain, was as familiar as his own skin, but deeper, richer. She was grown.

With a protector.

Just that word felt like a punch to his chest. He couldn't block the blow with his arms full.

How had Jack and Jackie not seen any of this? Dan didn't let them report every day, or he'd never get anything done. But if they'd seen Bess reeling, they'd have said so.

They'd missed both the drugs and the protector, so Dan had to assume they went together. What had he given her? When was she seeing him? Where?

A noise he'd never made before, a near-silent keening snarl, started in his chest. Dan stopped it.

Someone had given Bess poison, and she'd taken it. He couldn't imagine why.

He'd never give up on Bess' right to live her own life, never let anyone control her, not even himself.

But he also would not, could not, give up the responsibility that had shaped his whole life.

* * *

"His Grace the Duke of Oakland."

Vellot didn't bother to hide his maps marked with chess pieces, or the newspaper he tossed down.

The old man saw it all as he limped in, gave Vellot a snide smile. "Playing war like a child."

Vellot rose and gave His Grace his due bow; after all, he hoped to receive such honor himself one day. "Like a soldier. Though one who follows the principles of science."

"Science." In daylight, Oakland's wrinkles grew shadows and made him look remorselessly old. Still, his clouded eyes clearly saw Vellot's arrangement of troops on maps with game pieces, deduced, no doubt, from the paper he'd thrown down. "In all of history, surely mankind has studied war more than anything else."

"War by brute force." Silently implying that Oakland should sit by waving to a nearby chair, Vellot waited till he did, then followed. He leaned forward over his table. "The papers report on the movement of troops, but not on what matters. How do the generals *feel*? Or the troops? Have their battles toughened them, or worn them down? Do they seek glory, or only steady food?"

"Does it matter?" Oakland sat back in his chair, regarding Vellot rather than the map. "If they desert, they'll be shot. If they're generals, they cannot resign. Once war is in motion, its mechanism *is* brute force."

Vellot just shook his head, a small smile lurking behind his fingers as he rested his chin in his hand. "The forces that rule the mind are far more subtle, and more dangerous."

The Duke of Oakland wished Vellot would offer him tea, if only to wash the bad taste from his mouth. He wasn't here for pleasure, and more conversation would only make it worse. "You like to play games to hurt women and old men. Very well. I am old. Were I two decades younger, were this two hundred years ago, I'd raise an army and put England right myself. If one must employ war's despicable brutality, it should be swift and strong. Our king has never done that. Now he is mad, and his son that most disastrous thing in a prince. He is stupid. I won't enjoy bowing to Napoleon's choice of king, but at least Britain will *have* a king, and that's what we need."

"You have confidence the other allies will fold if Britain does?" Vellot ignored the insults. Oakland just needed to feel strong; Vellot let him have that. He had inhabited his title a long time, and had connections in royal houses all over Europe.

"Russia won't fold." Oakland shrugged a shoulder so bony the edge of his coat looked hollow. "For the Tsar, his best friend is whoever is in the room. But the coalition will abandon him; they all tire of expanding Russia's borders."

"You see," Vellot shook his finger with a playful look. "The mind matters."

"The mind of the Tsar?" Oakland snorted. "It is his throne that matters."

"A king is both a mind and a throne." Vellot left the matter there. "In four days I will see the ambassador leaving for Germany. By the time I speak with him, Talbourne will be dead. We shall change Britain's ambitions abroad. Napoleon *wants* to emerge from Dresden an unchallenged emperor again. He will be so grateful that he will give us—you and me —whatever we like."

"One ambassador doesn't make a government." Oakland still looked sour.

"One ambassador *is* the government, in the right, rare, circumstance. After a few hours alone with me, this one's orders will shift. Trust me, Oakland. If we steer the ambassador in a new direction, then the cabinet in a direction to match, it will all come together."

"I *don't* trust you. And I'm not at all sure that an assassination will sway the ministers the way you think." Oakland's fingers tightened on the head of his cane. "But I must try. Our useless princes make a mockery of the throne. The result will be hopeless democracy, and we saw in the Terror where that leads. I won't have it."

Vellot rose to pour the Duke a drink rather than call a servant into this very private conversation. "You are giving our country a noble gift."

* * *

Bess was climbing through a hot and sticky nowhere. She'd been hot forever, dreaming of things she didn't want to remember.

Finally she hauled herself over the edge of sleep into a world she didn't recognize.

This was happening far too often.

This wasn't the Silver Duke's house. *Why had she wanted to go there?* Just the thought made her skin crawl.

Then she remembered the carriage behind her. Feather rearing.

She blinked; her eyes still didn't work right. The room was dim, but too bright.

There was a washstand in arm's reach, and next to it a familiar figure. Too tall, too broad. He crouched down and reached for her; she flinched before she recognized the scar on the knuckle.

"Dan?" Her sleepy numbness faded.

He answered with a familiar *mm* sound, bending close and giving her the soft smile that had belonged just to her. His hand settled on her forehead.

Too big, but so familiar. Just like Dan. *Her* Dan.

The sight and sound of him were so familiar—even the warm wood-and-ink scent of his hand—that Bess sagged down quietly with relief. She pressed her hand over his against her skin.

"I knew you were dead, but I still wanted you to come home."

* * *

Glory could see that neither the girl in the bed nor the man standing over her wanted her anymore. "I'll go then," she said softly.

"Glory—" Dan only looked her way a brief second. It had been like that the entire time, him vibrating with tension while Glory bathed the girl and dressed her. Glory hated nursing, but she'd do it for Dan; she'd do anything for Dan, he'd rescued her and many of her cohort from lives they couldn't bear.

"I'll go," Glory said again, shaking out her skirt as she stood. "You'll be all right, Dan. So will she."

"I owe you," he told her, a wild note in his harsh-gravel voice, a sound he never made.

"No, you don't," she whispered as she slipped out the door. "We're even."

* * *

Bess just saw the door close. It was hard to string one thought after another. "What happened to my horse?"

He made a strangled sound. "What happened to *you?*"

Dan hadn't died. He was back; he was here. So *much* relief in that thought. Relief she should have felt at the theater. Why hadn't she?

Then the relief stretched thin. Why was Dan *right* here? Hadn't she been on her way to see the Silver Duke?

Why had she been on her way to see the Silver Duke?

Dan knelt next to the bed. "How do you feel?"

"Bad." She tried to rub her eyes and saw her own hand shaking. Beneath the sheet she wore only a thin chemise that wasn't hers. "How long did I sleep?"

"Two days." He gave her no time for shock, just a tumbler of water. His hand between her shoulderblades levered her upward. Astonishingly easily, when she felt *so* heavy.

But her mind was on the house of cards about to collapse at the Dunsby house.

"Two *days!*" she moaned, struggled to unwrap herself from the clinging sheet. "What happened to my horse?"

Dan plucked her hands away from the sheet.

"Jackie took him back. He explained to Madame Franck, who told Lady Dunsby you're ill in your room. Finish the water."

His voice had changed. It was deeper than she remembered.

It was still steady, certain. Immovably, eternally certain. The same, but different.

Bess remembered that moment on the road on her badly saddled horse, that clear moment when she knew what fear felt like, maybe for the first time in her life.

This felt a little like that. Like that, and like shame.

142

Bess had never felt ashamed before either.

"I'm sorry I was like that. The night in the theater. You're a liar and all, but I missed you so much."

She'd been so shocked, and it had been so dark. And she'd been ill with that fever, whatever had put her down this time too.

In the high window's fading light she could see. He looked older, his skin a little darker. He didn't look the same.

As if someone had painted a new Dan over the old one.

He said nothing.

Loathing her trembling, Bess wiggled her toes. She was weak, shockingly tired for two days' sleep, and thirsty; but that was all.

The toe-wiggling did not reassure him. "I never lied about wanting you safe. What did you do, Bess?"

She wanted to say *whatever I had to.* She wanted to make this his fault somehow. She was still angry with him, so angry for disappearing.

And she'd figure out how to tell him so, but couldn't stomach telling him lies in return.

"I was careless."

"No. You?" He scoffed with fake dismissal. That little soft smile, the one just for her, came back; she could see it even with him half-turned away.

"Well, you know..." She had to swallow the lump in her throat. What *was* going on with all these unwanted emotions? "A lone thief is a dead thief."

His choked noise was nothing like a laugh. His hand swung toward her face; she clutched at the neckline she wore.

He stopped with his hand halfway toward her cup, the smile gone now.

"A woman from the Bottle and Bird changed your

clothes," he said, voice as blank as his face. "That's her shift you're wearing."

That cut through the muddle in her head. Did he really think Bess could be frightened of him? His dark eyes lurking behind a slightly hooked nose, the half-twist to his mouth; they were home. Whoever he frightened away, she *wanted* frightened away.

She sipped the last of the water, handed him the cup. When he took it, she used both hands to try and squeeze her head into working.

Her fury was just... gone. The fury she'd felt at the theater, the fury she'd felt about *spinach.* She felt empty, and the air in the room felt brittle.

All she had left was a question. "Are *you* all right?"

He shrugged, handed her more water. As if he didn't matter.

Bess wanted him to sweep her up in his arms and carry her to safety. He'd done it so many times. She'd felt bare all these years without his arms around her even once. Now he was back, she recognized what she'd missed most.

But at the same time she wanted to carry *him* out of here, out of London, to somewhere bright and full of food and jewels and horses. Like Lady Dunsby's house but without the threat of the Silver Duke.

She wanted to dream for him the things he'd dreamed for her.

"I think I understand a little better now what you were looking for. The freedom you wanted."

His brows pulled together. Not a scowl, just a puzzled little frown. "Do you?"

"I still can't believe you left like that. I would have done anything to make you stay. But I could have listened to you in the theater. King and country." The words of the woman who'd just left—had her hair been dark?—bounced around in Bess's head. "I could at least—I owed you that."

"Don't *ever* say that." Harsh. And hard.

"I do, though." The water was cool on her tongue. "I wanted you with me. But you were still looking out for me. I didn't know you sent Madame Franck money. I don't know why she never said so, except..." Bess sighed. "Except I only mentioned your name to curse it."

He settled back to sit on his heels, rest his elbow on the cot, his head against his fist. His head was close to hers; she had an odd urge to touch it. "Was it so awful?"

"No." She sighed again. The unruly demons in her gut that other people called feelings had wrung her out. "I love the dance. I swore I'd never tell you that. But I do, and I've learned so much."

"So she kept that promise. And who taught you that pinch?"

"The *varma kalai?* Also Madame Franck, of course. Didn't you always say it was better not to have a weapon? Because they make people brave when they have it and foolish when they lose it?"

"I think I did." She'd so missed that smile, the gentle one just for her. "A soldier told me recently that they always take more than one weapon into battle."

So did Bess. "She's decent company—Wait. *Jackie* took Madame Franck a message?"

"Him and Jack. After they brought you here." Something made Dan restless, wiped the easy moment away. He stood, the light motion belying the lean muscle in his body.

"How did they know where to find me?"

"Because they were following you." As matter-of-fact as slicing an apple, Dan put his hands under her arms and lifted her to lean back against the wall.

His hands were big and strong like always. He bent her

knees, bracing her, and handed her water before sitting on the cot at her feet.

His wide shoulders leaned a little closer.

"I have never been far away," he said quietly.

What did that mean?

She wanted to be angry about how long he'd been gone. He felt miles away right now. She wanted back their easy connection, wanted this new Dan to feel as familiar as the old one.

Wanted not to be lonely.

Whatever was broken between them likely couldn't be fixed, so she might as well say what she'd waited so long to say.

"Not good enough." Bess' muscles shook, but she kept her voice steady; she'd waited so long to say this, she had to say it all. "All the time I spent wondering if you'd left England. If you'd gone to Ireland, or the colonies, or—or *prison*. Or—" Ruthlessly steady. "—if you'd gone to the Continent and died in the war. When you could have just stayed. With me."

His head bent until someone might have accused him of praying. Bess threw an arm over her eyes so she would stop looking.

Finally he said, "To hold you like that would've been obscene. After you spent your whole life following me? What kind of choice would that have been for you?"

He sent the words carefully through this new brittleness between them, as if him *holding* her would have been more prison than home.

It wouldn't have been, for Bess. Why *couldn't* he have let her choose that?

She said, "I always thought of it as you following me."

She kept her arm where it was. If she looked at him she'd know what he thought, she always did; and right now she didn't want to find out why that hadn't been enough for him.

Though it might just have been her prodigious collection of faults. "I sound arrogant."

"You're allowed. I was arrogant to choose your life. No excuse, but I wanted so much for you. Still do. How long did you try an honest life?"

"I'm honest."

She felt his fingertip touch her sapphire ring.

Mercy Bennett. She'd forgotten she wore the thing. She might as well wear a sign: *I stole this.*

Well, she had just as much right to disappoint him as he did her.

"Did your *protector* honestly give that to you?"

The way he said it, like *demon,* made her peek.

He looked calmer than he sounded. "I'm sorry I didn't visit. Didn't write. I knew some things and thought I knew everything. But if you tell me now what your life is missing, I will move mountains to get it for you. Your life is everything, Bess. You don't need a protector. And you don't need opium."

"*Opium?*" Her dizziness came back.

"Did he give it to you?" Now he sounded hard as iron.

What opium? What would make Dan think the Silver Duke had—

Bess' arms dropped and her eyes narrowed.

"Why am I sick, Dan?"

CHAPTER TWELVE

Dan shook his head. His hands clasped—no, *clenched*—around the knee he'd hitched up on the bed, his eyes on her. She must look awful, sweaty, disheveled, some woman's far-too-large shift falling down one shoulder. Wildly Bess wondered what he thought of the brown hair.

"It gives you a punishing hunger when you stop. I didn't give you any more. Bess." His voice grew even softer. "Is he the one who gave you the opium?"

Thoughts were sliding and shifting in her head as she said nothing.

The Silver Duke had fed her *opium?*

Of course he could have hidden opium in that wine, waiting for her on every visit. It would also explain why she'd always felt so at ease near the Silver Duke when it was clear he was not to be trusted.

And it explained that last night of sleep, which she didn't remember at all.

How *dare* he poison her?

For Bess, hatred was a frosty, logical thing. It was reasonable to be wary of the Silver Duke, and she was. But that was now outweighed by one cold blue fact, inscribed on her heart with a sharp fresh pen.

That man needed killing.

The drug had painted her senses. This Dan was larger, more wary with her, but he still seemed to be her Dan.

The Dan she knew would tell her killing was too simple an answer. One she'd regret, even if she escaped a hangman's noose.

But would she? Dancing was hard, but stealing was simple. Perhaps killing would be even more so. The Silver Duke was a problem; the problem would be removed.

That bloodsucker had spent months encouraging her to think about killing someone. Only fair if she did.

Did Dan really think she'd taken opium knowingly? Here she'd been soaking in the comfort of having him back again, and he didn't know her at all.

Of course laudanum could be had from any chemist, but the alleys were home to plenty of people thin as skeletons who dragged themselves to opium dens. They both knew better. *Bess* knew better.

"You look thin," was all Dan said.

Bess leaned back against the wall behind her, hands cradling the tumbler of water. Dan might not know her, but she knew him. He only showed his soft insides to her, and here they were, pure and honest. The exact opposite of the Silver Duke.

It made her tired, thinking how stupid she'd been.

"You don't have to do this anymore. You don't have to—" with a shaky wave, "care about this. I'm a grown woman. I can take care of myself."

"That story won't wash. You fell off a horse, Bess. You."

Her fingers hardened around the cup. "I'm not a child anymore."

"Nor are you safe. Look at yourself."

"Life in a theater isn't safe."

"Then forget the theater. Go somewhere else, do something else. Something honest. But you can't go back there. And you can't go back to him."

Bess couldn't tell how much of her nausea was still the drug, and how much was hearing him say things like *can't go back.*

Dan *wasn't* dead, he cared if she lived or died, and he had reappeared at the worst possible moment. She already felt guilty that Madame Franck was involved, and now, Lady Dunsby and Agatha.

The Silver Duke loved manipulation games. If he learned about Dan, he'd make Dan his weapon.

And if she dealt with the demon the way he deserved... what would Dan think of her then?

She couldn't lose him twice.

"Dan, even if things can't be like they were, I still owe you, by anybody's measure. For all this—" She swept her hand around to take in the room. "And being a swine at the theater. I'm sorry. For all the food I can never repay. I *know* I owe you. But I can't balance those books by letting you lock me in a cage."

* * *

Not a cage; a jewelry chest, you God-damned treasure.

"You don't owe me. Don't ever say that." That was twice, and if she said it again, she'd break him.

She lay in his bed, sick and pale and shaking, angry because he wouldn't let her go back where she'd been drugged, in more danger than she'd ever been in her life. Because he'd failed. And then she went and said something like that.

Her head thumped back against the wall as she sighed. "I

150

know I do, I really do. I'm not a child anymore. I *know* I owe you. But—"

He could stand her saying anything but that.

He'd sworn so many promises to himself, to her. It didn't matter to him he'd been tiny at the time; he still had to keep them. He only had one more choice. "Then I'll go with you." Fuck crown and country.

There, an actual Bess smile. For the briefest instant, then gone. Just enough to remember later, a sweet little torture.

Then she shook her head *no.*

"I thought you had to save Britain or something." She held out her cup.

So determined to go her own way. Littler Dan hadn't realized the double edge to his promise to keep her free and safe too. Hadn't realized she might choose to go where she shouldn't and do what she shouldn't.

Hadn't realized *free* and *safe* might contradict.

He stood to fetch her more water. Already her color was coming back, easing the tension that threatened to collapse his ribcage from the inside.

Halfway to the pitcher, he looked back over his shoulder.

She laughed. "I'm not trying to distract you so I can run."

He just shook his head, unable to stop the smile she brought out of him. Maybe not, but she'd thought of it. So had he.

When she took the tumbler again, she sipped it rather than gulping it down.

The part of his mind that recognized numbers in ledgers like faces also took in her every detail. The damp hair curled on her forehead; the slowly steadying little hands; the hollow of her collarbone, visible in the vast chemise.

Thank... Bess that Glory had come and helped.

Dan had done most of the nursing. He couldn't let someone else wipe away her sweat; he had to judge her fever.

He couldn't let someone else give her water; he needed to count every drop.

He'd rather have done everything her small body needed, but that would have meant taking liberties he had no right to take. Freedom started at the skin. He knew that, remembered vividly the feeling of seeing words on paper that meant someone else controlled Dan's life.

He'd taken too much from Bess already.

Dan had always found words pointless. No one cared what he thought; silence was a tool and a weapon. He'd never needed to use words with Bess; she'd take one look at him and know.

Now he found silence hard to break.

He ought to tell her *everything* he'd never said. But the habit of hiding what shamed him most was even harder to break than silence.

All he could say was the obvious truth. "I don't believe you are keeping yourself safe."

He saw her bite her lip, drop her eyes. Then look back into his, as if she weighed twelve stone and was ready to wrestle. "I made a mistake. My footing's back. I'm all right, Dan."

"I don't believe you." She'd been such a stubborn child, and loved deception for the game of it. He had to remember that. "I asked at the theater; they said the Tourmaline was ill. That's your bread and butter, Bess. So how are you earning your keep?"

"I'm visiting a friend. Which you know. Trying some-where new. Some*thing* new."

"Like your hair. And your new name."

Bess said nothing.

He needed her to talk. "Tell me you won't take opium again."

A flash of fury in her eyes. At him? It was gone too fast to tell. "I won't."

God, she should have been a diplomat; she gave away nothing. If she was someone's mistress, why the disguise?

How high up was her *protector?*

"You came here in a dress that cost more than you earn in a year, and you're making me guess how and why. If this is some long swindle, you could go to the noose and hang. I don't want that. If you're being kept—" He swallowed, clearing his throat. "If you're being kept, you're giving up any chance of a safe life. A husband. A home. You deserve a place of your own."

"I don't want a safe life. Especially not that way. Trade myself for a place? I thought you didn't want me to whore." Her fingers wove together, gripping her cup tight. It was her only sign of tension. Her voice stayed even. "We never had a safe life before. And I was happy, Dan. I really was."

He could pick her up, cradle her in his arms. It would be so easy. But to her it would feel like they were children again, when to him it would be completely different.

"I'm glad you were happy." No amount of throat-clearing would make his voice less hoarse. "Little girls should be happy. But it *wasn't* safe, and I..." He couldn't admit every-thing, but he had to admit something. "I was constantly worried for you."

She took the thought, turned it over, and with silence, accepted it.

The moment stretched, honesty between them now, after so many years of silence, too precious to break.

Then Bess broke it.

"I didn't magically become fragile when I came of age, Dan. Or become someone new. I know law-breaking bothers you, but it never did me. We're not the same. I have work to do, and I won't explain it to you."

"You're as much as telling me you're in the middle of some swindle."

She shrugged. "Apparently, I don't owe you anything. That includes the truth."

But I owe you.

More sentences he'd never say.

How could he keep her safe and still finish this thing with Fitz? It was the only way to buy her a new life *now*, when she needed it. Some sane, good man would marry Bess, whatever her history, if she had a large enough dowry. Dan knew enough of the upper classes to know that when what they wanted coincided with money, they bent their rules easily enough.

He'd clung to that idea so long he couldn't let go of it, even now, when she was right here, and the thought of her marrying this mythical good man twisted in his gut like a knife.

He wanted to watch her himself. Having her watched wasn't the same. But if the Grand H.'s warnings had done nothing else, they'd made Dan constantly question himself. The rightness of his actions, the source of his impulses. Watching her day and night would go way beyond anything right, not just because of the act itself, but because of what he'd be thinking as he did it.

And what other choice did Dan have? Short of locking her up.

What lock did he have that she couldn't pick?

Letting her go was the best he could do. If she knew everything he felt—if she knew everything he'd *done* all those years ago—she'd never speak to him again.

He'd boosted her over hundreds of windowsills, hundreds of walls. She still needed one more boost, into a level of respectability where she'd be safe forever. He needed Fitz' money to give her that boost.

"It's your life, Bess," he said quietly. "Try not to get hanged, I guess. Just remember." He'd allow himself this much.

He put out a finger and touched just the tip of her nose. Instantly pulled away.

"I'll never be far away."

* * *

YES YOU WILL, Bess thought. He took his touch away so fast, when she was so hungry for it. Instantly gone, it stayed alive in her skin; she squeezed her fist to keep from touching the spot. The sapphire ring hurt.

In another day or two, if she could salvage her place at Lady Dunsby's, she'd be in a carriage rolling to wherever it was the Silver Duke expected her to assassinate Talbourne. One way or the other, Bess would make sure he'd never know Dan existed.

"I'm *so* glad you've recovered." Lady Dunsby sat on the sofa in Bess' room, her lap festooned with delicate fabric. "Mrs. Frank must be an excellent nurse."

Her supposed excellent nurse only smiled while her hands went on folding Bess' heavy new coat into the vast open trunk.

She hadn't been silent helping Bess in at the garden door.

"You're not too cold from the river breezes?" she asked loudly enough for anyone to hear, as if she and Bess had just strolled through the garden. Took Bess' arm and shot suspicious glares at Jackie's departing back.

As they slowly climbed the stairs, she muttered under her breath. "Now you listen to me. Those hackney men won't tell me where you've been. But I'll tell you this. I'm *not* letting you rob Lady Dunsby."

If Dan still looked after her, Bess thought tiredly, feet dragging toward the bed, *why hadn't he sorted out Madame Franck?*

Because she'd spent five years whining about Dan to Madame Franck, that's why. Madame wouldn't believe a word he said.

Sitting was hard. Bess longed to roll herself up into the smallest possible ball. Maybe if she were a tiny, silent bundle, Madame Franck would go away.

Madame Franck surveyed all this with an unflattering amount of surprise. "You *have* been ill."

"Very." Bess just wanted water and sleep.

"And why couldn't you have stayed here to be ill, as any reasonable person would do?" She dropped her voice. "Is that Dan Fox planning to rob the house? Is *he* keeping you?"

Bess, still numb and hollow, had to think for several moments what Dan *keeping her* would mean. If it wasn't a delicate phrasing for stairwell games, hadn't Dan always kept her?

She shoved the thought away. Her guard, grocer, teacher, even compass—Dan might have been those. Never her *keeper*. And certainly not today.

She undid a few buttons of the riding habit, knowing she had to get out of it before someone saw her.

Maybe Dan left her because he knew how cold she really was.

Maybe she hated having a clear head.

"No one is *keeping me.* Or robbing Lady Dunsby. I have such a terrible headache," Bess whispered, slumping sideways on the bed.

Still scolding, Madame Franck reached to finish unbuttoning the habit. "Then why are his men following you? You said you hated him. That's why I put his money in a safe place. You said you wouldn't take an apple from him if he begged you to."

Batting her hands away, Bess undid the buttons herself, slowly. Mercy Bennett, she'd love an apple. "When people tell me money is somewhere safe, they've spent it."

"What do you want, a banker's duplicate? You think they

keep accounts for the likes of us? Usually you have so much sense."

Picking at her scratchy eyes, Bess looked sideways at Madame Franck. "So you were serious?"

"Child, if I couldn't keep money, I wouldn't have had two husbands and made it this far. The good ones go too fast; the bad ones, not fast enough. In all cases, you must hold on to your *money*. The theater is no place for beggars; only a high head can play a queen."

That made Bess feel worse. She hadn't suspected the Silver Duke enough and had suspected Madame Franck far too much. Why did suspicion have to be so finely measured? She hoped her excess had burned away with the last of the opium. "You shouldn't have come with me."

"I guaranteed you to the ballet master. You'd best believe you're going back. He's no doubt furious, if he's sober." Madame leaned closer, her voice dropping to a whisper. "But whatever it is you *have* to do, it better not be stealing from Lady Dunsby!"

"Don't worry," Bess had assured her from the soft bed. "It isn't."

Looking now over heaps of things to pack, Bess wondered why Madame Franck thought Bess would steal when Lady Dunsby was ready to stuff all of London in her trunk.

While Bess' attention had been elsewhere, her belongings had grown to include a silver *service de toilette*, with hairbrushes, trays and mirror, plus matching boxes for combs, powder, and three silver hairpins. She wanted to roll around in it.

Golden perfume oil lay nestled in the center of a heavy crystal bottle; its three-sided stopper was taller than Bess' hand was long, like a crystal spire. It reminded her of this house.

Hair ribbons and lacy *fichus* lay in a little sandalwood box, and underthings were everywhere. Bess only hoped the stays would fit.

Apparently she hadn't had to be awake to be the victim of shopping.

"You spoil me, Lady Dunsby." Bess sat on the floor among piles of boots. Almost all were too big, and past-Bess would have picked a pair and stuffed them with rags to fit.

But her ladyship insisted Bess make a feature of her small feet.

"Nonsense," she scoffed, "We'll have the coldest November I can remember, and I'm old as dirt. We're going to the country; you need boots, simple as that. They ought to be attractive."

Murder aside, maybe Bess should try to live a better life. It was pleasant, having people think nice things about her. "Shouldn't we choose some for your friend? Lady Carrollton must not get to London often." Bess was trying to ignore the pair tall enough to reach nearly to her knee. They'd destroy her ability to run.

But they were lovely.

It was fine to be small; it let her squirm into windows, and fly higher on stage. But constantly standing by Agatha's silvery-blonde perfection made Bess want to be just a little taller.

Bess put those boots aside with a little sigh. She wasn't used to passing up the opportunity to take something she wanted.

"Lady Carrollton manages her own shopping." Lady Dunsby waved away the thought. "The boat will be small for all our essentials."

That distracted Bess from the excitement of boots. "The *boat?*"

"Oh yes, dear. And you must be sure to be ready in the

morning. If you are truly well enough, we mustn't miss another one."

* * *

"THANK YOU, Mr. Watkins. Do be sure you've taken all the luggage; we mustn't forget anything in the carts."

Lady Dunsby took two canes everywhere, and employed them now in her visibly eager march down to the boat.

The tide was high, and the rope-bannered boat, as long as two carriages, bobbed nearly level with the ancient stone road. It would be a lively task, stepping aboard. It looked chancy to Bess.

Lady Dunsby must have caught her expression.

"It's much the fastest way to Gravesend; Londoners have taken these boats for centuries. Well, not this particular boat. I'm sure it's younger than that. Thank you, Emaya, I do appreciate your carrying that basket."

Bess never showed surprise as a matter of policy, but she let her eyes widen a little toward Madame Franck and mouthed, *Emaya?*

Madame Franck just waved her off with fluttering fingers. "Here, Hortense, give me that cushion. Mr. Watkins, can you settle this so her ladyship can sit? Bess, take these shawls. Do you have the rest, Lady Agatha?"

Agatha's arms were full of shawls. She just stood, wide-eyed, holding them and staring at the boat, the iron-brown lapping water, and the open gray sky.

"I'm sure it's perfectly safe," Bess murmured to her, trying to take the shawls from her.

Agatha only tightened her arms, apparently from ecstacy. "It's *beautiful.*"

Bess studied the crust on the boat's planks. There was a clear lack of anything to steal. "I suppose."

160

Madame Franck reached a long arm out the carriage door and yanked Bess back inside.

Her voice was a quick hiss. "Do you plan to sneak anything aboard that boat? Gold? Bodies?"

Bess blinked with wide eyes. "You think I have a body in my purse?"

"You shouldn't even be on a boat. When I think of what the air will do to your lungs. Are you coughing?" She narrowed her eyes suspiciously. "*Will* you cough?"

"Traveling through the everlasting passage of time, at some point, yes, I will cough. I'm fine. Are you?"

Madame Franck let Bess go.

Around them Dunsby footmen maneuvered their trunks and seemingly endless small pieces of luggage.

Which Lady Dunsby kept counting.

"We really must not forget anything in the carriages. Gravesend is perfectly pleasant, but not a *large* town, if you see what I mean. It is not the best shopping. Especially this time of year. Oh good, there's Mr. Burton after all! I had almost given him up."

Another small cab stopped on the cobbles, its horse stepping back and forth as if it didn't like the footing before the door opened and a man climbed out.

Bess never showed surprise in the middle of a performance. She clung to that. She couldn't be surprised. She wouldn't.

It was Dan.

It was surprising how Bess' insides swooped upward. Another symptom of too many disorderly feelings. The sky looked a little brighter, then dimmed again as she realized having him near only put him in danger.

Still. There was nothing more familiar, or more welcome, than looking out for Dan.

Though she'd never seen *this* Dan before.

Bess would've bet money she'd seen Dan every way he could look. She'd have lost.

He wore *green* snug trousers, bottle-green, above polished shoes, and a sky-blue waistcoat under a navy coat. His gray overcoat did nothing to dim all the colors, all of it as shocking as the sun falling out of the sky.

Not only were they entirely unlike Dan's well-worn black, they violated every current rule of fashion. He'd apparently saved all the fashion for his hair, because Dan's straight black hair was a riot of Brutus curls, combed slightly forward with pomade to hold them in place.

And he wore blue glass spectacles.

If that hadn't been enough, he spoke.

"Lady Dunsby! I apologize over and over for my lateness." Dan's gravelly voice had taken to the trapeze. It swooped and tilted, flighty as a very large bird. "It's my first time at sea, and I am at sea, if you know what I mean. I am so very pleased to meet you. Thank you so much for the place; I will prove out your faith in me, I assure you."

Bess could not have been more astonished by an actual ghost, but Lady Dunsby showed no surprise at all.

"Mr. Burton. Your timing is impeccable. If you would just ensure that no one leaves anything behind in the carriages. I'm so worried about shopping in Gravesend. I've even packed a ham." She handed him a basket. Likely the ham.

Dan nodded gravely as if he waited upon ladies like this every day.

"Absolutely I will, madame. And this must be Lady Agatha. Let me take those for you. And this is? I didn't know you had a second young lady in the family."

Dan would never show shock in the middle of a swindle, any more than would Bess. Nor did he betray by so much as the flick of an eyelash that he already knew her.

But Bess thought she saw something in the way he held

his mouth, just because no one was more familiar to her. Fury? Worry? Confusion? Might he even be pleased to see her?

She leaned toward fury.

"Oh yes," Lady Dunsby said distractedly, "Miss Page has been good enough to accompany my daughter, and brought Mrs. Frank with her. Emaya, do greet Mr. Nathaniel Burton. He is a new secretary to me, engaged by my banker but with excellent references. I always abide by my banker's wishes. We shall have plenty of time to get acquainted on the boat! Well, not plenty of time, because I expect we'll be at Road's End before supper. I hope you don't mind dining on cold food, Mr. Burton. I've packed chicken and butter sandwiches. Of course the boat has no oven."

Madame Franck was also very good at holding character. "Mr. Burton. We will be so glad of your help." She looked a bit lost without her feather and her insults. "I want to inspect the footmen's work, but promised Lady Dunsby to keep track of her last few things."

If she muttered something else to herself as she turned back and bent into the carriage, rear end in the air, searching the cushions, no one could hear it.

Dan—*Dan?*—bowed deeply to Lady Agatha, whose distracted curtsey showed she was still absorbed in the view of the water. He offered her an elbow; she smiled a little and shook her head, wandered toward the water, the shawls in her arms forgotten.

Bess gave him the fastest curtsey ever, and started down to the boat, hoping he wouldn't follow.

He followed.

They knew how to talk while barely moving their lips and never looking at each other.

"Go home." Bess kept her slight smile on her face and her eyes on the wet footing.

It didn't matter how pleased she was to see him. It was too dangerous for him to be here. Dangerous to him, and to his opinion of her.

In fact, he was already a lot less pleased to see her than she was him. The flush in his cheeks could have been cold, or it could have been anger. "*You* go home. I'm not letting you steal from Lady Dunsby."

For a moment Bess contemplated the predictability of a life of crime. No one expected anything else of her.

It hurt a little.

Madame Franck knew perfectly well that she could learn new things. She'd learned to dance, after all. And at least some *varma kalai.* Where was the faith that she might have other goals in mind?

Then she remembered her goals and dropped that train of thought.

And anyway, what was *he* doing here? Bess murmured back, "I didn't realize saving crown and country meant duping Lady Dunsby. I won't let you steal from her either. Or Agatha, come to that."

Dan let two more steps go by. "So no one is planning to steal from the Dunsbys."

Bess saw the trap. If she wasn't stealing, what was *she* doing here?

Well, what was *he?* "That costume is incredible."

"You look beautiful." The words snapped off as if he broke them mid-sentence. Maybe he was just a little pleased to see her? "You must feel better."

"I'm perfectly well." Truthfully, Bess felt miles better after a solid night's sleep, though still a bit wobbly. She wasn't about to admit that. Or anything at all. "Here we are, sir," she cheerfully announced to the man on the worn stone steps. "Where would you like us?"

He gave his name as Mr. Ledder in a way that said he

expected her to immediately forget it. "Master Hickey's seeing to the stowing. It's not that big a boat." He seemed alarmed by the mass of footmen and even bigger mass of trunks.

Used to coping with uneven footing, Bess still found it a trick to step onto the deck. Its damp boards pitched side-to-side and frontways at the same time. The motions weren't violent, but they were there. "We must be careful helping Lady Dunsby onto this boat."

The footmen slipped and slid into the cabin, squeezing past one another in and out. The master must be down there, tearing out his hair over balancing all this cargo.

As Lady Dunsby's new secretary, Dan—*Mr. Burton*—took charge. "Here, men, make a chain and pass things in one and a time. Give the master a moment." While the footmen organized themselves, seeing the logic of his suggestion, Dan took the chance to lean close to Bess, clearly working to lock down his expression. "What in *hell* are you doing?"

Bess felt no such constraint. She tossed him a pretty smile, happily awaiting Lady Dunsby, ready to pack her in with shawls. The wind picked up, cold enough to slice right through all her woolen skirts. She told herself she felt light not because Dan was here, but because she was alive, the poison was gone, and she had no idea what would happen next.

Bess felt *good.* "Do you enjoy sailing, Mr. Burton? I'm so sorry if you don't. It sounds as if it will be too many hours for a bad mood to last the whole way."

* * *

ON THE PAVEMENT, Lady Dunsby cocked her head toward the boat and said quietly, "Our girl isn't a lightskirt, is she?"

Madame Franck watched as Dan and Bess stalked down

the stairs together and on to the boat. They probably thought themselves unremarkable. But Madame Franck saw the way their steps stayed together, and when the boat pitched, Dan, never taking his eyes off the footmen, put a hand out to where he knew Bess stood, and just as unthinkingly, she took it.

They thought themselves clever sneaks, but middle-aged women knew how to see things.

"Miss Page is naturally friendly." Madame Franck added that to her inner ledger of the worst lies she'd ever told. "She has been through so many shocks, and we only find ourselves here through the kindness of strangers. Of course she is warm when she meets someone new under your roof, so to speak."

"Hmm. I've had excellent references for Mr. Burton, but he may have less obvious faults than his sense of fashion. I'll keep an eye on him, and do you the same for Miss Page. I have hopes, you know, for her in London. She's welcome to make a cake of it in Gravesend, as likely no one important will hear. But she must still be *unattached* by the time I bring her to London society, if we want her to make a good match."

Madame Franck inwardly bristled a little at her insinuations. "You have taken such care with Lady Agatha, I am sure Bess will follow her good example."

Middle-aged women also knew how to fire shots at one another without the explosions of guns. Lady Dunsby gave Madame Franck a look that conceded the accuracy of the shot. "You may think Agatha ought to be married by now, but she is young for her age. And I must say, uninterested."

"Is she?" Agatha didn't *look* young for her age, and Madame Franck wondered if that might not be the blindness of a mother who didn't want to lose her only company. Still, Madame would happily treat Agatha with kid gloves, as long as Lady Dunsby did the same by Bess.

She didn't know what Bess had planned, but looking at her on deck beside Dan, she felt like she could see something invisible connecting them.

They reminded her of home. Had they been different children, they might have smiled at one another while they chased parrots or played at the waterfalls. The British were not gentle with their children, certainly not in these big, sooty cities.

And the British seemed to lack any poetic guidance such as one found in *akam*. She would wonder more how they managed to stumble through life, if she hadn't seen for herself how they didn't.

Their Mr. Shakespeare had the right idea, of someone like her to carry messages between them and help their story along.

If only she knew what messages to take.

"Do take another shawl, Mr. Burton. Sea air is so harsh when you're unaccustomed." Lady Dunsby was packed all around with shawls and huddled against Madame Franck, who looked happy not to move. Both ladies wore a rug over their laps and deep woolen muffs.

Dan didn't correct her that they were on the river, not at sea. "No worries, my lady. I'm sturdier than I look."

Bess stifled her snort.

He still wasn't bulky, but his taller frame was packed with tight muscle. Those clothes hid it with a slightly loose cut. Certainly the greatcoat didn't show the narrowness of his waist, and definitely did not hug the shape of his shoulders.

She still had not recovered from the shock of his hair in curls.

She had the knack now of the boat's roll under her feet, and stood. "I'm going above. I've never sailed down the Thames; I don't want to miss it."

"Do be careful, Miss Page. Take an extra shawl. And see to Agatha. She loves this trip, but it's so terribly cold."

Dan fell in beside her as though he were just another shawl, something she surely wanted to take up on deck too. Bess was still trying to find a way to send him back as he gave her a hand up the steps she did not need.

Agatha stood at the boat's front—had Bess heard the mate call it the prow?—just below where the mate sat lookout. Bess' bonnet blocked the rest of her view. Despite the wind and the cold, she pushed it back.

The buildings of London were now the crests of the valley of the river. All around them big and small vessels slid, veering over the water, following invisible rules, avoiding collisions somehow while Bess watched. Stone walls and steps pocked the water's edge, letting people reach the flow of the river; and on their left, busy docks held enormous ships, bobbing slowly on their lines like giant wine corks.

Agatha stared across the blue-brown water as if her nose pointed the way.

"Mind yer step," the mate said lazily with a quick look back. "If you fall in while tide's goin' out, what's left of yer will wash out to sea instead of Kew."

Not even this grim warning affected Agatha. She cast Bess a little smile back over her shoulder, a few silvery-gold curls escaping in the wind. Bess pulled off her woolen glove to test the temperature of Agatha's cheek.

"You are freezing! Really, Agatha. Go sit with your mother for a moment."

"I don't want to miss anything."

Bess looked out over the expanse of water. The weaving pattern of the boats drew the eye; here and there great houses, like the Dunsby house, presided over spits of high land, and remnants of antique gardens fought for space alongside raw-looking warehouses.

Their boat's spread sails caught the wind and slackened in some mysterious dance Bess couldn't decipher. It was not like riding in a carriage, along a set road; they were moving back and forth on the sluggish water, part of the dance of all boats.

Bess had forgotten how much the world could surprise her.

But Agatha had seen it many times before. Bess decided a scolding from her companion was in order. "This cold is too much. Honestly, you could lose an earlobe. Take this shawl, go get warm, then come up again."

Biddable as always, Agatha smiled and went. Bess offered a hand to help, but Agatha's feet were sure across the deck boards.

"She must have done this many times," she said under her breath towards Dan. She knew he was there.

As they moved back toward the cabin, Dan took Bess' elbow. "What game are you playing?"

Bess kept her voice soft enough not to carry to the master at the rudder on one end or the mate at the other. She couldn't tell which way the wind was blowing. "Funny you didn't mention that you *work* for Lady Dunsby."

"It's new." He shrugged at her disbelieving look. "I just finally learned it today, in fact. *I'm* not the problem. I am responsible to Lady Dunsby now, which makes *you* the problem."

In fact, *Dan* was the problem. She felt lighter just seeing him, right here, close enough to touch. But if they traveled in the same direction, he would cross paths with the Silver Duke. On the one hand, she had to make sure that greasy soul never set his hooks in Dan. On the other, Dan wouldn't like the most permanent answer.

Best for Dan to come clean so Bess could work out how to get him gone. "*This* was why you wanted my help? Stealing something at Gravesend? For crown and country? Because you're in costume if ever I've seen one, Dan."

"Bollocks." Dan tried so hard not to swear in front of her; he must feel terrible pressure. "Talk about costume. I looked in your trunk. That's a full wardrobe, with a gown for evening. What for?"

Bess berated herself for not checking the trunk was locked. The miniature of the Silver Duke was in there.

Then counted herself stupid; if Dan wanted to see inside, no lock would have stopped him.

"Lady Dunsby is persuaded to introduce me to society. Alongside Agatha, I think."

"Who persuaded her? Who paid for the clothes?"

At least he was asking about the clothes, not the picture. He must not have seen it.

Bess gave him a sugary smile. "Sir, what makes you think you can ask such personal questions?"

She saw that muscle jump again at his jaw. Odd; she'd never seen that before. Or perhaps he just hadn't had that muscle.

"I should have—" He stopped.

"No, do go on! Should have what?"

Another jump, but his voice stayed even. "Should have done a better job of educating you."

He was welcome to be irritated and let Bess be the calmer one for once. She shouldn't be, but she was ridiculously glad he was here.

* * *

EVERY GIRL down the alley had a story about her proper parents, even though most of them lived with mothers Bess knew were probably theirs.

They scattered like mice at Dan's approach.

To Bess, his bent scowl was a familiar home. "Dan!" She wanted to put up her arms to be carried, but she didn't. He would do it, could easily do it; but at her age she wanted to act big, even if she wasn't.

He'd walked her toward the Grand H.'s cellar like he always did, dark eyes darting everywhere looking for trouble.

Bess chattered to him about Emily's stories, and Gertrude's. "They made me wish I had a story, Dan. You ought to tell me something."

"Don't know anything," he muttered like he always did when her origin came up.

"If you don't know about me, tell me about you." Bess was not above stealing his story and telling it as her own. Indeed, it sounded like fun.

"No."

"Why?"

"You won't like it."

It warmed Bess' little-girl heart that he didn't want to tell her a story she wouldn't like. "I'll like part of it."

"How do you know?"

"Because it has you in it."

The street smells faded a little as they drew nearer their sleeping-place. Bess never considered that home; other than talking about Dan, she never used that word.

A set of boys knocking away each other's pebbles on the road's packed earth scrambled away as they passed, suspecting Dan's scowl had something to do with them.

Finally he said, "My mother left me at the orphanage."

"Why?" Bess was still small enough that it was always her first question.

"Ugly."

"Why did she leave you just because she was ugly?" Lots of mothers were ugly; Bess had seen plenty.

"Because I'm ugly."

"You're not ugly! You're beautiful!" Indignant on his behalf,

Bess had grabbed his hand, yanked it hard, wanting his full attention.

He'd given her most of it, swinging her up in his arms to carry her even though she was more than half his size.

"Men aren't beautiful. They're handsome," he mumbled, as if her words had made him shy.

"You're so handsome, then." She'd switched to whatever word he wanted; her sentiment was the same. "It must have been because of something else, Dan. It must've."

They were old enough to have seen children left behind for many reasons. Because they couldn't be fed; because the parents were ill, or drunk, or lazy, or sunk in the despair poverty caused. Or because they died.

A few children had run wild so long that, like feral cats, they couldn't be tamed. But that wasn't Dan. No one had left him because of that.

Dan didn't answer, and Bess said nothing else, because even at that age she'd hated to admit when he was right. She didn't like that story, and Dan ought to make up another one.

* * *

BESS KNEW everything she needed to know, especially about when to make up a story. "Educate me? I'm very well educated about life. A lady's companion is an excellent place. I might yet be some lord's wife."

He winced as if she'd stepped on his foot. "I'm in no position to complain, if that's actually what you're doing. After all, I am the secretary."

She put up a mocking gloved hand. "Horrors! And it takes dressing like that?" Then she dropped the hand and the horror. "Do what you like, just don't be angry with me."

"I think it's my turn."

She had to admit the truth of that. Still. "I'm not angry now, *Mr. Burton.*"

"You were at the theater. One fit of temper from you leaves an impression."

"I was allowed some anger after the way you left me. It was one too many times." Bess felt foolish airing childish grievances, but he was the one who'd started the sniping.

"What are you talking about?" His dark head bent close. It was a curiously pleasant sensation, his profile blocking the river view, his body making a quiet space between them where no one else could hear. He barely whispered. "I've never left you."

In that private quiet, it felt safe for Bess to talk. "Remember that Christmas we had oranges?" Dates were never certain, but according to Dan, Bess had been around nine. So likely thirteen for Dan, though a weedy-looking thirteen. "You slept by the door, and I had to sleep alone." She'd been *cold,* that night and all the ones after.

Now she saw hot red burn across his dark cheeks. "I was too old. Sleeping with a little girl wasn't right."

"I'm just telling the truth. I was cold." *And you were gone,* she didn't add. It was the first time in her life she could remember feeling truly lonely. "And then three years later, you stopped sleeping in the cellar at all."

He was looking out over the cabin roof, at the water, not at her. "Not my idea."

"What?" Bess had *always* thought he'd just left her. Or could no longer bear the Grand H.'s snoring. "He made you leave?"

"Yes."

He must know his puny answers only made her more determined to find out the rest. "Why? He thought you'd done something wrong?" Dan should have said so. Bess could have convinced the old man to change his mind. She usually could.

"No." Clearly he knew she wouldn't rest with one word answers, as he sighed and added, "He was afraid I *would* do something wrong."

"With what?" Bess' mind ticked back. All they'd had was some food and a fire.

"With you."

Shocked, Bess forgot her *persona*, the boat, everything. "*Me?*"

Quickly cutting off anything else she might say at top volume, Dan's voice dropped till it was the next thing to silence. "Think about it, Bess. I was a bastard, from the orphanage. *Look* at me. I've looked like a devil all my life. That's what people see. He believed the same as everybody else."

"No! I mean, he *can't* have. He knew you."

"No, he didn't."

The fury rising in Bess now was clean and hot. "You're making excuses for him!"

"Not me. I fucking hated him."

They stared at each other, Bess awash with shock at the new view of her childhood, Dan immovable as always.

"You hated him?" Quieter now, Bess still shook her head. "Why didn't you—Why didn't we—"

"Live somewhere else?" The exhaustion on Dan's face belonged to a much older man. It was clear he was rehearsing worries he'd run over and over in his head for a long, long time. "The brothel, with Emily and her mother? Would that have been safe?"

"Where did *you* sleep?" Bess countered fast.

"The street. A doorstep. Sometimes a windowsill."

This shifted everything Bess thought she knew.

Pieces of her past broke, sliced into each other with sharp

edges, and made for more uncertain footing than the rocking of the boat. "Winters were cold."

"Better me cold than you."

"No, Dan." He might be immovable, but Bess didn't back down. "You were still too young. And we would have been warmer together. It was my fault."

"Never your fault."

For Bess, the Grand H. had been a long, slow disappointment. When she was little, he said what to steal, and she did. When she got old enough to know the value of the coins he drank away, she told him to stop, which he ignored; so she'd ignored him.

That last year, she'd refused him coins *or* liquor, because if he drank till he slept, he pissed himself.

He'd embarrassed Bess, so she erased him from her mind. There indeed was her poor relationship with emotions; she'd never thought how he'd affected Dan. Education indeed.

Good thing he was already dead, as Bess moved him into the *better dead* column in her head. "If he were still here—"

He could hear the ice in her voice, and he looked down. Looked softer than she remembered. More than she could blame on those absurd curls. "He taught you to read."

"I forgot that." She frowned. "He taught both of us."

"No, Bess. He taught you. I just listened."

"This is..." Bess felt pressing on her the whole weight of his childhood, so different from hers. She'd just taken what she was given and didn't look any harder. She had to say his name. "*Dan.* You should have told me. You should have given me time to hate him."

Dan just shook his head, looking tired. "Hate is wearing."

Bess disagreed. But she didn't want to fight.

These old men. Rotting puppet-masters like the Grand H. and the Silver Duke. Who taught them to act like that? What gave them the right?

Dan looked out over the water.

With her newfound determination to look a little closer at what was around her, Bess realized: he'd successfully used the past to distract her from the present.

"Dan." Bess couldn't let this go. Definitely not now. She was desperate to know he wasn't just here because of her. It would be like him sleeping in a windowsill again.

"It's Mr. Burton," he reminded her, near-silent, barely moving his lips.

She knew that. She knew it and had forgotten it, she'd been so swept away by the pleasure of having him near. When was the last time she'd forgotten what name to use?

He'd never meant to leave her. He'd said that before, but now she saw what it meant. Even these last few years, he'd had her watched, which was... ghoulish, really, but if it was still abandonment, at least it wasn't simple.

And then at the theater he'd asked for help, and she'd put him on the ground.

She'd rather he were as far from the mess she was in as possible. But he was here, and he needed help. That was why he'd been in the theater, after all; likely he still needed help. "You've done too much. For him, and far too much for me. Whatever you're doing here, it better be for yourself. Please tell me it's selfish."

* * *

EVERY TIME he was around her, he lost more precious control. He'd wanted her to think better of him, and look what happened. A walk down memory lane that endangered everything, and she hadn't been put off from the question at all.

He'd have to give a reason for his presence she'd believe, or she'd never stop digging for it.

One lie came to him as easy to sell, because it was true. God damn his soul to the hell it deserved, but it was true.

It was the last lie he wanted to tell, but that just made it uppermost in his mind. There was no time to think of anything else.

"Selfish in a way. It's for the woman I love."

CHAPTER FIFTEEN

It was true. He'd always adored Bess, put her at the center of existence. And that had been for little-girl Bess.

Grown-up Bess was even tougher, claimed not to need him, looked different every time he saw her—and he was hopelessly in love with her.

It was far, far worse than merely desiring her. Yet in its own way, it felt better. He *was* capable of a finer emotion... for Bess. And if he *had* a heart to give away, what else would he do with it?

He didn't expect her to take it so hard. After all, she didn't know he meant her. She rocked away, silent. Then she looked like she might speak, but didn't.

He was pretty sure she'd bought it.

Finally she pointed one finger at him. "Explain."

"Go look after Agatha, and tomorrow you'll go home."

She wouldn't be distracted. "All this... for some woman? Explain."

"Are you going to tell me what *you're* doing here?"

Bess didn't move.

"Dammit. I really didn't educate you at all, did I?" He shifted and looked out over the cabin at the other boats, wondered if they had such exasperating women aboard.

"We educated each other. You can't distract me twice. Explain yourself." He saw her twitch. "It's not *Agatha,* is it?"

Christ, now he had to distract her from the woman idea. He made himself that kind of quiet below a whisper, where even the *s* sounds wouldn't carry. "I'm looking for a ledger." It sounded stupid and small when he said it out loud, especially when it had taken over his whole life. "There's a man where we're going, with a ledger. I've got to find it, find out what it says."

"Why?"

"Money."

"Why do you need money? What woman do you know who needs luxury? Your room has four bare walls and little else."

So even with her fever, she'd seen his room. Dan squashed a rising embarrassment; as lodging, he'd honestly paid for it.

There was no comfort like *not* living under threat of a hangman's noose, and he needed her to have that.

"I'm trying to make something of myself so she can have a better life. Been trying for years. Now I'm close."

She folded her arms again, cocked her head, a birdling puzzled by him. He could see her running through names in her head, every woman they'd ever known. "*Five* years?"

He didn't answer. This was a very dangerous game he was playing. Getting Bess out of this mess was one thing; it was another to give up every secret he'd kept his whole life.

She kept going. "Make what of yourself?"

That was Bess. She kept going and kept going and kept going. She wouldn't stop. "Who gave you that sapphire ring?" Only an offense might distract her.

"Stole it. Make what of yourself?"

He was well and truly trapped. He'd have to tell her his plan. Way too soon.

This was the problem with a life of lies. One never knew when the next trap would spring. He'd hated growing up this way, hated lying to Bess and everyone else every minute.

He checked the other men. The captain was behind a flapping sail, the mate far ahead of him. They wouldn't hear.

"I've spent five years learning more than bookkeeping. I've learned about money."

She came a little closer, so he didn't have to try so hard to stay quiet. "What is there to know? Everyone wants it and only rich people have it."

"It's not so simple. The wars were expensive. *Very.* Plenty of gentry aren't rich any more. Hell, the Prince alone owes a king's ransom."

"I don't understand." She pulled her bonnet back on to help keep her voice between them. "If no one has any money…?"

"There are still rich people, Miss Page, people who aren't genteel." He let himself give her a little smile. "Merchants, and army men. Gambling on Britain's future. There's money, just not where you think."

"What's that to do with you?"

He'd have to tell her all of it. "These men make money selling things on paper. Say one man wants to buy coffee; another sells; they have to find each other. Negotiate a price. Someone has to put those buyers and sellers together. You can sell other things, too. Debt, and chance. Money is far more complicated than you think."

She frowned; Dan had tried to explain his beloved numbers to her a hundred times when they were young, but she wouldn't have it. He pressed on.

"Traders can be rough; some have reputations. A few too

many are swindlers. Two years ago, the market wrote down its rules, exactly how to trade. A man can *buy* a place in the exchange. Anyone can. You don't have to be born into it, do you see? You just need enough money, and a decent reputation. At least from swindling; other vices are fine."

"How do you prove your reputation?"

"Vouchers. Letters. The word of someone reliable."

Bess accompanied her shrug with a bitter snort. "To keep out people like us."

"But I've almost got that money, and the letters too. I just have to see that ledger."

She looked up at him, and he knew she believed him.

He saw it click. She made up her mind, and that scared him. Bess hated to change her mind.

She nodded. "Fine. I'll help you."

"*Help* me? You've got to get the hell away from me."

Another of those sugary smiles. Apparently that was Miss Page's style of argument, and Dan hated it. "It's a very small boat."

This was worse. Definitely worse.

But what could he do about it right now, except toss her in the water and hope she'd float to Kew? The mate already said she wouldn't.

He looked out over the cabin's roof again, at the water, and contemplated his sins. His mother had probably tried to explain them to him, same as the masters at the poorhouse. The Grand H. had reminded him often that nothing he touched would ever be quite right; that was one reason he tried not to touch Bess.

Now, one of the many.

Bess hopped up and down at his elbow, trying to see over the cabin roof too.

* * *

IT WOULD BE nice if Bess could blame all her selfishness on the opium and the sickness it caused.

But Dan had just proved Bess was selfish down to her core.

All those years he'd given her everything she asked for, right down to letting her hold a grudge. He must have fallen in love five years ago. It explained everything. He could have told her, but why should he have trusted her? She'd been a child and acted like one.

She'd like to think she'd have behaved differently if she'd known. Well, she could prove that by acting differently now.

Some girl—some woman—some *lady* had Dan's heart, and he was buying her a future with all this. It was a sobering picture, not of the boy Dan had been, but of the man.

He really did make Bess want to be a better woman.

Because she wasn't good. She *hated* this woman she'd never met. Hated the idea of her, right down to her no-doubt perfect toes. She must be good for Dan to be in love with her. Absolutely awash with morals. Mercy Bennett, Bess had just flat-out told him she'd stolen this ring. His mystery woman doubtless never said that, because she never *did* that.

Trying to imagine her pinched Bess inside in ways she didn't want to admit. She'd always thought of Dan as hers, but she'd been a child. For all his yapping about her life, he deserved his own. Deserved a woman who'd adore him the way he deserved.

That woman might know what his smile looked like, the one where his scowl and scars all let go and he got soft because he was looking at her. Bess thought of it as *her* smile, but maybe that woman got to see it too.

And she'd get to see Dan's hungry look, the one like the man in the stairway, the one Bess imagined Dan could match. That was another reason to hate her.

The idea made Bess' stomach knot even though the drugs were long gone.

Well, hate her or not, if Dan wanted her, he'd have her. Dan might not like Bess saying she owed him, but she did. She could pay just a little of it back by helping him now.

Besides, he clearly had a plan. Bess loved plans; she just didn't make them. She had none regarding her inevitable clash with the Silver Duke, but it didn't bother her; the Silver Duke's plan was all about killing Talbourne. She just had to foil it.

Dan's soft smile was just for her as he noticed her trying to be taller to see his view.

He looked forward at the mate, then casually back toward the master. Neither were looking. "Go on," he murmured, bending one knee forward and bracing his other foot at the join of the cabin wall.

With a genuine grin, Bess, fast, stepped up on his knee, then his open hands, as quick and light as she used to do over walls, or horses in acrobat shows.

His palms felt strong as a boat deck, but unlike the boat deck they went *up*. He pushed her higher with strength that seemed effortless, till she stepped forward over his shoulder to stand on the cabin roof.

When the sail swung past, Bess danced around it, and the boat master gaped at her perched on his roof.

She looped her arm around the mast, the hem of her gown whipping in the wind.

Dan could be right. Maybe bitterness helped nothing. It was just that, bad as she was at figures and ledgers, Bess thought in terms of accounts. And Dan had been robbed, both by her and the Grand H.

This horrible girl of his better be special.

The river looked wide, all the boats and ships like peculiar animals darting between and around each other. And the sky seemed very far away.

Bess wiggled her fingers at the staring boat master.

That gentleman, once his astonishment passed, did nothing, as if young ladies perched atop his cabin every day.

* * *

"I'm perfectly well, Mrs. Frank. Agatha, mind your hems. Do make sure we leave nothing behind, Mr. Burton. As I've said, the shopping here is not the best."

Bess didn't care about her hems. She couldn't stop looking in every direction. It seemed impossible somewhere so different could be such a short voyage from the depths of London.

She was used to buildings crowding and shoving each other. Here, the clustered facades on the water's edge seemed prim by contrast, as if they'd decided long ago to stay in their place.

Here, the steps down to the water were wood, and the buildings perched right next to them. The largest place wore FALCON and HOTEL signs etched below two wide water-facing windows.

And the Thames here was very slow, very flat. Its water creeped out between hillocks of grass and brush, escaping the main flow of the river and finding its own way to the sea. A squat fort sat on the opposite shore.

It was even more obvious here how the sea flooded in, mixing its salt with the fresh currents. There was a blue-green quality to the dark water that reminded Bess of a tourmaline. She told herself not to be superstitious, but it felt like a good omen.

The black and gray clouds stacked in the sky threw out

peach-colored wisps, as if in a hurry to get where they were going before the sun set.

She slipped a little on the first greenish step. Had the water been higher, she nearly could have walked into the hotel; but they'd ridden the receding tide out of London, and the boat almost brushed the sand. Bess saw it dimly through the water just below her. "Agatha, let me help you up first."

After Agatha, Madame Franck hung back, torn between glaring suspiciously at Dan, and minding Lady Dunsby's commodious basket. "No, Hortense, you go on. I can't be easy till you are on the boards. There, are your canes set firm? You aren't cold?"

"Of course I'm cold, that breeze is like an ice-house." But Lady Dunsby mounted each step slowly to stand tall on the wooden walk in her resplendent wool damask, so many shawls wrapped round her chest she had a mushroom shape.

The rest of them slowly joined her, lugging whatever parcels they could.

Around the ladies, Dan was attempting to play a sort of bookish milksop. He juggled three of Lady Dunsby's smaller valises. "Lady Dunsby—"

The *crack* was a sound Bess had never heard before.

CHAPTER SIXTEEN

What stopped her heart was the sight of Dan's head spinning and turning, his hat flying far away. The same instant, his luggage dropped, and so did he. The valises lay on the boards; Dan disappeared.

Only his fingers remained, hooked over the edge of the walk.

His other hand was somehow clenched in hers, a strong hand-to-wrist hold, as Bess stretched flat on the pier.

She didn't know if he'd pulled her flat, or if she'd dropped. Instinctively, she tried to pull him up.

It took several beats of her heart to realize *he* was pulling *down*.

Apparently Dan realized the same thing at the same time. He stopped trying to pull her over his secure wooden edge, and she stopped trying to pull him back on to the pier. Bess took a breath and evaluated their position.

She could have planted her feet and hauled him up—she'd done it before—but made a show of struggling with his weight, gripping uselessly at his coat and attempting to help. He *was* heavy.

He made a show too, of working himself up over the edge of the wood to flop flat on the mist-damp boards then roll over, gasping, when he could easily have pulled himself up with the one hand.

The gasping didn't seem for show.

Madame Franck had also thrown herself flat; only Agatha crouched on her feet, while Lady Dunsby stood as firmly planted on her canes as she had been a moment before. There was no one below in the shallow water, or in the windows of the buildings bellied up to the walk. A few villagers stuck their heads out their windows to see to the commotion, but that was all.

In the distance, an apple-seller, as calm as Lady Dunsby was, faintly cried "Apples for sale!"

Then boots came thudding around the hotel's corner, two men on the wooden walk.

"What the devil? Anyone hurt? Are the Russians back?" shouted one, his apron flapping.

"I don't think anyone is hurt," said Lady Dunsby. "Are you, Mr. Burton? No. He's lost his hat, though. We need conveyance to Road's End, can you arrange it? "

"I can, missus." The aproned man looked as confused by her calm as everyone else.

"The Right Honorable Countess of Dunsby," Madame Franck said faintly, still peering around.

"Madam," the innkeeper corrected himself. "Yes, I recall you now. Sorry, madam. It's been a bit glum. The Russian fleet has just gone, and there's men without work. Too much time on their hands, I guess. Phil, fetch up their luggage."

The boat's master and mate were clearly torn between tossing up crates and collecting themselves.

"Such an unfortunate welcome." Lady Dunsby tugged up her gloves, preparing to climb the slight incline up the boards to the street. "Someone hunting in the wrong place, no doubt. You *can* engage us a carriage?"

"Right away, madam." He dashed away.

"What the hell?" yelled the boat's master. "Is it safe to launch?"

Phil the porter, an older fellow with bursts of yellow-gray hair escaping from his black cap, just shrugged and waved his arms.

The master didn't wait. Heaving trunks chest-high to get them even with the walkway, he shoved them over, ignoring whether they crashed into boxes already there. The case that had held the cold dinner made a noise that told Bess the world had lost a plate.

"Slow down!" she shouted over to the boatmen, but they paid her no more attention than they did the cold wind.

At least the shouting gave her an outlet for her feelings.

Seeing Dan fly away like that had snapped something in her. Dodging her own danger was one thing. But danger for Dan—

Madame Franck took over shouting insults at the boatmen, and Bess used the chance to talk to Dan.

"We must get your hat!" She grabbed Dan's arm and ran down the walkway, following the hat's path in the water.

She wanted a good look at him. It came back to her all in a second how he didn't always admit he was hurt. How he'd once run home on a badly turned ankle. It swelled to the size of her head.

She couldn't see any blood, but that wasn't calming.

She hid it by shouting at the now departing boat.

"Can you flip the hat out of the water? Do you have a pole?" she shouted into the wind, all the while keeping a grip on Dan that would bruise. Over her shoulder to him, more quietly, "Are you hurt?"

"I just stopped my fall off a pier with one hand. Of course

I'm hurt." Dan waved too, with his good arm. "It's right there!" he pointed at his hat. "Perhaps you can get a paddle under it?"

The gray bowler indeed bobbed on the waves, but tilted, as if taking on water.

Her grip tightened. "Did it come close?"

"I heard the ball go past my head," Dan said grimly. "That hat probably has a hole in it."

On the other side of fear, Bess found, there was something even harder to understand, harder to admit. It made her hands cold, colder than the wind. And something in her chest felt sharp and icy.

A feeling like the world held only one diamond, and she'd nearly lost it.

The high whistling sound in her head wasn't from the water, Bess realized. It was in her ears. Someone had *shot* at Dan.

At *her Dan.*

Dan leaned toward the water as the boat's mate threw a hook toward his hat.

Bess grabbed the back of his coat.

"I won't fall."

"I have to do *something.*"

Her stuttering gasps caught his attention; he looked back over his shoulder. "Breathe."

She felt oddly angry at him. "Go marry your perfect shop-girl, but don't *die.*"

"I'm all right." Turned back to the water. Perhaps he hadn't understood. "Can you catch it?" he shouted at the boat.

Bess had never once felt like this before. Never. Like she could lose the whole world.

Because Dan never let you, that roil of tangled feelings whispered in her gut.

Nothing to do with the Silver Duke was worth a bullet hole in Dan.

"We must go back. Tell the boat to come back."

Just then, the mate landed his hook on the bowler. It sank.

Shrugging, the man pulled back his rope, with gestures that conveyed that he was out of plans, and the hat was gone. It was too far away for him to shout.

Dan sighed. "That boat's not coming back."

"We have to get another. Do you have money for the passage?"

"Miss Page, I'm not going *back*. I doubt that bullet was meant for me." Looking to make sure no one was near, he added, "I'm supposed to be here. How about you?"

She grabbed his wrist again and dragged him back toward the hotel. "Let me remind you I decided to help you. It would help to leave."

His grip on her after the gunshot had been like iron, but now he let little seven-stone Bess drag him back to the hotel.

Bess forced herself to drop his arm. And gritted her teeth. "This is intolerable."

"You've got more nerves than that, Bess. How many tumbles have I watched you take? You've no idea how many times you stopped my heart."

They approached Lady Dunsby in a weather-worn carriage; behind it, a cart piled high with their luggage, hitched to a bitter-looking donkey.

As they did, Bess murmured, "I'm sorry."

Just a few nights ago she'd felt a hundred feet tall. Like she held all of London in the palm of her hand.

Now she felt tiny and helpless. It hurt to think she'd ever made Dan feel that way.

Quite unnecessarily, Dan seized Bess by the waist and lifted her straight into the carriage, giving her a squeeze that felt intended to reassure her.

It only made Bess conscious of the emptiness around her where his hands had been once he let go.

Her ladyship was all contrition. "I'm so sorry about your hat, Mr. Burton. I doubt we'll find another. But some shop will have a cap or something, even if it's not as fine as your lost one. Do we have all the luggage?"

As Dan went to count it, Lady Dunsby reached a hand toward Bess. "Miss Page."

Keeping one eye on Dan, Bess stepped closer.

"A lady has emotions," said her hostess quietly, "but let's not let them run wild, hmm? You're a lovely girl. I expect you to do much better than a secretary, if you can only keep your head. You do understand?"

Bess bit back the urge to defend Dan. She tightly pinched the soft skin between her thumb and finger, an old trick for keeping her focus. "Apples for sale!" called the street seller, closer now and a useful distraction.

"I'll do just as you say, Lady Dunsby," she promised, as usual with no intention of keeping it.

* * *

ROAD'S END wore a dress of white columns, very fancy; but it was dark, asleep. Appropriately to Dan, who felt like everyone around him was performing, it looked like a theater in the morning when no one was there.

But it was night, when there should be an audience.

When they rounded the corner, the carriage wheels rocking in the rutted road, they found the real Road's End. It had a square face, plain and indifferent to water and sky; in fact, both water and sky had become all one color with the setting sun, a lost dark blue, and the house hulked black against the last of the color.

Only a few of its windows showed candle glow.

"I'm Able. Th' steward. An' butler," a sunburnt man told Dan at the door, answering his knock. "I suppose there's luggage."

"That's right, Mr. Able." Lady Dunsby answered him, already out of the carriage and on the ground. She might walk with two canes but she was always two steps ahead. "Do see everything is taken out of the carriages, will you? You know I hate to lose things. Never mind us, I'll take us through."

Her ladyship's familiarity with the house was obvious, as she stumped through a maze of rooms to the farthest one, all her party trooping after.

It was large, with French windows that showed a garden. The furnishings were plainer than the fine London homes Dan had seen from the inside; its wood was painted rather than gilded, with old-fashioned tapestries on the walls. The carpets were pleasantly worn but clean, and a cheerful fire made a cozy nook.

With two women sitting by the fire where Dan expected one.

The thinner one wore a yellow gown and on her lap, something *moved*. Dan tried not to jump.

"Come in, Hortense!" she called, petting the thing in her lap. "Excuse me for sitting. Ruby hasn't felt well, and I'm warming her by the fire." The apparent Lady Carrollton leaned over and released the whatever-it-was on the floor. It looked like a rat.

A fat, fluffy, ginger rat, with no tail or ears.

Dan surmised this was Ruby. She disappeared under a chest of drawers.

He hoped that was the last he'd see of her.

Lady Carrollton addressed him. "You're accustomed to guinea pigs, aren't you, young man? Never mind. They're no bother. They like to find each other; Mr. Pig is here somewhere. Hortense, you remember Arabella, don't you? I should say Lady Winpole. We've got a nice fire waiting for you. And this is Agatha? So grown-up?"

Dan only heard *Lady Winpole* and all the color fled from the room.

That must be her. The other woman by the fire. She was round and short, both rounder and shorter than Lady Dunsby, in carefully drab clothes betraying touches of luxury. A mink muff lay on her lap, and her large ring sported an orange stone, radiating enameled lines like a sun.

Or a spider.

He'd gone so senseless he barely heard Lady Dunsby's reply. "Of course! Lady Winpole has been kind enough to partner with me at bridge often this year. You haven't waited your supper, ladies, have you? We ate quite well on the journey. I brought ham."

"Of course we waited!" It wasn't clear if Lady Carrollton was scolding or reassuring. "It's so cold, and now the sun's down. You must have some warm soup. Isn't this weather a nightmare? I can't remember it ever being so cold."

An ancient animal deep in Dan's chest told him to toss Bess over his shoulder and *run, run, run.*

No one knew better than he the things Lady Winpole was capable of. The whole point of this was *not* to meet Lady Winpole. He didn't want her to see his face. He damn well didn't want her to see Bess'.

And there stood Bess on a pet-chewed carpet not three yards from this nightmare.

He hadn't imagined *himself a target;* he'd never been important enough to shoot. He still felt Bess was the one in danger. It was a familiar feeling, as was his determination to stay closer and closer until he could get her out of it.

But Lady Winpole's presence made that bullet real. Perhaps someone *had* intended that shot for *him.* And while it couldn't have been Lady Winpole herself—clearly she'd been sitting by this fire for some time—it could easily have been at her request.

Nothing about the shot made sense; even had Fitz's plan gone wrong, there was no reason to shoot Dan; he hadn't even done anything yet.

Still, the feeling of being a target settled into his skin and drew it tight.

Lady Dunsby, with her gout and two canes, stayed standing, introducing first Agatha, then, "Miss Page has been kind enough to accompany us."

Thank God Bess had dyed her hair. Dan wished she'd *shaved it.* She was too short, too memorable.

Too rare.

Dan's blue spectacles were not merely decorative; they solved the fault of his eyes, which saw everything far away but blurred things that were close. He'd thought everyone's eyes like his till he'd left behind Bess and the Grand H.'s memory, and sought other kinds of work.

The blue helped bookkeepers like him ease the strain of long hours reading ledgers by candlelight; but his were specially ground to help him see.

They also hid his eyes.

Bess ought to have spectacles. Dan fought down the urge to throw his spectacles, a bag, *something* over Bess' head. Bess was doing her best to go unnoticed, but eventually people noticed Bess; she couldn't help it.

Don't let that woman remember her. If he was praying to anyone, it was Bess.

The silence all around him, which he finally noticed, said he'd missed his conversational cue. Likely his introduction.

"So grateful, Lady Dunsby, thank you so much," he said in Mr. Burton's swooping voice. "Lucky enough to serve a lady like yourself and make a journey too. I've never been down the Thames; it's been an experience."

"Too true," Lady Dunsby nodded with dramatic emphasis she hadn't shown at the time. "Mr. Burton's *hat* was shot off at the Falcon Hotel, can you imagine? Just as we landed."

"*Shot off?* Oh, that can't be true." Lady Carrollton's thin colorless curls trembled. Her horror looked real.

As did Lady Winpole's calm. "That's an unfortunate welcome."

"Just what *I* said, Arabella. Isn't that just what I said?" Apparently feeling the niceties were over, Lady Dunsby stumped over to sit in the last upholstered chair by the fire. "Entirely unfortunate. The innkeeper blamed Russians. I'd no idea you had any."

"It's been a trying summer." Lady Carrollton slumped back, no longer watching where her guinea pig had gone. "The Russian fleet docked here for repairs. It's put everyone on edge. I swear I don't know if they're our allies or planning to attack us."

"Allies, for the moment, Lady Carrollton." A tall man with silvering temples entered by the French windows; an icy burst of wind came in with him. "Not that I've seen the latest papers."

Bess stayed in the shadows, nor did she move. But Dan felt the way her attention sharpened. As with Fitz' wife, it was palpable how closely she watched the man's movements.

Could this... older... man be her protector? Dan studied him from top to toe without moving his eyes. Memorized his face.

"Oh." Lady Carrollton seemed exhausted at the prospect of another round of introductions. "Lady Dunsby, here is Lord Vellot. Perhaps you know each other?"

Then three more suspects confused Dan's focus by charging in through the French windows too, one waving a brace of dead rabbits on a string. The little animals' limp bodies and muddied fur were ill-suited to Lady Carrollton's sitting room, as was the cutting wind they brought with them.

"Agatha!"

It was a brazenly familiar address that froze everyone there.

* * *

AT THE YOUNG man's outburst, Bess stopped worrying about how she should hold her hands. The three older ladies were clearly scandalized, and not by drafts or dead rabbits.

Bess wondered what they'd think if they saw him *in flagrante* in a stairwell.

"Close the door, Charles. I don't want my piggies to escape." Lady Carrollton weathered the awkward moment by wearily starting introductions yet again. "Lady Dunsby. You recall my son, Lord Waresham. He's kindly surprised me with a visit and brought friends."

Her tone made clear she welcomed neither his surprise nor his friends.

It was definitely the Charles Bess had seen ravishing a lady against a wall. Bess hoped her face conveyed anything but *I saw you in the stairwell.*

"Lady Dunsby," he said, boisterously cheerful. "Glad you've arrived. It's been deathly boring waiting for you. And Lady Agatha, of course."

The belated courtesy fixed nothing. Agatha blushed in the middle of the floor.

Lady Dunsby, who had just gotten comfortable, stood, drawing every eye in the room.

Her sudden declaration vibrated with genuine feeling, brief though it was. "We must settle ourselves," she announced in tones Caesar must have used about crossing the Rubicon. "I suppose Mrs. Frank is unpacking. We should help her, Lady Agatha. Do come with me."

"I apologize for my familiarity," Charles said with a too-informal grin. "We've all known each other such a long time. You'll be glad I'm here; my friends are useless at hunting." He displayed the dead rabbits.

Lady Dunsby said nothing, only gave him a curt nod as she clumped past.

Agatha followed, so Bess did too.

Bess thought of Agatha as someone obsessed with inexplicably dull things, the opposite of everything that happened on a stage. This Charles complication was gripping.

But she could hardly ask all the pertinent questions with Lady Dunsby just a few steps ahead.

Dan followed her out, and once they were out of earshot of the assembled guests, pushed her into an open doorway.

In fact, it was closer to lifting her up and depositing her there.

The feel of his hands on her ribs was immediately familiar and comforting. The strength of him moving her so easily was something else, something new. The way his warm hands almost scorched through her gown was delightfully direct proof that he was still here, whole, alive.

He didn't wait for her to turn around. He was looking out, Bess knew; if anyone watched, he would just fade away behind her. They'd done it a million times before.

But his warm breath against her ear had never felt like this.

"Say the word and we're out of here," he murmured. "There's not a trustworthy person in this house."

She looked back over her shoulder and up at his face, right where she'd missed having him all those years.

"Including us?" She gave him a smile she'd never given

anyone before; she'd never felt it before. Like the feel of his hands on her, it was something unnamed and new.

* * *

FOUR MEN IN THE HOUSE, any one of whom could have been her protector. Or he might have been back in London; but Bess was here for a reason, and the less she said about it, the more Dan worried.

That sweetly flirtatious smile was certainly something Miss Page was practicing for someone who wasn't him.

"One word," he reminded her, "and we'll fucking *swim* back to London."

"What about your shopgirl?"

"What shopgirl? You mean the *girl* girl?" Her interest in this supposed girl was heart-warming, even as more lies would just complicate matters. "Never mind her. I'll get the money another way if I have to."

Bess' smile faded as if that wasn't the answer she wanted. She gave a quick nod, drawing his attention to her bare slim neck. If he bent forward, he could kiss it.

Not that he would.

But he was that close, and it fired up his blood.

In fact, he was so distracted watching her walk away, so small, such a whirlwind of surprises, that it took him several more minutes to realize his real problem.

Storey wasn't here.

CHAPTER SEVENTEEN

The room provided for Bess and Agatha held their trunks and Madame Franck. Also two narrow beds, a washstand, and a dressing-table, as well as a worn carpet like those downstairs. Its only touch of luxury.

It was a deep dive down from her palatial chamber at the Dunsby house. Bess wondered what the rooms were like in the house's unused new wing. And whether if, with a little coal fire like the one in this grate, they'd be warmer.

Lady Dunsby settled herself on one bed's edge, interrupting the unpacking, and waved to Bess to shut the door.

"Ladies. I shan't lecture you how to behave," she began.

Madame Franck shot Bess a suspicious look.

Lady Dunsby went on. "I heard many lectures on how to behave when I was young, and I ignored them all. My mother did *not* lecture, which was wise. However."

She planted her canes firmly at her sides. Bess was on tiptoes waiting to hear what came next.

"Even in the country, even among friends, one must always take care with one's appearance. I don't mean whether your dress is dirty. I mean whether you appear to be the sort of woman a man can trifle with, or not."

This was as fascinating as a circus. Bess hoped for trick horse riders next. Perhaps out from under the bed.

"Agatha, I don't know what passed between you and Lord Waresham. But he's said nothing to me about his intentions regarding you, and I know you're aware that you should treat him as a childhood friend. *At a suitable distance.*"

Then Agatha—*Agatha*—talked back! "I recall many stories of your society seasons, madame, and I believe my father danced with you *everywhere* in public before he declared his intentions."

It had to be true, as Lady Dunsby sighed heavily and leaned back.

This was *better* than the circus.

Rich people were generally stupid, but these two were nice, and clearly had their own problems. Hardly urgent ones, compared to finding enough food to stay alive, but compelling ones nonetheless. They all walked on tightropes, where one wrong step sent you falling down... to live among people like Bess.

Clearly Lady Dunsby was aware of the situation's absurdities; still, it was truly dangerous. One couldn't imagine Agatha a fallen woman, living in the streets where Bess had grown up.

"It was a different time, and your father was honorable. I love Lady Carrollton but she never had the temperament to raise a boy like Lord Waresham. What's done is done, there he is, tall as a watchtower, but not... not the right kind of man. He isn't kind, not like your father was, Agatha, and that's the main thing marriages need. Everlasting kindness."

"Perhaps kindness isn't what I like most," said Agatha with an absolutely brazen toss of her silvery-blonde head.

Bess was agog.

"Oh, it isn't?" Lady Dunsby clearly wasn't as taken aback as Bess. Agatha must have unexpected depths. "Well, I can't lecture you, as I just said I wouldn't, but here's some advice. And Bess, you listen sharp, as you don't have a mother to tell you this. Firstly, excitement lasts a minute, or sometimes an hour. Marriage lasts year after year, and if you're tied to a man who isn't kind, you'll have plenty of time to regret it. Secondly, *society* isn't kind. Not at all. And once they think they have your measure, even once you realize your mistakes, they won't forgive you. You'll find yourself stuck on a path you don't want. Really, Agatha."

"Mother," Agatha's urgency seemed intimate among the four of them. "I haven't encouraged Charles, not really. But he *is* exciting. I can't just *ignore* him. I know you had your share of excitement when you were young. I *know* you did."

Bess expected her ladyship to refute this charge, but Lady Dunsby just smiled a little, shrugging one shoulder as if she were still a flirt about to dance. "You know too much. But that's my disservice to you, darling. I could be a bit wild, because my mother was very staid and quiet. You've inherited a mother who kicked up her heels through no fault of your own. If you give people the least idea you'll do the same, they'll take it all out of proportion. Think of your father's telescopes. A lens changes what you see."

"No one will see us here. Me, I mean," Agatha hurried to correct herself.

Lady Dunsby's smile faded.

"Lady Winpole can see. Don't forget that. Regardless. Lord Waresham is no one to trust with your heart. Or any part of you," she added swiftly, with a sharp look that told Bess she had once kicked up her heels indeed.

Bess wondered why Lady Winpole rated such a warning. She looked like every other matron in a gray dress. But given

Lady Dunsby's advice about appearances, Bess remembered she was not the only actress in the world.

"Very well, mother," Agatha said in her soft voice, but Bess didn't think the speech had swayed her.

When Madame Franck quietly said, "Your mother is very wise, Lady Agatha," without any dramatic flourishes at all, Agatha only smiled and moved to help with the unpacking.

At least Lady Dunsby had said something about this Waresham character first. If Agatha persisted in defying her mother, that example would make it easier for Bess to drop a word in her ear.

What word, she didn't know, because she couldn't explain how she, the country cousin, once saw Charles tossing a woman in a theater stairwell.

Oh well. One thing at a time.

She must concentrate on Vellot, the Silver Duke. Just being in the room with him had made her arm-hairs bristle.

The impulses he brought out in Bess were hard to square with her resolution, not three hours before, to be a better person.

No doubt Dan had been right about the cause of her illness, its poison. That she could simultaneously hate Vellot and struggle to return to him was proof.

Bess wasn't one for self-study, but she knew what she could do.

The better Bess would warn the Duke of Talbourne about Vellot's assassination scheme.

The worse Bess cared more about Dan, and Madame Franck, and herself than any duke. And that Bess had to find the moment, the opportunity, to put an end to Vellot's schemes entirely.

* * *

Distraught by Lady Dunsby's exit, her hostess shuffled after her using a foot-sliding gait apparently intended to keep from kicking any guinea pigs.

Lady Winpole left too, not bothering to pay attention to the floor.

Dan stood in the doorway looking as if he'd never left.

"Damme." Waresham threw himself down in the chair his mother had vacated. "I suppose I couldn't have done worse."

There were no servants about; his dead rabbits flopped on the floor. Dan saw what had worn the carpets besides the guinea pigs.

"No, you couldn't. Viscount Harman, by the way, heir to the Earl of Ayles." The brown-haired man tossed this in Dan's direction as he sprawled in a chair opposite Waresham. Apparently it was his introduction.

Kind of him, as Waresham's brazen greeting of Lady Agatha had put a stop to introductions when Dan needed them most. It was chancy enough figuring out how to talk to these people.

Dan stepped forth out of the shadows. "Nathaniel Burton. At your service. Apologies, sir, I do not know Lord Ayles."

"Nice to meet one man in England who doesn't."

"Please, Harman, we're in the country. Shake off your gloom. Zachary has."

The blond man stayed by the French windows, staring out at the fallen night as if he could make it lift. "That's because Zachary only cares that tomorrow he will paint, and damn the weather."

"Don't start tossing that wash again. It's the *country*, man. You need to breathe the air. By morning you'll be *begging* to hunt pheasant, see if you aren't." Waresham studied Dan up and down with a look of distaste that said he found Dan less interesting than the pattern in the rug. "I don't suppose you do much shooting in London, Burton?"

"Not of animals."

Even the man at the window grinned at the glass, and Lord Harman whooped. In the company of apes, Dan had proven himself an ape.

Dan clamped down on the thought. That was how he'd made a place among the fist-flying men of the streets and kept it. These weren't apes; these were the glittering people. With far more weapons at their disposal than words.

It had been men like Dan who, forty years before, had suggested the rowdy traders in stocks, notable for their bad manners and worse reputations, should band together inside their coffee house. Only ten years since, they'd built a fine trading room and hired a constable to toss out brawlers. Now they wore their coats at all times and tried hard to look honest.

Just last year, those formerly rough men began shaving like gentlemen and made themselves rules. They were full of greed, ambitious, ruthless. But they did have rules.

Rules meant fair games, and fair meant Dan could win.

Waresham made him tired. He was the kind of man always measuring himself by others, counting off money and women and every kind of trophy. Trying to put Dan in his place.

Little did he know Dan was the kind of man who would soon take his place.

He just had to find Storey.

* * *

"WILL you help me dress for dinner? I can't reach the tapes alone." Agatha sounded shy again. Her gown had all the pieces and ties of a fashionable dress, but they had no maid, and Madame Franck had disappeared.

"Of course!" Bess locked her trunk.

"We usually do bring maids, and a footman. But my mother said she wanted to limit herself to one boat. Truly, I think she wanted not to overtax Lady Carrollton."

Bess plopped herself on the bed. Slightly shabby, like everything at Carrollton House, but Bess had slept on far worse.

"Agatha. Are you honestly..." She couldn't think what word rich people would use for what she'd learned about in the streets. "What are you doing with Charles?"

Agatha always glowed, but now she had fire behind her eyes.

"Do you know him? I'm afraid what they say is true. He's an awful rake, isn't he? Oh—you didn't hope for him yourself?" Agatha frowned. "But you don't know him, do you? You've never been to London before."

Mercy Bennett. "Your mother made clear his reputation. It isn't good."

Agatha sank to the bed next to Bess. "I know it isn't. I think I *like* that. His eyes on me are so... *intent*. Like I'm all he can see."

"I suppose that's flattering." *He looks at every woman that way.*

"And he just... says what he thinks. Why can't everyone?"

Because people have too many secrets, thought Bess.

Stealing was so much simpler than this spying business. See something you need? Take it. No fuss, no lying.

Though Bess enjoyed fuss and lying, they'd lost some of their shine when that bullet had carried off Dan's hat.

And she didn't enjoy other people's double-dealing, certainly not Waresham's. How could Miss Page put it? "One can hide sharp lies under a huge pile of sincerity."

Blinking, Agatha slowly nodded. "I'll watch closely. I must tell you I haven't seen him since summer. We were at the same house party in Sussex. We did dance." The last part sounded a little forlorn.

"Agatha, you can do much better. How can you not know it?" Bess recalled Agatha saying she didn't mind if Bess outshone her. "You're beautiful."

"Am I?" She sounded more surprised than anything. "That's odd. I've only been to a few London parties, but no one notices me. Charles says it's because I'm a pearl among diamonds. That I don't sparkle, but I have a quiet little shine. He even quotes poetry about it. *Full many a flower is born to blush unseen.*"

Bess ground her teeth. Charles was a lying liar who liked young ladies to feel he was their only chance. "You could be a *lighthouse*. I think he's playing on your feelings. Making you think you're small."

Agatha reached over and squeezed Bess' hand. "You make me wish I had gone to school. I felt too shy, then Papa was gone; I wanted to keep my mother company."

"If your papa was here, he'd warn you off Waresham, I know it."

"I'm ashamed to say that's part of his appeal." Agatha untied her curls to brush them. Natural curls, of course. How had this Waresham convinced Agatha she was plain? "There's something appealing about a man bent on behaving badly, don't you think?"

Bess would never roll her eyes at Agatha, but she came close. How could Agatha fall back on the same old rich-lady excuses?

Bess thought about Dan's dark scowl. How it made alley girls swoon. They thought they knew what he was like, when they knew nothing about him. They weighed both him and Lord Waresham based on looks.

"No," she told Bess firmly. "I don't think bad behavior is appealing. Because it means you're playing games with fire to see if you get burned, without admitting that you're the same as women who've already been burned. I think you deserve fun, but what's fun about him? He's only out for himself, and cares less for you than a dead rabbit."

Agatha gasped.

"If that's not too direct."

"No," Agatha finally said, twisting a loose curl around her finger. "I see what you mean. Indeed, your case is clearer than my mother's. You're saying it's a little selfish to play with fire, and I'd be smarter to indulge myself with affection. That, and kindness," she added thoughtfully, thinking of her mother. "I'm going to think about that. But Charles is just so effortlessly attractive. As if he exuded a magnetic force."

Well, Bess was less inclined than usual to blame women for the lies they told themselves about men. The Silver Duke's charms hadn't been that he was bent on bad behavior, but he'd been delightfully aloof.

"I suppose we all have our vices," she muttered to Agatha.

* * *

DAN ONLY KNEW how skimpy Lady Carrollton's table was because he had seen fine tables before.

Mr. Able, the steward, was something new. He watched each dish arrive, peering at the few footmen who ran back and forth to the kitchen carrying plates for all the diners.

"I serve *à la Russe*," was Lady Carrollton's timid explanation as footmen set plates before each guest, already sporting tidy portions of food. "It is the new fashion."

"Indeed?" Lady Dunsby eyed her nearly bare plate. "Where?"

"Russia, I suppose," said Lady Carrollton in a small voice.

"I had no idea you loved fashion now, Hannah." Lady

Winpole looked annoyed and poked her tiny mound of baked clams.

"It was an extraordinary summer. The Russian officers came to dinner several times and were very interesting guests."

"Aye, interesting. Hungry more like," said unshaven Mr. Able, glaring at each plate like he could weigh it with his eyes.

It was easy to see why tyrannical Mr. Able liked Russian-style service. Since each plate was composed in the kitchen, he controlled their portions.

Very, very small portions.

The son of the house wasn't shy with his disapproval. "Mother, you can't eat like this. *We* can't. We're grown men. I ought to have tried for some pheasant."

"We saw a wild boar," Harman chimed in.

Fortunately, no one expected Dan to talk.

"There's a lamb carcass hanging in the barn for Fawkes day." Mr. Able looked annoyed by the impending expenditure of lamb. "Besides that, we got to be frugal. We've been feeding fat Russians all summer. Got to tighten up."

"You've a table full of guests, Mr. Able." Lord Vellot looked unimpressed by the steward's tight-fisted approach. "With more expected. The Duke of Talbourne always travels with a large retinue."

Mr. Able left the room muttering something about eating wallpaper next.

"I thought the Duke had already been?" Lady Winpole waved her hand to summon her footman, who jumped forward to offer her, and only her, a silver box of Eccles cakes.

The sugar pastries made Dan's mouth water. He'd stolen many in his day, right down to eating the loose sugar that rubbed off in his pocket.

Tough to burgle one at the table.

Clearly the Carrollton table was famous, as no one acted surprised when the next dish was a poached egg next to a bright red lump that turned out to be rasped cooked beets.

Dan almost burst out laughing. He was at the glittering table, one of those people. But the table was not what it seemed.

He'd just explained to Bess the new powers of money in this new world. Hadn't he believed his own story? This wasn't the same glittering world he'd witnessed as a child, his nose pressed against the glass; it was different. And so was he.

He'd learned from his childhood how to survive hungry; so had Bess, though she was probably the only person at the table for whom the meal was nearly a reasonable size. The other ladies persevered.

Waresham and his friends, though, clearly suffered.

"Where's the rabbits? Damn it, that's why I brought them!" Waresham downed his claret, which he'd likely also brought. Lady Winpole had a glass of port beside her, but no one else had wine.

Dan was in no danger of toasts.

The noise drew Mr. Able back into the room. "The cook is jugging them, sir," he said grudgingly.

"Charles, please," Lady Carrollton weakly admonished.

"I don't want them jugged, I want them here! On my plate! Boiled if need be! Is this how you keep my mother fed all winter? No wonder she looks like burnt paper."

"I keep the house just as Lord Carrollton requires," Mr. Able shot back. "He sends instructions weekly. Like he done for sixteen years." His out-thrust jaw said that if the son didn't like it, he could choke on it.

"Lord Waresham. Your father gives me a generous allowance for the house."

"Gives it to this barbarian, looks like. And just when do you plan to unlock the cellar? Give *us* wine, not the damned rabbits."

Lady Carrollton winced but did not give in. "Mr. Able runs the house just as your father would like."

"Yes, that's fine," Lady Dunsby put in, agreeing in order to derail the mother and son spat that threatened to go on forever. "I would take just such careful care of you, Hannah, should you be so good as to visit me."

Ah, thought Dan. Perhaps that was Lady Dunsby's reason for this visit. To spirit away her long-suffering friend.

Innocently, Lady Dunsby added, "I am very keen to try your plan of reducing, Hannah, as you can see I need it. The doctor prescribed for my gout just such a plain diet as you enjoy. I only mean that when you want a change of scenery, you must come stay with me. If the Russian fleet tired you, do come."

* * *

BESS FOUND it difficult to eat even the few bites of food on her plate with the Silver Duke sitting opposite.

Just being in the room with him stole away all the pleasure that had come back into the world since her recovery. Clearly his effect on her was not solely that of laudanum.

Hate was wearing, just as Dan said; but Bess couldn't just give it up. For long months the Silver Duke had given her something to look forward to, a fake echo of the real life she used to share with Dan. She had invested in their relationship; she had *believed* him. She hated him now, but she hated herself more. For falling for his rotted lures, jumping onto his hook.

His face across the table reminded her every second how stupid she'd been.

Plus, he was venomous.

He must have planned to give her more of the drug while she was still at Lady Dunsby's. Occasionally he glanced her way, as if puzzled why she was here, looking well, and ignoring him. No doubt he'd prefer her begging for more at his feet. Had he let Lady Dunsby foil his plans? Was he that feckless?

Did he think he still had his hooks in her?

Bess bet he did. He had enormous faith in himself.

He liked complicated games with himself in the middle, and he had no scruples. He could have shot at Dan. But had he?

He'd been out of the house; but so had Waresham and his friends, and all with guns.

If the game had been simpler, she might have made a simpler decision, to settle outstanding accounts with Vellot and sort the rest out later. But she found herself less interested in settling accounts with him herself than ensuring Dan wasn't in danger.

This many men made the situation foggier. Perhaps that was also Vellot's plan.

She was grateful to sit beside one of the ladies.

"I like an Eccles cake best when the currants are a little sour," she told Lady Winpole in the next chair. Of course the lady was rude not to share her cakes, but this dinner was more like meals among thieves, where everyone ate what they had and only the closest shared.

"Do you?" Surprisingly, her ladyship broke off a bit of pastry and put it on Bess' plate. "My cook does them nicely, and of course they travel well."

Bess put the flaky bit of butter and sugar pastry on her tongue and let it melt. She tried to imagine a bad Eccles cake. "Do you make this trip often?"

"I come see my friend once a year, and Lady Dunsby

persuaded me to do it now." She looked, and sounded, terribly bored. "For the sake of a decent bridge partner, I agreed; but I should have given more care to the weather." Lady Winpole fastidiously rubbed her fingertips against the edge of a napkin.

The weather might not have helped Lady Carrollton's stingy steward, but... "At least it would have been warmer."

"Precisely."

"I admire your ring." If Bess wasn't mistaken, its fine enamelwork alone was worth quite a bit; but its real glory was the sunny sparkle of its orange center stone. "It's a hyacinth, isn't it?"

Finally she'd hit on something Lady Winpole was willing to share: what she knew about gems. "It's a hyacinth from Africa, and I have high hopes for expanding the trade there. The Ceylonese have long held the monopoly, but I believe these African stones can rival the Ceylonese hyacinths in splendor. In fact, this orange color is so much more pleasing than Ceylon's red ones, I'm not even sure it's the same stone. I've seen one from the Canadas that rivaled it, and I suspect it may be something altogether new."

Bess was very much able to distract herself from a skimpy supper with talk of jewels. "Perhaps it is only the cut."

Lady Winpole leaped on the idea without ever really taking notice of Bess. If she had, she might have wondered how a simple country girl knew so much about jewels. But she went on almost as though she were conversing with herself. "I thought the same thing. But I do have quite a good Ceylonese hyacinth, a table-cut stone in the middle of a brooch I bought years ago..."

As she went on, Bess could hear that the gentlemen were also trying to distract one another from the light meal. "I had no idea the Russian fleet was here," said one of Waresham's friends to Vellot. "Did you?"

"I had an idea." Vellot's smugness was palpable.

So Vellot followed the movements of the Russian Navy and wanted to assassinate a duke.

That gave Dan's mission a new flavor. Dan said he wanted to find a ledger—for king and country. Yet he showed no interest in the Silver Duke, no more than anyone else.

Dan couldn't possibly be here to kill the Silver Duke himself, could he?

She dismissed the idea immediately. When Dan talked at all, he tended to show his cards. At least to her. If he said he wanted a ledger, he wanted a ledger.

His mission and hers could still be connected.

Lady Winpole's opinions on the cutting of hyacinth stones were plentiful and flowed freely till Waresham spoke over everyone else. "This is intolerable. Madame, I insist that you immediately purchase some decent beef."

Lady Carrollton waved a limp hand sparkling with diamonds, and Mr. Able thrust out his jaw. It was astonishing to watch rich people thwart each other. No one was getting any beef.

CHAPTER EIGHTEEN

The Grand H. had never cared for poets, but to Dan it instinctively felt cruelly poetic that he'd taken this mission to provide for Bess. A Bess *far away*. Not right here, swimming in this nest of vipers with him.

Were he inclined to poetry himself, he'd have written something about taking on providing for a little girl only to eventually find himself traveling with a woman.

One happily chatting with a traitor who had committed bribery, arson, and probably murder.

Neither Dan's old feelings for Bess nor his new ones allowed him to reach the logical conclusion that criminals made their own favorite dinner partners.

Bess should have been dancing at the opera house, only in danger of catching fire from the footlights. Bess wasn't like Lady Winpole.

He watched Lady Winpole offer Bess another bit of cake, and Bess laugh as she took it.

All right, there were *some* similarities between Bess and Lady Winpole. He needed to find Storey, and that ledger, and get Bess out of here before Winpole engaged her to pick government ministers' pockets.

He would search the rooms. It was the place to start. There wasn't time to make chums of the footmen, or find a maid susceptible to sweet talk. He just needed to read the ledger, not steal it. With all the guests recovering in their own ways from that joke of a dinner, and all the servants in the kitchen washing every plate that had ever been made, he should be able to move about unnoticed.

The older ladies now watched the younger ones with sharp eyes. Lady Dunsby especially kept leaning over the table to peer down it and make sure Waresham wasn't signaling Agatha.

Soon this dismal dinner would adjourn. Surely Dan could search and give up worrying over Bess for half an hour.

Not that he ever had before.

* * *

"I must talk to that girl." Vellot gritted his teeth as he dogged Lady Winpole's heels out of the dining room.

She looked to the young ladies far ahead. "What, Lady Agatha? Her mother knows you. She might otherwise indulge you, but she will not let you get her daughter alone."

"Not her, the other. Dunsby's an amiable twit," he snapped. "She'll do as she's told."

"Will she?" murmured the short lady with silk-rustling skirts at his side. Vellot looked more than agitated; he looked thwarted, and that amused Lady Winpole.

"Just make sure I get some time alone with the girl. Not just a few minutes."

"You may not *order* me, Lord Vellot. Nor do I know why I should arrange for you to vent your frustrations on that girl.

Your Duke is not here, and your plan has fallen awry, that's all. I never had much faith in it, or you."

"My plan has not yet begun." Still his face bulged red as if he clenched his teeth. Looking for someone to bite.

It was none of her affair.

"I'll do you this favor," she said mildly, "and you will cease giving me orders. I have provided *you* funds in exchange for the work you promised. If anything, I employ you."

* * *

THE YOUNGER LADIES settled into the parlor as the older ones went into the next room to visit its card table and miserly drops of sherry.

"Come, Agatha, help teach Mrs. Frank to play cribbage. She's willing to be a fourth, but doesn't know how to play." Lady Dunsby's voice roused Agatha from her contemplation of the vast outside dark.

Agatha would rather have talked with Charles—Lord Waresham—but he was closeted in the library with men and port, and paid no attention to her now that Lady Dunsby was watching him closely.

That was a bad sign. She sighed a little as she backed away from the telescope.

She only wanted distraction from the emptiness in her life where her father had been, and Charles was wonderfully distracting. What she really hoped for, every time she looked through a lens, was the sensation of putting her eye against the cold brass after another dearly familiar eye had warmed it. She still missed her father so badly, she spent hours looking for whatever he would urge her to see if he were there.

She could easily face the fact that Lord Waresham did not reward close examination. It just left her more alone.

Her mother waited at the door.

In a soft winged chair by the coal fire, Bess had fallen asleep.

"Should I wake her?" Agatha asked softly as she went to her mother's side.

"Better not. She's been ill, and the Thames voyage can be tiring. You feel well enough to play, though, don't you? Come through. Lady Carrollton's best table is in here, and it's delightfully warm."

So Agatha went into the next room with her mother to day-dream of younger men and lose games to older women.

At the card table, Mrs. Frank sat across from her, laughing at Lady Dunsby's observations about the ease of playing cards.

None of them noticed when Lady Winpole rose to draw the window curtains, as if against a draft, and in passing, nudged the door so it drifted shut.

* * *

FOR ONCE BESS was pleasantly warm, the warmth seeping into her and making her drowsy.

She could have slept there all night, but she was wakened by the small slide and rattle of a page turning.

Another new, unfamiliar room. And behind her—

She heard another page turn. Bess leaped from her chair.

"I'm sorry there's no bath for you, but there's wine," said the Silver Duke, sitting far away with his face in shadow.

Bess' heart knocked so wildly in her chest it nearly tipped her over.

It only beat harder, faster, as she took in the scene. He'd put a small desk beside him. It bore a pen and an inkwell. A blank cut sheet of paper lay there, and only one candle shed any light.

It was all so horribly familiar. *Too* familiar.

Her body felt confused, as if she'd told it to spin then chained it still. As if she had clockwork inside, and the gears were grinding. The sameness of it all turned her mind, her feelings, in directions she didn't want them to go.

"What are you doing to me?"

"Me? I'm reading this book. I rarely read novels, but this one captured my attention. It's called *Self-Control.*"

Bess gripped the wing of the chair for balance. She'd had no wine. She couldn't be drugged again. "I don't feel right."

"You do, though." He turned another page. "I brought you wine, you know. All the way from London. Lady Carrollton has an abominable cellar."

Bess closed her eyes, then felt she was falling. She forced her eyes open again.

He'd never been her safe harbor. He wasn't one now. All the familiar things repeating, repeating, clutched at her mind and twisted it like a key twisted the tumblers in a lock.

But she refused to be unlocked. She would *not* undress. He was no duke. His name was Vellot, hers was Bess, and...

And Dan would hear if she screamed.

She would never; she wanted to help *him* for a change, and drawing him to Vellot's attention was the farthest thing from help. But she felt better, just knowing that she could.

The horrible man just sat in the shadows, turning the pages of his book. As if he had nothing to do with the roiling feelings inside her.

A lifetime of uncertainty had made Bess practical as hell. She didn't believe in magic or demons.

But somehow that man had the power to affect her with these signals: the paper, the candle, the book.

She didn't need to explain it; she only needed to escape it.

One heavy masculine hand waved toward a sideboard. Yes, it held a crystal goblet of wine. Next to it a delicate porcelain plate held a cut apple. Her favorite. "You must be hungry," he murmured, still looking down at his book. "Why not drink?"

"Drink it yourself. Choke on it." Bess moved behind the heavy chair. The fire was at her back, which wasn't perfect, but she felt better with some barrier between them.

His tongue *tched* behind his teeth. It was more menacing because he didn't look at her. Didn't see her. "You're feeling ill. You must have been ill lately. Or did you buy yourself medicine from some chemist? Lead pills? Laudanum? You must look after yourself. You're an *artist*, Bess. Grand in *everything* you do. You could—"

"Stop it. Just stop." She had nothing nearby as a weapon. She would have to trust to the *varma kalai* if he came close; she hoped he kept his distance. She didn't feel in control of the distance between them, or of herself, and it was the most sickening sensation she'd ever had. "Stop winding me like a clock."

"Ah, Bess." He turned another page; he wasn't even reading, she could see that now. Maybe the repetitive sound was the purpose. "Cold feet about your grand finale? The Duke of Talbourne hasn't even arrived yet."

His utter faith in his control of her, of the room, made it worse.

But unless she was prepared to try to strangle him with her bare hands, she could only listen or leave.

She'd *followed* him here.

He tapped the blank paper, and her eyes focused on it. Like looking through one of Agatha's telescopes, it looked empty at first; she would have to find her target. If she kept searching, she'd find it.

She blinked. It wasn't a map to a target, just a blank sheet of paper. Everything, *everything* he did made her feel floating and calm as she had with him so many times before. How did he cause it with only words?

How did he make her doubt her own mind?

She didn't move. "You can't still expect me to help you."

"I need many kinds of help."

"How could you need anything from me?"

He smiled. She could just see it, in the shadow, and even in the warmth of the fire it flooded her with cold.

"You're an *artist*, Bess. You do *great* things. No one suspects you could even *kill* a man to change the world. Couldn't you, Bess?" Just what he'd said before. What he *always* said. He hadn't just asked her that once. He'd asked *many* times. She remembered that now.

Repetition. The repetition must matter. Bess tried to think of distractions, but her mind was blank. Like the paper.

She'd fallen into his web before and found her way out. She could do it again, as long as she didn't panic. She knew the workings of the trap, or some of them. She *had* to trust herself.

She didn't.

But Dan did.

She clung to the thought. He went on, "Your time's almost here, Bess. Haven't you always wanted to matter?"

Her insides settled. She took a free breath. It was miraculous relief, because Vellot had made a mistake.

After all this, he knew nothing about her. He thought every opera dancer was the same. He needed her to feel special because of *his* attention. Like Waresham did with Agatha.

But Bess had always *known* she was special, because Dan had always treated her so.

That thought held her up, made her strong enough to play the role she had to play.

She crossed to the sideboard and took the wine. The spot

between her shoulderblades itched when she turned her back on him, but she made herself do it. Made herself sink back into her chair and look into the fire.

She was a great dancer, an even better actress. The way out of his trap was to be what he expected.

He thought he controlled her utterly. Even her swearing at him hadn't given him pause; he expected her to crumple.

Expected her craving for opium to crumple her.

He was right. She wanted it right now, that feeling of fake peace, that momentary calm. She'd take the sick stomach as a fair exchange. Maybe even the shame.

But Bess only enjoyed lies when they were hers.

She settled back in the chair, cradling the glass. When she tipped it to her lips, she knew that, with the light of the fire behind her, it would look like she drank.

"There," he said with a purr. "Sometimes a girl needs good wine. You should rest; you'll feel better." His voice had a low, insistent rhythm, and Bess could just imagine how it would lull her towards oblivion if she'd taken the opium. "You're important to me, Bess. You're important to *everyone*."

How mortifying that she'd once enjoyed listening to this.

She wriggled down into the big, heavy chair. "There," he murmured. She heard him put down his book. "You're asleep now, aren't you, Bess? Comfortable and asleep. You'll wake up far more calm and ready for your grand performance."

"So I will." Despite the pounding in her chest she kept her voice low and even.

"Are you ready to tell me what man has your attention? Who are you thinking of more intently than you think of me?"

How did he know Dan even existed? It didn't matter. "The Duke, of course."

"Of course." He sounded smug again. It was the right maneuver, reassuring him he knew all there was to know. "I haven't given up on His Grace, Bess, and neither should you. He'll be here."

"Mmm." She only cradled the glass in the crook of her elbow and pulled up her feet, pretending to fall asleep.

She heard his chair creak as he rose. If he came any closer, she'd have to spring.

But fortunately, he seemed confident his work was done. That he controlled her. His quiet footfalls trailed away, then the door closed behind him. He left her to dream his poison dreams.

Bess peeked around the wing of the chair.

He was gone.

Trembling, she leaned into the fire, into a heat so hot she almost felt her eyelashes singe, and poured the drugged wine into its heart. Waited till every drop had sizzled away.

She still felt cold.

Nothing remained in the glass. She let it drop onto the carpet. He must mix his brew in the bottle, using very tiny doses. He thought she'd had enough to sleep through his words. His everlasting words.

She'd come here to take her life back from him, but she didn't know how to fight his weapons.

Shivering, she silently acknowledged the difficulty of it because his words were hers. He'd drawn them out of her. Spun her dreams into chains.

Chains of which she was ashamed.

It was impossible to outrun her own dreams; nor could she destroy them.

Bess tucked her knees under her chin, wrapping herself into a small ball, trying to get warm.

What artist didn't want to be great? She wanted her performance to mean something more than a moment's flash of ankle; she wanted it to stay with the people who saw it, make them remember it, remember her. It must be so obvious that even he could see it. Her vanity. Ambition. Greed, and pride.

The Grand H. had moralized about such things and she'd ignored him. They'd sounded fine to her.

Now, and without the veil of drugs, they looked ugly.

She stayed knotted up in the chair, reminding herself that he didn't know her. She barely knew herself. He could say it till the sun came up, but she didn't have to kill a man because he said she would.

Nor had she said anything about Dan. He couldn't make her do that. He'd never make her do that.

If she just kept repeating that, maybe she'd believe it.

An oddly muffled *squeak* made her look down.

A furry potato had trundled up to her tipped wine glass, sniffed at it. He ruffled his black-and-white fur, looked up at her and squeaked again.

This had to be the famous Mr. Pig.

Quickly she leaned over the side of the chair, rather like Lady Carrollton had done, and scooped up the glass. She might be ugly inside but she didn't want to accidentally poison a guinea pig. Lady Carrollton's hospitality was horrendous, but it would still be a poor return for it, poisoning her pet.

Its little black eyes looked up at her, and its nose twitched. Clearly, it did not care for the smell of the poisoned wine. "Wheek," it said.

You're right, she silently told Mr. Pig, feeling utterly grateful. *I didn't drink that bastard's wine.*

She just had to keep moving. Find someone new to be. The Silver Duke couldn't control everyone she could be; Bess could barely do that herself.

She was still too shaky to hurry. But she crossed the room, slid the blank sheet of paper off the small desk, then returned to the fire to lay it in the grate and watch it burn.

Mr. Pig watched too, with great interest.

Bess was from London; she had no intention of picking up a fat rodent. But she gingerly patted his furry little back, showing her thanks. He'd been company in one of her lowest moments, and she needed that.

It felt raw, admitting that truth.

Admitting that she needed someone else. Company. Realizing that more than fame or diamonds, what she wanted most right now was Dan.

* * *

NONE OF THE SERVANTS' rooms yielded anything interesting to Dan's search. They had nothing worth stealing, which surprised him. If he worked for someone as tight-fisted as Lord Carrollton, he would definitely lift some silver.

Even if he had to walk to London to sell it.

He rushed through Waresham's room, full of scattered clothing. Zachary's held drawing paper and a neat unpacked valise. Lord Harman's appeared empty; his leather case was under the bed. Clearly the young men had come without valets to rusticate in the country, just as they appeared.

Vellot had taken the master's room. Dan wondered what the absent Lord Carrollton would think of that.

It held nothing beyond obvious toilet items: his razor, damp linens, his clothes. The lack of valet clearly taxed him. Crumpled neckcloths lay on the chest of drawers.

At Lady Winpole's door, Dan slid inside, then paused. He didn't even want to touch anything of hers; but there was little *to* touch. Her small locked writing desk and two locked trunks foiled casual observation. He'd have to come back when he had more time.

He'd rather be caught by a servant than a guest; they'd

likely share his lack of patience for rich people. But he didn't want to be caught in Lady Winpole's room at all.

Atop one trunk sat a dress doll, the kind Dan would never steal. Only fine ladies ever had them, and they were out of fashion. It looked odd there. Lady Winpole's gowns were plain, and the doll's bright, ruffled dress was old.

Gingerly he checked under its skirts; it would have been the perfect spot to hide a key. But no, nothing.

He doubted the ledger was with Lady Agatha or Lady Dunsby. Nor did he suspect Madame Franck. Maybe that was misplaced faith, but he only had a little, and using it was his prerogative. There were things to doubt about her, but colluding with Storey, or Lady Winpole, wasn't one of them.

He approached Bess' things with restraint. It would feel... vicious to paw through her finery. It wasn't as though the name of the man who'd endangered her would be written on her stockings.

He still had to search the public rooms, and below stairs. Road's End had that whole unused wing, plus its kitchen at the far end, and apparently a cellar.

And a stable, a barn, a coop for chickens, and...

He could spend a week searching it all.

He needed Storey to show himself, he thought as he slipped back to his own room, stepping on ends of floorboards so they wouldn't creak. Dan was no master of disguises. He did not fit in here, and the longer he was here, the better his chances of saying something that would betray him.

Hopefully rich folk expected London working men to retire early.

His room held a small desk; he tossed upon it half-written letters he'd brought with him, evidence of Lady Dunsby's correspondence. He'd also brought a half-filled ledger, and a wallet of purchase duplicates. Fake, but there.

The hand did not match his, but then, he was a new secretary.

His room showed Mr. Burton to be just as he appeared: a bit vain, a bit ambitious, reaching above his station in life.

Dan admitted he was two out of the three, and suspected he might also be vain. Because it pained him to set his curling iron in the fire.

* * *

WITH EVERY STEP Bess took toward Dan's room, she wanted him more. He was everything she now knew the Silver Duke was not. She wanted his calm, his certainty; but mostly she wanted *him*.

Wanted him so selfishly that she felt ashamed of it.

She'd missed him for five years. Wasn't that long enough? Hadn't she paid for it already? Though she wasn't sure what she'd paid, or to whom.

It steadied her a bit to creep across the long flagstoned corridor that led out to the depths of the kitchen. She heard the servants gathered there, still dealing with Mr. Able's curious method of serving dinner.

"A la rooss, says he. I'll rooss a plate over his head."

"If this wedder keeps up, we'll be eating pongers noon and night, and he'll tell us to dig 'em ourselves."

"Go on, Mary, them peas are hot."

Gathered as they were, it was easy to slip past them, easy to glide through the empty dining room to the wide stairs that led up to her room, and the rest of the guests, and Dan.

Dan's room at the end of the hall shared two cold walls with the outside. It should have been on the top floor with the servants; but then, hers should have been too. Perhaps life was more uncomfortable in the between-places where Miss Page and Mr. Burton tried to live.

He'd been *shot* at; he deserved to sleep. But there was a faint light under his door.

And she had nowhere else to go to shake the clammy sense of horror Vellot left behind.

The faint light under his door drew her forward. She tapped their old code at the door, softly, so it wouldn't carry. Tap. Tap tap tap tap. Tap. Did he still sleep lightly?

It took too long for him to answer. Long enough she half-formed a plan that if he didn't answer, she'd go in anyway. Even seeing his shape, his hand, one ear would make her feel better.

Even though the idea felt a little... wrong.

She felt grateful all over when he opened the door.

To, admittedly, an astonishing appearance. A vast night-shirt fell all the way down to his ankles. She'd never seen him wear anything like it.

Atop his head bunched three little twisted papers. He'd made *papillote* curls, where the curl was laid in paper and pressed with a hot iron. That was how he'd changed his hair.

It wasn't what she'd expected. It wasn't what she knew.

Covering her mouth with a suddenly shaking hand, she felt her wavering confidence die.

"Are you hungry?" he whispered. "I'm sorry. We'll get to that apple-seller tomorrow; Mr. Able likely guards the larder with guns."

"I'm not." She glanced down at her empty hands as if they surprised her. "I didn't bring you anything."

His puzzled frown would have looked scary to anyone else; Bess found it wildly comforting.

He glanced down the corridor. "I didn't find it. The man isn't here. If you get caught—"

Suddenly remembering how Bess didn't worry enough about getting caught, he reached out and turned her as if to send her back down the corridor; but stopped at the touch of her arm.

"You're freezing."

He pulled her back against him, folding her into him, moving for both of them as he shut the door.

He felt blissfully, blazingly warm. Every lean muscle radiated heat like the sun shed light; Bess curved her back, leaning into him.

"What have you been doing?" It was a little scolding, a little worried, and everything Bess wanted to hear right then. "You could freeze to death in this hellhole."

Sweeping his nightshirt over his head, knocking off the few hair-papers, he wrapped it around her like a blanket. Sideways, it came down to her knees.

She turned in his arms and found herself facing a wall of tight, lean muscle. Marked here and there with puckered scars and darker than her skin would ever be. She could see the slight curves of his chest contract as he pulled her close. Her cheek fit perfectly against him there.

He smelled of water and starched linen and something shockingly, intimately new. This was grown-up Dan's scent, Bess realized.

The sensation was familiar yet *not*, and Bess wanted more.

As if obliging her unspoken thought Dan swept her up against him with one arm under her shoulders and the other under her knees, carrying her towards the room's one chair, at the desk.

Twisting in his arms, Bess reached out and caught its top rung, swung it into a new spot, defensible, against the wall between the bed and the too-cold windows.

Dan didn't argue, just pulled her more tightly against him as he sat.

"What happened?" he murmured, the gentle rasp of his

voice soothing against her skin. His lips brushed close to her temple, seemed to settle against her hair.

Bess just shook her head. She didn't want to think it or say it, didn't want any of it to touch him.

As long as he held her like this, she could pretend it was years ago. Pretend they still had their old life. When she could be certain about who they were and what they did.

She reached up to his half-curled hair, ruffled it, making it stand up crazily. "I never had to do those." Talking would break her. The Silver Duke's smothering spell was fading, yet the more air she drew in, the shakier she felt.

Supporting her effortlessly with one arm, he touched her hair, wrapped one ash-brown curl around his finger. Fit its natural shape against his skin before sliding away and letting it go.

"I know." His voice was deep and comfortable in the dark.

He knew. He knew her, her hair, her faults. He was all her certainty. And he'd finally come back.

Turning into his hard chest, hiding her face against it, Bess gave in to the urge to cry.

It was not like being a little girl again. Not at all. She was a grown woman, she'd had dozens of London's finest wait behind stage for her, panting for her attention.

They'd never be Dan.

His arms came around her, all warmth and hard muscle. "All right." Always accepting, never wavering, motionless, immovable Dan was everything she craved right now.

More certain of him than the spinning of the earth, Bess wrapped her arms around his lean, muscled chest and hung on.

CHAPTER NINETEEN

Christ, had he done that by touching her hair? He'd known not to, and did it anyway.

Some hellish impulse had made him do it, and now she was weeping. Bess never *wept*.

His body exulted over the feel of her in his arms, only half-satisfied, wanting far more; but he forced himself to remember that this was already far more than he deserved.

Slowly he turned, reached around her to ease her into his arms. Whatever had happened wouldn't be solved by an apple. "What's wrong, Bess? Did something happen?"

"I'm not *good* at being frightened. You never let me be frightened. I never had to do it before."

When he reached to push her hair back, she flinched.

Dan had always known that someday she would learn to fear him. That she would see what everyone else saw. His sins, his guilt, his twisted devotion. And, ever since he'd seen her on stage, his helpless desire. Because everyone else was right about him, and their mutterings couldn't help but come true.

He wasn't ready for that day to be today.

He tried to lock all that down inside him so she couldn't see. "It's all right, Bess," he said quietly. "You can be frightened of me."

She pounded one small fist against his chest. "Of course I'm not frightened of *you.* I'm frightened of the *paper.* Even though I didn't drink the wine. Why did I ever like those things? Why did I ever like hearing it? I don't want to be addicted to opium, I don't. And I don't want to change the world. Not like he means. *I don't want to do it.*"

He felt his heart flutter free. She wasn't frightened of him. That was all he needed. That and to keep her safe.

He just had to find out what she needed him to do.

"You don't have to do anything you don't want." He tried to keep his voice soft, soothing.

"Keep talking," she murmured, then rattled on. "I'm sorry. Here you spent all those years sleeping in the snow because of me and someone *shot* at you and really that's what frightened me first, then there was the candle and the paper and I must sound insane to you. I just really needed to see you because you make everything better and that's just me being selfish again, isn't it?"

One of his hands settled on her cheek, so big next to her delicate face, his thumb just under her jaw, adjusting, lifting.

Then he was kissing her.

All the noise stopped. All her chatter, her fear, it just... stopped. He could feel it drain out of her.

Everything was so quiet between them, the taste of her lips on his, caressing his, tasting his, was silent.

He'd policed himself so tightly that he'd never imagined this. Not even these last few days, *knowing* he wanted her exactly the way he shouldn't.

So everything about it was a complete surprise. The way she tasted, the strength she packed in that little body, the hands he knew could deal pain smoothing around his neck and up into his hair.

He meant to steal the kiss; she foiled him by giving it instead.

* * *

ALL HIS SELF-LOATHING took a step to the left and Dan felt free.

If this made her feel safe? He could do that.

A mistake he couldn't help making. Only Bess had ever worried for his safety.

She melted against him, a tiny velvet angel of sweetness, and though he'd never thought of Bess that way before, he'd think of her that way forever now.

Twisting herself in his arms, wiggling up her skirt, she managed to wrap her legs around his waist, shocking him to his core. Tightly he gripped her hips against him so she wouldn't slide any lower and feel the evidence of how quickly and how hard he wanted her there.

She never held still, looking for more, and it stunned him how he'd always known that about her yet never expected it in her kiss.

He didn't know what she expected, but he knew it was his job to stop this. She thought herself selfish? She didn't know the meaning of the word.

* * *

AFTER WHAT SEEMED LIKE FOREVER, time started again. Dan's mouth, as steady and sure as the rest of him, left hers. Bess found her heart had slowed, her breathing synchronized with his.

"Bess," he breathed against her cheek. "You're perfect."

Everything inside Bess began to unfold. Like a thousand paper ornaments, sharp edges transforming into beautiful order spelling out the words *of course.*

His kiss confirmed everything she knew and reshaped it, turning everything she knew slightly sidewise and slotting itself into a whole new machine of reality.

So many things made sense. Of course she had no use for other men. They weren't Dan. Of course she'd waited five years for him to come back. Only he made her feel wanted and safe, and now, *desired.*

How had she failed to recognize it the second she saw him again? Opium? The Silver Duke?

Or had she played so many parts she didn't know herself at all?

The thought re-lit the flame of uncertainty that had driven her here in the first place. It was selfish to want Dan back where he used to be, every minute by her side. Also foolish. The Silver Duke would never let her go; tonight proved that. She ought to push Dan away and keep that distance.

She hugged him tight, all wrapped around him, and his hand caressed the back of her head.

She whispered, "Why'd you do that?" Wasn't he here risking his life so some shopkeeper's daughter could have nice plates? He was in love with that girl. He wouldn't risk his life unless he loved her.

She'd never thought Dan was one of those men who could be in love with one woman and kiss another. But then, she'd never imagined him kissing anyone.

Now she found it impossible to imagine him kissing anyone but her.

"I wanted to." His hand went back to smoothing her hair. It was blissful. Unable to keep her eyes open, she tilted her head again to lay it against his chest. He went on, "I'd like to say I thought it would help, but mostly, I wanted to. I'm not perfect."

He was, though. An infinitely kind fountain of slightly surly, steadfast support. Lady Dunsby could have used his image to illustrate her lecture on kindness.

To prove it, he said, "Whatever you're doing, you don't have to do it alone. I want to help, Bess. Tell me how to help."

It wasn't the desire to be a better Bess that drove her to speak. Her sudden burst of honesty came from a simpler place. Perhaps the same one as that kiss.

"There's a man who wants me to do something bad."

The way the weight in her chest floated away once she made the admission was another revelation. A much smaller one than Dan's kiss, but still.

Saying it aloud didn't make it more real, but it helped her see how it fit into the world. That how she acted, for or against the Silver Duke, would make her one kind of person one way, and another kind of person if she went the other.

It was a little worrying how long Dan said nothing, but she was willing to wait.

Being Dan, he asked the only pertinent question.

"Are you going to do it?"

How like him. He could have asked what, or why, but he only wanted to know what she was going to do next.

So he could be there to catch her.

"No." In his arms, certainty was easier. Maybe it soaked into her from him; she felt it in her bones now. "I don't *want* to."

"And you don't have to do anything you don't want to do."

* * *

THAT WAS all Dan had ever hoped for in his life. Bess had to do so many things she shouldn't have had to do; eat coarse bread, live with the Grand H., steal for a living. He should have saved her from all that. If he finished this mission, he still could.

He'd be damned if he'd let anyone force her to do anything. After all, he was damned already.

Having Bess followed had been worthless. Somehow, traveling only between the players' boarding house and the theater, she'd gotten entangled in something very dark indeed.

But just as clearly, this wasn't the time to press her for the whole story.

He'd seen her laugh in the face of big, burly men, and take on any kind of challenge just to win it. Foot races against boys in their street, vaulting over horses that could crush her under their hooves, even learning to flip open a knife one-handed to cut a purse quicker than Dan could.

He'd never seen her scared, and whatever scared her would have to go to hell before he did.

"Who do I need to watch for?" The heat of him had flagged with the conversation, but he could still feel it banked like coals inside him. As long as she didn't know, he'd be fine.

As long as he kept her cuddled against him like this without kissing her, she wouldn't know.

She drew a shaky breath, and half-laughed in his arms. He was grateful she could. "I'm not telling you to start swinging your fists. If I need that, you'll know."

"Is it that Vellot?"

She didn't answer.

Everything inside him hurt. What had the bastard done to his Bess? "He's your protector?"

She turned her face into the skin over his heart and said quietly, "I don't have a protector."

He should not have felt so explosively, powerfully glad.

"Yes you do," he promised her, arms crushing her to him as he kissed her again.

She'd been frightened nearly witless, and with Bess, that was practically impossible. He should be out tearing someone apart, not kissing her again. But he couldn't help it. She was in *his* arms. She had come to *him* for help. She'd hated him for years, and still when cornered, she'd come to *him*.

This kiss wasn't gentle, and Bess only spurred him on.

Had he let himself dream of her kiss, he'd have dreamed of this. Dimly he knew her fingers clutched his hair, her arms winding around his neck, her back arching to press her chest to his. He reveled in it, his arms full of the soft little bundle of strength that was his Bess.

Reveled in the sweet taste of her as she kissed him, as determined as he was, pulling his mouth into hers in a way that wouldn't be denied.

As if he'd try.

It felt like it had only taken moments for the idea of kissing her, *loving* her, to take root and wind itself around every muscle, every tendon, every vein inside him, until it couldn't be separated from him. It *was* him.

It always had been. He should have known.

He would never deserve anything Bess gave him. He owed *her*. And that included putting some distance between them, from her lips flushed from his, her eyes trusting him.

That trust that gave him strength to pull back.

"I'm sorry," and his voice caught in his throat because only half of him meant it yet he forced it out anyway.

"Don't be. I feel better."

He smiled, taking a shaky breath. "Good." Maybe he could convince her he'd only meant the kiss to be medicinal.

"You should have told me."

"What?"

"That you—" She waved between them. He let her go a little more. "All this."

"It's new."

"Like, I just discovered I'm Lady Dunsby's secretary this morning new?"

No, yet... "Yes."

He'd loved her all his life, yet loving her like this was new.

"Oh." Completely ignoring the way he'd tried to put some space between them, she snuggled against his chest again. "I think I've wanted this my whole life."

His heart pounded harder than it ever had, a *thump* so deep he thought he might die. But he couldn't, for the same reason as always. He couldn't leave Bess alone.

He couldn't stay with her, and he'd never tell her why, but he'd never leave her alone.

"I told you how wrong that would be." He'd never tell her she couldn't love him—he didn't have it in him—but he could try to dissuade her.

He was thrilled and worried in equal measure to remember how Bess hated changing her mind.

Bess just waved an airy hand and settled in against him more firmly. In a second she'd have proof of what she did to him, and wouldn't that be everything he'd feared from years ago? "And I told *you* I never thought of you as in charge of me. I've always thought for myself. If I thought you should bugger off, I'd say *bugger off.*"

He closed his eyes. He could get used to this kind of torture. He rubbed the tip of his nose into her hair. It was softer than silk. "Except you're not allowed to say *bugger off,*" he reminded her, knowing she could hear the smile in his voice. "And that's the problem. We haven't just grown up together. We were all we had." He could hear her voice in the theater saying *and you left me.*

She must be thinking of that moment too. "I don't see the problem, if you don't leave again."

He'd never realized before how much he needed someone to want him.

"You deserve someone better. I—" He couldn't admit his worst fault. After all these years, it was impossible. "You don't want me."

* * *

THAT MADE no sense to Bess. Wanting to be with Dan was like breathing air. Part of existence.

So many things made sense to her now. That hunger she'd seen in the stairwell? Now she knew how it felt. Of course she would never trust it to anyone but Dan; he was the source of everything good.

Of course the men with their hothouse flowers hadn't interested her. Of course she kept her distance from the *ballerinos,* the dance masters, the ushers in the theater. Of course she rolled her eyes at the men in fine coats on the street.

None of them were Dan. And they'd never match the measure of him.

"You must let go of this idea that you're awful, Dan. You've never done anything awful to *me.* You have been wonderful for as long as I can remember."

Why couldn't he just let her be sweet? She wanted to be, just once, here in his arms. The other dancers talked about kisses being *earth-shaking,* but Dan's kiss made the earth stand still.

She was hungry for *more* of him, the feel of his arms, his

taste, the sound of his breath, the sound of his heartbeat. She didn't want to let one bit go, and she definitely wasn't ready to leave the fortress of muscle and bone and, yes, too-saintly morals that was Dan.

She'd wanted things all her life, but never anything as much as she wanted him now.

He was silent.

Maybe he was regretting this impulse. Maybe he'd remembered that stupid shopkeeper girl. Bess learned the depths of how cold she could be, just thinking about the nameless woman she'd never met.

"I'll stop now because of this girl you love." She didn't mean it, but it was the lie she should tell.

When he still didn't say anything, and his grip loosened, she realized he believed her show.

Reluctantly, she stood.

He ought to have looked ridiculous with his hair half-standing on end. He'd have to re-curl it; the papers had gone.

Instead, he looked hard and flawless as a Roman statue, the faint dark shadows coloring the dips and swells of his skin. All the hard edges of his crooked smile had softened just for her, his lips lush and red from her kisses.

If people didn't think him handsome, it was because they didn't get to see him like this.

That little half-smile around the corners of his eyes, that especially belonged to her.

She didn't know much about men, but his hungry look matched the way she felt. And she was the only woman here. If he was hungry, it was for her.

Well, he might not realize it for a while. Feelings were difficult, especially hers; his must also be tough. And hadn't she always leaped through doors first?

He probably did love this nameless woman. Bess was building up more and more details for her now. She was a shopkeeper's daughter who ate jam at every breakfast, drank tea with sugar all day, and never cared what he got for dinner because by then she was full. She was surely pretty, but in ten years she'd be fatter than a house. Not the luscious kind of fat, the lazy kind.

Yes, Bess could see it all, but she wasn't particularly worried.

She *was* well-versed with the feeling of wanting something that someone else owned.

And she was very good at stealing.

* * *

DAN WASN'T sure why it gave him an uneasy feeling to see Bess standing on her own two feet again, confidence restored, but it did.

For now, he'd ignore it.

"We should leave the house. Now. You can sleep under a tree, and I'll keep you warm. The first ferry back to London in the morning, you're on it."

"So *we* leave but only *I* go back to London?"

"You're not safe here."

"And you are?"

Cuddling, adult Bess was a revelation; diplomat Bess was perhaps his least favorite. "I can take care of myself."

She folded her arms. "So can I."

"I have work to do."

"So do I," she said grimly.

"Go back to bed," he tried, the way he had when she was little and just as difficult, "take what you need to stay warm, and be ready for the first boat in the morning."

"All right, I will." Perfectly sheepish, as if just seeing the wisdom of his words, even slumping her shoulders in defeat.

"Dammit, Bess, I know you're lying."

She straightened right back as solid as she had been. "Then why make me *say* such a stupid thing?"

She had a point there.

She went on. "You should get on that boat, but I have to stay. I have to, Dan, I really do." She'd softened a little now, but he could see she meant it. "I can't just run back to London and look over my shoulder the rest of my life. And I have to warn a man who's in danger. He's not here."

"Neither is mine." This was a hash. Spying was far stupider than stealing, and Dan had hated stealing plenty. "Just tell me who to watch for, and I'll handle it."

There was something lurking in her eyes, something like a smile. Dan saw no reason for it except that she was looking at him. "You honestly think I'd go back to London and leave you here?"

It was hard to admit that Lady Dunsby was about to do what he couldn't: introduce her to fine society. "You'll have better prospects for a future if you keep your distance from me," Dan admitted. "And if you stay, you must stick with Lady Dunsby. I mean *stick*. Close by, and not be alone for a minute with the man who frightened you tonight. Because I know you. You won't tell me who it is, but you know I know. I'll kill him before I let him hurt you."

"I'd never make you do that," she murmured, still looking at him the way she had when she was little, with a new edge to it. Like he hung the moon.

He had to tell her the truth about him before this went any farther. She had to know. He just wasn't ready.

"You win, go to bed," he said gruffly. It reminded him unpleasantly of the fight they'd had when she'd woken from the opium fever. "You can't keep winning, you know."

She smiled. Not Miss Page's sugary smile, a real one, just for him. "Yes I can."

* * *

ARGUING WAS FAMILIAR. It was *comfortable.*

It made Bess forget why she was here, and she liked that.

In the room she shared with Agatha, she wriggled out of her fine dress with its ties where only servants could reach and into her heaviest night-rail. The thick portrait frame she'd stolen from the Silver Duke shifted in the bottom of the trunk, and its soft thump made her jump.

A heavy night-rail wasn't as pleasant as being in Dan's arms. She crawled between icy sheets and waited for them to warm.

This couldn't be what young ladies felt when they succumbed to a rake's charms. This was how rakes felt. *She* was the rake.

Bess didn't have to strut or flirt. She just knew exactly who Dan was, and he seemed to like that. She liked how much he liked it.

She'd used the word *desire* before but now she knew what it meant. It called to something inside her that answered *of course.*

When she closed her eyes, the world started spinning again like it had when the Silver Duke tapped the empty paper. She opened them again. The plain plaster overhead had a certainty to it, but it wasn't as certain as Dan. The dressing table with her silver toilette set, even the icy wind rushing past her shutters... If she fell asleep, would they stay the same? Where would she be when she woke?

For once Bess wanted the world to stay still.

Her mind flooded with images of Dan from recent days. Wary, in the theater; worrying over her, in his own bed; telling her all those things he'd never said before with the rocking deck planks under both their feet. She'd missed him for so long, yet she'd never really known him before.

Or herself.

A rare phrase from the Grand H.'s reading lessons came back to her. It wasn't even a whole sentence. *Your confidence in yourself, from your right knowledge of things.* The rest had been a jumble of words; that one clear idea had struck deep in her mind and taken root.

She had right knowledge of Dan; she was sure of that. Less so about herself, and none at all about the Silver Duke.

She needed confidence in herself to do something about Vellot.

At minimum, she would have to warn the Duke of Talbourne; that she knew.

And she'd have to help Dan find his ledger, whether it helped him win his lazy shop-girl or not.

The most certain confidence would come from putting an end to the Silver Duke. It wasn't just a grudge; it was a cold hard certainty. He would haunt her as long as he lived.

But if she disposed of him, would she lose the chance to steal Dan away from his shop-girl? It was a maddening thought that led in maddening circles.

When Agatha came to the room, Bess pretended to be asleep, letting Agatha undress quietly and crawl into her own cold cot. Even the comfort of a larger bed, where they might have shared their warmth, was denied at Road's End; but Bess preferred it that way.

Though she wanted, *needed* to stay awake till the world made sense, eventually her own mind, the traitor she'd least suspected, dragged her down into sleep.

Her thoughts still prodded her in her dreams, making her imagine the Silver Duke was leaning over her. Every creak of the shutters yanked her from sleep, and the long windy night was not restful.

The sun was not yet up when she heard Agatha turn over,

making the rustling noises that said the other person in the room was awake.

"Agatha?" she whispered.

"Yes?" came back the quiet answer.

"I'm not who you think I am. Let's find some horses and ride."

CHAPTER TWENTY

*D*an might have slept for a few minutes at some point in the night, but if so, he couldn't remember.

He'd never taken the time to hate himself with this kind of depth and fervor. He had no patrons to meet, no secrets to chase, and he was in a cold cell-like room at what felt like the ends of the earth. There was nowhere to run from himself.

He'd been right to stay away from Bess all those years. All in one night, he'd proved the Grand H. right.

There was no converting him to a better kind of man. Only doing his work, and getting Bess back to London. The sooner the better.

He curled his stupid hair, put on his stupid clothes, and wrote a little on one of the fake letters as he watched the sun come up. His disguise could only be better for fresh ink on his hands.

But the act of writing was a dangerous channel into thoughts he would not admit. When he found himself writing *She wishes to decide on my behalf,* he broke off mid-sentence. That was not about Lady Dunsby.

The light was high in the watery sky when he finally put down his spectacles and pen and ventured out. He'd run out of time to hide.

Lady Dunsby sat with her friends in the receiving room, where frost was just disappearing from the French windows.

He wanted to ask after Vellot. Dammit, he would. His disguise, Fitz' whole mission, none of it was as important as Bess. "I thought I saw Lord Vellot come down before me."

Lady Carrollton's denial was a tight shake *no.* "He never rises before noon, even in winter. I don't know how he can bear it. There are so few daylight hours."

If Vellot was still abed, Dan would pretend to work. Bess and Agatha must still be abed too. "Speaking of daylight. You wished to write letters, Lady Dunsby?" Fitz had been uncommonly careful to give him a list of the lady's correspondents and suggestions for urgent-seeming business. It was obvious now it had been because guests to Road's End rarely brought servants.

"I ought to, Mr. Burton, but I'm in no mood. It's too cold for needlework, and I was about to read aloud. Unless you'd like to read for us? Some of Madame d'Aulnoy's fairy tales?"

No, he bloody well would not.

"I'll find an occupation, never fear," he said in Mr. Burton's changeable voice, trying to make *never fear* sound fearful.

"There goes Lord Zachary out the garden," Lady Carrollton said, draping herself over the side of the chair in truly liquid fashion, no doubt a common practice in the catching of guinea pigs. "Perhaps the young men have found entertainment."

Rather than explain why he preferred to keep his distance from young men who weren't imposters, Dan took her veiled suggestion and followed him.

He had no intention of joining some country shooting

party, but it was good to escape the house. The cold air was a welcome slap to the face.

He found the young men not shooting.

"Do play, Zach," Waresham pleaded as Lord Zachary rounded the corner of the house. "Harman's a weak pigeon. One match has wasted him."

Lord Harman only waved a hand as he crossed the packed earth beside the barn. He was puffing. "Better a broken-winded pigeon than a swindler of cream-pots. How are you so good at the game when you spend all your time chasing every skirt from dairymaids to the Queen?" The spoon-shaped racket in his hand told what game.

Waresham spun his own racket in one hand and tossed the small ball in the air with the other, caught it. His grin was unrepentant. "Zachary, do play. With one it's a boring frig; with two it's a game."

"Just what you tell the dairymaids, I imagine." Lord Zachary picked up a curious frame with an uncut sheet of paper pinned to it, and pulled a stub of pencil from his pocket. "I'm on the verge of something important, Waresham. I told you that when you dragged me out here."

Waresham scoffed. "You've been puddling about with chalks and paints as long as I can remember. It's a fair way to burn your candle, I suppose, if you've nothing better to do."

"Ask Mr. Burton to sacrifice himself on your altar of rackets."

Dan thought he was unseen, and perhaps he had been; Waresham looked at him now as if he'd just appeared. And looked disgusted.

But he must be desperate for play, because he said grudgingly, "I'll show you how to play it, Burton, if you want a try."

Dan knew he ought to wave off. Waresham was a pompous clown, probably impressed with himself for playing at common taverns, unaware it had a much rougher history.

But Dan felt like a tiger wound tight, and needed release.

"If it pleases you, Lord Waresham," said he, taking off his coat.

That made Harman's eyebrows go up, because the cold wet air instantly chilled the skin.

But Dan had slept in alleyways a long, long time. And he didn't intend to hurt the coat.

"You know the game?" Waresham asked, as much mocking as asking.

"I think so." Dan tugged at his sky-blue waistcoat, even put a little quaver in his voice. "Let's try, anyway." He surveyed the wide barn wall. "You play in the open? With no other wall?"

Waresham sighed. Even he, apparently, wouldn't enjoy triumphing over someone new to the game. "Yes. Haven't you seen it done?"

With no further explanation, he tossed the ball in the air, and whacked it toward the side of the barn.

Dan barely had a moment to sweep up the other racket where Harman had dropped it on the ground and use it to flip the ball back toward the wall. He expected it to dribble, but it rebounded respectably. Straight back toward Waresham like a child's toss.

He thought he heard Waresham's disgusted sigh as the man returned it at an angle that aimed it straight at Dan's head.

This wasn't Dan's first game of rackets.

Swerving back, he smashed the ball toward the wall for a good bounce and sent it rocketing at Waresham's chest.

Harman, the only spectator, shouted.

Fortunately—or unfortunately—Waresham wasn't too bored to watch the ball. He dove out of the way, landing on his rear, and the ball went flying out of the yard and into the grass.

Waresham stared as Dan pretended to fiddle with his racket.

"Sorry." Dan could lie sometimes. "Isn't that how it's played? I thought that was why one used an alley. So it bounced off the back wall."

Standing, Waresham dusted off his trousers. Dan could almost see the cloud of ire gathering around his head.

It cheered him up tremendously.

Waresham took off his coat, folding it ostentatiously over Lord Zachary's drawing board. Zachary shoved it off to the ground and went on drawing.

"What do you say to that spot there?" He pointed to a packed-earth expanse between the stable and the black-smith's shed.

It was not enough yards wide for a serious game; he must have thought Dan's first strike a fluke.

Or simply intended to kill him with the ball.

"Very good," was all Dan said.

Having returned the last ball to Waresham's failure, it was Dan's turn to serve. Uninterested by rules, Waresham tossed the ball up again, his racket slicing forward to drive it into the wood.

Only the slight natural bounce provided by the horsehair core let the leather sphere hurtle off the wall and back toward Dan. It was dense; when it hit, it hurt.

Dan suspected they both knew that.

When he got behind the thing and bashed it back against the wall, so hard its rebound flew straight between them to the wall behind and bounced again, the real game was on.

It was a flurry of smashing blows. Both of them proved better than the other expected at predicting the flight of the ball as it careened through the too-small space.

Waresham did, however, let a volley go when it looked like too much effort, while Dan was merciless.

Waresham also cared little about getting out of Dan's way. After losing points twice avoiding careening into his lordship, Dan decided that if that was Waresham's game, he could play that too.

On the next point, when Waresham's solid form got between Dan and a return volley, Dan simply crashed through him.

"I say!" Harman had appointed himself a kind of umpire, as if it were a wrestling bout, watching the flight of the hard little ball with squinting determination.

"My apologies, Lord Waresham." Breathing hard, Dan went to help Waresham up off the dirt again.

Glaring, Waresham bounced up.

Dan didn't wait for an excuse, only offered his own. "I was only watching the ball."

Waresham's lean face was red, whether from anger or effort Dan didn't know. But when he took a step forward, intending to loom over Dan, Dan simply stayed put. Waresham might think the threat of a fight would make Dan cower, but Dan had grown up in a world where that could happen at any time, and he was more than ready.

Perhaps to break the tension, Lord Harman called out, "Will you play?"

Huffing, Waresham turned again to the wall.

Dan wasn't letting him steal the serve twice. "Service is mine, sir."

"*What?*"

Dan was tired of games. He didn't have it in him to pretend to salve Waresham's conceit. He'd pretended too much for too long, and he only had so much in him.

He simply reached out and took the ball out of Waresham's hand and served it.

With a snarl Waresham returned it, using his longer reach to whip the thing at an angle that would once again send it straight for Dan.

Ignoring that Dan had already proven himself faster.

These men were stupid, thought Dan to himself as his return sent the ball at an angle that was low and hard to hit. At least Waresham was stupid.

But hadn't Dan known that already? Wasn't that the basis of his plan to join the Exchange and beat such men with cleverness, not force?

The foolish anger drained out of him and he realized that his brain was also his best path to the pleasure of beating hell out of a lordly idiot.

Head slightly cooler, he studied the geometry of their too-small space and began to plan out his strikes.

The points grew as he knocked ball after ball at angles that forced Waresham to duck low, the disadvantage of his height, or think, which was also not his strength.

Seeing himself lose only ratcheted Waresham's temper higher. At one point he raised his racket as if to strike Dan instead. Lord Harman only shouted "Oy!"; Lord Zachary never looked up. With no one to egg him on, Waresham abandoned his threat.

Perhaps it was the warm blood finally pumping through his head, or perhaps it was the beat of his heart, but Dan realized something. These were the men he thought deserved Bess more than he did. He'd *believed* the Grand H.'s claims that Bess deserved them, deserved their life.

Bess deserved to be draped in furs and jewels, she probably deserved to be queen, but she didn't deserve this. She deserved better than this.

His last ball bounced just a foot from the wall, with no way for Waresham to return it.

"That's the match!" whooped Lord Harman, clearly exercised just by watching. Lord Zachary glanced over from his drawing.

It cleared Dan's head. He was puffing, but the heat under his skin was comfortable. Ready. He could take on anything.

It felt like glittering.

He smiled to himself.

Waresham threw his racket as far as he could into the grass. Probably expecting some servant to fetch it.

Dan slid back into being Mr. Burton. "What an excellent game, your lordship. Very bracing. I'm so glad you asked me to play."

"Excellent," Waresham muttered between his teeth.

Harman clapped Dan on the shoulder. "Well *done!* And without your spectacles, too. I feel a fool for underestimating you."

That cooled Dan fast. He was giving himself away.

Bess could be someone else for days on end, but Dan didn't have it in him. He was no Mr. Burton. He had to find that ledger and leave before someone unmasked him.

"We'll shoot again today; you should come." Apparently the game had loosened Harman's friendliness.

Or perhaps he just wanted more company. Waresham was an ass, and Lord Zachary certainly didn't look likely to tear himself away from his drawing.

Dan decided Mr. Burton's stamina had run out. "I'm terribly spent after all that effort. I was just about to lie down, in fact. I'm not as robust as all of you. I suppose you're going after more game?"

"I'm killing something bigger than a rabbit," Waresham gritted out, hands on his hips.

Guns were a game Dan couldn't play. Pistols, rifles, and all the various parts of their ammunition were too expensive for people like him.

Perhaps a bookkeeper wouldn't be expected to shoot.

"You might instruct me before holiday's end," he said, bowing in his shirt-sleeves in the cold wind.

"Perhaps." From Waresham, it sounded like a threat.

"We'll have to go into the woods to shoot." Harman didn't look eager. "The young ladies must still be abed; it would be rude to wake them."

"They're not." Lord Zachary didn't look up from his drawing board, but he did at least speak. "Saw them riding this morning just after dawn. Would have made an interesting picture, if they'd waited and let me capture it."

"Good lord, you were drawing at dawn? You're obsessed." The idea of working at dawn clearly scandalized Waresham.

But Dan didn't hear him; he was already gone.

* * *

Keeping her things in order was the maid's job; Lady Winpole she didn't concern herself.

Except with her Pandora doll.

She took it everywhere she traveled, as it provided company, as it were, when people were dull or disappointing.

They were *always* disappointing.

When she returned to her room to rest after a boring morning of listening to Dunsby gossip and Carrollton chase her guinea pigs, she noticed Pandora's crooked skirt.

Pandoras mirrored fashion, but Lady Winpole kept this one as it had been when she acquired it, a fixed moment of time, like a perfect jar of jam. Its ruffles and lace might have seemed a jumble to someone else, but Lady Winpole knew exactly how they should look.

The edge of the doll's overskirt turned inward.

She always left the Pandora on that chest to guard such notes as she trusted herself to have. Even she could not run a mercantile empire from memory. She used code, like she did in her letters, to track current holdings, like her copper and her furs.

If someone had seen those lists, she might have lost too many secrets.

"Nelly," she summoned her maid. When the girl arrived nearly at a run, Lady Winpole said, "You're discharged. Go back to London." As the girl's face crumbled in horrified shock, she added, "Stop at that hotel on the way and tell them to send me a maid for the next few days. Someone honest."

Simultaneously tasked with leaving and finding her own replacement, the girl just stammered through her tears, "Yes, madame," curtsied, and left. She almost tripped over her own feet in her hurry.

Lady Winpole didn't rush.

It likely wasn't the girl who had trespassed, but discharging her sent a message to the rest of the servants. She knew Lord Vellot would not dare venture in here, and the ladies were too vapid. Hortense was down there right now describing how best to frizz hair. The stupid girl-children were likely out gazing at Waresham with cow-eyes.

That left Waresham, his friends, and that secretary.

Their rooms were right at hand, making very little work for Lady Winpole.

After only one night, Waresham's chamber was a storm of tossed belongings. Well, the house belonged to his family, and he had possessions. No pen or paper, though; no record-keeping at all. Not that it was definitive, but anyone looking for her records would make notes.

His friends' rooms were bare. Lady Winpole did not run her fingers along every crevice in the furniture, but she came close. Their simple luggage held only a few collars, razors, shirts. Nothing of interest.

The last room on the hall belonged to that secretary. His desk was indeed strewn with cut paper, some of it bearing excruciatingly correct handwriting that recorded Lady Dunsby's maunderings. The letters stopped in too-obvious places, as far as she was concerned. As if someone wanted to label them *unfinished*.

This room she searched thoroughly. She examined every curl-paper, checking to see if any bore writing; she checked under every drawer for anything tucked against its bottom. There were no shreds of paper in the fire.

None of his ridiculous clothes bore any ink-stains.

This Mr. Burton might think himself fashion's peacock. The clothes were new. But he didn't have a fashionable face.

The hair-curling suggested he wished to impress ladies, yet she'd seen no attempts at charm, either toward the older ladies or the younger.

He'd also immediately taken Lady Carrollton's suggestion he join the young lords, when a real secretary would have known his place.

She'd have to watch him carefully. Pandora's ruffles didn't lie. Someone had searched her room, and it was most likely this Burton. It didn't matter who he was or what he wanted; her privacy was absolute.

Perhaps there was a way to send him that message.

Picking up his spectacles, she dropped them to the floor.

One blue lens cracked.

Unsatisfied, she ground her heel into it until she felt it shatter into tinier pieces, then dust.

She left it there.

He had no servants to disturb it. Let him discover it for himself.

CHAPTER TWENTY-ONE

"So you see." Bess had warmed to her story with the rising sun. "Once the consumption had taken my mother too, I had nowhere to turn but to the man who'd promised to marry her, then abandoned her."

The more distance she put between herself and Road's End, the more distant she felt from the Silver Duke's mind-spinning. The swaying of the horse and the damp smell of water soothed Bess in a way that was completely new. She could see why rich people came to the country to rest.

Of course, the more she pushed the Silver Duke out of her mind, the more it filled with the startling revelations of the night before that had to do with the more important man.

Nothing about men had ever appealed in the same way before, and Bess doubted they ever would again. The appeal of that bristly edge to his chin as it rubbed her skin, the taste of the corner of his mouth against her tongue, the heat of him all around her, those things weren't *men*. They were *Dan*.

And Dan was in love with someone else.

She had to find out more about this woman. Was she *here?* Was she the sort of woman who would follow him?

Bess couldn't just go around killing people, and if she did, she'd have to start with the Silver Duke.

But wouldn't that just push Dan farther into the mystery woman's arms?

Mulling over the problem, Bess kept her face masked with this cozy new persona, the one gossiping about the Silver Duke. He was the root of her problems. Thus the consumptive mother who had been abandoned by...

"Not Lord Vellot!" Agatha was rapt, ignoring her reins. Luckily her horse seemed inclined to follow Bess'.

Bess nodded solemnly. "The same."

"Ah!" Agatha sat back in her saddle. "The scoundrel. But he did find you a place. For here you are, and he *is* the one who sent you."

Bess tread carefully into the necessary murk. "He is, but... he alarms me. He can do things, Agatha. Convince people to do things. Sometimes when he speaks to you..." She must just admit it. "When he spoke to *me,* I didn't know my own name for a second. It's as if he can direct the movements of your soul."

"Oh!" Agatha's soft exclamation was salted with horror. "Is that what it feels like? Everyone knows he studied some disreputable sort of medicine abroad. Apparently he lectures at parties, but I haven't seen it."

"Medicine? Like the kind you drink? What about the mind?"

"Your mind is in your body, so I suppose it is all one." She thought for a moment. "I remember; he calls it *magnetizing* his patient. Lady Villeneuve told me she is very suspicious of it, and him."

"Tell her she's right." Just thinking about him in that darkened room reminded Bess it was winter-cold. "She shouldn't let her charges talk to him alone."

Agatha nodded vigorously.

When Madame Franck talked about *varma kalai*, she talked about the body's life force, how it flowed. Today that felt confirmed. Her mind, her blood; everything in her had surged toward Dan last night. That was what had made the experience so... overwhelming.

Madame Franck was right; she'd been a poor student. Surely all these invisible waves were connected. The Silver Duke seemed to have some way to control these forces. He had clearly magnetized her, or tried.

Dan hadn't; that wave had come from within her. She'd reached out to the hard muscled heat of him, but also the gentleness inside. And he'd responded. Hadn't he?

She put aside the problem of the Silver Duke, receding behind her, to contemplate the problem of a Dan in love with someone else.

Agatha had already moved on. "Lady Villeneuve might be a good friend to you. Don't her girls live with her? You could go there. She's an excellent—"

"Last chance?" Bess smiled and finished as Agatha broke off her own words. "I think I'm fine where I am. If I may stay with you another day or two."

Agatha waved her whole arm, dismissing the question widely. "I was about to say *matchmaker*. My mother finds your prospects very exciting, but we really seldom socialize. Of course I'd rather keep your company. Continue."

"Yes, so. The boy I mentioned? The one I'd grown up with. I think he might... feel something for me. Romantically." Bess suppressed a wince; it was too tepid a word for the way she'd felt last night. For Dan's hard heat against her body, making her feel soft. "But he cares for someone else." It was truly useful in this moment to have so many lines from bad plays stored up for Miss Page's use.

"Romantically?" That had Agatha leaning forward in the saddle again. Her horse trotted forward in response, bouncing the basket Agatha insisted on looping round the saddle horn. Agatha had to straighten, letting Bess' horse catch up as she settled her basket. She was as attached to luggage as her mother. "You mean he loves you?"

Bess summoned that moment again when he'd kissed her. The second kiss, which had seemed to come straight from a... a *vehement* heart. She rehearsed it over and over again so nothing the Silver Duke had said or could say would shake her memory of it.

Bess didn't think she had much imagination, but she'd easily conjured this friendless-girl story, and just telling it let her think more clearly. "Well, he wants me. I *know* he does. So it's all right, isn't it, to steal him away from someone he's known for a few years, when he's known me all my life?"

"Hmm." Agatha gathered up the reins as if that would help her grip the complex situation Bess described. "My father would have suggested we imagine the possible answers. Isn't it a question of things proceeding in order? For instance, if he'd declared his love to you, then saw another woman and decided in an instant he loved her and wished to abandon you, that would be wrong of him."

"Well." He hadn't declared his love for her, but Bess always knew what Dan was thinking.

Didn't she?

Of course, she'd thought she'd known what the Silver Duke was thinking, and she'd been disastrously wrong there.

"On the other hand," Agatha went on, "if he knew her for, let's say a year, then declared his love to *her*, surely you would rather release him from some nebulous connection to you than marry a man who loved someone else."

Trying to be a better person involved a lot of complicated details. And words.

"We're not betrothed," Bess admitted grudgingly. "He hasn't even said he loves me. But he doesn't have to!" she rushed to add when Agatha clucked her tongue just like her mother. "And maybe he's said nothing to her either!"

"That *is* complex."

"Surely not. I am sure I want him more than she does."

"But how can you measure such things? Scientifically, I mean."

"Lady Agatha." This wasn't helping at all. "I have far too many concerns just now to start learning science."

"Well. I mean, one can do a thing, like steal someone else's beloved, but I thought you were worried about the morals of it."

"Not really. If morals are all there is to the problem, then it's easily solved by just doing it."

Now Agatha's mouth fell open. Swaying up and down with the horse's walk, she looked silly. "You just asked me if it's *all right!*"

Mercy Bennett. So she had. Dan had taken over her thoughts and slipped in some of those morals without her knowing. Bess frowned.

She'd been horrified by his admissions on the boat. It could be cruel to ask him to give up one more thing. For her.

Bess would have to feel guilty. Not terribly, but at least a little.

Agatha added, "Really, the only people with a right to say what is fair are the man, and you, and this woman."

"Forget the woman."

"Well, at the *very* least, him and you."

This was getting Bess nowhere. It wouldn't help to ask Dan if she could steal his heart; no one agreed to be robbed.

He *had* kissed her. That meant something. She supposed she'd have to ask him what.

It wasn't just words that were difficult; all these questions about souls and letting people manage their own were everlasting work.

* * *

AT ROAD'S END, even as midmorning passed Dan in his game of rackets, a messenger came with an announcement that caused even sour Mr. Able to lurch into action.

The Duke's arrival was upon them.

Expected as it was, it still launched a rush of furious activity among the servants. Mr. Able, chasing every farthing, hadn't wanted to open the grand wing in such wintry weather till the last possible minute.

Now Lady Carrollton was nearly fainting from tension and Lord Waresham nowhere about.

Madame Franck offered to ease her hostess' distress by supervising the servants' work.

The new wing was grand, with Greek columns and tapestries; but it had few embellishments, mostly carpets, and it was dusty. Madame Franck could feel dust on the mantelpiece of the parlor behind the grand ballroom, and it had to be removed. Lady Carrollton was determined to entertain the Duke in style for bonfire night, and this parlor would doubtless be called into service.

A maid rushed out, truly running, with gathered dust cloths in her arms, and almost collided with Dan Fox.

Or rather a sweating *Mr. Burton.*

"Mrs. Frank!" he called out, keeping hold of his *persona* if not his temper. Slamming the door behind him, he charged toward her like a bull. "Your job was to keep her safe, and now you've—"

He looked surprised as he stumbled past her, gripping his arm in sudden pain, and caught himself against the mantel before he fell. As though he hadn't even seen her move.

"Have a care, child. Remember who you're dealing with," said Madame Franck, standing tall as if she still wore her peacock feather.

Slowly, he pulled himself to his feet. Spread his hands wide, even as one arm hung lower than the other.

"My mistake," he said, slowly and clearly. "I'm sorry. I'll start again. Where did Bess go?"

"Where does she ever go? She goes where she likes." Madame Franck wished she could give a better report of Bess, and of herself.

"Why didn't you do something?"

"Why didn't *you?*" Number five, the teacher, propped her up, gave her the voice to answer. Otherwise she would have crumbled. Bess was so dear to her, and this boy so thick-headed. "I've lived with her for five years and I had to fight for every scrap of her she would let me know. You, she trips along after like a little lamb."

He blinked. Unwittingly stretched and relaxed his arm, which still pained him. "Bess isn't lamb-like."

"For you she is. Oh, I hate him! Oh, he never writes! Oh, do you think he's gone to France? Do you think he's killed? Practically the only sentences I heard from her for a *year.* She learned to hate you because it was all she could do and go on. Then you reappear, *poof,* and want a little chat, like you'd just gone yesterday. No *good to see you,* just *I was wrong about ethics, come steal with me.*" All her anger from the theater came back, and she folded her arms across her chest, hard. "If we'd been alone, I'd have shown you exactly what I thought!"

"Madame." He whispered it, dropping his hands, but not moving closer. "We both care about Bess. She's connected herself to someone dangerous. And now she's out wandering the countryside alone."

"*I know!*" Her waving arms might be theatrical, but they came from what she felt in her heart. "I cannot keep that child on a straight path, not even a slightly bumpy one. I cannot keep her on *any* path, because she doesn't give a fig what I think! The only thing, the only person she cares about is you. So *you* do something."

"Do *what?*" He looked lost. "I told her not to come; I told her to go home. She does what she likes. Am I supposed to lock her up? That's the *last* thing I want for her!"

She couldn't restrain herself. She gave him a little slap to the side of his head. "You tie her to earth with the only thing that holds her. You."

His cheeks reddened.

For a second he looked like a little boy, then he leaned close, shoulders hunching forward, black eyes glittering, in that way he must have learned as a child to look like a menacing animal. "If you're suggesting that something like marriage would hold her, you don't know Bess at all. Did you tell her that? Is that why she went looking for a protector in the first place?"

Some of her anger drained away. They were young, these two, and they had suffered much. They simply didn't know.

Instead of bristling at his bristle, Madame Franck patted his hand. He let out his breath.

"Love doesn't look for ways to put chains on people. And you don't want that for Bess. But I think you might love her, and she loves you, such a fiery love. She is hard, our Bess, but she burns for you. Admit it. Stop pretending you two have paths apart from each other. It's only hurting you both."

She hadn't touched him again, but he looked like she'd landed a blow.

"You don't understand." These weren't words he'd practiced before. They came ripped from him, raw. They hurt him. "I can't."

"I traveled halfway round the globe for love, then he died. I understand *everything*. Tell me."

He looked at the floor. Wouldn't meet her eyes, like an ashamed little boy.

"You don't know what I did. All this, trapping her in this life, it's all because of me."

His breath came heavy like he'd been running. She waited for him to say more, but he clearly couldn't.

Some deep wound in the boy had been inflamed so long that it poisoned him. She could only hope lancing it would help. "If you wronged her, tell her."

"She'll hate me."

"I don't think she can."

Slowly he breathed in, then out. "Bess can do anything. You know that. Except keep out of trouble. Please do something."

She patted his hand again. They were good hands, strong. He had it in him to be a good man. Not as good as her beloved, but fair, and kind. "I'm doing what I can, and if she's gone out, at least it's with Lady Agatha. It's far more dangerous for Agatha than Bess. Trust her, and try to trust yourself a little."

His clenched jaw softened a little. It smoothed his little permanent sneer from the scar over his lip and loosened the shadows in his face. "There are so many dangerous people here. Be careful. We should all be careful."

"Sound advice anywhere, child."

* * *

"So much depends on the woman." Lady Agatha dove into Bess' ethical dilemma like a surgeon after a bullet. "The fellow's connection with her only matters if he's made her some promise. If he has, there's a true problem. Any man so dear to you is unlikely to be so perfidious as to break it. Faithless," she said when Bess looked confused. "He'd have stolen *her* affections by giving nothing in return. Why, he could do the same to you!" Agatha looked horrified by the prospect. "What a terrible thief!"

Bess choked back laughter. "He's definitely a thief. I don't look to blame him for it."

Agatha's approach made it all seem lighter.

If she practiced saying how she felt to Agatha, perhaps it would be easier with Dan.

Slowly, Bess said, "Romance always seemed like a robber to me. It's some man taking something from a woman she doesn't want to give, or will be punished for giving. It's like letting a man pick your pocket. But this affair is all different. I suppose if he's in love with her, and I take him away for myself, that makes *me* the robber."

"I know nothing about it, but I'd always hoped romance would be like discovering a new world." Agatha looked like her thoughts had gone far away, probably to her parents' example. "Finding excitement in each other. In the sweetness. And of course in bed," she ended on a decidedly non-ethereal note.

Bess' sudden shift made her horse's step stutter.

"I have to say, Lady Agatha, I didn't expect you to talk that way."

"Please call me Agatha, I feel we're such friends. But keep to the topic. You must see him again and perhaps meet this other woman. What if she doesn't care for him at all? Perhaps he *is* trying to rob her."

Bess airily waved the accusation away. "He's too moral for that." *These days,* she thought to herself. "I don't want to meet her." She didn't. She didn't care at all about the shopkeeper's daughter, who had grown much taller and plainer in her imagination. Gawky, even.

If Bess met her, she'd be tempted to do something Dan definitely wouldn't like.

"Well, she may give him up, I suppose; or what if it is all much simpler? Perhaps he will give you *himself*." This idea clearly enraptured Agatha. "I'm not sure hearts can be stolen. If love is anything, it's a gift." Agatha said this with the kind of certainty reserved for stating that the sky was blue.

Maybe people with families and homes knew these things. Maybe Bess would know, if she were really a country girl with a consumptive mother. And a silent, sturdy father. A county clerk, perhaps.

Telling tales to Agatha was Bess' first experiment in imagining a family in a long, long time. It was comfortable enough spinning the story, but now that she had to wear it, it fit badly, leaving her cold in some places, cutting into her in others.

Women with consumptive mothers wouldn't go around stealing men. "I don't know enough to be sure I'm right." Confidence came from the right knowledge of things. Conjuring stories about relationships out of thin air wasn't right knowledge.

"That is why it is an adventure." Agatha's serenity teetered on the edge of annoying.

Bess loved adventure. Doing more, being more, having more than anyone else.

That was how she'd become entangled with the Silver Duke.

Right knowledge of things would indicate she shouldn't indulge those impulses any more.

"This boy—" Dan was no boy, but the word fit the story she'd told. "I can risk anything but him. I can't lose our friendship. For so long, it's been all I had."

"Is it the kind of friendship you can lose?"

No. Agatha had a point there. Bess couldn't lose his friendship; she was just greedy. She wanted more.

Perhaps this other woman did too.

* * *

BESS DOUBTED she'd find Dan's gawky shop-girl hiding in the Falcon Hotel, but the ledger she might.

Dan hadn't found the ledger. If he'd known she was asleep in a chair, he'd have stayed nearby. So he'd searched last night while everyone else played games.

He'd also said the man with the ledger wasn't at Road's End.

The ledger-man wasn't likely to be a villager; probably a traveler, like them. If he wasn't at Road's End, he must be in the village; and if he was in the village, odds were he'd stopped at the hotel.

They trooped up to the Hotel's top riverside room with Agatha's everlasting basket.

"I never imagined he would let us a room!" Agatha had been matter-of-fact about lovers, but the boldness of taking a hotel room made her blush. She was too fair for it; she looked blotchy.

Bess shrugged. "He let us because you paid for it."

The shocked innkeeper had asked after their horses, their husbands, and their business; Bess knew he recognized them from yesterday's arrival.

But in the end his work was to let rooms, and he'd been no match for sheer determination. Bess simply insisted that they were exhausted and required a room. Now. With the day barely begun.

"People who aren't rich need to work their trade. Here." Bess moved a chair so it looked out the window that faced upriver. "You look out for the next boat. I must search the hotel."

As Agatha watched, Bess stepped out of her woolen petticoat and pulled it over the skirt of her riding habit, tucking up its train. With a heavy shawl crossed over her chest and tied behind her, her riding habit disappeared and at first glance, she could pass for any plain villager.

"So clever! Never tell me you fear adventure." Agatha pulled a piece of hard biscuit from her basket. "You ought to eat first."

Murmuring her desperate gratitude, Bess snatched the dry thing and munched a bite, pointing it at Agatha. "You've visited Lady Carrollton before."

"Quite. It's from London. Sailors take it to sea."

"Your love of water is so puzzling." Bess peered out all the windows. One overlooked the wooden walk where they'd landed.

It would be an easy place from which to shoot at someone's head.

Dan's ledger meant money, and that was a thing Bess understood from its right nature. Putting aside all questions of gawky girls and the Silver Duke, she'd like to find it for him.

She'd also to find out who had taken that shot.

She didn't forgive, and she didn't forget.

"You'll be all right here?" Leaving Agatha alone felt like dropping a baby chick to the floor where someone might step on it. "You must keep an eye on all directions."

A lone thief was a dead thief, after all.

"I shall be perfectly well." From the basket, Agatha drew a small brass cylinder. She waggled it at Bess. "I shall be able to see everything."

"You're a wonder." Her rare grin flashed and faded as she examined the door lock. "Keep the key. This code will mean it's me at the door. One, four, one." Bess tapped it out. "If anyone else opens that door without the code, bash them in the head with the telescope." With a quick nod, she went out.

* * *

AGATHA LOCKED THE DOOR. "It's a spyglass, and I won't; it could break," she muttered after Bess was gone.

* * *

TWO INN ROOMS hung over the water, and they seemed likeliest to hold what Bess wanted: a ledger, a smoking gun, or both.

She slipped two of her three silver hairpins out of her hair. She'd tucked them there this morning after deliberately, and heart-rendingly, bending the ends.

She adored that *toilette* set. The mutilation of her silver pins made her a bit sad, but they did make adequate lock-picks.

Slipping inside the room, she said quietly, "Did you want breakfast, sir?" as if she were a maid for the inn.

But no one was there.

Keeping her steps light, Bess went to the bed first. People loved hiding things where they slept.

But she found nothing under the straw tick.

Her lips grew thinner and thinner as she rummaged through rumpled bed linens, then the clothes in the open valise. A razor and soap by the wash-basin; nothing underneath any of them. Nor was anything tucked behind the paintings or under the bed.

The room held a wooden coat-stand, two chairs, a small scarred table bearing bread crumbs, and a desk. Nothing in any of them, though the pen-stand was crooked, as though

270

recently used, with a pen on it; a corked inkwell stood nearby. She gently sloshed it. Liquid.

What had he written if not the invisible ledger?

The room's side door led to the valet's closet, as Bess expected; but there were no signs it was occupied, no linens upon the small cot. This room housed no gentleman, then. But someone.

There had to be something to find here. It was too meticulously neat for a room the man had tidied himself. This was a man with something to hide.

Wary of soot-marks, she knelt to peer into the fireplace.

There. On its floor, hidden under a thin coat of ash. Someone had burned a piece of paper in the little coal stove, and a piece remained. A small scrap, smaller than two fingertips.

Bess used her fingernails to pick it up, gently blew it clean.

It might not relate to the ledger at all, but the second its surface came into view, she knew Dan had to see it.

* * *

Scrap tucked in her pocket, Bess' muscles sang with tension as she opened the third door. She couldn't waste the chance to finish her search.

The scrap was something, however small. In some sense it belonged to her, and Dan, more than most. It wasn't the ledger, but it might lead that way.

She'd still like to know who shot off Dan's hat.

"Breakfast, sir?" It had worked in the last room, and expecting it to work again, Bess let herself be surprised.

An arm reached out from the side, aiming for her neck.

Quicker than thought she pinched it hard and blocked the flow of force. The pain made the arm jerk away, hard.

"Aggh! What did you do, Bess? I just wanted to keep you quiet."

"Jack?"

The burly man, shaking his arm to shed the pain of it, lifted his wrist with the other hand. "What'd you do, girl? You've got lightning in your fingers."

"That's because you're a jackass. Bess! So good to see you again." Jackie, brushed-back hair flawless as always and a big grin on his cheerily handsome face, came forward to take Bess' hand in a much more civilized way.

She grinned back. Seeing them made her feel lighter, even with a proverbial hot coal in her pocket. "This hotel is stacked with reprobates. Your wives let you out of London?"

Jackie put a hand on his heart. "I pine for her constantly."

Jack just shrugged. "Mine didn't fuss."

"Dan planned this?" It was the only possibility. "What are you doing here?"

Jack looked at Jackie.

"You're the plan, Bess," Jackie shrugged.

"She was the plan in London. This is a different plan." disagreed Jack, still shaking his hand as if it stung.

"If Bess doesn't know the plan, we shouldn't tell her the plan." Jackie grinned as he said it, but poked Jack in the side as if in reminder. "Bess didn't even know the plan when the plan was about her."

"That's what I'm saying. This plan isn't *that* plan."

"Say *plan* again and I'll get the fire iron." Quickly Bess studied the room. "Dan brought you, and you've been here a while. That much is obvious."

"See? She doesn't know the—" Jack cut himself off, respectfully swinging his stinging arm from his broad shoulders, and nodding towards her in acknowledgement.

What stung Bess was that Dan hadn't said anything about these two being here. He hadn't trusted her.

Mercy Bennett. Agatha was right. They had to actually talk.

It was also plain that one of them would have to stop telling lies, and since she was best at it, it might be her.

"Are you two alone?"

A silent silver-haired pixie, Jackie just poked Jack's side again.

Jack stared at the ceiling. "I mean, if you have a best friend, you're never alone."

Bess folded her arms. She'd been dealing with these two all her life. "So do your wives know what you're doing? In a *hotel?*"

Jackie's hand flattened against his chest in theatrical dismay. "I'll have you know my wife adores me more than the day we were wed!"

"That might still be very little. You tell me if you're alone here or I'll tell her about the time you stole a beef roast and used it to—"

"There's a girl downstairs." He cracked immediately. As Bess expected.

"A girl?"

"That's all we know." Jack used his good elbow to whack Jackie in the ribs. All that poking, and Jackie was the one who opened his trap. "Weasel. This is why we can't paint King's notes anymore."

"I want to meet this girl." The fake anger she'd used to cow her old friends was simmering into reality. What *girl* had Dan brought all the way out here? And for what?

Was it *the* girl?

"She's downstairs. I wouldn't go in there alone. She's not charming like you."

Just then the door creaked. Bess whirled. Jack had so startled her, she'd forgot to lock it.

An eye squinted in the door's crack. Agatha's.

At Bess' beckoning she thrust in her head and whispered, "The Duke is coming."

"That's not the girl," Jack told anyone who was still listening.

"Mercy Bennett." Maybe she could get Jack and Jackie to watch out of Agatha's room. She'd have to tell them someone shot at Dan from there.

Unless they were the ones who...

No. Suspicion must have limits, and Bess found one. These old friends would never hurt her, or Dan. Some things couldn't be bought.

Like Agatha. Bess hissed to her, "How do you know it's a duke?"

"There's a footman with him, in his colors. And a soldier, judging from his coat."

"On the London ferry?"

"No. From the fort across the river."

Bess didn't know how to read a rich man's colors, but it sounded like Agatha could. "Is it Talbourne?"

"No." The shake of Agatha's head was certain. "I know the colors well. It's the Duke of Gravenshire."

CHAPTER TWENTY-TWO

ow Bess had two urgent things to handle. The paper in her pocket, and the wrong duke.

But first, she wanted to see this *girl downstairs* for herself.

Agatha should stay safe. "Jack, go with Agatha back to her room, would you?"

Jackie waggled his eyebrows. "Why not me?" He smiled at Agatha. "It's never a waste of time to squire a pretty girl."

"That's why. *You* take me downstairs to see this girl."

"I could go too!" Agatha wasn't keen to be left out.

"You'd best limit yourself to one friend below your station," Bess told her grimly, and opened the door to check the corridor was empty before waving her out.

* * *

AGATHA DID NOT TAKE her advice.

Bess supposed it didn't matter if no one watched out the window above. She'd *like* someone to take another shot, so she could catch them in the act.

What really fired her temper as she stood, stupidly obvious, in a crowd of four while Jackie tapped on the door, was that it was their same old code.

One, four, one.

He could at least have kept our number ours, Bess grumbled silently to herself.

The door squeaked open. "Jackie," said the girl who'd opened it, throwing the door wide.

She had a pistol in one hand, and unfortunately, she was beautiful.

"I'm so glad you've come," she said, heedless of who might hear, ignoring Bess' and Agatha's unexpected presence. "Did you bring me breakfast? I'm out of port."

She also ignored how all four of them trooped in and Agatha closed the door.

Her dark hair tumbled around her shoulders in glossy waves. She wore the kind of silk wrapping-gown ladies wore in the morning before they truly dressed, and the room was full of bits of metal and glass Bess didn't recognize or understand.

Heavy leather gloves lay abandoned on a cast-iron ring on the desk, sufficiently small to hint that they were hers and she'd just shed them.

Agatha's eyes were wider than anyone's. Bess regretted letting Agatha come down here. She regretted getting Agatha out of bed this morning.

"It's the middle of the morning," was Jack's comment on the request for port, with a religious man's disapproval.

"Is it? I thought it was still yesterday. Didn't you bring all these friends from a party?" She winked one dark eye at Bess.

Jack just looked to the heavens again for patience. "No. This here is Bess."

The girl's spine straightened. There was a burnt spot on the side of her robe, but she ignored that too. "*Bess* Bess?"

"Yah."

"Well!" She curtsied. The burnt spot was still smoking. "This *is* an honor. Our introduction should be more formal, but I'm afraid it's not Jack's strength. I'm Schuyler Thorpe. Very happy to meet you."

Behind Bess' elbow, Agatha gasped.

The woman looked over Bess's head as if noticing Agatha for the first time. "I see you've heard of me. So kind of you to keep my reputation to yourself."

Agatha opened her mouth.

"So. Kind."

Agatha shut it again.

"I'd like to hear something about it." Bess wasn't leaving without some idea what the girl was doing here.

"My apologies," said Miss Thorpe in a tone that said she wasn't sorry at all. "I am here because my services have been engaged, and once my services are engaged, I keep the details private." Apparently losing interest in her visitors, she went back to the mess of metal on the table by the window, looking through it for something.

Her window was smaller than the ones upstairs, its curtains flung open so that anyone on the boardwalk outside could see in if they cared to. The only reason Miss Thorpe wasn't on full display was that no one had stopped outside in the riverbank wind.

Her view was the slow-flowing water beyond the narrow boardwalk. On it, a boat with ten men at the oars approached, defying all current. A broad-shouldered man stood in its center, blocking Bess' view of a smaller man behind him, and alongside a man in a scarlet coat. An officer.

Bess' wrong duke was about to land.

"Agatha. You know this woman?"

The dark-haired woman threw a look at Agatha over her shoulder, then turned back to her search. "Aha!" she said as her fingers connected with something which she drew from the pile.

It was a piece of cheese.

She bit off its end.

"Miss Thorpe was new to society when I first started attending assemblies myself," murmured Agatha, clearly reluctant to cross her but loyal to Bess. "I believe after that first year her reputation... declined."

"True," said Miss Thorpe, turning to lean against the table and gesturing agreement with the cheese. "I disappointed society, and it disappointed me. Still very rich, but not welcome in drawing rooms. Fortunately, I've found other ways to occupy my time." She put the cheese back in her mouth so her freed hand could slap at the still-smoldering spot on her dressing robe.

"I believe Miss Thorpe no longer receives invitations," Agatha whispered in Bess' ear, easily heard by all.

Bess' eyes narrowed.

Miss Thorpe wasn't gawky *or* fat. Nor did she look lazy, but she definitely looked loose. She was also lovely, which Bess hated.

And she had a pistol.

Bess turned to her colleagues. "Get out."

Agatha, startled, backed away, and Jackie followed, but Jack tried to object. "We better—"

"Out." Jack was much larger than she, but unwilling to push; Bess had no such qualms.

She shoved his muscled bulk out the door and shut it.

Then pointed at the pistol now on the table. "Have you fired that lately?"

"Define *lately*." Miss Thorpe cocked her head, chewing her cheese.

"Did you fire it yesterday?"

"No." She stood, and Bess saw in her the grace that went

with being raised in fine houses, with propriety-minded people. "Who was shot?"

"Dan Fox hired you?"

Now Miss Thorpe was quite alert. "Has something happened to Mr. Fox?"

"Did you shoot him?"

"Shoot my employer? No." Her shoulders went limp. She leaned back on the desk again, dropping the hand with the cheese. "Frog's knuckles. I suppose I won't be paid then."

If she thought Dan was dead, she definitely hadn't been watching from this window. Not long enough to see him run after his hat, anyway. She seemed genuinely both surprised and disappointed.

"You said you were rich."

"Oh, I am," some of the woman's careless energy came back. "But one likes to be paid for one's work."

"Which is?"

"Are you paying me?"

This was logic pure as gold in Bess' world. Of all the women she'd ever met, if there was one Dan might find attractive, it was this one.

Bess wanted to push her into the river. All that stopped her was that Miss Thorpe might be able to swim.

"Mr. Fox is fine. Someone shot at him out of the window above." She pointed upward toward the suspect window. "If I were you, I'd be careful."

"Oh, I'm always careful." Reassured, Miss Thorpe thoughtfully chewed more cheese. Bess wondered if she ever fully dressed. "Well, that's good news. Fine. I'm glad he's all right."

"How glad?"

About to begin the scientific measurements she'd told Agatha she had no time to learn, Bess was interrupted by Agatha herself, once more at the door.

Behind her Jack waved, wide-eyed, to convey that no one should blame the interruption on him.

"Do you not wish to get to Road's End before His Grace?" whispered Agatha, as softly as would carry.

Bess did not wish to get to Road's End before His Grace. At the moment, dukes and murders were the least of her problems. She wanted answers out of this Miss Thorpe person right now.

But she supposed, based on her previous conversation with Agatha, that it would be premature until she knew more of what Dan thought.

Words. Words and this confounded consideration for others were her enemies.

She pointed at the woman. "I'll see you again."

"No doubt!" Miss Thorpe just smiled, a very pretty rose-lipped smile that did nothing to help her case, and waved her cheese.

* * *

JACK AND JACKIE HAD DISAPPEARED.

"They're in there," Agatha whispered, nodding toward a door. "The innkeeper came past. Flirting with Charles is one thing, but obviously I ought not be standing with two men in a hotel."

She was absolutely right.

Having Agatha and Lady Dunsby to worry about meant even more care than not stealing from them. It was a lot to carry.

With no sign of the innkeeper about, Bess tugged Agatha with her into the room with the waiting men.

It was a linen closet.

Quickly Bess ran her hands under each folded white square, squeezing it, looking for guns or ledgers.

And looked from one Jack to the other. Pausing her search, she pointed overhead and didn't mention the paper she'd found. "I want you watching that room night and day, understand? I need to know everything the man in there does. *Don't* let him leave."

They promised, extravagantly in Jackie's case, before Bess waved them to go back upstairs. Agatha copied her, silently doing as Bess was doing, looking for anything and everything.

They found nothing.

After a few minutes of dedicated quiet, Bess peeked out.

Fortunately, the innkeeper was deeply involved in conversation with someone in a waxed coat that reminded her of yesterday's boatmaster. Both men glared at a sobbing girl beside them.

Bess waved to Agatha to follow her; they crept out along the wall.

"I must engage my own passage to London. I'm not a *night woman,* sir! I arrived here with Lady Winpole!"

Bess stopped, melted into the shadows. She pressed Agatha back with her, hoping among the bustle of travelers and villagers trying to sell things, they wouldn't be noticed.

"Well, I don't see no Lady Winpole now! This is a respectable hotel. Your lot needs to come by night or not at all."

The innkeeper seemed to have grown sensitive on the topic of whores, Bess thought with some guilt. Forcing him to let two ladies take a room in the early morning had cracked him.

The girl was devastated. She stomped a foot, still sobbing, her voice carrying. "I am *not a night woman!* I was engaged under *perfectly* respectable circumstances, and I—"

Apparently realizing she was about to say something rude about Lady Winpole in public, she cut herself off.

Well, Bess admired self-control, and rather admired Lady Winpole, who could clearly control others at a distance without the Silver Duke's methods.

She hadn't noticed this girl at Road's End, but there was no reason to make up such a shocking tale as being dismissed in the middle of a journey. The girl wasn't on stage.

Bess told herself that she too had become sensitive on the topic of strange women and stepped out of the shadows.

"There, there, Millicent, no need to cry. I'm so sorry you must travel alone! Why don't we stay with you till the boat leaves?" Surging forward, she took the crying maid by the arm and led her away from both the boatmaster and the innkeeper, Agatha at her heels.

Despite the weather, she led the girl out of doors, making her pull her shawl tight.

"My name's not Millicent," the girl said, sniffling.

"Wipe your face," murmured Bess under her breath. "It is till you get back to London. Nothing wrong with that name, I've always liked it. What happened?"

"I don't *know!* I did nothing wrong! I always keep everything just as her ladyship likes it. I never touch anything I shouldn't! And then out of nowhere she discharges me! Heaven help me." She did not wipe her face. She started sobbing again. "I can't go home again, I can't! And I won't get another place with no letter of reference. She sent me away with no reference!"

Feeling both frustrated and helpless, Bess turned a longing look to Agatha. People. Feelings. Perhaps Agatha could do something with them for a while.

Agatha, to Bess' relief, stepped forward and rummaged in the girl's bundle for a kerchief. This she pressed into the girl's hand, practically forcing her to blow her nose.

"All right," said Agatha in a soothing tone Bess tried to memorize in case she needed to produce it on stage. "Never fear. Here's a guinea. Take the boat to London and make sure the boatmaster engages you a reputable-looking cab. Go to Dunsby House in Greenwich—can you remember that?"

Still leaking tears, the girl nodded.

"All right. Just wait for us to come home. I'm sure we can find you a place. Tell Mr. Watkins I sent you, and to find you some employment till we come home. That should be enough for a perfectly honest reference. All right?"

"Oh *thank* you, miss. Thank you! You're a right sugar lump you are, not like that—" Again she cut herself off from saying anything about Lady Winpole, which Bess found interesting. "I'll do a good job, I promise you. I'm so glad I came straight here instead of looking for a new maid first."

"New maid?" Bess prompted.

"I'm to find her ladyship a new one before I get on the boat."

"Never say so!" Agatha's eyes, usually so gentle, had that fire back in them, and not about Lord Waresham. "That's cold of her, I must say."

Bess thought so too, and it surprised her; she'd had a lovely conversation with Lady Winpole.

Just then the same voice she'd heard at a distance sounded close.

It was the apple-seller. She called into the inn, some language Bess didn't recognize, and several ragged men, some showing deep scars on their hands or face, came out to greet her, their low voices making strange sounds.

Agatha had the maid who wasn't a Millicent well under control; Bess drifted away to join the apple-seller.

The streets of Bess' youth had been filled with every kind of language. French and Italian since she was born, and Spanish, since Napoleon seized their lands. There were clusters of Jewish people too, from all countries, and they had their own languages with their own soft sounds.

These sounds were different.

This wasn't a girl Bess suspected of stealing Dan's heart. This girl knew something else Bess needed to learn, though she wasn't sure why.

Her mind belonged to *her,* not the Silver Duke. And tossed in among the feelings, the *impressions* inside her that Bess liked to ignore, little burrs of something—dreams? Memories?—caught against the sounds of the girl's voice.

The men slunk away at Bess' approach, making the girl look up. Her face was thin, with big dark eyes, and she wore a warm shawl draped over her head.

"Apples for sale?" She offered Bess the basket.

Nothing could distract Bess from apples... except the sounds from this girl's mouth. "Say it like you said it to them. Say apple."

The girl looked confused. *"ee-Ya-bluh-kuh?"* she offered, clearly not understanding why that was what Bess wanted.

Bess didn't understand why it was what she wanted either. But she knew those sounds. She knew how they should fit. *"Yabloko,"* she told the girl.

The girl's eyes widened.

A flood of sounds followed which Bess didn't understand at all.

"You speak English, though, don't you?" asked Bess.

Immediately the girl switched back. Her eyes became more guarded. "Yes."

"What language is that?"

"Russian." More suspicious now. "I am not beggar. My father died working on ship. We do not have moneys to get home."

"I didn't say you were." Bess had too many worries at the moment, and when she looked over her shoulder, Agatha jerked her bonneted head towards the side of the hotel. The

Duke had surely landed, and he'd be at Road's End before them. "You're selling apples?"

The girl just offered the basket again, as if the question were stupid.

"Will you come to Road's End today, and I'll buy all you have?"

"Buy them now."

Bess beckoned to Agatha.

"I'm so sorry," she whispered as Agatha handed over several shillings. Agatha could do magical things even without money, but here Bess was draining her purse.

"Don't be," Agatha whispered back, with a cheerful smile. "We need more food at Road's End!"

* * *

THE SAD LACK of whores in Gravesend had driven Storey down to the last hut in the row, as close to an alley as the waterside village could muster.

Belinda was lush and often drunk. She knew no card games, and her most alluring garment was a stained linen shift.

"It's appalling," he told her for the twentieth time as she sat across her bare wooden table from him and poured him a shot of the horrible swill brewed in the village. The French still refused to ship Britain brandy.

"Look," said Belinda, tired of hearing about her shortcomings, "I ain't got no lace, or Burgundy wine, and I ain't gettin' any either. You can shut up and take what's goin', or you can shut up and leave."

It was a mark of the lack of choice in town that she could talk that way, Storey mused as he sipped the liquor, then swiftly set it back down on the table. That stuff could make a man blind.

What this town needed was someone to bring a few girls together, dress them properly, keep their manners, and make sure the sailors in and out of town knew where to go.

Mr. Storey loved the business of prostitution. It never went out of fashion, and done right, it made money hand over fist.

He never questioned Lady Winpole's methods. She'd made herself very rich, and by following along in her wake, she'd made him financially comfortable too.

But one never knew when one's fortunes could turn, and as far as Storey was concerned, a good whorehouse was like a bank.

He pulled a slim volume out of his pocket, one he'd owned years before he'd ever met Lady Winpole at the Temple of Books.

Belinda rolled her eyes in her plump cheeks. "Not that bollocks again!"

He fixed her with a look. She hadn't given up her attitude, but she'd learned to quiet when he gave that look. She'd be a fine addition yet to the business he had in mind. "Poetry," he said under his breath, forcing her to listen, "is the way a man learns to speak so men above him will hear."

As if in illustration, he turned to the book and intoned, "How rarely reason guides the stubborn choice, rules the bold hand, or prompts the suppliant voice; how nations sink, by darling schemes oppressed, when vengeance listens to the fool's request."

"So then," Belinda downed her glass of the burning liquor in a swallow, "what does it mean?"

That flicked him a bit raw, because he wasn't really sure. It was the sound of the words, the way they went together, that had let him climb to the place where he was. That and listening to the way fine men spoke even in the dirtiest of places.

There was one part close to the end of the poem about how to live a moral life, but it didn't interest him as much.

No, what he liked about the poem was how its hero conquered everything he saw. He loved that and ignored how the hero ended. That wasn't the part of the story he liked.

"Just listen," he told his tiny audience. It was too cold to sleep alone, and if he were to be here all night, perhaps he could coax some words out of her that didn't sound like the cacklings of crows.

* * *

DAN WANTED TO BATHE. The exertion of rackets had warmed him, but then the sweat cooled on his skin, and his conversation with Madame Franck had left him clammy.

If he wound up forcing Bess to stay close under the guise of keeping her safe, he *deserved* eternal torment. Because it was a guise. He didn't want her beside him to keep her safe. Not only to keep her safe. And saying so would be a dirty lie.

He had to secure her freedom above all else. It was the only way to balance the scales after what he'd done to trap her in this life in the first place.

Road's End had meager hospitality, but it did have water.

With all the servants rushing about the new wing, there was no one to help Dan to the means to bathe. But surely even a gentleman in such rustic conditions could be expected to find his own bucket of water and a quiet spot in the barn where it was warm.

When he went to get clean linen from his room, he did not notice at first how it was not as he'd left it.

Not until he passed his desk, and something crunched underfoot.

He knelt.

The twisted wire of his spectacle frames made a distinct shape on the floorboards. Its details were blurred; that was why he needed the spectacles. To see things close. Some of its blue glass shards were ground to powder.

It was not an accident, and the message was clear.

Lord Waresham wouldn't have soothed his masculine pride by crushing a pair of spectacles. This was someone else.

Lady Winpole.

London men with titles were no better than he; he grasped that now. But they were still richer. They had more. They could do more.

He was still just Dan, carrying the weight of what he'd already done to Bess, carrying it close enough to kiss her. He couldn't have more.

His destroyed glasses said as clearly as a letter that if Dan crossed Lady Winpole, she'd kill him. But he'd already crossed Bess in ways she didn't know, and if she ever found out, he'd rather be dead.

CHAPTER TWENTY-THREE

Road's End was alive with torchlight and people buzzing in and out, the new wing open and welcoming. The Duke's arrival had lit it afire.

Returning from the village on their horses, it was like returning to a different house.

Bess would have gone straight to find Dan, but Agatha had one of her fits of firmness, insisting they dress, and quickly.

Bess saw the wisdom of it when they darted—in ladylike fashion—into the huge gold-trimmed parlor, its candles lit to dispel the wintry afternoon gloom. There were no guinea-pig holes in the carpets in here.

Road's End had put on a costume and become someone totally different, and a duke had joined it onstage.

"This is Lady Winpole, and Lady Dunsby, and of course her daughter Lady Agatha, whom you may have met. And her companion Miss Page." Lady Carrollton's hand fluttered toward them both.

They'd arrived just in time for their cue. Bess and Agatha both curtsied.

"Ladies," the Duke said gravely, and bowed very slightly.

He was thick through the chest, his bulk sailing high like a ship, with steel-and-silver hair springing up even though he'd brushed it back. Instantly Bess thought of several dancers who would like to make his acquaintance and wondered why he never visited their opera house.

It would only have made sense for his eyes to linger on Agatha. Even opera dancers knew how the Duchess of Gravenshire had died, tragically, many years before. His Grace was surely lonely.

But if he was, he showed little interest in Agatha.

"I am most grateful for your welcome," he told Lady Carrollton. That lady clutched her lace shawl tightly. "It must disappoint you that the Duke of Talbourne could not make the journey. But I can assure you he and I are equally entertaining, which is to say not much; and I, at least, travel with a smaller retinue."

"We are very grateful for your company, Your Grace," quavered Lady Carrollton. "And I trust your men are comfortable."

Bess wondered if *they* had carpets chewed by guinea pigs.

"Quite comfortable," the Duke assured her soberly. "Captain Clark must feel the same."

"I shan't be staying," the tall man in the red coat said quickly. "Lady Carrollton entertained many of our officers while the Russian fleet was here. I would not further impose."

Bess' eyes sought out the Silver Duke. She had missed his introduction.

His face was easy, but his body was rigid with rage.

He'd not expected the Duke of Gravenshire. Clearly, he did not *want* the Duke of Gravenshire.

Bess wondered why.

Lady Carrollton trilled on. "We will have a party in the

Duke's honor tomorrow on Bonfire Night. You must bring your officers then, Captain Clark."

Bess' eyes traveled around the edge of the room looking for Mr. Able. The lady's invitation should send the steward round his last bend.

She couldn't see Mr. Able.

But she did see Dan.

To her, he shone among all these simpler, boring people. His black hair still reflected no light, but his shoulders looked as lean and strong as she knew they were, his hands clasped behind his back as he surveyed the room.

When his eyes lit on her, he smiled.

Just a little smile, but it was *her* smile, the soft one no one else got to see.

Bess felt her own expression grow soft in return.

It was dangerous, but unavoidable. As if only they two waited for one another on opposite sides of the big bright room, finding each other by instinct.

The conversation they held with their eyes was quick and familiar.

Bess glanced at a door.

Dan shook his head.

She knew her expression said *we must.*

Knew he would give in, by the way his half-crooked smile bent.

That smile had always been dear; now it was everything.

Tearing her eyes away, Bess turned to Agatha.

The Duke had moved on, with Waresham and Vellot following behind him. Lords Harman and Zachary stayed, conversing over glittering glasses of wine that the cellars had suddenly produced.

Poor Mr. Able must be apoplectic.

"Agatha, I must speak to Mr. Burton."

"Really?" Completely without art, Agatha looked over

Bess' shoulder to where Dan stood in the shadows. "You know my mother wants you to leave him alone. I thought you devoted to the boy from your childhood."

"So I am." She was. "But I must speak to Mr. Burton. May I give him some of your apples? And sea biscuit?" Bess glanced toward the party around the Duke. They were all sipping tall clear glasses of small beer, and pale as it was, with no other fare they'd soon be stupid or sleepy or both.

Dan needed nourishment too.

"Of course," said Agatha, generous as always. "You mustn't be gone long. My mother is no doubt wondering where we've been."

* * *

"We can't speak like this. They all saw where you went."

The small drawing room must have held gold-colored things but Bess' eyes locked on Dan. She came toward him as if drawn by a string.

"I'm going to put apples and biscuit in your room." She was drinking him in as if she hadn't just seen him the night before. "I missed you."

He waited for the clean, familiar guilt. It didn't come. "Where were you all day?" It was more than the five years they'd spent apart. He'd missed her too, missed her now, would miss her until she was in his arms again.

He saw how they drifted closer to one another, wondered if she noticed.

"I searched the hotel, and I found something." Her face changed. "And a girl. Who is that girl?"

If she'd been to the hotel, Dan knew exactly what girl.

But this wasn't a game. Lady Winpole had sent a message. She sensed somehow he was there to find out about her, and she'd do whatever it took to strike back at him.

He could not risk her connecting him to Bess.

They'd drifted closer still. He didn't need to touch her to know the shape of her back, of her hands. He could imagine rays of warmth coming from her and landing on his skin even across the space between them.

Softly, the way he'd talked to focus her attention when they were children, he said, "You must go back to London. On the next boat. You'll have to go alone."

Her eyes snapped, then narrowed. "I won't. If you insist, I'll make Lord Harman take me."

"You wouldn't." Despite his every resolution, she roused his ire. "Is he your protector? Would-be? Or past?"

Because even though Bess had said last night that she didn't have a protector, Dan knew better than anyone how she could split words to avoid telling the truth.

"Whichever. The situation would change if I went back to London with him. Who is that girl?"

"None of your affair."

Bess' face grew hard. "Whose affair is she?"

Dan wanted to needle Bess that the girl could be Lord Harman's affair for all he knew, but he owed Miss Thorpe a debt. It would not be fair to play with her reputation. It was already in shreds.

"Bess, I am here as part of a plan. That involves thinking ahead. Miss Thorpe is here to assist in the plan, which I will not endanger by spilling to you."

In fact, Miss Thorpe was here to help Dan make an escape worthy of the stage.

"I'll find out," said Bess, all too knowledgeable about stagecraft.

"I doubt it."

It felt so familiar, just like the two of them as children teasing, throwing challenges back and forth, but also all new.

Because for the first time, Dan contemplated kissing her quiet.

Even if it didn't work, he'd like to try.

"Is she *the girl?*" Bess asked with dramatic emphasis.

"What girl?"

"The one. The one you are doing this for."

She really did not know. Even after last night, Bess honestly thought Dan was in love with someone else.

It was a relief. Partly. It would make her easier to send back to London. She *had* to get away from whoever had so shaken her last night, as well as Lady Winpole.

It was also another lie piled onto the heap on Dan's soul, but compared to some others, it was small and he could live with it.

Keeping Bess' suspicion alive required only that he not answer her questions.

Then Bess said, "You love *me*, you know."

She dropped it there, like a pile of treasure right at his feet. As though she knew but he didn't.

I know, he wanted to say.

"Bess." When had they drawn close enough to touch? One of his hands moved of its own accord to follow the shape of her head without touching, wanting to tilt her into him, wanting to hold her.

Instead, he traced a stray glossy hair and tucked it behind her ear.

Under his breath he said, "Nothing is more important than you being safe. I wouldn't ask you to go back to London if I didn't need you to go."

"You need me here more. That job you took? To find that ledger? It *has* to be you." She was so confident; then she proved herself right. "I found you this."

From her pocket, she pulled a scrap of scorched paper.

It had a few numbers. Curved and slashed so they could be clearly read, the way bookkeepers wrote them.

Alongside the thieves' symbols they'd used in their childhood.

Dan stared.

Without spectacles, he had to squint to make the marks clear. But they were there.

The five circles that meant money. The up-and-down slash that meant man.

On the back, another that was unfamiliar but easy to guess: a cup-like curve with a line up from its bottom that would remind anyone of a ship without ever using the word.

"What the—Where did you find this?"

She told him the room at the Falcon Hotel. "It's like they left a letter for you."

"*No one* wanted me to read this."

"But you can! Can't you?" Now Bess didn't sound quite so sure.

Neither was Dan. The ship was easy to read, but other new symbols were mysteries. It was a little like reading a stranger's ledger. So many of the merchants devised their own ways of recording income and expenses; Dan was used to deciphering their peculiar marks.

But this was even harder still, because there weren't words, only symbols.

It was a chance. Dan wanted to whoop out loud, thinking he might soon be done and Bess' future secured. Then his insides sank just as fast. "Did anyone see you with this?"

"No, of course not. But it was there, in that hotel full of our old Jacks and *that girl,* and I'm the one who found it."

"So you did!" Forgetting everything but her, Dan swept her up against him in both arms, spinning her around up off the floor till she laughed. "Because you are the cleverest woman in London."

It was hot gold in his veins to see her smile.

As he slowed, her smile faded. One hand caressed his cheek, then both her hands cradled his face, soft fingertips brushing the stubble on his cheeks. "Please," she said.

He'd never told her no.

Capturing her mouth with his he drank in the taste of her, like champagne, like breathing.

Her hands splayed against the sides of his head, holding him to her with the smallest touch, turning him the way she wanted so she could taste him. It was a kiss that made Dan's eyes close, made his heart melt, made his muscles tremble.

Desire whispered in his ear to *lay her down right here, to have her entirely, that she was his, she'd always been his and she always would be.*

It shook him enough to let her lips go.

He didn't want to. He wanted to curl around her and touch all the places he wouldn't let himself think about. But he loosened his crushing grip.

"Thank you," he whispered, as if he'd been the one begging for a kiss.

Her feet fell back down to the floor, but she stayed on tiptoe, arms around his neck, her eyes looking into his. "The best thing about being a thief is that if you really want something, you can take it."

She couldn't mean what she thought she meant. The idea that she might gripped him like a hot fist. His voice was thick. "You ought to know better than to say things like that. Don't tempt me."

"I'm *trying* to tempt you."

"You know better." She had to stop saying such things. Dan was only human, and she was all he'd ever cared about. Now he had her taste on his lips and he wanted so much more she couldn't imagine. "Don't tempt me to break you open like a vault and steal all you have. You're too clever for that."

"It can't be stealing if I hand you the key."

She really didn't know what she was doing to him. How he would fall on his knees for the chance to love her completely. To *keep* her like the treasure she was.

He'd risk fire and brimstone for that. He'd risk the hangman's noose.

But he couldn't risk her trust.

"Tell me you'll go back to London," he murmured against her lips, hoping the kiss had devastated her as much as it had him.

"I'm never going to leave you," she said, her eyes drifting closed, and she kissed him again.

He could barely keep from swearing into the kiss. If she wouldn't go till he did, then he had to get to the hotel and find that ledger.

And he didn't want her to know how impossible it was for him to leave when she did things like that.

Finally, they released each other. Her open eyes so close to his set a spell on him that held him tight.

"Then stay close to Agatha and Lady Dunsby," he said. "You'll have to lie. Tell them I'm ill in my room. Don't let them check on me."

He wanted to warn her to stay away from Lady Winpole, but this was Bess. If he told her not to do something, she would definitely do it.

She bit her lip again. "Dan. That duke."

"Yes?" He expected her to tell him of some new shocking connection, with a duke of all men. Did he have a weakness for ballerinas?

"Never mind," she said, frustrating him more than it did to put her perfect-to-hold body away from his.

Which he did. Loosening her arms. He regretted it as

soon as they were gone. "Why is it so hard for you to keep your distance from these rich people?"

"Agatha's not a bad sort. Nor Lady Dunsby. I feel sorry for these ladies; they're so lonely and dull."

He had to risk it. "Bess, I'm begging you. Stay away from Lady Winpole. She's dangerous. She's not what you think."

"Why, what is she?" Bess pressed her lips closed, then bit her lip as if it actively pained her not to argue. Dan tried not to smile. "She said she was just here for Lady Dunsby, for the sake of a decent bridge partner."

"Decent?" That rang a bell in the back of Dan's mind. "Lady Winpole said that?"

"Yes, why?"

"Because I was told in confidence that Lady Dunsby isn't particularly good." The rest of the conversation at Mercywall House, Fitz' house, came back to him. "Yet Lady Winpole has been winning."

"Interesting. A card sharper?"

"Sharpers usually win. So, Lady Winpole? Yes. Lady Dunsby? Likely not. Stay alert, Bess, and keep safe. Promise me you will."

Wide-eyed, she nodded. "I will," she told him.

Dan just looked at her.

"I will. I'm telling the truth. Honest."

Searching her eyes, Dan let out a small sigh of relief.

Bess went on, "As soon as I keep my promise to the apple-seller."

"*What?*" He had to duck his head to force himself not to yell.

"I just made a little promise to the apple-seller that I must discuss with Lady Winpole, and then nothing, I promise."

"I hope the promises you make to me matter half as much as the ones to an apple-seller."

"They do, Dan. I promise." Bess winced a little, hands

clenching. She shook one small fist as if he'd threatened her with a fight. "Honestly, Dan. I want to do this right. We should have a long quiet talk, but there's nowhere to talk, and no *time.*"

"We don't have to talk about anything." He knew she'd felt just as he did when their eyes met across all that space full of light. They didn't have to talk. They knew. Too much. That was why this was so difficult.

"We do. I need to understand how you feel about this girl who's got you putting yourself in danger. I need to know how much she matters to you. I need to—" She cut herself off, made herself start again. "I need to know how to make you happy."

Christ. That was the last thing *he* needed.

"You don't need to know anything more than you know, Bess." He couldn't bear all the space between them; he pressed his lips to her temple, reveling in the feel of her soft hair.

* * *

He put a finger under her chin, drawing her face up. "Do you have any idea how many times you've made my heart stop?"

She felt hers pound in answer. He'd said that before, but this time the words sounded different.

It felt like she had waited her whole life to hear these things. From *Dan.*

"Every time you climbed out of sight. Every time you fell. Every time you charged into danger as though you had nothing to lose."

Those weren't what she was longing to hear.

He'd always wanted her safe, but Bess wanted him to want *her.*

Because Bess was selfishly certain now that everything

she kept leashed inside, all the worst things she could do, would be unleashed if something happened to him.

"Don't go to the hotel alone," she said. Ordered. *Begged.* "You know you shouldn't."

"I won't be alone," he reassured her. "Jack and Jackie are there, and they'll watch out for me." Now he bumped his knuckle softly against the bottom of her chin, and Bess liked that a lot less. It felt like she was little again and he was leaving her. How could those men keep watch better than Bess did? They'd been forgers; they didn't have a ruthless bone in their bodies.

If Dan were relying on that Miss Thorpe to watch his back, Bess was going to need more weapons.

"A lone thief is a dead thief," Bess reminded him. "I'll come with you."

"We can't *both* disappear claiming to be ill. They'll notice. I'll be fine."

"Dan," she said, forcing herself not to throw her arms around him again. "You were never a very great liar."

Surely he felt some of this same pull she felt. The need to stay close enough to touch. Bess desperately hoped it wasn't just her.

It must not have been, because after a reluctant minute Dan said, "Dammit. I think I can arrange something. Keep your cloak at hand and stay alert."

She hovered near him, even as he took her hand in his. He didn't seem to want to leave either. "Why?" asked Bess. "What will you do?"

"I'm going to take a lesson from the Tourmaline and cause a distraction," he stage-whispered to her, his unexpectedly bright grin making her smile before he disappeared.

CHAPTER TWENTY-FOUR

*D*an might not think it, but Bess took his warnings seriously. He made her wish she wore armor instead of her demure rose-pink gown.

This gown *was* a kind of armor, though, for the company she found herself in. The fine people circled each other, and her, like live lions, and the dress was the fake fur that let her wander among them without looking like prey.

The room's most dangerous predator, the Silver Duke, stood on one side speaking low to the Duke of Gravenshire. Just the sight made the hair stand up on Bess' arms.

Perhaps he gave others the same sensation, as no one drew close enough to hear what the Silver Duke whispered to the real one.

Bess, however, wanted to know. Badly enough to pretend an interest in a narrow painting of a hanging pheasant.

Unfortunately, this attracted Lady Winpole, who came to stand beside her.

Hoping to prevent any more difficult conversation, trying to eavesdrop, Bess only said, "That's a lovely turquoise in your ring."

"Yes." Her ladyship did not look down. "It's not the ring I wished to wear in honor of His Grace, but it will do. My maid stole the other, and it's lost."

"A ring stolen?" Not-Millicent had done no such thing. Bess knew a thief when she saw one, and not-Millicent was not a thief. "You haven't lost the hyacinth, I hope."

"Not at all. I'll wear it tonight, as we must all be pretty and march for His Grace."

Bess pretended to study the pheasant. "I suppose that's what dukes require."

"Gravenshire more than Talbourne," Lady Winpole said with a shrug. "Talbourne only cares that everyone revel amongst themselves too much to comment on his flirty wife. Gravenshire has no wife, and his addle-pated daughter is married now. He must be bored." She nodded a little toward Lady Dunsby. "And there's Hortense bursting with joy. No doubt she imagines Agatha can catch him."

"Really?" Bess pretended to look shocked. "He's twice her age!"

Lady Winpole made a noise that struck Bess as a strangled chortle. "You're delightfully innocent, girl. Perhaps I'll take you to the Continent with me once peace settles in. You'd be entertaining company if you keep saying fool things like that."

Bess had the chilly feeling that it wouldn't matter much if she *wanted* to go to the Continent. "Thank you, madam."

The heads of the dukes, the real and the false one, bent together as if in serious conversation. But Bess noticed that Vellot, as she must remember to think of him, was doing all the talking.

Desperate to hear, Bess had to get rid of Lady Winpole. "A Russian girl came back from the village with us; she said your old maid told her you wanted a new one." Best not to reveal her own involvement in the maid discussions. After all, not-Millicent would be on her way to London before Lady Winpole found out any more about it.

"So I do." Lady Winpole's eyes were nothing noteworthy; a colorless color, lost between brown and green and gray, and neither sleepy nor awake. But when they fixed on Bess, they held her.

"Shall I send for her?"

"She'll keep. I'll see to her eventually."

If Lady Winpole wouldn't leave, Bess still had to get closer to the gentlemen. Making sure her back was to them, she drifted nearer, and as she studied a painting of two familiar guinea pigs, she heard why Vellot wanted to speak to His Grace alone.

"It must be difficult," Vellot was saying, "being in company without the wife you loved so much. You must still miss her. I am sure her last thoughts were of you."

Bess turned and openly watched.

Vellot reached out and smoothed the gold knot pin on the Duke's lapel. It was a slower gesture than one would have expected. "She likely thought of you. Her last thought was of you."

The horrible familiarity of his voice, his slow gestures, his repetition, spurred Bess into action.

Throwing manners to the wind, she flung herself between the two men. After all, she was small. "Have you seen the guinea pigs, Your Grace?"

Vellot's face reddened visibly at her outburst.

The bushy-browed Duke blinked, as if waking. "What guinea pigs are those?" he asked, but without surprise.

Whatever it was Vellot did, he'd been doing it to the Duke.

"I meant this painting, but you may have also met Lady Carrollton's actual pets?"

The Duke was tall and broad, but the weight of him came

from more than his size. His was a heavy look. She was glad of it, because it made him seem less lost, less foggy.

He scrutinized the floor with utmost seriousness, apparently for guinea pigs. He must know their habits. "I don't believe I've had the pleasure."

"You must while you are here. I did not expect them to be charming, but they are."

He was a man around whom the air seemed to stop a good two feet away. Still, Bess pushed through the invisible barrier around him to take his arm. "I won't feel right until you meet them."

He allowed himself to be led aside, and Bess did not look back to see how Vellot took that maneuver.

Nor did Lady Winpole appreciate Bess bringing her the Duke. She sniffed, dropped the tiniest curtsey to the Duke to convey that she did not want his company, and sailed off.

Bess wasn't sure what she ought to say. "I believe she's been called away," she said weakly.

She wished she'd seen more plays with dukes in them.

He was silent a second longer than she expected, then said, "No matter. I wished to pay her my respects, but it's the lady's prerogative not to want them."

In Lady Winpole's absence, he studied Bess so closely she began to wonder if he doubted who she was.

"Is Lord Vellot a friend of yours?" She led the big man to a spot before another portrait, this one of a man in a buttoned coat. The world was made of old men ordering each other around; perhaps he'd feel more comfortable.

Instead, he looked down at her.

"I spend much of my time on parliamentary matters. I make it my business to establish common ground with all my peers. I beg your pardon, miss, but I've forgotten your name."

Go right on forgetting it. "Miss Elizabeth Page. I'm no one to remember, sir."

He was staring down at her, at her body, so intently Bess had to consider how to tell a duke she didn't return his interest. It was not a situation that called for bluntness.

But what he finally said was, "That's a lovely sapphire you wear."

He was looking at her *hands?* Confused, Bess wondered for a moment if he'd overheard her and Lady Winpole discussing jewels. Why should he notice her ring?

The *why* followed quickly. "It is a very old tradition for kings to identify themselves with rings. Did you know that?"

"No, sir." If he wanted to lecture Bess about rings and history, she'd happily listen, even while she felt her heart follow Dan down the road to the village. She hoped he was safe.

She didn't believe Vellot could do magic, but the very inexplicability of it meant she had to wonder how he did it, and if he could do it at a distance.

His behavior just now suggested that he needed to be close, so Dan was safe. So was this Duke, as long as she kept Vellot away.

Gravenshire looked better now, in fact, less mired in memories of his dead wife. Roused by curiosity. Unfortunately, about rings.

"For instance," he said, "an old friend of mine gave his ring to a child he wished to protect. She has few friends in the world, and he gave her his ring to prove that she has his support. Rather like a letter of introduction."

"I can imagine, sir." She could. Like the thieves' symbols, such a ring said everything necessary without words.

"It was gold, bore his crest. So you might say it bore his signature."

"I can just imagine it, sir. Like a medieval king." Bess could. Exactly like the gold crest ring she'd lifted at the opera house at the Silver Duke's request.

The one she gave him.

"My friend gave the child a ring of his mother's, too; less recognizable, not *signed* you might say, but just as precious because it was his mother's. Perhaps more so."

A sinking feeling started in Bess' stomach.

"It was an ancient sapphire, set in quite heavy gold. Sideways."

Bess did not look down at the ring she wore. A sapphire, set sideways in quite heavy gold.

She said, "That used to be the fashion, wasn't it?"

His eyes bore down on her. "Yes. It was."

She took the bull by the horns. "It sounds much like my mother's ring. This was in her family for hundreds of years. It's a humbling responsibility."

"It must be." His eyebrows yanked together. "The girl I speak of lost her family rings, and is in rather dire straits without them. The old gentleman who offered his protection has taken it away, suspecting the girl of selling the rings; and worse, it puts him in a bad position. As anyone who has his ring can claim to have his letter of introduction, so to speak."

"That is a sad story." She meant it. "You make me want to lock this ring away in a vault. I always thought it was safest on my hand."

"It ought to be." His Grace straightened, and Bess felt it a little easier to breathe. But he did not stop his piercing look. "But cutpurses are everywhere these days."

Bess wasn't sure what she was supposed to take from that, so she shivered for him. Whatever he suspected, the more helplessly delicate he thought her, the better.

"I'm very sorry for this girl. I wish there was something I could do for her."

"I'll keep that in mind, Miss Page." From him, the name sounded almost threatening. Bess knew that unfortunately, the Duke of Gravenshire would remember her, and that ring.

"If there is anything you can do to help the girl, I will be the first to tell you."

Perhaps he'd stop worrying about the ring if she just told him his life was in danger.

"I wished to ask you about Lord Vellot." She needed some cleverer way of introducing the topic; none was coming to mind. In plays, uncovering the villain came with a dramatic gasp in the last act and everyone knew who he was. She had to be more subtle. "I've overheard some things he's said. About Lord Talbourne."

He studied her face this time. And said, "His Grace is addressed as His Grace, the Duke of Talbourne."

Bess did not let her face show her dismay. What a silly mistake. Of course dukes were different.

Mercy Bennett, she was making a hash of this.

"Sir, your life may be in danger," she whispered.

His bushy eyebrows flew up and he once again studied her small length from top to bottom. "From you?"

Too right you are. He was stupid on top of it all. "Of course not." She ought to flutter her eyelashes or something to look more helpless, but she was too annoyed. Miss Page was slipping more and more all the time.

"Sir," she said crisply, "assume a lady hears things. Lord Vellot has plotted against His Grace's life. I'm telling you this so you safeguard your own, as you've come in his place."

Now he'd likely think her Vellot's mistress, but she'd done it. She couldn't be any plainer. If he was too stupid to take the warning, that wasn't her fault.

At least he didn't brush it away. "Interesting," was all he said, and turned to address Lord Waresham as he approached.

Bess, not wanting to stay beside either of them, curtsied and left.

If Lady Winpole could do it, she could do it too.

* * *

THE SMELLS of the impending supper were incredible. Unlike the night before in every way. Candles blazed all over the house, and Bess had no idea what Dan was up to, only waiting for whatever signal came. She felt faint with hunger. She wished for more of Agatha's sea biscuit. And apples.

"Have you got an apple in your pocket?" she felt moved to ask, as staying near Agatha seemed safest.

Agatha looked down at her flowing silk gown. "If I did, it would show."

In a room full of candlelight reflecting off the glass and gilt, in a room with a duke, no less, Bess just wanted Dan and some food. In that order.

How long would she have to wait for Dan's so-called distraction?

CHAPTER TWENTY-FIVE

$\mathcal{D}$an's mind was back at Road's End with Bess.

That was the only reason he made the stupid mistake of rapping on Miss Thorpe's door, then pushing it open without tapping the code.

He found a pistol's barrel aimed at his nose.

"You're right. I apologize." Reaching up, he gently pushed the weapon's muzzle toward the floor before slipping inside.

"Mr. Fox. You don't follow your own instructions?"

Sorry, distracted, he wanted to say. But in this odd situation, he was her employer, and didn't want to admit his distraction. "Miss Thorpe, I need you to visit Road's End."

"I haven't been invited." Her dark hair shone where it fell against her shoulders, and though dark had fallen, she still wore a dressing-gown. One with a scorch mark on the side, he now saw.

"Exactly. I need you to cause a fuss."

"Mr. Fox." She folded her arms. "You promised me not to implicate me in your scandal. I have enough problems with my own. Once you make good your escape, if I'm seen here, people will draw conclusions."

"No, they won't. No one knows yet about your... interests. Do they?"

Annoyed he was right, she shrugged. "Not yet. I've been experimenting in Shropshire. Sheep don't talk."

"So go to Road's End. Cause a stir. The biggest drama you can, like on the stage."

"Even if I wanted to, sir, I am not dressed for supper in company." She twirled a lock of hair between her fingers. "Even if I find something suitable, who will help me dress? You?"

That made Dan flush a little red; he could feel the heat in his cheeks. "If you'd rather have me tie your tapes than Jackie," he growled, trying to make himself menacing again.

"Why, Mr. Fox. You're secretly a big ball of sugary fluff, aren't you?" She fluttered her eyelashes and smiled like she knew something.

"Dammit." To deny it further would make him look foolish; he felt foolish already. "Just dress. I'll send you a tavern maid. Go. I don't care what you do with your frills or your hair. I need the household so upset by your arrival that they lose track of who's there and who's not."

"Lady Carrollton?" Miss Thorpe had been told only what she needed to know, but she had been in society once, and everyone in town knew the local gentry.

He swallowed. "Well, the Duke of Gravenshire is there now too."

"*What?* You want me to make a spectacle of myself in front of a duke?"

"Miss Thorpe. You told me you were done with society. Did you mean it?"

He knew he had her there. He'd warned her this business would put paid to any further attempts to enter good society. She'd claimed she wanted nothing else to do with it.

Like many people, once she saw the gate shutting her in—or out—she likely wished she'd made different choices.

Fortunately Miss Thorpe was made of stern stuff. "I meant it." She said it a little grudgingly; Dan knew she was taking a blow.

No titled match for her. No society. No fine wedding.

No doubt she'd already bid those things farewell, but she'd still feel the loss. Women like her did.

Bess had apparently never thought of them. Shockingly, she thought of him instead.

The dark-haired woman looked up at him through calculating lashes. "And I thought you secretly gallant. You're quite willing to throw a lady under the carriage wheels if it helps a girl you..." She paused and looked him up and down. "...like. Aren't you?"

He wasn't about to bare feelings to her he'd hid from London for years, even from himself. But they were trying to break free. He could feel them, hot in his veins. Like hope.

"What do you think of justice, Miss Thorpe?"

"I don't," was her swift answer.

"I used to think justice was people getting what they deserve. But it doesn't happen much, does it?" He gave her part of a smile that would have looked rueful if not for the scarred sneer. "I'm starting to wonder why that doesn't happen to me."

Why couldn't he be one of the millions who got what they wanted instead of what they deserved? Why couldn't he have Bess?

Why couldn't he simply keep his mouth shut and live happily ever after?

Miss Thorpe looked at him with a cocked head and thoughtful eyes. An expression that said she was deciding what to think.

Dan couldn't finish this without her help. "It's all right if you don't want to do it. I can send Jack—"

"No no, you don't want the boys associated with you. They have jobs to do once they get back to London." She caught up the bottle of liquor on the table. It was open; she swallowed a mouthful of its contents. "I'll go."

"Are you sure? If you don't want to make a scene—"

"Oh, that's one thing I do enjoy." She looked around her. "All right, get out and send me that maid. I hope she can do something with my hair."

* * *

DINNER WAS WHOLLY different from supper the day before, so different that Bess assumed Mr. Able could not come to the table because he'd died of despair in the pantry.

The new wing's dining table was vast, with full, flaming candelabras flickering in every window, light glowing on the silk-striped wallpaper.

Nerves stretched, waiting every moment for Dan's promised distraction, Bess watched the parade of arriving food with awe.

Lord Waresham's jugged rabbit finally appeared, brown and luscious, next to cubes of carrot as bright as Lady Winpole's hyacinth jewel, and Bess would have been happy to have only those.

Yet beside them came whole chickens. Stewed mushrooms and French beans. Almond cheesecakes, white sprigs of cauliflower, wine and butter sauces, and apricot jam tartlets. An entire roast turbot, the fish platter mounded with its meat, and a whole bowl of tangy olives.

It was as though the gates of plenty had spewed forth a whole table of deliciousness for the Duke's pleasure, and Bess eagerly rode his coat-tails all the way.

Lady Winpole sat on Bess' right, no more inclined to share than ever; people passed dishes around her. Her silver box of Eccles cakes, however, did not appear.

On her left was Lord Harman.

Bess thought him attractive in a plain way, suitably boring for gentry. Why couldn't Agatha interest herself in someone like him?

Shuffling platters, he addressed her. "I trust Mr. Burton is not ill from his crushing game of rackets."

"Excuse me?" Bess' forkful of tartlet paused halfway to her mouth. When all the dishes were served together, she didn't see the harm in eating the tartlets before someone else did.

"He quite put Lord Waresham in his place." Lord Harman's dark eyes looked amused as he gestured with his chin across the table at Waresham, who glared silently at the Duke from his seat.

"Did he? I didn't hear. Lady Agatha and I were shopping in the village."

"So I gathered, as Mrs. Frank charged all over the house looking for you this morning."

Bess surveyed him again. There was a twinkle in his eye.

Bess had no talent for flirting and no desire to practice. If she had either, she supposed, she would practice on him.

"Were you looking for Lady Agatha too?" Bess tilted her head in Agatha's direction. Her friend's pale blonde curls positively sparkled in the candlelight, and for once the room was warm; Agatha was blushing.

She expected a flippant answer, but Lord Harman regarded the pretty picture Agatha made very thoughtfully.

He said, "I wish I were."

"You'd be wise. After all, she's right here."

"Have you heard of my parents, Miss Page?"

"No, sir. But I am not familiar with London society."

"Everyone else I know, *everyone*, is *very* familiar with them. I have been compared to my father all my life. It is the nature of life as an heir that everyone expects me to take his place." He leaned a little closer. "But what if I don't wish to?"

Rich people and their problems. "If you don't wish to, do something else."

Lord Harman shook his head, a lock of dark hair falling over one eye. "Britain is built on shoemakers' sons taking the place of shoemakers, and kings' sons the place of kings. And so on for everyone in between."

Bess speared a French bean on her fork. "Mercy Bennett, you make it sound like a privilege to be orphaned."

He twitched with surprise. "A grim thought." Then he let out a laugh. A long, sincere laugh, so sincere that it made Bess like him a bit better, though she wished he wouldn't draw so much attention.

"Sometimes I have them."

"I'm glad I was most inappropriately seated next to you this evening, Miss Page."

"Really? Who should sit by me?"

"What, next to Lady Carrollton? Lord Vellot, I suppose."

Bess stilled, and did not look toward that gentleman. He sat at the other side of the table, next to the Duke. He was not far enough away.

And it couldn't be too soon for Dan to be finished with that awful ledger. "Then I'm glad too, Lord Harman."

* * *

THERE WAS no sign of Storey or his green coat in the hotel room, but it had to be his. Even Dan could admit that Bess had some shortcomings—her arithmetic was not the best—but her sense of direction was perfect.

Sending Jack to watch the boardwalk and leaving Jackie outside the door, Dan could finally concentrate.

Think like a criminal. Where would Storey want that ledger? Within reach, but not easy to find.

Carefully, methodically, Dan examined all the walls from above his head to the floor. Every piece of furniture. He flipped over the straw ticking, untied it, rummaging through.

He was so close. Not just to the ledger, but to finishing this for Bess.

His old plan had turned to dust. He could no more deliver Bess into the arms of a money-hungry London merchant than he could cut off his own head.

But give Bess her own home? With him in it?

The Grand H. was dead. No one to judge him but Bess. And if he made her happy? That was all he'd ever wanted, after all.

Wouldn't it be all right then for him to be happy too?

He wanted her to want *him*. Even now he could taste her lips, the feel and the smell of them like apricots in sunshine. He was hungry for another taste. For her to wrap her arms around him again like she had earlier, and last night. For her to lean into him and trust him.

So hungry for her that an apple and some sea biscuit was all he needed to keep working into the wintry night.

* * *

HE FOUND NOTHING. Nothing under the floorboards, even in the nearby rooms. There was no trace of the ledger, and as the moon rose higher and higher, his spirits sank low.

He *would not* come this far and fail.

But had no idea what to do next.

One foot on the chair, he balanced to the side of the

window frame as he looked out, checking to see Jack was still there.

Jack was, and he knew his job. He wasn't just lurking in the shadows. No, he'd struck up a conversation with some cove in a boat, pointing and having a fine time as the boat bobbed just below the edge of the boardwalk. The tide was high.

If Storey had arms a few yards long, Dan would bet he'd have hidden his ledger just under the edge of the boardwalk. Sure, some sailor might see it when the water was low; but it was more likely they'd never pay it any mind.

Looking around himself again, Dan tried to imagine what Mr. Storey could have done without leaving this room. He *didn't* have arms yards long, so...?

Nothing under the chair. The floor was spotless. The glass panes in the window, slightly waving his view with their nearly invisible changes in thickness, were spattered with sea spray, but they hid nothing.

The nearly full moon ducked behind a thick cloud, dimming the night. Dan opened the window and leaned out.

The cold air was wet; it slapped him with salty mist. He slammed down the sill. Neither the taste nor the temperature appealed.

Then he paused.

Under his hands. Had the windowsill rocked?

He pushed slightly. It had. Its frame had, to be more specific.

Looking around to check no one was watching, mindful of his silhouette in the window, Dan rocked the window's sill again. It moved.

Grasping it, he gently pulled.

It came up.

There within the wall, between the shingles and the lathe, wedged a worn book with a gray, bent cover.

Swallowing, fingertips grasping it carefully, carefully lest he drop it into the wall and lose it completely, Dan lifted it out.

Then ducked below the window so he couldn't be seen.

There was just enough light from the candle to see the pages.

But, ugh. They were so hard to read without his spectacles. It was like being a boy again, but worse, because he knew the writing should be clear. He pushed his eyes into every kind of shape—tight, wide open—trying to find the right one to see.

Yes, there were symbols he knew, as well as the familiar shape of numerals, some done in new ways. It was funny how a person's handwriting showed even when drawing symbols. The five circles appeared everywhere, still oval like seeds.

This hand had written the scrap Bess found in the fireplace. The five circles looked the same.

They still meant money.

He could do this. He could read this. He just had to force his eyes to work.

And he had to take notes.

Taking slips of paper out of his pocket and laying them on the floor with a pencil, he began.

BESS WAITED SO LONG for Dan's distraction that when it came, she nearly didn't recognize it for what it was.

The commotion in the hallway made little sense. The servants had raised voices.

"Miss! The family is at supper."

"If you'll wait here."

"Let me take that bottle for you."

"Won't you have a seat—"

The door burst open, and the dark-haired woman from the hotel leaned an arm against the door-jamb, a graceful leaning *S* with a bottle of nameless liquor in her hand.

She surveyed them all coolly and announced into the silence, "I heard the Duke had arrived!"

The gentlemen all stood, rattling the long table.

Her dark eyes raked up and down the formidable Duke. "Well, that must be you."

Bedlam immediately broke out.

Waresham charged at the woman, so fast that Lord Harman had to move quick to put himself between them. He and Waresham started a low, intense argument while Lady Dunsby, hands fluttering, wrestled herself out of her chair and moved slowly toward Agatha.

Bess joined the ladies, dinner gloves clutched in her hand.

Lady Dunsby ducked her head. "Isn't that—"

"It's Miss Thorpe, madam," affirmed Agatha, shooting a guilty look toward Bess as she incriminated the woman. "You remember her. There was a scandal...?"

"And here's another," said her mother briskly.

From inside the fray, Miss Thorpe's voice rose. "It's a cold night at the end of England; give me some supper. I'm not here to seduce anyone's sons."

Lady Dunsby's eyes widened. "You and Bess must retire." She looked about; there were no footmen. "Take some platters and amuse yourself in your room. Don't come out."

The argument around Miss Thorpe now included Madame Franck, never one to miss an opportunity to scold snot-filled young men. The Duke watched as if he were a soldier at the theater, standing with his hands clasped behind him, wide chest thrust forward. Vellot scowled in his seat; Lord Zachary slouched in his, blond head leaning on his fist as he watched as if composing a painting of it all in his head.

Lady Winpole served herself more rabbit.

No one saw Bess scoop up a chicken and the rest of the tarts.

Agatha followed her lead, snatching a small bowl of French beans from the table and dashing after her through a side door.

In the little withdrawing room, Bess used the napkin she'd lifted to wrap the tarts. "I must go out," she said, a little breathless, which startled even her. She hadn't been running. Only waiting to go to Dan's side. How that had taxed her she didn't know.

"Not really!"

"Yes, really." Bess handed Agatha two of the tartlets, stacked the chicken platter atop the beans. "I must take some dinner to Mr. Burton."

"Isn't he just above?" Agatha looked as interested as she was confused, silvery curls bobbing by her face as she watched Bess' quick movements.

"No," said Bess firmly. "He isn't. Unless anyone asks after him. You understand?"

"Enough."

Bess darted away without another word.

In the hall she saw a maid helplessly holding a cloak, as if wondering what to do with it.

"I'll carry that for you," she hooked a finger in the fabric and had it before the maid could react.

And disappeared down the hall.

CHAPTER TWENTY-SIX

It took seconds to hide herself in the stolen cloak and let herself out the French windows.

It was a longer journey around the entire side of the house toward the front. But at least if anyone saw her they wouldn't know it was Elizabeth Page, Lady Agatha's companion.

Even at the front of the house no one recognized her, because no one was there. Only the Russian apple-selling girl, looking longingly at the waiting cab and its driver. No doubt Miss Thorpe's.

"Get in," Bess muttered behind the girl, making her jump.

She scrambled to obey, though, and Bess paused name the Falcon Hotel to the driver, then climb in after.

The little cab only had one seat. As it rattled along the rutted road, Bess twisted sideways and tugged on her gloves. "What's your name?"

"Why?"

"So I can use it."

"How?"

"Are all Russians this suspicious?"

"Yes," said the girl, hitching her now-empty basket higher on her lap. "Why don't you tell me *your* name first?"

"Bess," and it felt like the first time she'd ever introduced herself.

She wasn't Miss Page; she wasn't the Tourmaline. With no disguise at all, she was going to see Dan, her Dan, and that was more *her* than anything else she'd ever done.

"Bess," repeated the girl, musingly. "Bess. Sounds like sack of flour hitting floor. So short."

Bess wanted to laugh, then she didn't. Questions of her name stirred up wonderings Bess had put aside years ago. "It is short for Elizabeth, sometimes."

* * *

"THEY LET YOU STEAL THAT HAM," Dan said as he showed Bess the bread he'd nipped from the street-seller's basket.

Since it was illegal to sell bread in the streets, Dan considered that fair.

"It's better than begging," shrugged Bess as she tore her thick piece of mouthwatering ham in two and handed Dan the bigger part. Then she grinned and held open her pocket. Three Eccles cakes sparkling with sugar were tucked inside.

Suppressing a whoop, Dan tilted his head to say they should walk down the street.

They ate on the way; stopping made them vulnerable. It risked being caught, and it risked someone else wanting what they had.

"Is my name Elizabeth?"

Dan choked on his bite of ham.

They had to duck into an alley to be out of sight as Dan coughed, Bess keeping a hand on his arm as though it would keep him safe.

Once he could breathe, he ducked out of the alley to look around, then down at Bess. "Why do you ask?"

"The maid at the inn. A man slapped her rear and called her Bess, and she whacked him in the chest with a tankard and said it's Elizabeth or nothing, that's her name."

The grimy stone around them framed Dan like a painting as Bess looked up at him, waiting for answers.

"I don't know," was all he said.

"Would the Grand H. know?"

"You can ask him," said Dan with one of his fierce-looking scowls.

"He showed me the paper with your name on it. Just Dan. I thought mine would say Elizabeth, but he doesn't have one for me. Why doesn't he have one for me?"

Dan's sharp-edged face looked younger for a moment. "He showed you that?" Like he was embarrassed.

"Why do you look upset?"

"I look mad, not upset."

"That's what you want people to think."

Dan sighed. "He paid money for me. To put me to work."

Bess' own little brows furrowed into a frown. She wasn't trying to dig into Dan's past; she wanted to know about her own. "So he must have done the same for me, right? But he doesn't have a paper."

"He didn't pay for you."

"So where did I come from?"

Babies appeared, Bess knew that. They sprung up all over the mud-spattered streets. People had them everywhere. She must have happened somehow.

She didn't know the details, but she was pretty sure the Grand H. hadn't produced her single-handed.

"I don't know," said Dan, and she knew he was lying.

But he looked close to tears, and nothing made Dan cry, not even the time in a fight when a man twice his size had pulled his arm bone out of its socket. The Grand H. hadn't known what to do, and it had hung like that all day till a forger, Jack by name, had pulled it right.

Bess wanted to know, but not enough to make Dan cry.

Dan always told her what was what. He was bigger than her, and stronger than a whip, and he'd faced down fists, even knives, a hundred times to keep her safe. If he said he didn't know, then she'd take it as truth.

He gave her everything. She could give him that.

* * *

BESS STUDIED the dark features of the girl next to her. "Are you going to tell me your name?"

"Varvara," said the girl, grudgingly.

"Well, that's elegant compared to *Bess*." She looked out the window, stolen plates of food balanced on her knee. She was still hungry. "I wish you had those apples, I'd buy them again." She'd kill for an apple.

Varvara snorted. "With the silver girl's money?"

"Well." When had it ever embarrassed Bess to be taken for a swindler? "She's my friend."

"Such friend I should have." Varvara wriggled a little in the seat, and from some deep pocket pulled a garnet-red apple.

She offered it to Bess a little sheepishly. "I asked too much money anyway. *Voz'mi yabloko, Yelizaveta.*"

The strange sounds tugged at her, in her belly, in her chest. Bess took the apple and turned it over in her hand, studying its skin as if she could read it. "Thank you." It felt hard to say.

"*Spasibo.* Is what you say."

"*Spasibo.*" That felt odd in her mouth too.

"You have good ear. Sounds right."

It sounded right to Bess, too, and that was more

confusing than anything. "So will you work for Lady Winpole?"

"I met her." Varvara just shook her head in a dark cloud of something like revulsion. "Staying in room with her is like throwing barrel of salt on floor. Who needs so much bad luck?"

"I'm sorry for that." Bess was. Money was hard to come by, and at least Lady Winpole had plenty. "You need money to go home, don't you?"

For the first time, Varvara's thin lips settled into a softer shape. "To send mother home, if possible. Me, I would stay. There is an English boy..." She shook her head.

"He wants you?" Bess had to know.

"He wants me," Varvara confirmed. "I know. He says is too poor to marry, but he never see poor in Russia." Then she shrugged, a deeply emotional shrug. "I never see poor in Russia again either if I work for Lady Winpole."

"My—" What was Dan? Her English boy? Her other half? Her air?

She pulled her mind back inside the carriage. "Someone else warned me about Lady Winpole. I don't know why; I rather like her."

Even in the deep shadows around the girl Bess could see her serious expression. "You like fooling yourself about what you see?"

It was a curious thing to say to Bess of all people. She had seen everything in her life; she knew what was what.

Dan had told her so.

Bess just left the girl to her own thoughts and the grassy marsh view till the shapes of the village floated out of the gloom.

When the cab rocked to a stop before the Falcon Hotel, Varvara reached for the door, but Bess motioned to pause. "Good luck."

Varvara gave her a crisp nod. "You too." Then she went.

But Bess didn't need luck. She needed Dan, and he was inside.

When she climbed down from the cab, she unlooped the cloak from around her, letting the icy air claw at the bare skin above her gown.

Its silken blue folds topped with seed pearls around the neck wasn't as showy as some of Agatha's things, but it was finer than anything else she had ever worn. It had been made for her. It was hers.

The only times in her life she hadn't been playing a part was when she was with Dan. She felt that now; it felt like all the other times put together.

She left the cloak on the seat. "Go back for Miss Thorpe," she called softly up to the round cab driver.

She hoped to steal something much more important from Miss Thorpe tonight.

* * *

THE WHISTLING wind cut straight through his corduroy coat and Mr. Storey realized he'd soon have to purchase an overcoat or get out of here.

"How deep is the water?"

"Deep enough," said the surly boatman beside him. He looked up and down the water edge as though measuring it with his eyes. "The Russian ships had no problem as long as they were light."

The light sloshing of the water was the only sound in the night besides the wind and their voices. "It won't be light," warned Mr. Storey. "Any ship I land here will be loaded."

"Then don't land here," the tar said with a shrug. "Take it on up to London. Ye wouldn't unload here if ye had sense."

Mr. Storey already knew that. Gravesend wasn't the place

to unload a ship if he had his way. The marshy land made poor roads, and hauling anything heavy—like timber, or copper—over land all the way to London could double its price.

He was asking because Lady Winpole wanted to know, and when she asked a question, he did not tell her *no*.

"What if a ship needed to drop anchor for a while?"

The tar shrugged again. "Good a place as any."

Perhaps that was Lady Winpole's plan. The ships shouldn't even stop in England, by Storey's reckoning. Cuban owners forced their slaves to dig day and night for copper so Wales had enough to smelt when it ran short of its own ore; the British wanted copper for their entire fleet. Copper had helped keep Napoleon down at Trafalgar, and the Navy was almost superstitiously devoted to wrapping their ships in it. That trade was set.

The way to make Connecticut copper pay would be to sell it to people with no access to the slave-dug stuff. Straight to China, Storey figured.

But ultimately those ships would do whatever Lady Winpole said to do, and so would he.

It put him out, a bit. He had lived and breathed her fortunes for years now; it was past time she took a suggestion of his.

So when he finally slid out of the sailor's donkey cart by the village road, instead of turning toward the Falcon Hotel, he stopped at the dirt corner that led to Belinda's hut. He wanted a little something for himself.

She was poor company, but she was soft, and she was warm.

* * *

IT WAS ABSURDLY difficult to walk into the hotel, not as Miss Page, nor the Tourmaline, but Bess. Just Bess.

She tried putting on one of her characters' walks, or the way they flicked their eyes. Nothing fit. She was Bess tonight, or no one. Before, it had always been easier to be someone else; now it felt impossible.

She passed close by Jackie, wrapped in wool as he lounged by the door under its low rafters, watching the inn's comings and goings; he raised his silver eyebrows. "And who are we tonight?"

She just smiled, kept walking.

He'd never know.

Only Dan would.

She knocked on the right door. *One, four, one.* And waited.

Slid in before it opened very far, placing her dishes on the floor with a quick crouch before standing straight.

To offer Dan her garnet-red apple.

* * *

FOR THE FIRST time in his life, Dan understood some of those old vicar's stories they'd beaten into him at the orphanage.

When they'd talked about the temptation of Eve, they didn't mean the apple.

Dan didn't notice his own steps as they carried him closer, one step, two; then his arms went round her. Bess. Small; strong; soft; impossible.

His whole life since the first moment he saw her.

She melted against him, lithe muscles bending back, letting him fold her into his arms, against his heart.

She must feel how she lit a fire in him, must feel the heat that Dan felt radiating from his body into hers. He whispered, "You're cold."

"Not anymore."

He laid his ear against her ear, warming it, then gave into temptation yet again and turned his face into her neck.

His entire life had been an inescapable chain of yielding to fault after fault, dragging her further and further into a life she didn't deserve.

Like he had all his life, he told himself this would be his last mistake.

He'd wanted to hold her like this since that first moment in the theater when she'd floated across the stage. He'd wanted more than just to hold her, and damned himself to hell.

Now she was here. Some angel, some devil was trying to trick him into believing that dreams came true.

He kissed the soft skin behind her ear, restraining himself from devouring her lips, or the rest of her, the way he wanted to do. He could still make a hash of this. He likely would. But oh, the moment was heaven.

She shivered.

It was his cue to let her go. He tried, but she held on.

"Why did you come?" he asked, so quietly only she could hear, forgetting he was the one who had made it possible.

* * *

WHY HAD SHE COME? To be with him.

It was that simple, and so complicated Bess couldn't say it with words.

So instead she said, "I thought I might help."

He let her go, which she didn't want. Had she said something wrong?

She'd thought for a second she already had him. The sensation of his breath against her skin had made her tremble right down to the bones; she still felt it.

But then he released her when for once she wanted to be trapped.

He looked ragged, worn. He rubbed his eyes with one scarred-knuckle hand. Mr. Burton wore gloves; right now, Dan wore none. "I wish you *could* help. My eyes are nearly crossed and my brain is blistering."

She laid her hand on his forehead. She thought she felt him flinch. Maybe he was afraid of her. Like Madame Franck had been, for a moment.

Well, she'd been afraid of herself last night, for a moment, till he'd reminded her who she was. What was real.

With him as Dan and her as Bess, she had no lines from old plays to deliver. No words for all the things she *wanted* to say. But she could still help, and she owed him. "Are you ill?"

"No, my blood—my spectacles got broken."

More accustomed to seeing him without them than with them, Bess now saw they were gone. "What happened?"

He shrugged. "Bad luck."

That was what he'd always said when some bigger boys caught him in an alley, or some footman landed a few blows during his escape. That was what Dan said over his bruises. Bess' eyes narrowed. "Who turned your luck bad?"

With his one-sided smirk, more of a grimace tonight, he just shrugged. "Like usual. Me."

As she'd done the day before, Bess went and lifted the carved wooden chair. Set it against the wall, too far back from the windows to see.

"Careful," murmured Dan, reminding her that the guttering low candle might cast her shadow on the window despite the heavy curtains.

Grasping his forearms through his coat, trying not to be distracted by their hard warmth, she maneuvered him to sit, then handed him the platter of chicken.

He looked amazed, and suddenly lean from hunger. "There's a whole chicken here."

Seeing his hunger made Bess hungry too. But she'd let him eat first. She'd let him do anything, if it meant staying by her side rather than someone else's. "Eat. I'll read."

And delicately drawing up her blue silk skirts, she sat by his knee the way she had when they were little, and scooped the ledger up off the floor.

As soon as her eyes fell on the page, she felt her soaring spirits sink. It was a mass of scribbles, that was all. How had Dan read any of this? None of it made sense.

Then she noticed a pound sign, a particularly florid example of the familiar slashed *L,* and from there she saw the *p* and *d* that meant pence and shillings.

Then the five hastily stroked ovals made sense. They were supposed to be circles. Those were money.

"Bess, you don't have to," said Dan, devouring nearly a quarter of the chicken in a few bites like a starving wolf.

Or fox.

Wishing she were the better person she'd tried to be for, oh, an hour or two, Bess also wished she'd captured that fox on the green at Lincoln's Inn. She wished she'd carried it out of the city with her own two hands rather than let it be hunted again.

She also wished she'd paid more attention when Dan had tried to teach her arithmetic.

The lines in front of her weren't solely numbers, nor was everything familiar. "What does this oval with two loops mean?"

"I've been trying to decide."

"Let me think." It wasn't a boat; the picture for *boat* was clear enough. She couldn't think of another thing that had that shape. Certainly not with a loop on each end. What had loops like that?

She looked at the platter in Dan's hands, trying to ignore Dan's strong, scarred hands to see the porcelain. It was oval, not round. And it had no handles.

Handles.

"Dan, could it be a kettle?"

"Who does business in kettles?" His brow furrowed as he ate, thinking; she watched him think. Who could possibly think him evil just because the lines of his face fell a little crooked? "Maybe not kettles exactly. Iron?"

She couldn't look away. His tongue swept across his deep bottom lip, and she felt herself flush as she realized he must taste of chicken, but better. Still her mind ticked on. "Copper pots cost more."

"*Copper.* Bess, you're brilliant." He reached for the ledger in her hands, then stopped himself. "I can't leave it for Storey to find covered in greasy fingerprints."

"I'll hold it for you."

Bess had the uneasy feeling that she was one step away from the role of a foolish woman being robbed of her virtue in a stairwell. She found she didn't care about her virtue.

She didn't even care about looking foolish.

The feeling was new, and not entirely welcome. But it explained words that had never made sense to her before.

I can't help myself.

* * *

EJECTING Miss Thorpe from Road's End proved surprisingly difficult, even though several people gave it their concerted effort. Lord Harman, in a fit of chivalry, refused to let anyone lay hands on her, not even Waresham.

It was all more fuel to the fire raging inside Lord Vellot, the fire that was burning down hopes and dreams he'd spent decades putting into place.

Eventually the maids of the house, overseen by a firm Mrs. Frank, safely packed a loudly singing Miss Thorpe into her hansom cab. They sent the cab down the road, gleeful choruses about sailing away from Spanish ladies escaping its windows.

This caused the British ladies Carrollton and Dunsby to retire to their chambers, overcome with nameless emotion, while the young men went to the front parlor to steal Lord Carrollton's cigars.

Vellot had only Lady Winpole left to stand inadvisably close as he stared into the dining room's small fire, trying to rearrange the ashes of what was falling down all around him. She tossed another match into his soul. "I don't see your plans developing as you expect."

He kept tight hold of his fury. She was not a suitable target for it. "I'm not through yet."

"I imagine Napoleon feels the same way. Is that your sympathy for him, do you think?"

Vellot clenched his teeth. "My plans require only slight modification."

"I don't think so. Talbourne must have had wind of your intentions, or he'd be here. Gravenshire has no interest in matters abroad. Everyone knows it."

"Yet Gravenshire *is* here. And was at the fort. Talbourne may have an inkling, but he sent Gravenshire to do his work. So the ministers' plans have not changed. Nor have Lady Carrollton's; her bonfire night *soirée* tomorrow will celebrate the ambassador's departure. Just before he goes, he'll be here, within my grasp."

"Intending to do just as he was told in London. He'll get no last-minute orders from Gravenshire."

"He'll get them from *me*." Vellot's fists gripped the air, his mind already imagining the persuasions he must use to convince the man quickly. It wouldn't be easy to make the man believe his orders were the exact opposite of what the ministers had instructed him to do. Vellot's persuasions would have to be tied to something the ambassador desperately wanted; Vellot would have to find out what that was. In very short order.

"And Gravenshire?"

"The unfortunate assassination of a duke was always meant to convince wavering friends to be firmer in their convictions," Vellot reminded her, in a voice of quiet iron. "One duke serves as well as another for that purpose."

The Duke of Gravenshire had a dark shadow inside him that was easy to see and easier to touch. With a little more time at his disposal, Vellot might well convince him to put an end to himself.

It would be an interesting experiment. But at this moment in history, Vellot needed an assassination.

He had many weapons in his arsenal; if his first choice didn't serve, he had another. No one went into battle with just one weapon.

"Have another cake and go knit with your friends," he told Lady Winpole before he strode from the room.

Leaving her looking after him with narrowed eyes that said she did not appreciate his tone. Not at all.

CHAPTER TWENTY-SEVEN

Much as she wanted to help, Bess had to turn the ledger back to Dan once he'd wiped his hands clean. He wanted to read so much faster than she could puzzle the meaning.

As when they were children, she couldn't keep from hanging over his shoulder.

"Is that a man?" She hoisted herself over him, pointing at the book.

"No, *man* is the slash that looks like a numeral *one*."

"So what's this?"

"I don't know." Sighing, Dan put the ledger down on the floor again and rubbed his eyes. "Fuck, I can't see."

He was so hunched over. The Dan of her memory was constantly crouching, leaning, hunching. It had to be painful.

She eased off his coat so he could stretch his arms gratefully in the cold room.

Before he could sweep up the ledger again, she put her hands to the sides of his neck.

He froze at her touch.

Silently, she squeezed the rod-like cords of muscle there. They were locked solid.

Calling to mind the parts of *varma kalai* that hadn't interested her before, Bess tried to trace what should be a flow of life through his skin, his muscles.

Found a place that needed release. Pressed it with her fingers.

Dan grunted. It sounded surprised.

Surely he'd say if it felt bad. Bess did it again.

The hard knots of his spine chased each other down. She tried to picture each bone. She'd seen the spines of animals, at butchers'; Dan wasn't an animal, but in common with them, he was flesh and blood and bone.

When she found another locked place and released it, he made a small, muffled moan.

The sound made her knees weak.

How could it cut through her like that? It was such a curious combination of man and animal, pain and pleasure. And it spoke straight to her insides without using one word.

"You've done enough," she murmured and, mustering the sort of courage it took to climb a house in the dark, draped herself around his shoulders, her ear against his.

He'd always been her guiding star. Surely he knew by now she would always return. That all she wanted was to be here, with him.

She couldn't help herself.

She couldn't see his face, but his voice was hoarse. "Bess, don't tempt me more than I can take. Don't you want a home? Safety? Regular meals, damn it all?"

"I want someone who thinks I'm perfect."

* * *

HE'D NEVER BEEN able to tear himself away from her. Not from that first minute.

His hands knew the shape of her and were hungry to feel it again. His gut, his mouth, his heart felt hollow; he was desperate to fill himself with all her fire. She should be in his arms; he should wrap himself around her and never let go.

It was like a slow dance where they both knew the steps. He reached for her; she let him lever her around his body, into his arms, hers around his neck.

It *must* be his fault they fit together like two trees who had grown this way.

She deserved better than those marionette boys with their flapping collars and inflated pride.

She also deserved better than Dan.

After all, the only thing he knew for certain he'd never done wrong was loving her. It was his finest feature.

"Bess," he said, and then the rest of the words didn't mean anything anymore, so he kissed her.

She was perfect; the kiss was perfect too, fast and dangerous and sly, like Bess.

And shy too, and hesitant, and that came close to breaking his heart.

She kissed him like she wanted to learn the shape of him all over again. Her fingers trailed down over the muscles in his neck, then up into the ends of his hair; her thumb brushed the edge of his ear, making his blood pound.

She had never been so soft, and he wondered how she was doing it.

Then her muscles clenched, and with the agility of an acrobat and the grace of a ballerina, she pulled herself up into him, up, his shoulders her windowsill to cling to, twisting, trusting him to help.

In a movement he'd never imagined anyone could do, and that he would remember for the rest of his life, she folded one leg close to her chest then extended it under his arm so she could wrap her legs around his waist, using all four of her limbs to hold him close.

With a maneuver she couldn't have learned on the stage she settled fully onto his lap and hiked her gown high, as high up her thighs as the garters of those black stockings she'd worn on stage must have been. Dan's mouth watered. He'd never been as hungry for food as he was for her in that moment.

He couldn't help but support her. His hands spread under her strong thighs, pulling her close, holding her up.

Some shocked piece of his brain mumbled that she didn't know what she was doing, but that was too stupid to say. She knew what she was doing. What she was offering.

And she kissed him again.

She wasn't only kissing his lips; she brushed against the tip of his nose, smoothed a kiss over the edge of his cheekbone, too. As if his face were as lovely as hers. As if *he* were perfect.

It was the sweetest thing she'd ever done, and it did break him.

"Bess, we can't," he whispered against her lips, breathing in her breath.

And Bess, who always charged ahead, blinked in his arms, confused. "Then why did you kiss me?"

"Because I had to."

"Don't stop. I can be good, Dan, really I can. I won't steal any more. Nothing to get me tossed in prison." She winced, and he thought she'd cut herself on him somehow; then he realized she was looking at her hand. At the sapphire winking on her finger. It flashed out of the corner of his eye. Bess studiously ignored it. "I'll even take that ring back."

"Do you know whose it is?"

A thoughtful pause, her expressive face looking into the

distance over his shoulder, like she was composing the lie she had to tell. He'd never blame her. *He'd made her the way she was.*

Then she met his eyes squarely and stuck to the truth. "I'll find out."

It was this glimpse of her, the Bess she could have been, should have been, that pushed Dan over the edge. His selfish plan wouldn't work with an unselfish Bess. He couldn't lie to her.

He couldn't lie to her anymore.

"Bess, your whole life is my fault."

* * *

BESS SHOOK HER HEAD. He must get over this mad need to heap himself with scorn. "You *gave* me my life. You give me everything." Why did Dan think that made a difference at this moment, when Bess felt like she was about to dive off the stage into reality?

"No," he said heavily, "you don't know."

The way he looked, like he was in pain, cooled Bess' skin. Where a moment before she was ready to discover anything and everything he could do to her that could be called *inappropriate*, now he looked like he wanted to be anywhere but here with her, and that, more than anything, made her slip out of his grip when she'd rather stay.

She slid off his lap, feeling small, feeling foolish, and sat back on the floor, only inches away. Folded her legs under her on the chilled oak beams, and stared at him.

"I—" He met her eyes and started again. The pain in those dark depths changed them; the diamonds there shimmered like tears. "Everything you've been through, it's all my fault."

"That doesn't make sense." It didn't. "You always fed me and found me. I'm still angry with you for not saying a word after you left me with Madame Franck, but it wasn't so bad." She hated to admit it, but she was trying to be good.

"It's my fault you were there in the first place. With the Grand H. In the gutter. You never should have been there at all."

Bess began to feel the cold of the floor. "What do you mean?"

"I stole you."

The words made the world spin.

The sensation was too similar, far too similar to the way she'd felt when she was in a room with the Silver Duke. The world was gone, and so was she. Like the blank white paper had carried her away and she didn't know where she was or why.

Dan kept talking, and it was like falling.

* * *

HE'D STOLEN BEFORE, when ordered, or out of desperation. This was the first time he had a choice.

He had no idea of his age, but he was little, and quick.

No one saw him steal the apple, and no one saw him give it to the tiny girl with golden ringlet hair.

She was crying, pushing back into the knobbled stone wall behind her and crying. Calling for mama. Breaking Dan's heart.

It helped the crime that most people were watching the carriage accident in the middle of the road. Pushing and shoving and trying to see and, in some cases, when they did see, screaming.

The screaming didn't help anyone's composure, not Dan's, and certainly not the little girl's.

The tears weren't from hunger, as she refused to take Dan's apple.

Dan had no memories of his mother. He remembered the orphanage and its packs of wild children, dirty and hungry and frightened all the time, and sad-looking women tossing bread to him. Until the Grand H. took him in.

But he was smart, smart enough to know this little girl's mama had left her there, or, as it seemed likely, had just died in the middle of the street.

The orphanage would have her soon.

Dan couldn't have that.

Even though he was so young, smaller children shied away from Dan, with his permanent air of angry distance and his burnt-black hair.

But this little girl wasn't frightened of him. When he leaned down to pick her up, she put out her hands.

The crowd was growing, people elbowing each other aside to see. If he left her there, she might be trampled.

No one who deserved her would leave a treasure like her on the pavement. He was too little to know all those words, but he knew the truth.

She laid her head against his shoulder. She stopped crying for her mama. Maybe because mama wasn't coming.

Dan knew what that felt like. The beginning of hopelessness.

No one stopped him.

So he took her.

* * *

"The Grand H. was angry as hell."

Dan just kept talking, while Bess wondered if she'd lost her mind.

Had he given her opium, like the Silver Duke had done? Was that why she was spinning in this lake of impossibility, unable to understand what he said?

"He tried to find your parents, or said he did." Dan sounded bitter. That made no sense either. "By the time he got back to the corner, or what I thought was the corner, nothing was there."

"You... took me?"

"You see what I did to you? Someone would have come. Someone would have found you. If I'd just stayed there. I should have just stayed *there*."

"You said I could have been trampled."

"I thought so then. I've lived it again a million times since, wondering how I should have done differently. You'll never know how I wish I could do it over again, do it different."

"A million times?" None of it made sense.

A little boy who'd found a crying little girl, that made perfect sense. An accident; an apple. Bess had seen accidents; they happened. Children lost their parents; that happened too.

It made no sense that Dan had remembered that story a million times and *never told her*.

She pushed herself to her feet. She felt heavy. Even awkward.

She'd felt like this before, like she might fall off the world.

She'd felt like this the night by the fire, with the Silver Duke talking, telling her things she didn't want to believe, always telling, telling, till she didn't know *who* she was. Till she didn't know what was true or even real.

Then, she'd been able to think: *Dan.*

Now she had nothing.

More lost than she'd ever been before.

Bess wanted to say something, but didn't know what. What could she say? What did words matter?

The Silver Duke's betrayal had made her feel sick, stupid, hollow, frail.

This one made her feel as if she didn't know her own name. *She didn't.* The world *had* no center. Spinning without a center sent a person flying, and Bess felt like she was doing just that, flying into senseless space. She was lost, not just now, but always had been, and always would be.

The Silver Duke was evil. He needed killing.

But Dan?

She had no words. They froze solid and fell away, and it felt like they took her skin with them.

Raw, aching, she left him there.

* * *

"BESS!" hissed Jackie. "Didn't Dan give you a coat?"

Bess just walked past him, her eyes seeing nothing. None of the feelings had words. *Lies* were top of mind, and for once, none of them were hers.

Jackie trotted after her.

A million times. She could have imagined Dan forgetting the story. Perhaps remembering it when he got older. But he'd remembered it all, remembered it every minute they knew each other, all their lives. And he hadn't told her.

He'd lied when she'd asked.

"Here, sir." Jackie waved at the sleepy driver of a rickety cab outside the Falcon. It wasn't Miss Thorpe's cab, but apparently the little town had at least two.

Bess just stood in the outside air; it whipped against her, but she didn't feel it any more than would a statue.

Lies were normal; Bess lived in lies. This was something different. She'd always felt like Dan had known her. Here was something he'd known *about* her and hid.

Stealing her indeed.

"Take this." Jackie slid his heavy coat over the shoulders of her thin gown. She felt the warmth instantly envelope her, but it didn't get past her skin.

At the last second, he climbed into the cab with her. It set off.

Too rickety to seal well, its window shades flapped in their frames, letting the icy fingers of November air reach through.

That Bess didn't feel either. She saw it, though, in the little cloud of ice roiling in front of her face when she breathed. The icy air felt like *morals.*

"Bess."

She desperately wanted to borrow someone else's emotions right now. The awkward girl she'd pretended to be in the theater audience; quieter Miss Page. Unfortunately, what she had stored inside that came pouring out were the feelings of the wronged Queen Dido, who hadn't cried either, just crawled off to die.

"Bess."

It wasn't that she'd put too much faith in Dan's honesty. She'd put too much faith in *Dan.* She couldn't imagine the Dan she knew keeping something so important from her for so long. Forever, really.

He hadn't just kept it from her. He'd made her *not want to know,* and that was far worse.

She'd *picked* the Silver Duke from the throng of her admirers. She'd also always stuck close to Dan wherever they went. She'd *chosen* to let them twist her, shape her. There was something wrong with her. She was strong and fast, but her mind was too easy to mold. No wonder she *couldn't help herself.*

She felt hands taking one of hers, and she jerked.

When she looked, really looked, Jackie had both his hands high as if she'd warded him off with a pistol, and her hand was pointed at his throat.

"What do you want?" It didn't feel like her voice.

His usually sparkling dark eyes were serious under the lock of white hair peeking out from his bowler hat. "What happened?"

"I don't know." She didn't.

"Did Dan—" He paused at an unvoiceable thought, then voiced it. "Did Dan hurt you?"

"Yes."

He made a sound like *he'd* been shot, and shifted in his seat, still with his hands up. "What should I do?"

"Nothing. Leave me alone."

"I can't just leave you like this. Bess. Whatever Dan did, whatever he said—he didn't mean to hurt you."

"Yes, he did." That was the worst of it. Dan had kept the truth about her from her all those years on purpose. Trained her not to ask about it on purpose. Like a puppet. A toy.

A pet. Like a guinea pig.

Bess dropped her hand.

The cab rolled on, frozen ruts in the dirt road making its seat rock.

Jackie, never at a loss for words, seemed to search for them now.

The shapes of the village faded away around the edges of the flapping window shades before he found something to say. He hunched himself down, near but keeping his distance.

"Then we'll kill him together," he said, and the words jerked Bess out of her stillness, flattened her against the thin wall next to her seat as she backed away from him. "Sometimes it's the people closest to you that deserve no mercy. They show the rest of the world one face but you know the truth of it. Just tell me that's Dan, and I'll believe you. Because we've known each other since you were tiny, and I've no right to tell you what you know."

From Jackie, who had known Dan just as long, it was more than a kind offer.

It was as if her childhood gave her permission to be, to think, in a drowning ocean.

It let her talk.

"Dan doesn't deserve killing," Bess heard herself say. "He didn't hurt me like you think." She banished the memory of his arms from her mind, trying to stuff it down into the dark unquestioning deep where she'd put her wonderings about where she came from. "It was more than hurting my feelings." She tried to find the sensation and put a word to it. "He hurt my trust. No, I think he destroyed it."

"Ah." Putting his hands down, Jackie looked no less sorrowful. He seemed to understand exactly how bad that was. Then he put into words what she wanted to say. "Between the two of you? With all you are to each other? That's too much. Hurts too much."

That was it. It hurt too much to bear.

"What *have* we been to each other?" The cab was rolling near the front of the house, and Bess opened the door while it was still rolling. Called to the driver, "Stop here." It lurched to a halt.

She turned back to Jackie. "Was I only ever a pet to him?"

"A pet?" The man's round little cheeks weren't smiling now; he shook his head somberly. "Child, I'll believe whatever you say. I know you can tell the truth; but you know Dan even better. You know he's been at your beck and call all your life."

"There are people," Bess choked out, "who disguise themselves that way, but secretly pull the strings of you. Using you the way *they* want."

"And is that Dan? Only you would know."

Feeling she had no answer, Bess slipped out the door.

"Keep the coat," Jackie said when she tried to offer it to him through the open cab door. "I'll fetch it tomorrow."

With no more words, she shut the little carriage door and latched it, and the driver took that as his signal to move on.

She faded back into the dark grass and watched the cab leave Road's End.

It rolled past the new front door and its pillars, and with a sick jolt she saw the Silver Duke—Vellot—open the front door himself, and peer out as it rolled by.

As if he were waiting for someone. Maybe waiting for her.

Jackie leaned out the rolling cab's window and blew Vellot a kiss.

* * *

DAN TRUSTED Jackie to look after Bess once she walked out his door more than he trusted himself.

He'd said it. She hated him now. It was done.

It should have been a relief; he'd waited to do it his whole life.

He felt no relief. Only bone-crushing sadness. It was done, she'd gone, she wouldn't come back. His whole life, dust in an instant. The one person who thought he was worth something now knew he was worthless.

Time would only make her realize more. How every pain, every hungry night, every dangerous minute of her life had been his fault, not the Grand H.'s.

She'd never know how he owed her *everything.* Every good impulse he'd ever had. He realized stealing was dangerous, then wrong, because he saw her doing what he did and he feared for her. He looked for clean food because he wanted it for her. He'd taught himself arithmetic so he could count coins... for her.

He'd have swung from the hangman's noose long ago had it not been for what Bess needed. What Bess was.

It was easy to be cynical in the streets; everyone wanted, everyone needed. There was generosity, but there was more greed. Desperation bred vehemence.

He'd had the gift of one truly innocent person in his life

who needed him.

He still thought of her that way. She liked to steal, yes; she liked to cross the law, and she liked to lie. But from the minute he'd seen her, she'd been in his power. She'd shown him without having to lift a finger that if he didn't do the right thing, *she* would pay the consequences.

She'd been more than his heart; she'd been his conscience, the victim of his greatest sin, and his reason for living.

All without knowing what she did. He'd put it on her.

Or the Grand H. had put it on him.

Unable to let his horror out by breaking anything in the room, his long-honed animal instinct reminding him *he'd be discovered, it would show,* Dan sank down to the floor in the same spot where he stood, hunched into himself, hands sinking into his own hair, pulling it till he felt it start to tear.

This was why he'd turned to numbers. They were clean. Simple.

Never his fault.

He'd felt a conviction that day, the second he'd picked her up off the pavement, out of the shoving and screaming, that she was safer that way. It was hard to think back and realize how young he'd been, how small. Hard to give that little boy mercy. He should; that little boy had been right.

He just hadn't known better than to carry the child away.

Dan could blame the Grand H., and he did. He'd taught Dan to steal, to put anything valuable in his pocket and carry it off. Dan had known Bess was valuable and he'd taken her. It could be that simple.

But it wasn't. He'd known all his life it hadn't been that simple. He'd wanted her to keep. Wanted something of his own. Some*one* of his own.

She'd given him the first hug he could remember, and he'd wanted more.

Greed. It was what made men steal, what made them lie

to their ledgers, what made them cruel. It was why he'd had to leave Bess with Madame Franck all those years ago. He knew himself. He knew his own greed.

Now Bess knew it too.

His eyes fell on the ledger.

He could still get her the money. She could still live her own life. Married or not. To whomever she chose. If Dan earned Fitz' pay, he could give it to Madame Franck at least, and trust her to set up Bess properly.

Bess couldn't ever know who she'd been, because of him. But she could become anyone she liked... as long as he got her the money.

The ledger was just far away that he could see a page of it clearly. Had his tears worked like lenses over his eyes? Surely they couldn't help.

But he saw, as if lit with flame, that several signs he had taken to mean *plus* were longer at the bottom, dipping below the ledger line.

Like a cross.

Like a knife.

Falling on the book he gripped it in both hands. It was nearly impossible to see. They were blurs close in, and he shoved the book away.

Stood and stared at it.

Those weren't pluses.

The slash up-and-down that looked like *one* and also like *man* stood beside each one, and they didn't end at the line like a plus sign. They dipped below it. Every time.

In Mr. Storey's meticulous hand, they didn't mean *plus one*. They meant *kill man*.

The problem of Bess discovering his guilt had been brewing since they were children. It was done now, the limb cut off. His heart ripped out.

But he could still ensure her freedom.

CHAPTER TWENTY-EIGHT

*B*ess couldn't risk crossing paths with the Silver Duke. Not now; perhaps not ever. She felt too raw for that, and had just run from Dan for the first time in her life.

In the freezing cold, she darted lightly through the grass, soaking her slippers with frost.

At the end of the old wing stood the kitchen. Servants still stirred in there, washing, cooking, making life more pleasant for the owners.

She wanted to scream at them, *you're foxes; run!* But they wouldn't understand.

And she didn't want to say *fox* ever again either.

A spiderweb of vines spread over the bricks joining the old house and the kitchen corridor. A spiderweb that went up.

Vines were not to be trusted with her weight. Dan had told her that a million times.

Faith in Dan destroyed, she could do whatever she wanted.

As she felt for the roots, testing their depth, feeling they might hold her slight weight, she considered the idea as she climbed toward the high perch.

She could do *anything* she wanted. Go wherever she wanted. Steal whatever she wanted.

Kill, if she took the notion.

She caught the hem of her dress, heard it tear. It didn't matter. The dress wasn't hers. Nothing was.

At the edge of the roof, Bess' fingers just barely caught on the slate. Cold, the stone's edge felt sharp enough to slice her skin; that too she ignored.

Instead, she swung an arm into open air, trying to catch the sill of the window in the main house wall just opposite. She couldn't quite reach.

Recklessly, she let her weight swing back, then pulled herself forward again, building up the motion of her own weight so she swung back and forth like a self-winding pendulum.

At the last second, she let go.

The windowsill was just enough below the arc of her falling upstretched arm that, as she fell, her hand caught. She stopped her own fall, breathless with the knowledge that no one stood below to catch her.

That slowed her. If she was truly alone, she had to take care. There was no one to save her.

There never really had been.

Carefully she pulled her weight up, pushed on the window.

It didn't open.

She'd finally run into a spot she couldn't escape. There was no one below her and no one in front of her. She'd come round this way to escape the Silver Duke's poison, forgetting that also meant no one expected her inside.

Bess looked down. If she fell, she might avoid breaking

her legs; there were rosebushes below the window. Bare, thorny rosebushes.

If she hit them wrong, she could claw her own eyes out.

Swinging on her fingertips from a windowsill, Bess asked herself why she hadn't simply brazened it out. Walked in through the kitchen. What did she care if the servants thought her a hussy? They weren't writing her letters of reference.

Dan had been right about some things. She moved too fast, she didn't think things through, and she shouldn't say she owed him.

Mustering a great effort for a last one-armed heave upwards, she struck the metal glazing of the window with her other hand, hoping desperately it would open, not break.

Slowly the glass swung out. She watched to see if it would scrape her fingers; when it got close, she reacted, moving one hand out of its swiveling path, then the other.

Madame Franck leaned out and looked down.

"The windows open outwards, child," she said. Number one. Disapproving housewife.

* * *

BESS THOUGHT her humiliation complete until Madame Franck finished hauling her over the windowsill. There was another tearing sound. She winced.

The gown didn't feel *hers* any longer, as she wasn't sure who *she* was. But it had been pretty.

Then her humiliation dropped to a new low, as just behind Madame Franck stood Lady Dunsby.

Her ladyship's sausage-like curls trembled with agitation. "What are you *doing*, Miss Page?"

Madame Franck, with more presence of mind than Bess had at the moment, gestured toward a door. There was clearly going to be conversation, and it shouldn't be in a hallway.

Lady Dunsby shook her head. That was Dan's door, at the end of the hall where Lady Carrollton had put all of them as guests. Bess tried to find it funny.

And whispered, "He's not in there."

Lady Dunsby's eyes widened more.

Madame Franck just ushered them in and closed Dan's door.

She hissed rather than shouted. "Where have you been? Your hands are nearly blue. You'll catch your death of cold, and how can you dance if you're dead?"

"Dance? I wouldn't hear of it. Miss Page, if you expect to marry *anyone* of substance, you shall not dance tomorrow night at all. Dancing is a means of putting yourself on display, and the dancing would only shine more light on your..." She looked Bess over as if trying to find one feature on which to pin fault. "On your everything."

"I don't want to marry. And I don't want to dance." She turned as if to leave. Her limbs were all freezing cold, and she didn't want this lecture.

"You *must* be ill," fretted the Madame, "Dancing is your life!"

That made Lady Dunsby turn her consternation on Madame Franck. "Miss Page is not a chorus girl, Mrs. Frank!"

"Indeed, she is not! How dare you think such a thing? She is a *ballerina!*"

Under the circumstances, number three, protective mother, felt a bit much.

Bess turned back to both of them. "I am not a dancer. I am not a thief. I am not a temptress or a companion or anything at all. I'm no one."

She'd never been no one before.

At the very least, she'd always been Bess, the one right next to Dan.

Madame Franck hugged her fiercely, torn gown at all. In Bess' ear she whispered, "You are all those things and more."

The hug felt nice, but its warmth didn't penetrate.

Bess contemplated for a moment the mechanics of a woman made of ice who could still walk.

Lady Dunsby did not give up. Balanced on her canes, she stood, firm as a castle. "Miss Page. These moments of despair are natural, especially when one has..." She glanced toward Bess' torn hem. "...strayed. That does not put a home of your own, a kind husband, *love,* out of reach."

"Lady Dunsby, I apologize. I never wanted a home of my own, or a kind husband, or love. Not as such. I only wanted—"

She would not say his name.

Madame Franck saw something in her face. "Did you two fight?"

"Who two?" Now Lady Dunsby's plump cheeks nearly eclipsed her eyes, narrow as they were with suspicion.

"No." Bess felt her head hang. It hadn't been a fight.

"Child, if you are lost—"

Bess' head blazed up. *"Don't* say *in the wilderness.* I'll scream."

"If you are lost, where do you want to go? What would be home?"

This confused Lady Dunsby again. "London, obviously. What are you both on about?"

Dan would be home.

She *had* no home but Dan. She never had. Maybe there had been a house once, with a parent or two, some sort of place to which she belonged, but she'd never known about them. Never *thought* about them, not really, and that was partly because Dan encouraged her not to, but also partly because she'd never needed to.

Dan had been home and that had made everything simple.

Now that was gone and she should be furious with him, murderously furious, but she wasn't.

She only felt lost—yes, she did feel lost,—and lonely, and cold, and poor. For the first time in her life.

And hungry. And alone.

Dan was all she'd ever really wanted, more than sapphires or silks. But how could she trust him now? After he'd spun her around and made her feel the same way as the Silver Duke?

After he'd taught her what a lie could really be?

"I don't—" Lady Dunsby hushed when Madame Franck stopped her with a raised hand.

"Bess," her teacher said softly, so close they could have touched forehead to forehead, "no one knows the road home but you."

When Bess looked up at Madame Franck's face, she felt, finally, the tears come.

So many women she'd seen betrayed by their longing, their trust, their foolishness. In a second, in a lifetime, they were turned against their own best interests by some man who pulled their strings.

Was that the choice every woman faced? Choosing who would betray them?

Now the tears were so thick she could barely see Madame Franck's face. No numbered roles, just the woman who had housed her and taught her and cared if she lived or died.

"He's not the man I thought he was." Bess' voice broke with a sob.

Madame Franck's hands came up to frame her face. Dry, and warm; strong, and familiar.

"We all contain multitudes," said her teacher. "If you saw a side of him you never expected, that is the nature of courtship. A time to discover what we take with us for the rest of our lives."

"Courtship of who? This is preposterous!" Lady Dunsby thumped a cane, then ducked her head sheepishly, clearly hoping no one downstairs had noticed.

"He might not be what you thought," whispered Madame Franck, "but is he what you need?"

Madame Franck was a foolish romantic. But at her words, the whirlwind in Bess' gut slowed, settled like snowflakes.

Bess did want rings and stage lights and applause. And apples. But all she really *needed* was Dan.

He wasn't what she thought. She didn't owe him anything. She could walk away from him tomorrow; she'd find a way.

But she'd never forget him and she'd never stop needing him, and under her confusion and pain he was still really the only thing she needed in the whole wide world.

She didn't have to submit to that; but she must wrestle with it.

Unwilling to admit anything she didn't fully understand, Bess patted Madame Franck's hands with her own. "I'm not sure yet."

Lady Dunsby tossed her curls with finality. "Well, *I* am sure that this pantomime has gone on long enough. Are you betrothed, Miss Page? And if so, to whom?"

Madame Franck's hands dropped.

Bess curtsied, very sincerely. "I apologize, Lady Dunsby. I never meant to upset you. You've been nothing but kind. I am not betrothed. And I am not Miss Page."

"*What?!*"

This was a bit too far for Madame Franck, who couldn't

countenance breaking character in the best of times. She fluttered in front of Bess, hands waving away the words as if she could make them unsaid. "She means—"

Bess eased her aside.

"I am not Miss Page. I came to settle accounts..." *tell the truth, Bess,* said a quiet voice inside her that sounded a little like Dan, "...I came for revenge on the man you call Vellot. He's hurt me, threatened me, and threatened Madame Franck. I didn't know Mr. Burton would be here. We knew each other... before. In the past. He didn't come because of me. He's here because of—"

It wasn't her secret to tell, but Bess didn't have another lie in her.

"—Lady Winpole."

"Whaaaaat?" Where before Lady Dunsby had nearly shouted, this was quiet. Under her breath.

Bess rushed on. "You mustn't blame him, he's doing something good. Maybe. I don't know anything else about it, but you must let him." Of course she had only Dan's word that it was good, but stupidly, Bess still believed it. Maybe she wanted to believe it. Hopefully Lady Dunsby would let Dan be.

Her ladyship dropped into the room's only chair, staring, open-mouthed, at Bess.

Finally she spoke. "Yes. I know."

Bess' knees couldn't take one more shock. She sank down at Lady Dunsby's feet.

Madame Franck covered her mouth with both hands.

Lady Dunsby stared at Bess as though through one of Agatha's telescopes. Searching. Measuring. Bess did not expect her next words, either. "But how do *you* know? Are you here to help him?" Her soft face hardened. "I won't let you stop him."

"I'm sorry, my lady, but—you *knew?*"

With the same assurance with which she selected lace or engaged a cab just after a gunshot, Lady Dunsby pinned Bess with a level look. "I hope you think better of me than to be used unawares. Yes, I knew. I'd do a great deal more to cross Lady Winpole. I owe her a very old debt. She hurt a great friend of mine whose life was all too short. My friend lived happily all the days she had, but I missed so many of them. We had too few." Her gaze coming back from far away, she added, "Arabella is grasping, unprincipled, and cruel. I've known that longer than you've been alive."

It was Bess' turn to gape. "You never let on!"

"It's useful to be thought stupid, especially around her. I've let her use me to cheat at cards all over the southern counties, just to keep her unsuspecting. She's very dangerous to anyone she thinks a threat. I'm sure she killed that horrible husband of hers; I don't know why, and I don't want to know." Lady Dunsby's lips pressed tight. "I did not think she associated herself with Lord Vellot."

"She doesn't. Or at least, not that I know. Truly. I'm here because he required I be here."

"I'm well aware of Lord Vellot's peculiar corruption." Now Lady Dunsby looked kind, and sad. "Don't worry yourself if he made a fool of you. He's done the same to too many girls. If I wasn't in time to keep you apart, that's not your fault. I wish I had met you sooner." She flushed. "Unless there's a child?"

"No, no! He never... He knows where I live. And Madame Franck. All because I was stupid, and vain, and... I can't spend the rest of my life watching over my shoulder. Trying to keep Madame safe."

Madame Franck's hand settled on her shoulder. "Child, you are not responsible for me," she said softly.

"I'm responsible for *being* a fool. For falling into his trap."

"Well, men offer plenty of those." Lady Dunsby looked

like she wanted to get up and hobble off to bed, then she thought again, settled back. "So, wait—*did* you see Mr. Burton?" She looked about Dan's empty room. "Where is he?"

Bess didn't want to tell.

She also wished she didn't know.

If only she could forget him, wipe him out of existence the way he'd wiped away her questions.

Lady Dunsby waved away the question of Dan's whereabouts.

"Never mind. You stay far away from him, Miss Page, and yes, I'll continue to use the name as it's the one I know. He is engaged in very dangerous work. I have safeguards in place for Agatha should something happen to me, but nothing for you. Anyway, he's still poor." She looked at Bess again with the same fondly calculating look that she'd always had. "You're pretty, you know. Gentlemen don't always care much about the pedigree of a pretty girl. Lord Harman's a bit above your reach, and Waresham's a horror, but Lord Zachary might well be caught. Or the dashing captain across the river."

Standing, Bess carefully avoided her torn hem to curtsey and take Lady Dunsby's hand in her own. "Thank you, my lady." She was well aware Lady Dunsby was offering options that wouldn't require her sponsorship back in London; nor did Bess expect that. "Thanks to Madame Franck, I'm well able to provide for myself. I never wanted any man before, and now I think I'm done with that."

Starting for the door, she looked down at her destroyed gown. "I suppose Agatha will have to help me undress. I don't know what to tell her."

"Tell her whatever you like. She might seem light-headed but she's remarkably sensible."

"Like her mother," Bess smiled over her shoulder as she silently left.

Lady Dunsby just sat, shaking her head till her curls danced around her plump face.

Then she turned to her remaining companion. *"Madame Franck?"* she inquired.

* * *

DAN DIDN'T KNOW how long he stared at the pages with their blood-marks.

Finally he gave his eyes a rest, looking out the window.

From where he sat on the floor he couldn't see Jack, likely freezing his arse off on the dock. He couldn't see the water, or the fort across the river with its torches and haze of smoke.

He could only see the sky.

It was black and empty, the gray of the clouds obscuring all the stars, even themselves. The moon had fled. He might have been riding the globe into a dark void alone.

He'd imagined once the tie was broken he would no longer feel it in his blood. In the back of his mind, ridiculously, he faintly imagined he'd simply lie down and breathe his last.

But the tie wasn't gone. He could still feel it. Every thump of his heart in his chest said *Bess.* Every breath wanted her breath. His eyes, his hands, his whole body was still hungry for her.

It made him pathetic.

It also made him worth something.

He looked back at the book.

Every one of those crosses was a life like his. A life no one thought mattered. They'd still had feelings, maybe even dreams. They'd been as much a man as he was; more. They might have had someone to live for too.

His dreams had floated away in the starless night, but theirs might have come true, if they'd had more time.

He couldn't just take notes and testify. It wasn't enough to convict Lady Winpole of a few bribes. She needed to learn what prison felt like.

Let her find out how to play rackets against its walls.

Scooping up the book, he stuck his head out the door. Jackie was still gone.

"Innkeeper!"

He shouted at the top of his voice; it rang against the rafters. It wasn't long before the little man came bustling up in his shirtsleeves, eyes swollen from the smoke at his hearth.

"Sir?" He rubbed his hands against the dishcloth pinned across his belly as he came.

"I am sorry to put this on you, sir, but I must. You see how I am not the person who took this room."

Just noticing, the man puffed up like an angry bird. "Sir! I must insist...!"

"Keep still. You see I'm here. I have found this book in this room. Take a long look, sir. You see its contents?"

The innkeeper swept his eyes over the open pages of the soft, worn ledger. Dan held it open so he could see; even turned the pages.

"You see these marks? This here?" He showed the tree for *timber.* The ovals for *copper.* "And this?" He pointed to the marks for death.

"I do, but—"

"Just remember you saw them. Remember my face." For once it would be useful. "You can do that, can't you?"

"See here." The man trembled. "I don't want trouble."

"No one does." Dan let his hands fall, one still grasping the ledger, the other clapped the man's shoulder. "I'm sorry to involve you, but if I must, I will. You're the owner, aren't you?"

"I am. And I've a wife and son, so if you think to harm anyone..."

"I don't." Dan hoped he didn't lie. "Go on down; I won't disturb you again. Just remember you saw me, in this room, and what's in this book."

He waited till the man disappeared before following him down. With silent footsteps, just another shadow in the dark.

Knocked the code quietly on Miss Thorpe's door.

When she didn't answer, he swung open the door.

She lay upon the bed, sprawled bonelessly in her crepe gown, and for a moment he feared she was dead.

Then she raised her head slightly. "Shut the door, from the other side."

"Miss Thorpe, I'm sorry to bother you again."

"You should be."

When he went to raise her up, the smell of the whiskey hit him hard. It was heavy stuff. His toe kicked an empty bottle on the floor; he hoped it wasn't the one he'd seen earlier that was half full.

"Miss Thorpe."

She was limp, and uninterested.

"Never mind," he muttered under his breath, letting her fall back to the ticking. Slipping off her shoes, one, then the other, he rolled her till he could peel the coverlet from the bed below her and drape it over her body.

Drunk as she was, he doubted she'd feel the cold till it was too late. He'd seen plenty of people go that way.

"You wouldn't remember anything I told you now anyway." He tucked the edges of the coverlet around her gown, hoping whatever she wore beneath it would be comfortable enough to sleep in.

"I'll remember."

Seeing her eyes open was like watching someone come back to life. He almost stumbled back from superstition before he got hold of himself.

"Will you? Because it's important."

"Yes." She struggled a little towards a more upright position, then just gave up, throwing her arms wide across the narrow bed. She seemed lucid; just very, very drunk. "Important things are easiest to remember, though I doubt it's important to anyone but you. Try me."

"You're going to take Miss Page out of here tomorrow. Not me."

"What?" She struggled again. Gave up again, lay on her elbows giving him a wide-eyed look. "You engaged me specifically to provide you with escape."

"And you will. Escape for her. Her, and a book."

"See here." She fell back again, seemed to feel dizzy; she pressed her hand against her head, then stared at the hand suspiciously. "Oh, it's mine. See here. You seem nice enough, bit thick over your girl, but nice enough. You can't just stay here after that book disappears. I might not know all the details of what you're doing, but that much I can guess. Even drunk as a lord."

"Better me than her. You understand it's not negotiable, right? Because you do want to be paid."

"I do. Heaven help me, I love the money." She narrowed her eyes at him. "You know I'm rich enough not to need it, don't you?"

"That's what I hear. Yet you want paid pretty badly."

"That's right. Miss Thorpe is still rich. You can tell anyone that. Tell everyone you like." Slowly she covered her face with her hands, as if swimming underwater; then she sighed a fat plummy sigh.

Dan had misgivings. "Your escape will work, won't it?"

"Do you think I've been working night and day out in the

marsh—in the *marsh,* Mr. Fox, *in the marsh*—if it won't even work?"

"Yes."

"Well, it will work. Don't you worry about that. Of all the things you have to worry about, that is not one." She rolled her head blearily towards him, shifted under the coverlet. "There's a duke at the manor, you know. Doesn't do to come to their notice. You won't like it."

"I don't plan to," said Dan, and, his future arranged, left her to sleep off the liquor.

CHAPTER TWENTY-NINE

Agatha had been full of quiet questions Bess hadn't answered. She was too empty of these horrible feelings, or too full, and she was dead out of words.

It might not be right to blame Agatha for encouraging her to talk to Dan, but Bess did love a grudge.

Not expecting to sleep, once she lay down on the crisp linen sheets, the world faded away and she sank into slumber like it was her last escape.

When she woke, the watery light of the November sun flickered through the room, and she ruthlessly pushed away the memory that all her dreams had been of Dan.

A wooden tray sat on the table.

The day before she would immediately have thought of it being provided by Dan. He'd fed her so many times. Saved her from starving. He must have done that every day since he found her in the street, a little boy himself.

How old had he been? He couldn't have been more than six or seven. So tiny himself. So tiny to make such a big decision.

Had he really blamed himself for it all this time? He said he had. Why had the Grand H. let him blame himself? He'd been so little.

That answer was easy to guess. The Grand H. must have preferred Dan blamed himself.

Bess lay in the bed staring at the whitewashed plaster ceiling. The smell of tea was enticing, but she wasn't hungry.

She'd never once in her life wondered about the origins of the Grand H., but now it crowded into her thoughts. Had he been born in the alleys? In a village house? His words, Bess now realized, spoke of a place like Road's End. It seemed unlikely he came from some white-pillared Greek temple like the new wing; it seemed logical he had been born and raised in some room like this, with its plain plaster ceiling and bare wooden floor, a kind of titled puritanical poverty.

His voice. She could remember it well, the rich plummy tones in which he gave directions about which window to use to enter a room. It had not sounded like Jack or Jackie, or the hosteller, or Mr. Able. He'd sounded more like a duke.

That must be why Dan's voice was like that too. More silver plate than stone—not the sound of it, which was always rough and gravelly, but the shape of his words. And perhaps she herself, though she had always been good at adopting the speech of the people around her. Except the swearing Dan wouldn't let her do.

For some reason the Grand H. had been born to a place like this and wound up with his philosophy books in the London gutter.

It wasn't hard to imagine, now; she could see it happening to Lord Waresham. Wished it would. Even Lord Zachary with his zealous pursuit of art to the exclusion of everything else might be in danger of it.

Had it all been for drink? He'd bought Dan to do his stealing for him, as far as Bess could see, so he'd always have something to drink. Could it have been that simple, and that low?

Feeling even now the sick craving for something that would make her float and forget, Bess well imagined how it could.

Could the drink have made the old man blot out the existence of the little girl under his roof, made her Dan's problem and never his? Of course.

Yet, as Dan himself had recently reminded her, he'd taught her to read.

Had he expected a reward for her? Had he planned to sell her on to someone else? Had he only been waiting to make good on his investment, stopped short by his own death? Or had he hoped she'd find her family, her place, someday, and wanted her to be prepared for anything?

That Bess didn't know.

She couldn't ever know what was in someone else's mind. Vellot thought he knew, but in actuality, he only wanted to bend them to his will. In someone else's hands, Vellot's horrible magic might be useful or fine; but he'd perverted it.

Had Bess then been able to use some paper and drugged wine to get the Grand H. to tell the truth, she'd still only know what he was able or willing to tell her.

He'd been a grown man who could have done something to find her family.

Or perhaps he'd tried.

She had to judge by the actions she saw. The Grand H. had risked her life hundreds of times; Dan had been there to save her. That was the difference between them, and all she really knew.

The door latch rattled. "Oh good," breathed Agatha. "You are awake."

She looked with consternation toward the untouched tea but hurried to the desk and scribbled something down with the paper and pencil there.

"What on earth?" asked Bess, tired of thinking about Dan, Dan, Dan, always Dan.

Agatha waved a spidery-looking metal instrument. "I've been taking a dawn reading. Why haven't you risen?"

Bess didn't want to ask what a dawn reading was. She'd get an exhausting and uninteresting answer. "I was about to."

Agatha dropped her pencil and moved to pour tea. "It will be too strong," she warned.

"Good," muttered Bess. "I must speak to the duke. Will you help me?"

* * *

JACKIE STUMBLED into the room he shared with Jack shortly after dawn, knocked the code on the door of the closet where Dan slept on the unused valet's cot.

Dan emerged, yawning till it looked like his head might snap in two. He just gave Jackie a questioning look.

Jackie yawned back. "Storey never came back all night."

Well. This plan might work after all. Assuming he stayed out of Storey's way till tonight, Dan would get Bess and that book back to London after all.

Fitz knew where to send the payment.

The best way to avoid Storey's suspicion, and keep the book hidden, was to go on about his business as Mr. Burton. He'd even swapped the candle back in Storey's room, his own just a stump in his pocket and the wax cleaned from the candle holder. Storey should find no evidence that anyone had been in his room for hours poring over his ledger; only the ledger gone.

The knot in Dan's gut could have been anything. Simple hunger.

But it wasn't; Bess had brought him food the night before, their last meal together, no doubt.

* * *

"Where has the Duke gone?"

Agatha dogged her steps as Bess openly searched every room for Gravenshire. "He must have gone with the younger men. They're out shooting again."

"Where?" Bess had no more time for games. She had to convince the Duke of his danger, or at least try one more time; then she had to find a way to quiet Vellot once and for all.

She didn't know what kind of person that made her. But she couldn't think of another solution, and it wasn't because Vellot could threaten Dan or Agatha or Madame Franck.

It would be for herself.

She couldn't go through the rest of her life wondering what was real and what wasn't. Wondering if she did what she did because of his tricks in her mind.

The feelings inside her might be dangerous and strange, but if she'd listened to them sooner, she would have never crossed paths with Vellot. They'd told her; she'd spited them on purpose, playing with him like a child played with fire. Well, she'd been burned and would have scars, even if only on the inside.

Bess' life had always been forward, forward, forward. She couldn't keep looking back over her shoulder. Not for Vellot; not at all.

Looking backwards had only been to see if Dan was still there. And she was done with that.

Agatha trotted along behind as Bess opened the fine

pillar-framed front door, letting icy breezes swirl around them both. Both peered past the few ornamental plantings to the tree-lined drive. For an instant, Bess thought she saw Dan's shape dart through the tree trunks.

Any other day, she would have been sure. But now she felt unsure of Dan and everything she thought about him. Who knew where he was, or what he was doing? Or why?

Agatha only saw her searching the tree-trunks. "I think the men went to hunt, they would have gone farther into the woods. Out this way is only trees for ever so long. There's just an old barn beyond them that floods in the summers. It's too wet there to shoot." Agatha pointed.

No, no sign of Dan after all. Nor any duke.

"We must follow."

Agatha's pretty eyes widened. "The hunting party? We don't have deep boots."

Bess thought fleetingly, longingly, of the pair she'd put aside in London, trying to be a *good girl*. To curb her greed. Well, look what came of that. "We can't just sit around all afternoon waiting for the men to return."

"That *is* what we do in winter. There are books to read, and there's knitting."

Bess would rather hang by the neck till dead. "How do you pass the time in summer?"

Agatha bit her lip. "There's one amusement we could try."

* * *

"I'm making a hash of this." Even as she spoke, Bess let the arrow fly.

It flew with conviction toward the old whitewash circle on the barn wall, thumping into the gray wood on the circle's edge rather than its center. The sound of it sent the chickens in the yard flapping.

"It's your first time," Agatha soothed her, stepping up and drawing back the string of her own bow, taking careful aim before letting it fly.

Her arrow struck considerably closer to the center, and Bess felt an entirely immoral sting of jealousy.

"First or last time," Bess muttered as they trudged out of the tall grass to retrieve their arrows, "I have no talent for this."

"It can take a lifetime of practice. Lady Diane is the best archer in London, and she has been practicing since she could walk." Agatha grimaced as she pulled her arrow out of the splintered gray wall. "At least, I assume she is still the best. She was lost at sea last spring."

"So she's dead." Bess didn't feel like being gentle.

"I find that hard to believe without a funeral," said Agatha, showing her stubborn streak.

"I bet she doesn't find it hard to believe at all."

They were using the side of the barn that faced the old wing. There was a smaller shed next to it, with some space between them, but not nearly enough paces wide for an archery shoot.

Bess turned her side towards the barn and raised the bow the way Agatha had.

She was warm from exertion, at least, but her brain spun like the gears of a clock gone mad. She kept seeing Dan's blue coat out of the corner of her eye, but he wasn't there.

Between his lies and the Silver Duke's, had her mind broken?

"Ahoy the barn!" Lord Harman strode toward them from the farther stand of trees to their right, swinging what looked to be the gray-white bodies of waterfowl.

"Oh. Gulls." Agatha pretended not to be disappointed in the hunting take. "They can be quite toothsome once they're soaked in seawater."

Bess wasn't listening. Behind Lord Harman, several paces behind in fact, Vellot strode with a disgusted expression through the tall brown grass.

She could turn and let an arrow fly right at his rotted heart this moment.

She breathed in, then out, tracing his path like any hunter would their prey, wondering if she were the kind of person who could send an arrow through his body right now.

If she could pretend afterwards that it was an accident.

Who knew? She was the kind of person who could say *yabloko*, and fell for Dan's lies her whole life. She had no idea who she was.

"Careful," called Harman, and Vellot looked up. Met Bess' eyes across the expanse of wintry meadow.

He knew her arrow was aimed at his heart.

The thoughts that ticked through Bess' mind as time grew slow were ones he put there. *You can do anything,* he'd told her over and over. *What crimes have you committed? What else could you do?*

That was why she lowered the bow.

That, and the humiliating admission born of the last hour that she could not hit the side of a barn with any real intention.

"You should have told me you wished to learn archery," said Lord Harman with good humor as they grew closer; Bess saw Lord Zachary coming out of the woods, with Waresham and the Duke trailing behind. "I'd be happy to teach you."

Bess didn't bother to point out that Agatha had been a perfectly fine teacher. "You weren't here."

"Any of us would have happily tutored you to avoid facing down a ready weapon," laughed Harman.

"It only puts you in the same position as the birds you've

chased all afternoon. Isn't that what you deserve?" Bess put pressure on the word *you.*

And let the *deserve* hang between her and Vellot.

Who only said quietly, "Aren't there people who deserve it?" Just as he had done when he had her in his power. In his fist.

He didn't think she'd do anything to him. He was sure she wouldn't.

"There definitely are people who deserve it." She kept her eyes on him, not letting him go.

The awkward silence stretched between them, till Bess broke it with some cross between a laugh and a sneer. "I think I've heard that somewhere before."

"Common knowledge," he said, but a breath too late.

She had him startled. She had *him* worried for once.

She could tell he didn't like it.

But she did.

* * *

AGATHA WOULDN'T LET her speak to the Duke.

"You're too peculiar today." For the dozenth time, she placed Bess opposite her in the grand new ballroom, and curtsied as if a new dance had begun.

The rich polished wood glowed around them both, and Bess was bitterly conscious of the setting sun. Dinner wouldn't be till after dark, then hours more till the ball, which Lady Carrollton was determined to make as fashionable as possible. She probably wouldn't even serve supper till midnight.

Bess would have preferred to pass the time until she could settle accounts with Vellot by playing with the guinea pigs.

"I'm not peculiar." She stepped forward, arm raised to

greet Agatha's arm as if each of them had a gentleman by their side, as if two other couples flanked them. Agatha insisted they do some of the dance practice they'd had no time for in London. "No more than any day. I'm just restless."

"Then learn the dance! You'll have many chances to try it tonight."

"This, a dance?" Bess scoffed aloud.

Agatha stopped, huffed with frustration. "My goodness, then dance on your own!"

"I will!"

It was just what Bess wanted. To dance, and ignore all of this. Russians with apples, dukes, Dan and his dangerous eyes. The Silver Duke in front of her arrow.

She didn't know if she could kill a man, but she knew she could dance.

She turned in place, willing an orchestra to appear.

Agatha huffed again. "Uh... Perhaps you could try..." She started humming an old Scottish tune.

It was so old that even Bess knew it from the grimy underparts of London. She hummed a little too, letting the slow music swing her from side to side, her arms carving an arc in the air then her leg as she spun.

She could extend her leg farther than her skirt would go. Bess took a few moments to find the limits of her costume, staying within its boundaries while dipping, swaying, a shep-herdess dancing in the heather on a sunny day. She whirled.

Happy to see Bess do something other than grumble, Agatha went on humming as loud as she could.

In the vast polished room glowing with golden light, Bess raised her arms, framed herself, framed her turn. With little flicks of her foot, delicate cat steps, she ventured forth, retreated, then fully committed, with tiny leaps that looked airy, perfectly balanced, perfectly strong, dust motes dancing with her in the sunbeams.

When she stopped, one arm above her head, muscles in her leg locking her in place while still looking cool and graceful, her eyes settled on the door, and Dan stood there.

Agatha's humming stopped.

Had Bess conjured him with dance steps? Were they like books and blank paper?

Or with her mind? Her heart?

She'd seen him everywhere today, and here he was, back as straight as an arrow, strong leg muscles flexing as he stepped closer, then closer still, slipping off his coat like a fairy prince would his cloak. Tossed it to the side.

He was real, and he was here.

And as always, he knew what she was thinking.

He put out his hand. "Go ahead," he said so softly Bess could barely hear, but she heard. "Dance however you like."

Agatha covered her mouth with both hands. Before either of them could notice her, she hummed a little again, random startled notes that had come to her from nowhere out of the air.

Then she began to actually sing the song.

Since thoughts of thee doth banish grief
When from thee I am gone,
Will not thy presence yield relief
To this sad Heart of mine?

Dan wasn't looking at Agatha. He wasn't looking at anything but Bess. Those black diamond eyes glowed with things she couldn't name, feelings she didn't understand.

Since you have robbed me of my heart,
It's reason I have yours;
Which Madame Nature doth impart
To your black Eyes and Brows.

Like hot honeyed water, Bess' feelings refused to stay tamped down. She felt like they flowed out of her soul, out of her fingertips.

Dan was no dancer, and yet he moved perfectly in time with her, taking his cues from her expression, her body, twirling her one way and then, after a perfect pause, reversing her, displaying her, supporting her, making her dance possible.

He danced because she did.

He was so strong that the slightest touch of their fingertips was enough to balance her whole body. Her skirts whipped around her legs as she spun.

She balanced on one leg and bowed, the other leg behind reaching impossibly high, never minding staying covered, or who might see.

She straightened, and he caught her eyes. Nodded. Whispered to her, "Do what you want."

It was as though his words wrapped a string around her chest and sent her spinning like a child's toy, flying away from him, too filled with light to fall down. When she stopped, chest held high, her arms reaching back, she gave in to the urge and she ran.

Leaping into his hands she flew, and he caught her. Lifted her above his head, balancing like a bird, like stars.

Slowly he lowered her, his impossibly strong arms bulging under his linen shirt with the power it took to let her come down slowly, her leg, her body sliding against him, her skirt catching between them, falling, unheeded, both of their souls bare in their eyes.

But yet I wish the gods to move
That noble Heart of thine
To pity since ye cannot love
For old lang syne.

Neither of them saw Agatha backing out of the ballroom, standing in its doorway. The music grew fainter, but Dan and Bess moved as if an orchestra surrounded them still, slow reeds blowing heartbreak through the heather and mournful horns crying like human hearts.

If e'er I have a house my Dear,
That's truly callèd mine,
That can afford best country cheer
Or ought that's good therein;
Though thou wast Rebel to the King,
And beat with Wind and Rain,
Assure thyself of welcome Love
For old lang syne.

With the last slow turn, her arms drifted down to balance her hands on the breadth of his chest.

He let his hand skim down over the edge of her hair, her cheek, around the back of her shoulder to rest lightly, irrevocably, against her back, pulling, holding her close as he kissed her.

Agatha covered her mouth again, hiding her *oh* of surprise, then, blushing, closed the door.

Dan's kiss held every part of her, calling to her blood, her skin, her muscles, her bones. These were things Bess understood more than feelings or words. They made her; they made sense. And Dan held them in the palm of his hand, in every way.

They set her words free.

His mouth parted from hers, the tiniest space, and the breath she drew in was the breath of his body, the smell and the taste of him. Those gave her strength too.

She said, "I can't cut you away; you're the blood in my veins. The other half of me. I see you everywhere. I will for the rest of my life. And I can't trust it. I can't trust you."

His black eyes widened, looked like he was searching for what to say in her eyes.

Finally he said, "You're the sun and the moon and the

stars, Bess; you always have been, and you always will be. Trust *yourself*. I always have."

SHE HAD THAT PUZZLED LOOK, the one where her brows drew together because she didn't understand and thought she should.

"But I don't—"

The music room door creaked open.

Swiftly he bent and whispered into her ear, "You're the treasure. You."

"Miss Page."

Lady Dunsby stood in the door, with Madame Franck peering over her shoulder. Agatha lurked in the background, crestfallen.

Lady Dunsby thumped a few steps closer with her walking stick, then stopped.

"Miss Page, whatever it is you are engaged in, it will not *help* your cause, or Mr. Burton's, to be caught in such a compromising position."

Dan looked at his coat, tossed aside on the floor, then a flushed Bess haloed with sparkling curls.

It did look compromising.

And enticing. Tempting. His Bess, unleashed.

He'd never regret this dance.

"Lady Dunsby." He bowed, not bothering to disguise his voice. "I only assisted Miss Page in practicing the cotillion."

And then he bowed to Bess, hoping she saw the encouragement in his eyes.

I'm going to get you out of here, he mouthed silently, knowing only she would see and understand.

Then louder, to Lady Dunsby, "I do not wish to compromise either young lady in any way. You have been most gracious, and I beg your indulgence for just one more night."

Then he swooped to gather his coat and left. If he looked back, he would scoop Bess up into his arms instead, and run out of this damned house with her and never look back.

He would have, if he hadn't so disastrously done it before.

CHAPTER THIRTY

Mr. Storey's trembling was not due to the brace of stalwart red-coated soldiers marching behind him toward the party at Road's End.

It was because he had torn apart the Falcon Hotel, nearly to its beams, and could not find his ledger.

Lady Winpole had never exhibited even an eyelash of mercy in all the time he'd known her. Indeed, he was the one who'd arranged for the final disposition of several men who had disappointed her. He knew several places in London where bones rested as best they could without benefit of a grave.

Despite his use of poetry, Mr. Storey was not a man of arts, so his mind did not recognize the composition of a dire situation he could not escape. But he felt it in his gut, and as he swept off his hat and handed it to a harried footman, then stepped into a glowing world of candlelight beyond the oak beams of Lady Carrollton's front door, he felt in his core that he was going to his own end, and he hated it bitterly.

* * *

THE LACK of green corduroy coat nearly made Dan mistake Storey for someone else.

His cheaply-acquired evening coat fit him ill. It looked as though he were trying to shed his skin.

But Dan knew him well from following him day and night, taking weeks to learn his secrets for Fitz, never guessing that they would wind up here. He had the man's whole life in his grasp; quite literally, as the ledger was wrapped in linen and stuffed along his spine under his vest.

Storey came straight for him.

"Is Lady Winpole at the party?"

That was how Dan knew the man was badly rattled. He would never have openly asked for Lady Winpole otherwise.

"I couldn't say," Dan said carelessly, as if he'd never met her. It was the performance of his life. He knew exactly where she was, twenty feet behind him to his left, draped in gray bombazine and mingling with the brighter colors of the other ladies in the Carrollton party. "Wouldn't recognize her in such a crowd."

That seemed to rock Storey back on his heels. "No? I'd swear *we've* met before."

Dan's coat was black, and his spectacles gone. It was the wrong moment to be so close to Storey. He cursed the scar over his lip and his inborn sneer. Had Storey ever caught a glimpse of Dan on the street—and surely he had—Dan would have looked too much like this.

Storey's kind of crime depended on a memory for faces.

Dan hoped Mr. Burton's swooping voice would be enough to save him. "Never say so! Wouldn't want to insult a man by forgetting his name, but yours isn't coming to mind. Is it Wallace? Buffington? You're not from Scotland, are you?"

"No, no." Storey's interest faded away, and he went back

to examining the room for Lady Winpole. Dan saw his gaze connect; he blanched.

Dan almost felt sorry for him.

"Friend of her ladyship, are you?" Dan pretended to squint in the same direction. "You should have joined us last night. Or did you just arrive from London?"

"Had a warm night in the village," Storey said absently. "Belinda by name. I can tell you her direction, if that's your interest."

Dan instantly knew a lot of things Storey hadn't realized he'd given away. He knew whoever Belinda was, Storey planned to put her harder to work; that Storey would take her money; and that Storey would likely find other women to add to the business as well, because that was his habit.

Dan didn't feel sorry for him anymore.

"Lord Zachary." He hailed the young artist as the man strolled past looking bored. "Aren't you always looking for new subjects to paint? See who's joined our party. Doesn't he have an interesting head?"

Storey's eyes darted back and forth as if searching for a place to run as the young man's eyes skimmed his bland features.

"No," Lord Zachary pronounced. "I'm not much for portraiture, I'm afraid."

"Never hurts to try," Dan needled Storey by keeping Lord Zachary engaged staring at his face. If ever a witness were needed, Lord Zachary would make an excellent one. He displayed no bad habits except his tendency to ignore every-thing else in favor of art. He likely *could* draw Storey, and that was threat enough. "After all," said Dan in Mr. Burton's voice, "what landscape offers the variety you see in the human face?"

That pulled the young man out of his ennui. "You may be

right," he said, peering at Mr. Storey's ears with genuine interest.

"Excuse me," said Storey hastily, and bowed as he withdrew.

Dan hoped he slept badly every night of his life.

* * *

MORE SOLDIERS MARCHED IN, heads high, guarding a man in their midst; even scattered, they kept their eyes upon him.

Usually Bess preferred to be the center of attention.

Only Waresham fixated on her at the moment, and his gaze was clingy, unwelcome. "I hope you have a dance free for me," he said, leaning over Bess.

Across the room, Agatha cast glances their way. She was resplendent in virginal white linen embroidered with flame-like tulips, each one sporting a sparkling crystal at the tip of each petal.

Bess' own gown was trimmed with swathes of white lace, gathered around her chest then falling narrowly to the floor, making her look taller. It was the miraculous new lace made by machine, and Bess had pounced on it when the dressmaker explained it made the price of such a gown quite reasonable, even for a lady's companion.

At Lady Dunsby's insistence, it featured its own bit of sparkle; tassels of crystal beads swung from her sleeve's outside edge, catching the light when she moved.

Waresham seemed to be trying to peer through the lace.

Bess didn't have time for him. "I believe Lady Agatha would like to dance."

"I believe her mother would rather I not."

"When has that stopped you?"

"When the mother in question is close enough to see."

On stage, mused Bess, *that line would be charming.*

It had never been so important to distinguish play-acting from what was real. Dan's lies had made the world twisted and strange. None of the corners in the room really felt square. Bess would never admit it to Madame Franck, but she did feel as though she had walked down from a mountaintop into a pathless wilderness.

Perhaps Bess was losing her taste for stages.

Certainly Waresham's performance bored her, and it went on. "Are you looking forward to London, Miss Page? I have quite a neat townhouse near St. James Square."

Of course he did. "Lord Waresham. Lady Agatha has hopes of you."

He shrugged a loose, careless shoulder. "The more fool she." Then he slipped her a grin. "I blame you for looking so pretty in that dress."

Even if Bess had a new appreciation of how persuasive men could be, that line was unforgivable.

"Please excuse me," she said without further ado, and slipped away to the Duke of Gravenshire while the rest of the room followed the movements of the newly arrived gentleman.

She could tell there was a rhythm, a deferential dance to the way people approached the Duke, bowing and saying a few words, then moving on.

Bess didn't have time to learn it.

She was grateful the earth stayed predictably flat as she moved toward the man whose diamond-white shirt shone almost as bright as the million candles in every corner of the ballroom.

Of course Dan watched. She could feel his attention following her. As if her footsteps were his.

The invisible dance between them was an endless circle, a *pirouette* that should have had Bess spinning...

...yet made everything still.

She couldn't trust him, but he trusted her, and that helped. It was power humming in her veins, the same confidence that told her she could catch a windowsill with her fingertips or somersault over a moving horse and land without breaking a bone. It was a universal rhythm, a certainty in the way everything fit together that extended to her, too, and balanced her on her feet.

It was funny how he could sustain and betray her at the same time.

Was that how it worked for all women who loved faithless men?

The Duke of Gravenshire pulled himself to his full height, and Bess was quite aware that he towered over her.

Still, *she* approached *him.*

"Your Grace," she said as she curtsied low.

"Miss Page." She could see him take in every detail of her gown.

It was not a wanton costume, but she had confronted him alone.

Then she drew too close.

"Sir," she said, keeping her voice very low, knowing the room would notice, not caring one fig, "I must convince you that you are in danger."

He surveyed her again, from the top of her arranged golden-brown curls to the hem of her gown, likely not caring that it would look to watchers as though he considered an improper request. She had not been circumspect; neither would he be. "I believe I'll take my chances."

That made Bess' blood burn so hot that she raised her otherwise decorative fan and fluttered it before her face. Her flush wouldn't help how this looked either. Her gaze up at him might look adoring to anyone who couldn't look straight into her eyes at that moment.

In fact, the look she turned on him would suit any queen

in the ballet's *repertoire.* She held his eyes with hers till the faint smile around his eyes faded, then held it longer. "If it was me who wanted you dead, you wouldn't see me coming."

She'd seen him carelessly dispense awkward pauses to others; it was satisfying to see him flounder through one himself.

"Miss Page, I flatter myself that aside from my title, I am broad-shouldered enough to be my own protection."

Bess stopped herself from rolling her eyes with the long practice of an actress. Men and their convictions about themselves.

Instead, she forced herself to smile prettily and brazenly laid her hand on his.

In so doing, she slipped him the key to her trunk.

"See for yourself," she said. "There is a miniature of Vellot in the bottom of my trunk. No one else knows it's there. It should prove I know what I say. He wants Talbourne dead, and believes it will change the world."

The phrase *change the world* sharpened his attention. Now Gravenshire's bushy brows lowered a little. He appeared to lean closer to absorb more flattery. "The miniature only proves you have some intimate relationship with the man."

She was losing patience with his determination to be thick-headed. "And why would I reveal that unless I had a dire reason?"

Now that she had his attention, Bess played upon it as she would in a scene where her partner had forgotten his lines. "Tell me, how would killing Talbourne change the world? Whatever it is, he wants it. He won't give up even if Talbourne's too smart to show himself."

"It's hardly seemly for a young girl to refer to a duke with such familiarity."

"It's hardly seemly to be dead." She'd done her best with this man. "I can't do all your work for you. I'm only telling you to watch your back." Frustrated, she glanced around the room. "That person everyone's watching—is he titled too?"

"He is the ambassador to France. On his way to meet the emperor and draw an end to this war."

That plucked a string in Bess' head. "A man who could change everything. Change the world."

"Indeed."

There. Out of the corner of her eye she saw Vellot making his way toward the man. It was only obvious to her, perhaps, how subtly he moved. Like a snake sliding sideways to get closer to its dinner.

She kept him in her sight.

To the Duke she said, "If you value your country, do not let Vellot speak to that ambassador. Not alone; not at all. Tell Captain Clark too, since you might soon be dead."

* * *

"You've got balls of iron, I'll give you that."

Dan pretended to look surprised by the sudden appearance of Lord Waresham at his elbow. "Thank you," he said as if he knew whatever had set the man to raving.

Waresham kept going. "You do know the girl has nothing, right? She's only Lady Agatha's companion. No brass at all. If you're only out to bed her, I commend your taste... but I saw her first."

As a youth, Dan had convinced himself he could stand aside and let Bess marry some wet-nosed lord. So she'd be safe.

He was no longer willing to stand aside. "What makes you think I care what you want?"

"Because I know who you are."

* * *

LORD HARMAN'S cheery arrival forced Bess to break off her *tête-à-tête* with the stubborn Duke. "Miss Page. I wondered if you might be free to dance."

Could she? What if she spun too hard and flew up off the earth into space? In a world where Dan and the Silver Duke both had her turning, anything was possible.

She let Harman lead her away from His Grace, smiled up at him. Tried to be Miss Page. "It would alarm me to dance before all these people."

"It's not for them to watch; it's for us to enjoy. Allow me."

He did not grasp that she needed to stay with the Duke.

Dan would have read her from across the room; but then, so had the Silver Duke. *Perhaps she was only susceptible to being understood by a certain kind of man,* Bess thought a little wildly.

Against her will, she looked for Dan.

Even with everything such a muddle, if anyone could help her, Dan could.

He'd lied for his own ends, just like the Silver Duke; confused her and controlled her too.

But it didn't change how they understood each other with a look.

He stood near Waresham, back straight, and his eyes came to hers through the milling guests, unerringly. As if he felt her thoughts.

Even with all the bizarre distance between them now, they were two halves of the same whole.

The very set of his muscles, the subtle angle of his arms, said that he was ready to follow her lead. Ready to do anything Bess needed.

She flicked a look back to the Duke, and Dan lowered his head but nodded, almost imperceptibly.

He didn't even know what she'd told the Duke, but he would support it. That was what he did. He shadowed her, and he caught her when she fell.

For a villain, he was trustworthy that way.

Bess had a wild impulse to run to him and grab his hand. To drag him out of Road's End and race for the horizon. To forget about dukes and ambassadors. Forget how he'd lied.

Lord Harman paused with her, leaned closer for a private word. "Are you so determined to land yourself a duke?" he asked lightly. "We don't know each other well, but that seems unlike you."

"Why is my romantic life such a popular topic of conversation?" Bess countered, almost a snap, covering her exasperation with a brittle smile.

"It is usually all that concerns a young lady."

"I have other worries." She pushed away possibilities that could only exist if she could control time itself. If she could make this yesterday. If she could un-know what she knew.

But she couldn't, this was now, and her immediate problem was Vellot. "You know Lord Vellot considers himself a physician of sorts."

Harman's faint smile faded. "Yes, I've seen him display his work."

"He intends to affect the ambassador. I don't know how he does it or what he can do, but I assure you he intends to do it."

"You're not serious."

Bess moved to face him, cocked her head as though he'd said something amusing, and, building on the performance she'd just given the Duke, put all her cold anger into her eyes, just for him.

She said, "Be the one gentleman in Britain who takes a woman seriously."

He blinked, and bowed slightly. "My apologies, Miss Page." He did not look toward Vellot, but offered his arm. "Let us greet the ambassador."

Sure enough, by the time they reached the ambassador's side, Vellot was next to the man.

Next to him and about to lead him toward the punch-bowl... or somewhere else more quiet.

Harman greeted them exuberantly, as if he'd already imbibed many cups of the dangerously strong punch. Without introducing Bess, he clapped the ambassador on the shoulder. "You must be eager to sail away from Britain again, eh?"

The man looked down his narrow nose. "Aren't you Lord Ayles' son?"

Harman's fake grin faltered. "So they all call me," he said with a little grimness.

"You have a reputation for sober quietude, sir."

"I know." Still a bit grim. "I hope to repair that. Tell me, for what are you most eager?"

He led the ambassador into a conversation about Belgian ales, ignoring Bess but keeping her so close at his side that he often turned to guffaw her way.

That made it impossible for Vellot to speak to Bess alone. If Vellot broke away from the ambassador to move around Harman's broad body, people would see him approach her.

The impotent fury in his eyes was delightful.

"Lord Harman," said Vellot, breaking into an exchange about hops, "the musicians are about to play a *quadrille*. Surely Miss Page wishes to dance."

Again Bess fluttered her eyelashes and gave a tiny shake of her head. "Oh no, I couldn't dance in front of all these people."

Had the man contained a grain of humanity, he'd have smiled. It was funny. He knew who she was. He'd *courted* her as the Tourmaline.

But there was nothing. Only furious anger as she reiterated her intention to stay right where she was.

There was nothing human in him. Only a power-hungry demon whose look promised Bess she'd be sorry.

Well, she already was, but not about what she had to do to him. Her heart felt numb, while Vellot had no blank paper, no drugged wine. And she'd survived his tricks before. Survived his control. In fact, he'd never had any.

Bess felt the same cool calm she'd had with the arrow trained on his heart. *She* was in control, of far more than he knew.

He had abilities she didn't understand, but then, the reverse was true too.

It was an illuminating, terrifying thought. She felt more true fear of Dan. Because he mattered.

Vellot tried to drive her off again. "Isn't that Lady Dunsby looking for you?"

"Is she?" She didn't even bother to turn. "I'm sure she doesn't plan to dance either."

"You seem to have torn your dress."

"No." She gave him the same look she'd given him over the arrow. "I haven't."

She could see his puzzled fury. As if his puppet had started speaking on its own. Unable to pull her aside, or the ambassador, Vellot retreated.

Bess watched him go.

Still beside her, Lord Harman exuded so much welcoming *bonhomie* that more of the soldiers had clustered around, and he had them laughing about ales they'd drunk both here and abroad. "Now in Amsterdam, I drank a beer that made me piss blue—"

"There's a lady present!" one soldier objected, offering Bess a sweeping bow.

"Don't let me keep you gentlemen from your fun!" fluttered Bess and curtsied. It was safe to leave them. The ambassador was deep in the discussion now, and Harman had proven his worth; he wouldn't abandon his post.

I'm going to get you out of here. She hadn't forgotten what Dan said. Broken as they were, he was still determined to protect her.

And still some kind of conscience for her. Perhaps that was why she still wanted to persuade the Duke to do something about Vellot.

She glanced over her shoulder.

The Duke had not budged.

The bastard. Well, if he wouldn't go see the miniature himself, she'd get it for him.

* * *

DAN WAS LESS of an actor than Bess, but faced with Waresham's accusation, his expression didn't waver. "Everyone knows who I am. Lady Dunsby's secretary."

Lord Waresham's body settled into a dangerous curve. Like a bow being drawn.

He said, "I know you're here after the same quarry I'm hunting."

Dan's heart thudded in his chest. He didn't mean Bess, surely? He wouldn't *kill* her? Perhaps he only meant bedsport, but the man's trigger finger twitched and his eyes had an empty stare that called darker things to mind.

Dan shook his head. "I'm not hunting any quarry."

Waresham stepped close. He towered over Dan; Dan didn't budge an inch.

"I know Lord Vellot brought a second weapon. I know it's you. I knew it by your looks, the second you stepped off the boat. But this is *my* chance for greatness. I won't let you take my place."

A chance for greatness. Hunting his quarry. Dan's mind

snapped back to that shocking night with Bess in his arms, somehow frightened. *I don't want to change the world. I don't want to do it.*

It all fit together in horrible ways.

Had Vellot brought Bess here to kill someone?

It could only be the ambassador or the Duke. She'd clung to both men for the last hour.

She'd said she didn't want to do it. Dan didn't think there had been time from last night to tonight, as everything between the two of them had fallen apart, for someone to make his Bess into someone completely different.

He knew Bess better than anyone, and she was no murderer.

This had to be the most dangerous high wire she'd ever walked, and Dan wanted to be there to catch her if she fell...

...or someone pushed her.

"So you shot at me on the dock." Dan's voice was low, almost silky. The man could have hit *Bess*.

"I could shoot you now and no one would care except to avoid the puddle of your blood on the floor," hissed Waresham. "He didn't need to bring you. I'm a thoroughbred. Rare. You're as common as rocks. This is no job for the likes of you."

There were breakable things in Lady Carrollton's ballroom. It was no place to take Waresham apart.

The man should learn that firing a bullet toward Bess wouldn't do.

"You ought to know already," he said to Waresham in the same low voice, "that I can beat you at any game you'd like to play."

CHAPTER THIRTY-ONE

It was easy for Dan to walk Waresham out of the torchlight around the new front door to Road's End.

Easy to walk with him over the drive, as if they were making a quick jaunt to the trees to spit snuff, or relieve themselves. Easy to wait for Waresham to try to land the first blow.

He tossed his own coat on the grass, the ledger wrapped inside it. It made a dark shape in the frost. He still had enough speed in his hands to slip it there without Waresham's notice.

He tossed his own coat on the grass, the ledger wrapped inside it. It made a dark shape in the frost. He still had the speed in his hands to slip it there without Waresham's notice.

Dan had always been good at these things, because he'd had to be, not out of misplaced pride.

He ducked under Waresham's flying fist.

"Tell me you shot at me again." It was hard to want to do it, though. He'd never wanted to, only had to.

"Like shooting at ducks," sneered Waresham, flicking his hair back out of his eye, ripping off his own coat.

It was hard to want to do this.

Dan felt ripped away from his own heart. That was why he'd followed her today, to watch her shoot, watch her dance. Why he'd danced with her. He hadn't known he could dance at all.

"Tell me you shot *toward Bess*."

"I'm too good to hit her," Waresham said carelessly, raising his fists and shrugging one shoulder at the same time.

He didn't care. Didn't care if he shot Bess.

"Apparently not," said Dan, "you missed me."

With that, he closed the distance.

Waresham swung at his face, but Dan was closer, faster, *fiercer.* He never planned to hit just once.

Right, left, his fists thudded into Waresham's jaw, spinning it one way, then the other. Right, left, the spot under the ribs that made it impossible to breathe.

Then, as Waresham choked, pulled his face down into Dan's knee.

He backed away, watched the man stagger, blood dripping from his lip. "You've never seen her," hissed Dan. "Never heard of her. You wouldn't know her again in the street. You forget you ever met her, or I'll pull out your eyeballs and feed them to you. You follow me?"

Wordlessly, surprisingly, Waresham caught his own balance, lunged back at Dan.

* * *

LADY WINPOLE HADN'T BOTHERED to discharge Storey after he told his sad tale of losing his ledger. Just let him run off like a dog with his tail between his legs. Apparently to the kitchen to look for a bone.

This always happened. The most stalwart servant eventually folded like paper. What was wrong with the lower classes that they could not remain dependable?

Without cards, the party was dull. The two silly girl-children had disappeared, and in their absence the men milled in circles, looking for amusement. Lady Carrollton was doing her best to entertain them, but if the punch continued to flow, Lady Winpole expected there would be fisticuffs.

So her ledger was lost. At least it was written in code. She knew that for sure; she'd seen it, and she could not read it. The chance it could incriminate her was small.

Still, Lady Winpole did not make her living by ignoring small chances.

She silently climbed the stairs to the old wing and marched into Waresham's room.

Waresham was a predictable child, as careless with his toys now as he had been in the nursery. As suspected, his pistol lay on his desk. She took it up and let the ball roll out; it was loaded.

Hopefully correctly. She'd prefer the thing not explode in her hand, and she intended the shot to be at close range.

It had been decades since she'd been fox-hunting herself, but she never forgot a skill that might one day be useful. The powder bag had been tossed on the table as well; gently she tapped a little into the priming pan, preparing the pistol to fire, and held it upright.

Glancing out the window to see if Storey had walked through the kitchen and kept going, she saw Burton and Waresham circling each other beside the old wing, in the dirt drive between the trees and the house.

Burton.

The one likeliest to abscond with the ledger.

From above she saw him wipe blood from his lip. One of

his sleeves hung in tatters, and his shirt was nearly split down the middle.

He threw himself again at Waresham's torso. If he fell, she could shoot him where he lay. But it would be a difficult shot.

It was quite possible he'd win the fight; he was bestial, brutal.

But if he did, he wouldn't be able to return to the party in rags. Either he'd run off to the village—in which case her aim might fall short—or, more likely, he'd return to his room up here.

She looked about. There was one comfortable chair in Waresham's chamber; she took it.

Lady Winpole could gamble. She'd wait to see if she'd made the right bet.

* * *

THE SECOND he let Waresham stagger away, declaring through escape that their fight was over, Dan wished he hadn't.

But his point was made. Waresham, now wearing many raw wounds, would keep his distance from Bess or get more of the same, and he didn't look eager for more.

Eye swelling, jaw swelling on both sides, shirt ruined, raw places underneath, Waresham wobbled on his long legs back toward the Greek door of Road's End. Dan wondered if he planned to go back to the party.

He'd like to see that, but he had far more important business.

He'd promised Bess he'd get her out of here, and he would, or die trying.

The sky was completely dark. He was running out of time.

* * *

BESS WENT to the dressing table first for her trunk's key. The tin-backed mirror reflected an image of Bess looking like no one but herself. Drawn and tired. Bess looked down, not wanting to meet her own eyes.

The key wasn't there, of course; she'd entrusted it to Gravenshire. Foolish to think a titled man would do as she asked.

She'd take her silver hairpins and pick the trunk's lock; it would only take a moment.

Then in the mirror she caught sight of his reflection.

She turned.

"Lord Vellot."

"So formal." He stepped in quietly, heel and toe. As if he hadn't just been glaring daggers at her downstairs.

Bess mused that she had never really given him full credit for his ability to act.

"I'd prefer it formal," she said, slipping sideways to get the wall at her back. "As it turns out, we don't know each other very well."

"Of course we do." With all the calm of someone who expected what they said to be true because they said it. "Our midnight suppers? Warm baths? Cut apples?"

For a moment, the thought of cut apples nauseated Bess.

She felt shame as his big body drew closer. Shame that she had trusted him. Teased him. Told him who she saw in the theater.

Shame that she had stolen him a ring.

He wore it now, the gold signet ring he'd had her bring from the theater. He must have wanted it to convince someone, likely the ambassador, that he had the backing of someone very powerful. Gravenshire's old friend, no doubt.

He'd neither known nor cared that Bess had hurt the girl

by stealing that ring and the sapphire one she still wore. One girl's pain was beneath his notice.

It hadn't been for Dan.

Not as a tiny boy; not as a wiry youth; not even as the man he was today. Dan would do anything to save a girl in pain. He *had* done, for Bess.

Dan had lied to her for years. But his lies had scarred him inside; she knew that. They hurt *him.*

The Silver Duke never lied. Only assumed she was there for him to use, like everyone and everything else. Like someone else's ring.

Vellot drew closer. "I still have faith in you, Bess." With one big hand he closed the dressing table mirror in its oak frame. He began, oddly, to spin her hairbrush face-down on the table. Its glowing silver surface winked as it went round and round in a circle to the rhythm of his words. "I'm giving you the chance you've always wanted. To commit a truly great crime."

He thought that was what drove her. What she liked.

He didn't know her at all.

But Dan did.

Back to the wall, Bess leaned her head back to meet Vellot's gaze, refusing to watch the silver brush.

"What I like," she told him, "is to do whatever I want."

She saw it hit, saw him lose his grip on his calm. The fury back in his eyes. They crumbled so easily, these kinds of men.

"You don't get to decide that." He grabbed her arm, shook her so hard she felt her bones creak. "What you want doesn't matter. I have great plans, *grand* plans, and they aren't for the likes of you to contradict!"

Like a puff of smoke, the soulless girl he wanted, the girl she might have been, popped and blew away, disappearing like smoke through the cracks in the walls of Road's End. She didn't belong to him and she owed him nothing. He only knew she liked apples.

And that was nothing.

It was only thanks to years of street fights that Bess stayed calm in the face of Vellot's anger. Waiting for his grip to shift. Waiting for a chance to strike.

She wasn't soulless, but she was cold as hell.

Her toilette set rattled as he shook her again. The crystal perfume bottle made a dangerous *tink* noise as her silver brush fell to the floor.

For a moment he let go. Her fingers scrabbled on the polished wood of the table beside her.

Then his hand closed again, this time around her throat.

"No more time to play," he said, his face mottling red as he ground the words out through his teeth. "You'll go down there and lure His Grace into some room, with whatever you've got, and you'll kill him like I told you to. I've got another gun I can bring to bear, but I'm not wasting it unless you fail, and you haven't even tried yet." His thumb tightened against her artery; Bess felt it pulse. "You want to see a deserving man get his finish. You've wanted it for a long time. So get down there and do as you're told, or I'll have that native woman you live with hanging from the Tower."

Bess felt her fingers going numb and saw spots dance before her eyes. She forced sounds out past his fist. "Better let me go."

He ignored her. "And that secretary you make cow eyes at will be picking salt off his eyelids, scrubbing a ship's deck all the way to the antipodes. Bet he doesn't make it past the equator alive."

It could have been hard, but... "Thanks for making this easy," choked out Bess, bringing her hand up and down again, the dagger-like crystal stopper of her perfume bottle clutched in her fist as she drove it into the flesh at the base of his neck.

Recoiling, his fist opened; Bess dropped, choking, to the floor, bringing the crystal stopper with her.

Eyes bulging, he reached for her again, his heavy frame staggering against the dressing table.

Half the things on it flew to the floor, including the open perfume bottle, which landed with a thud. A thick smell of jasmine suffused the room.

The blood pouring down his neck stained his shirt a reddish-brown; the iron smell of it made Bess cough as she crawled away from his tottering form.

He couldn't seem to find her, or anything. Just leaned against the wall and then, in what seemed like only moments, crashed to the floor like a tree.

* * *

THE SOUND of something very heavy falling drew Lady Winpole into the corridor, peering up and down, trying to determine the source.

It had been nearby; she knew that.

Carefully she stepped out into the corridor herself, closing Waresham's door behind her and gripping his loaded pistol in one hand.

* * *

BESS HAD TO *LEAVE*. She didn't want to be in this house, in this room, one second longer.

But Vellot's blood stained the front of her crystal-tipped dress and her hand, which still clutched the spire-shaped top of her perfume bottle.

She'd changed her clothes plenty of times today; she

would again. She'd wash. But not here.

Recalling her trunk was still locked, she fumbled one-handed with the lid to Agatha's. Drew out a walking dress and a petticoat. It was all she had time for.

* * *

DAN SAW that one of the town's two cabs waited beside of the old wing of Road's End, no doubt waiting for a chance to take someone back to the village and earn some brass.

Forgetting about Waresham or the party or anything else, Dan wrenched a handful of the last bit of green grass out of the scanty Road's End lawn, then another, and another.

Then he went at the cab in a run.

Flipping the reins out of the driver's hands, he led the horse forward half a dozen steps so the roof of the cab was positioned under his own window.

Dropped his little heap of grass on the ground.

The horse bent his head. With a running jump, Dan vaulted with his arms up to its back, and from there jumped up to the seat, then the one spot on the cab's roof, its corner, that could bear a man's weight at speed.

"Thank you!" he called back towards the sputtering driver as he reached up to swing out the window casement, then pull himself up over the sill.

Faster than lightning he dashed into his room without looking around, grabbed a fresh shirt and his navy coat, fore-going the bright waistcoat, forgoing anything that slowed him down from reaching the hallway, finding Bess, and getting her out of here.

His plan with the Jacks and Miss Thorpe had a strict timetable, and it was Bess' only chance to disappear like a magical stage effect before anyone could trap her here.

That was all he wanted, and damn the—

As he swung open his door, he remembered the ledger.

Hidden back on the dirt of the road under his evening coat.

Just as the barrel of a pistol swung to stare him in the eye.

A pistol in Lady Winpole's hands.

* * *

CRAWLING TO HER DOOR, Bess opened it just a crack, peeking out from the bottom the way Dan had taught her as a very tiny girl.

She couldn't see anyone on the stairs.

Slowly she twisted till she could look down the bare boards of the floor toward one end of the hall—Madame Franck's closed door—then the other...

Lady Winpole, at Dan's door.

Lady Winpole, training a pistol...

...on Dan, who stepped out of his room.

Throughout the fight with Vellot, Bess had felt calm, cool; but this sight put frost on her bones.

Throwing open the door, she dropped the bundle of clothes on the boards. "Oy."

She let Winpole see her blood-soaked gown, the improvised crystal knife in her fist.

Lady Winpole whirled at the sound, and her eyes flew open at the sight.

Then the growl Dan made forced her to turn back toward the menacing sound.

"Bess." His was a voice from the pit of hell. "Tell me you're—"

"I'm fine." And she was.

Flooded from top to bottom with a feeling she'd just learned to name.

Dan was complicated, and so were most of her feelings. But not this. This was simple, pure, and icy clean.

Dan belonged to her.

Nothing else in living memory had ever been truly hers. But Dan was. And she'd walk into hell's own fires before she'd let anyone take him from her.

In fact, she'd go all the way to hell and crawl back out.

"Lady Winpole." Bess pitched her voice to carry just down the hall, but sound firm. Commanding. Unnerving, she hoped, from a blood-soaked woman. "You have something that belongs to me."

CHAPTER THIRTY-TWO

"*B*ess, go—"

She just raised one hand, the one not holding the bloody crystal spire. Silencing Dan.

"My lady," Bess said again as if they were sitting down to cards. "You have something that belongs to me. I'm taking him with me."

"Don't be silly, girl," said Lady Winpole, also as if this were a normal dinner at Road's End and the guinea pigs were about to make an appearance. "He and I have business."

"No, you don't." Insisting his version of reality was true had worked for the Silver Duke, up to a point. Bess decided to try it.

Lady Winpole only sighed, hefting the heavy pistol in two hands. Its muzzle wavered up and down, still pointed towards Dan; Bess' breath caught.

The older woman said, "He's got something of *mine*, and I can't let him leave with it."

Bess' eyes swung to Dan's. Black, glittering, telling her plain as day to *leave. Get out of here. Run.* "Do you?"

Seeing Bess calm and apparently whole straightened

Dan's back. Slowly, he raised both hands, dropping the coat and shirt on the floor. Their soft *shush* sounds made clear they were empty. Dan turned in place, letting Lady Winpole see through the rags of his shirt that nothing hid next to his skin.

The sight did nothing to calm Bess, though. She could see marks through the torn edges of linen, blood here and there, and it frosted her to her core.

But Lady Winpole clearly hadn't done this to him, and Lady Winpole had to be dealt with first.

"You see." Bess made it a statement, not a question. "So let him go downstairs."

"I'm not going without you." Dan clearly meant it, but that helped nothing.

"I'm not inclined to simply let him *go,*" said Lady Winpole with deep disgust.

Bess flicked her eyes toward the window behind Dan. The one she'd climbed in last night. "What if he jumped out the window?"

Dan slowly backed up to the glass.

"You don't understand." Lady Winpole clearly thought if Bess simply paid attention, she'd stop joking and grasp what was happening. "He's crossed me, and I won't have it."

"But if you shoot him, you'll cross *me.* And trust me, you won't like what I'll do."

That clearly hit home with her ladyship, who studied the macabre picture Bess made standing on bare wood as Dan slowly, slowly backed toward the window and, sliding one hand up the sill behind him, swung it outward.

Bess pressed her advantage.

"You and I understand each other," she said. It was partly acting, pretending to the Silver Duke's kind of grandiosity, and partly tapping into her own confidence, which had come rushing back with Vellot's death. She hadn't realized what a shadow he'd put over her life. She'd never let anyone control her again. "We're two of a kind, you and I. Surely we can arrange something."

"Girl, I don't bargain with beggars." The pistol swung up again toward Bess' chest.

A wild light came into Dan's eyes and he crouched, once again an animal poised to spring. Bess gave him a tiny shake of her head.

Lady Winpole saw it and swung the barrel back.

Bess' laugh was like frozen bullets. "You may feel you have the upper hand, my lady, but in truth you're in a very bad position. Trapped between two dangerous people."

She waited while Lady Winpole realized the truth of that, backing toward the wall so she could see Bess out of the corner of her eye.

"A pistol shot will kill one of you," said her ladyship, clearly grasping the untenability of her situation.

"But not both."

* * *

DAN'S every muscle was poised to go however he had to go. If Winpole turned that gun on Bess again, Dan would topple her before she took aim.

His Bess, his tiny blood-stained Bess—his hands ached to prove she was whole and well—picked up the clothes at her feet, stepped forward, then forward again. The muzzle stayed trained on Dan, but Bess was getting closer.

The longer this went on, the likelier someone would be shot.

He no longer felt the battering Waresham had given him. His skin was humming with anticipation. Any move—

Bess stepped forward again.

Another step, and even with her short arms, she'd be able

to reach Lady Winpole. "You're going to have to choose quickly," she said in a poisonous, logical voice that made even Dan's blood cold.

Proving herself a merchant at heart, Lady Winpole flattened her back against the wall and bargained. "What would you do for me in return?"

"I?" Bess' slow, slow dance moved her quarter-inch at a time closer to Dan, around the barrier of Lady Winpole and her dangerous weapon. "Why, I'll owe you a favor. That's worth something, isn't it? A favor from someone so much like yourself?"

Surely Bess didn't really compare herself to Lady Winpole. Ice-cold nerves, that much was true, but there was nothing else alike between them.

Lady Winpole had only sought to fill her own pockets, while Bess—

Well. Dan dropped that line of thinking.

One which Bess clearly expected Lady Winpole to follow. "So many people overlook a small woman, don't they?"

That little badge of kinship seemed to decide something in Bess' favor.

Lady Winpole let her move another foot closer to Dan, then another foot. Bess scooped up Dan's clothes in the hand that held her own.

Then Bess and Dan were together at the end of the hall, almost close enough to touch.

Dan knew what she was going to do by the look in her eyes.

"Don't," he said, but it was already too late.

Swinging her body downward like the ballet dancer she was, Bess shoved up and out, *hard.*

Catching Dan right in the center of the chest and sending him flying backward through the open window.

* * *

LADY WINPOLE's finger tightened on the trigger; Bess could swear she heard the metal creak.

Lady Winpole just looked disgusted. Disappointed, as always. "I should shoot you right now."

"Ah, but then I won't owe you a favor."

"You think there's a place in London I can't find you? In England? The world?"

"I have a feeling you'll have plenty of problems of your own." Dropping the crystal spire with a rattling *thud* to the floorboards, Bess let herself grin. She'd put her money on Dan no matter what, and Dan was about to cause Lady Winpole many, many problems.

Bess' pleasure made Lady Winpole sigh. "I have a great many tools at my disposal. Men in the courts. Men in the Tower. The kind who will do anything for a little ready money."

"Really?" Bess enjoyed pretending to be impressed. "Do they like you better than I do? Because when I promised you a favor, I lied."

With a squeal half-outrage, half-anger, Lady Winpole swung the sagging pistol barrel upwards again.

Bess only wished that she and Dan had had more time.

But Lady Winpole seemed to want to haggle. That, or simply vent her ire. "How dare you? Look where you are! What do you think you're going to do now?"

"Whatever I like," said Bess, and dove head-first out the window.

* * *

Flipping backwards out the window, Dan barely managed to catch its sill with his fingertips. It had been a lot of years; it hurt, but he hung on.

"Goddammit, Bess."

Letting his toes catch on the brick, Dan stopped his momentum, then shoved himself, twisting, off the wall to the shale roof beside him.

Just managing to land his worn boots on the shale edge, by some miracle of motion he pushed off, flipping backwards again so his legs swung up overhead before winding up below him on the firm ground below.

The cab driver shouted his shock.

Dan would have waited lifetimes, but it wasn't long. In moments, Bess came soaring through the air towards him, one hand clutching their flapping clothes like a flag.

He caught her, rolling with the blow.

"You used to be smaller." His hands ignored the ruined gown, feeling her arms for broken bones, feeling the shape of her delicate head.

"You used to be bigger." Yanking him toward the cab.

Dan shook his head. "I have a plan, remember?"

"You have a plan for *this?*"

"Amazingly enough, yes."

He took her blood-stained hand and pulled her along the drive.

Dark had fallen, but the night was bright. Dan ran to the dim heap at the edge of the drive he knew was his evening coat.

There it was, and yes, gloriously, it still contained the ledger.

He looked back toward the house.

The torches burned low by the Greek-columned entrance, but the moon shed silvery light everywhere.

By it, Dan saw the casement window on the front of the old wing swing open.

"Run." He yanked Bess forward, cutting across the spindly lawn.

* * *

LADY WINPOLE WANTED to fire the pistol. But she hadn't amassed a smuggling fortune by giving in to impulse. Her aim was likely poor, it was night, and she only had one shot.

Foolish to waste it.

She'd find those children one of these days; that was a given. But the gun in her hand gave her another idea of how to solve a more pressing problem.

* * *

IT WAS ONLY natural for Waresham to want a little coddling after Burton had so sorely abused him. He wanted a poultice for his crotch, and his head, and the spot on his ribs where Burton had planted a heavy boot.

So naturally he avoided the ballroom completely as he staggered back into the house.

Thinking only to keep away from anyone who might see him in such a sorry state, he limped on through the sparsely furnished rooms his father was so sure would raise his place in London society.

The man was a fool. No one would ever come to Road's End who was more elevated than the men here tonight. A duke, an ambassador; and they weren't here because of his father. They were here because of him.

Waresham was going to be the right hand of a duke, beloved of an *emperor.* His name would be—

He spotted a tiny, delectable figure ahead of him, by the

window in a flower-papered parlor, swathed in drapes of white lace. A shawl was pulled over her head against the cold air, but he recognized the crystal-bead tassels at her shoulders.

Nothing would be more pleasant right now than to give Burton's precious whore the gift of his company. That would teach the bastard to assault him. *Him.*

And perhaps she knew how to dress a wound. He could use some pampering.

"Miss Page. You'll forgive me for importuning you in so quiet a room. I've had an accident and I must rest." Sighing, he sat in the closest chair. "You wouldn't mind nursing my wounds a little, would you? I confess yours are the hands I thought of first, and I'm quite willing to reward you for the attention once my fortunes have improved. A night at the opera, perhaps."

She turned. "You really will chase anything in a skirt, won't you?"

Waresham hopped up, wincing as his bruises clutched. "Lady Agatha! I was not aware it was you."

"Obviously. Miss Page loaned me her gown." She let the shawl fall about her shoulders, clucking her disgust. "She was right about you all along, and I so foolish, thinking you would ever have a truly tender feeling for me. Or anyone."

"Really, my lady." Waresham felt his ire rising. "You are the one lurking here in the dark, no doubt waiting for any man to come and meet you here."

"Get out," was all Agatha said.

* * *

AGATHA REALLY WAS DISAPPOINTED, both as Waresham limped out and after the door closed behind him, but not enough to cry.

Passion, she decided, was only pleasant in the imagination.

She could go back to the party, and try to flirt with a soldier, or even the Duke. But it held little appeal.

She stayed where she was till she happened to see something remarkable, something she wasn't supposed to see. Two figures running in the dark, one in black, one in smudged white. Her tulip gown. It wouldn't be coming back.

Perhaps she'd order another.

* * *

HALF-STUMBLING, half-sprinting to the lawn's edge, Bess and Dan passed the Jacks, both in brown burlap coats and bending over a brace of wooden tubs.

"All right?" gasped Dan, out of breath. It had been quite a night and wasn't even close to over.

"All right," said Jack, saluting with a stick he pulled from the tub before him. It held a pointed cylinder lashed to its end.

Jack surveyed the both of them with worry, but went on pulling things out of the tub, thrusting the ends of the sticks into the ground.

"You know what to do, then," said Dan, and, taking the bundle of clothes from Bess and clutching it against his side along with the ledger, he pulled Bess on.

She ran with him. "What will they do?"

"What they do best," he assured her, trying to help her fly over the clumps of sedge grass clustered under the trees. "Make a fuss."

"I don't see how that helps." Still calm, Bess was winded too; when Dan looked over, he could see her breath in the moonlight. "They'll be after us, you know. All the way to London. Anywhere we go."

"They'll be looking," said Dan, "but not where we are."

* * *

THE WRECKAGE IN BESS' room told its own story.

But stories, Lady Winpole knew, changed, depending who told them.

She could not afford any stories in which her relationship to Vellot came to light. Smuggling was one kind of treason; conspiring with Napoleon was entirely another. She could buy her way out of a great many things, but not a sentence to hang for that.

Vellot's heavy carcass lay slumped on the floor next to a dressing table, one that had scattered many of its *accoutrements* across the floor.

She noticed the heavy diamond-shaped crystal perfume bottle. Its precious liquid had dribbled out onto the floor.

Much like Vellot's blood.

Yes, this was a useful situation.

Taking the bottle, she sailed back down the hall to the window outside Mr. Burton's room. There she threw it as hard as she could out the window to shatter against the shale roof of the kitchen below. She followed it with the blood-smeared spire, no doubt its stopper.

The thuds and shattering noises would no doubt be heard in the kitchen, but who cared? No one listened to the stories of servants and anyway, now the thing was gone.

Then she marched back to the room and awkwardly pointed the muzzle of the pistol at Vellot's fatal wound.

And fired.

The sound in the little room had her ears ringing. It was very easy to drop the thing—it had stung her hands with its recoil—and run into the corridor, and scream.

* * *

IN THE WOODS, both Dan and Bess heard the gunshot.

They might have heard a faint woman's scream after, but they couldn't be sure.

Especially since the next noise also sounded like a gunshot, then another.

Bright flashes of golden light burst overhead, again and again. Bess had to turn back and look.

Jack and Jackie had lit fireworks. Even as she watched, another fizzing candle fired into the air and exploded, scattering motes of light.

Glittering sparks of fire shot high into the black sky and rained down on the grass behind them.

"There's a great deal happening back there," observed Bess.

"Keep moving," and Dan pulled her forward again.

* * *

THE SOLDIERS, drunk, rolled out the front door like buckshot balls, followed by the ladies.

"I don't recall arranging any fireworks," said Lady Carrollton. She had found and stuffed the guinea pigs in a basket she carried on her arm. Possibly so they wouldn't run under the feet of the drunken soldiers.

Mr. Pig poked his nose out, and surveyed the scene with suspicion.

"Well there they are, Hannah," Lady Dunsby said with eminent logic, as her daughter joined her and they both peered out into the icy night.

Another pair of golden fireballs exploded over the grass, which looked black in the moonlight.

"Drrrr," said Mr. Pig with obvious disapproval, then dove

under the cushion in the basket, where Ruby wisely hid already.

"It's very pretty," Lady Carrollton admitted. "Here," she told a footman, "take them inside. The fireworks will only upset them."

Behind her, the Duke of Gravenshire moved silently toward the stairs.

* * *

"You'd better come with me," he told Lord Waresham, as that young man limped out of the back of the house, taking in but not mentioning the younger man's state.

Waresham knew the sound of a gunshot when he heard it, and it hadn't been fireworks.

Silently he followed the Duke of Gravenshire up the stairs.

He wondered if this would be his moment. His pistol lay loaded on his desk. It would be the work of seconds to retrieve it and put paid to His Grace even as the guests gathered below, gaping at fireworks like a bunch of ducks.

But at the top of the stairs, he found they weren't alone.

"I saw him," Lady Winpole gasped, pressing a hand to her chest. "Mr. Storey, his bookkeeper. He ran out of the room. Do go in, Lord Vellot is in there and I think he's dead!"

With a few long strides the Duke of Gravenshire followed the point of her trembling hand, disappearing into the room.

Waresham regarded her with suspicious dread.

He was no judge of theatrics, or old women, for that matter. But to his eyes the Winpole woman looked fairly cool for someone who had just discovered a murder. If anything, she seemed impatient for Gravenshire to return.

If this was true—if Vellot was dead—Waresham had lost his prize opportunity to vault over his father's reputation straight into the waiting arms of an emperor who could give him any favor in the world.

He'd spent years following in Vellot's footsteps, currying his favor, even giving up choice bits of skirt when Vellot had taken them for himself. It couldn't all be wasted in a second. Burton could have done away with the Duke; but someone murdering Lord Vellot was unimaginable.

Gravenshire's shoulders filled the dark doorway.

"He is dead," he announced.

"It was Mr. Storey, I'm sure it was." Lady Winpole leaned against the wall, presumably to keep on her feet. "I've seen him a dozen times at the card table. I know his face perfectly well. He's a *bookkeeper.* Why should he do such a thing?"

"Why, indeed." Gravenshire didn't twitch an eyelash at the woman, but looked Waresham's way. "See if he's still in the house, will you?"

And with that, he went back in the room and shut the door.

Both Lady Winpole and Lord Waresham heard its key turn in the lock.

* * *

It was dim in the room with no candle, but still bright enough by the moonlight for Gravenshire to make his way to the closed trunk against the wall and try the tiny key from his pocket.

The trunk was full of delicate lacy things, and he pushed them aside in some discomfort, for it had been many years since he'd laid hands on so many feminine things. It felt awkward.

But there, at its bottom, lay a linen-wrapped bundle right where he expected; and when he removed its shroud, he did indeed find a miniature of the late Lord Vellot, embedded in a heavy bronze frame.

"Well," he told Vellot's corpse. Someone had clearly taken matters into their own hands. Who, and how, he didn't know. But he'd guard his own back a little more sharply, and alert Captain Clark, too.

The ambassador would leave tomorrow as prescribed, and he would indeed change the world. Soon Napoleon would not be emperor, and Britain would stand tall as his staunchest enemy.

Reaching down to the corpse, the Duke of Gravenshire removed the gold signet ring from the dead man's little finger, wiping it clean on the man's coat before slipping it into his own pocket.

* * *

"HAVE YE HEARD? A Storey man shot his lordship! Worked for Lord Vellot, he did!"

The maids' whispered traveled down the corridors faster than fire, every servant repeating it to every other one till the few people not on the lawn watching the fireworks were buzzing with nerves, wondering where the murderer was, hoping he'd get caught.

Then Lady Winpole herself followed the gossip down the halls. "We must turn out all the servants to find him," her voice drifted down the corridor toward the pantry.

"Hear that? We're all to turn out the woods for him!"

Silently, Mr. Storey, standing by the fire waiting for his fate, grew still.

Mr. Able came barreling out of the pantry, grains of salt falling from his sleeves; he'd been weighing it. "No more gossip, you lot, get back to work."

"But Mr. Able! We can't work if there's a—a *murderer* in

the house!" A weedy footman voiced the thought, but several others and all the kitchen maids nodded and agreed.

"Yer daft. Like a murderer would hang about trying to snatch up cakes. No, he'll be in the woods, or making for the ferry; the soldiers will get after him. I'm sorry, sir, I didn't see you there." His notice of Storey, lurking in the kitchen corner, brought the buzz in the place to a halt. "You're one of her ladyship's guests?"

Feeling pinned like an insect under glass, Storey nodded. "Yes. Sorry, I'm Mr. Samuel. Sorry to startle you. I was in search of an honest ale. Can't drink any more of that punch."

"Oh, the punch'll kill ya," said Mr. Able wisely, clearly deploring both its excessive existence and its excessive consumption.

"I'll just be a moment."

Leaving them to think he had to step out for some basic purpose, Storey walked out and around the kitchen wing and climbed into the hansom cab waiting by the vine-covered walls. He gave the driver Belinda's direction.

CHAPTER THIRTY-THREE

"We can't run all the way to London."

Bess was out of breath and out of ideas. Escaping Vellot, then Lady Winpole, had been more than a night's work. She hadn't even gotten any jewels out of it.

Dan didn't seem fazed at all. "Seems familiar, doesn't it?"

It was. Put that way, the very familiarity of it lightened Bess' mood. She had a stitch in her side from running over clumps of earth and through puddles of water besides. Her slippers were soaked, her feet freezing; but knowing that she and Dan were running somewhere together made it feel worthwhile.

He slowed as they reached another line of trees, looked back at her, black hair blowing across his forehead. "I'm sorry."

She slowed, laid a hand on the tree's bark to steady herself. Looked up at him in the moonlight. The lines of his face, more familiar to her than her own. "It might be all I've ever really wanted," she said before she could stop any horrible feelings from coming out.

His jaw dropped open and she whirled away, horrified by

the burst of feeling at a moment like this, and suddenly nauseated by the smell of blood on her. That Dan should see her like this.

"I've got to get out of this gown."

* * *

"Of course." He tossed their wad of cloth over a low branch, and tucked the ledger in the back of his trouser waist.

His own shirt, in the dark, was smudged black from when he'd caught Bess; he knew in daylight it would be another color.

Reaching under her own arm, Bess' fingers fumbled at the tapes tied there. "Agatha's gown is too long," she mumbled. "Don't know why I haven't tripped yet."

Dan did; because he'd been pulling her along nearly like a flag behind him. They were close to escape, but if the night had proven anything, it was that plans were only a tiny part of a man's luck; and Dan never thought himself lucky.

Wresting off his shredded shirt, Dan dropped to one knee, uncaring that it was immediately soaked through with marsh water. The ground was sandy and heavy, but he could move some of it aside, as long as he was careful not to slice open his hands on the sturdy grass roots.

He shoved the bloodstained shreds of his shirt into the hole he'd made, then looked up.

Bess stood as bare as a goddess in the moonlight, its glow lighting every lock of hair, the curve of her shoulder, the swell of her hip.

Like a silk-and-silver statue.

She crossed her arms before her, not from shyness, but from the cold. Perhaps a little shyness; she turned halfway around, looked back at him over her shoulder. "Can you get the gown in there too?"

He'd forgotten what he was doing. Forgotten anything but this sight. People glorified the wrong gods. Some power had made this happen, and Dan would remember later to be grateful.

He snapped back to his senses. "Here. Get into the fresh one."

Bess gracefully crouched and washed her hands with the wet grass, stood and slipped into the petticoat and gown she'd fetched like she was dressing for a normal day.

When Dan grasped her hand, it was cold as ice, and he could feel her shivering.

Throwing on his evening coat, he pulled her against him, inside it with him. He tried to take her chill into himself. "What can we do to get you warm?"

Gasping, she pushed herself away from him, and Dan thought he'd gone too far. But all Bess said was, "We can run!"

* * *

PAST THE TREES that circled Road's End, the marsh went on perhaps a mile or two; Bess couldn't guess at distances without pavement or houses.

Another stand of trees, and Bess wondered if they were running all the way to the sea.

But no. Past the trees was another meadow, this one sloping gently upward; Bess felt the ground under her feet get drier, firmer, even though she could no longer feel her feet themselves.

The barn Agatha mentioned was there, the one she said flooded in some seasons. It seemed high enough to be dry enough now, and its open doors showed a scene from a peculiar hell.

Inside sat something that looked like a blacksmith's forge.

No, two forges, but without wells for shaping metal. Instead, iron bars lay over the coals, glowing red; and above them perched curious hats made of glass. Or so they looked; as Bess drew nearer, she saw that the hats sprouted copper tubes that led to a pipe hung from the barn's rafters.

And over this hellscape-contraption presided Miss Thorpe, hair haphazardly tied behind her neck with string and soot stains all over her cheeks, hands, and scorched dressing gown.

Bess couldn't understand anything she was seeing. Not the forges, not the glass or pipes, and certainly not Miss Thorpe. Just the sight of her, blowing water over the forge-grids with a bellows in both hands, made Bess' stomach sink.

She hadn't been lying when she'd told Dan that running somewhere, anywhere, with him was all she really wanted out of life.

She couldn't explain that around Miss Thorpe. "You're out here building a fire?"

That made Miss Thorpe whip around to see her, then grin a maniacal grin and dash across the barn to throw open its far doors. "No," she said, with a trembling note of exultation in her voice. "I am out here creating miracles."

Poised beyond the barn—no, *floating*—a shape loomed in the dark, round, colored with stripes of a hue Bess couldn't discern in the moonlight.

She reached a hand back towards Dan, though whether to protect him or for reassurance she wasn't sure. "What *is* it?"

"*C'est une Charlière!*" When Bess just impatiently shook her head, Miss Thorpe grunted impatiently. "A gas balloon. Are you bereft of knowledge?"

"Probably." Bess turned to Dan. "What is it?" she asked again, as if only Dan would tell her the truth.

"Escape," he said, with that ground-gravel voice that made things real.

Bess did thread her fingers between his and dragged him forward as she moved to examine it.

A basket was slung below the thing, she saw now; its net of ropes captured the bubble-shape, and supported the basket below.

A basket big enough for a person. Or two.

Miss Thorpe was wrapping a thick woolen shawl around the top of her dressing gown. "All right," she said cheerfully, "get in."

"You're taking Miss Page, not me." The same real voice.

Miss Thorpe's actions jittered to a stop.

The soot-streaked woman fixed Dan with a haughty glare. "We had a bargain."

"Dan, no."

He heard Bess, but answered Miss Thorpe. "You'll get paid the same whichever carcass you float out of here."

Faced with inescapable logic, Miss Thorpe shrugged. "True. All right," she gave Bess a dubious look from head to toe, "in you go."

The basket, floating unnaturally off the ground, had a door, fastened with wood and leather toggles; Miss Thorpe opened them with her gloved hands and threw the door wide, one arm arcing to convey that Bess should climb inside.

"No." Bess held on to Dan's hand with both her own. "I'm not going without you."

Trying to copy Miss Thorpe's jaunty attitude, Dan also waved toward the basket with the hand he still had free. "As you can see. Bess, it's the only way. Winpole and Waresham are both killers. You need to get away from here."

"Perhaps they should fear *me*."

Dan shot a wincing look in Miss Thorpe's direction; she pretended not to have heard. "Get in."

Bess was not calm now. Her heart seemed to be trying to

beat its way out of her chest. She could not feel her feet, they were so cold, but the very air seemed to burn, and it wasn't from the frost.

"Dan," she half-whispered, "As pathetic as it sounds, I have been trying to talk to you for days. Years. I've almost worked out how to do it and I am not leaving you here until I do."

"Oh God," swore Miss Thorpe under her breath. "Not a lover's tiff. People, a miracle of science awaits."

* * *

SHE LOOKED SO BRAVE, tiny and brave. Hair tumbled all around her, without gloves or shoes, about to take a more dangerous leap than she'd ever taken before, she was thinking of him.

"Steady," he said, his voice softening against his will as he took her waist in his hands. She felt fragile, and so cold.

He swung her up into the swaying basket. "Hasn't it got a blanket? A rug?"

"In the hamper." Miss Thorpe was folding her bellows into a trunk of her own that the Jacks would presumably retrieve once she floated away.

"Dan." Bess took one of his hands as he tried to reach past her for the hamper, forcing him to meet her eyes. They were... He'd seen her look every way but hurt, until now. "We both know I'm not letting go of this, of you. Don't make me hunt you down, because I will. I won't be sitting in the theater. I'll be following you everywhere you go. I'll be searching every gutter for you, every garret, and everywhere in between. Don't make me do that." She swallowed. "And don't make me beg."

Dan was too worn down to curse Fitz, or fate. "I wish it wasn't like this. I'm sorry. For everything, always."

Quick as ever, Bess knelt in the basket, making it sway. She clutched the lapels of his coat. "It's not over. It might be, if we really hate each other and have five whole minutes alone to say so. But we haven't yet."

"Bess." He leaned in to take her face in his hands. Too much cold between them, and too much heat. "I'll never be far away."

She didn't close her eyes. Stared into his from an inch away. "Then get in this basket. So you'll be there to catch me if I fall."

That was everything he was.

He closed his eyes first.

Then swung around to ask the woman behind him. "Will it hold three of us?"

"No." Straightening, Miss Thorpe wiped hair out of her eyes, smudging the soot on her face further. "You're not honestly contemplating—"

"What if we put three in anyway?"

She snorted, packing away what looked like sharp and shining brass instruments, wrapping them in oiled cloth before laying them in her trunk. "Never. If you must die, you won't do it by sinking my balloon."

Dan didn't want to sink her balloon. But he didn't want to put Bess in it and watch her float away, either. He wanted to be with her.

That wasn't a small want, like food or air. It was yawning, cavernous; it felt like crossing a desert and standing by the ocean, staring at everything he needed.

Bess must have seen something of it in his face, the way she could always read what he thought. She still leaned toward him, making the basket sway. "Do you want to?"

"You know I do."

She had that sparkle in her eye that always meant she was

about to do something particularly bad. "Then, Dan, have you ever done something purely for yourself?"

Never. And if he could, he'd start with this. But...

"Miss Thorpe, can you show me how to control this thing?"

"Once you're aloft, you *don't* control it. But it's my balloon."

"I'll buy it from you." The mad thought came out before his reason caught up with it, and he felt the power of money singing through his veins. Fitz' money, but his to dispense for this mission.

And to Dan, the mission had never been Lady Winpole. The mission had always been Bess.

"What the—" Miss Thorpe drew closer to see how much he meant it. Her own face went through horror, then anger, then a kind of calculating resignation.

Dan's hands slid down again and one wrapped around Bess'.

"Do you have any idea how high this will go?" asked the balloon-woman.

"Does it matter?" Dan shot back. He wasn't looking at her.

He was looking at Bess. And she didn't look frightened. She looked *excited*. Ready to fly.

"I'm ready," she said, knowing his thoughts again without him speaking. "If you'll come with me."

"I hate you both," Miss Thorpe scraped a lock of hair back from her face, smearing her cheek with soot. "I love this balloon. I love it in a way you cannot possibly understand. In a tender way, like a lover."

Dan felt himself grin.

"I might be able to understand," he said, smiling the soft smile that was only for Bess, and climbing aboard.

* * *

BESS WAS grateful he didn't make her hit him over the head and throw him in the basket. She could have made the effort, but she'd already made quite a bit.

Places were sore that usually weren't, not usually, and a lot of things hurt.

She also planned to give up on being good. It hadn't done anything for her, and here was Dan climbing into the basket with her despite her worst behavior.

Not that he knew that yet.

The basket rocked a little, and Bess tried not to feel like a loaf of bread.

She knelt so she could see up over the basket's edge. Miss Thorpe was working at a tied rope with her fingers, and giving them hurried instructions. "Don't lean out once you are in the air, obviously. Don't panic. There's champagne in that hamper." She jerked her chin toward the little bin built into the side of the vessel they sat in. "You give it to the peasants when you land so they don't tear apart the balloon."

"Would they?" Dan asked from his side of the basket. As always, accepting but ready.

"Try not to let them," said Miss Thorpe. The basket-vessel swayed, and she gave them a last look. "Pull this," she showed them a narrow cord, "when you want to go down. *Gently.* Don't yank at the thing unless you can bounce."

She was bitter, and resigned, and somehow wistful all at once. She pulled the last knot out of the rope that held the thing to the ground.

The balloon rose silently into the night.

Bess hadn't expected how it felt; she hadn't expected any of this. It felt as if she weighed nothing. As if she could fly. She *was* flying.

The world had fallen away, and it was the most natural thing for her to go *up.*

Part of her felt angrily dizzy and demanded to be returned to the ground.

Bess recognized it, a part of her that was afraid of the Silver Duke's handling. It was built into her now, that fear, and she wondered if it would ever completely go away. It went with the faint, faint craving for a poisoned sleep, and the feeling of no cares at all.

But there was no paper, no book, no fire, no wine. She had to tell herself she was fine.

The basket rocked, a little crazily, and Bess gasped, fingers clutching the edge.

Then it settled. She looked behind her.

Dan had moved to lean against the basket's far edge, his weight balancing hers so she could be where she was. The black of his features blended into the black sky like it was his natural home; he looked quite at ease. "It's fine, Bess," he told her in that voice woven through all her days and dreams. "You can do whatever you like."

Always Dan's answer, but tonight it had a wild edge. As if he didn't care if she stood and jumped over the edge; he'd catch her or follow her down.

Now that they were alone, the wildness in him made Bess feel a little shy. She wanted so many things, none of which she could steal.

She wanted to understand things, and have them be different too.

She peeked over the basket's edge.

They were already higher than the trees, higher than she'd ever been before in her life.

A small figure disappeared into the row of trees below. "Lord Harman," muttered Dan, and she realized he'd knelt and peered out too. "He's too clever by half. He's going toward the barn."

"It's all right." Bess had to start trusting her instincts again sometime, and right now, with Dan beside her, seemed the easiest time. "If he sees Miss Thorpe, he'll make sure she gets back to the inn. He's all right, really."

"Is he?" Dan asked with a funny tone in his voice that was new.

Smoothly they drifted over Road's End, covering in what seemed to be seconds all the distance that they'd run.

From the air they could see its big new wing and its old one, forming a fat letter L on the ground.

They were sufficiently far behind it that they ought not to be noticed, though Bess saw the red coats of some soldiers moving below, behind her improvised archery field, searching nearby trees. Maybe for her.

Then heat suffused her again, and it was Dan's arm around her waist, pulling her back to the center, away from the edge where she might be seen. She sighed before she thought. He was so very warm, and she was so cold.

They knelt there, looking out of the basket, as they floated past the exploding golden and red sparks of light from the Jacks' fireworks.

"Nobody has ever seen them like this," Bess whispered. No one else could hear; still, as they drifted so high above all the people below, she wanted to whisper.

"Likely not." Another burst of fiery red, and then a whole handful of candles, one after the other, exploding with sound and color.

They were too far and too high to really worry, but... "What if a firework hit us?"

"The balloon would burn instantly." His arm tightened around her waist, sending a silent message that he would not let that happen. As if there were anything he could do about it if it did.

Reassuring her, warming her, there with her.

Her icy limbs warmed from his heat as they floated up

and away, the fireworks growing fainter, smaller, and they drifted into the black sky like pieces of the night.

* * *

IT SHOULD HAVE FELT UNREAL, like a dream. But it felt very real, so real Bess had no question whether she'd been magnetized or not.

She only questioned whether she was really as foolish as she felt. Because she *couldn't help herself.*

"Dan, why did you do it?"

He took it as a reason to move. Slipped his coat off his bare shoulders, tried to drape it over Bess.

She shook her head *no.*

"Why did you do it?" she asked again.

"I wanted you," he whispered. "I wanted someone of my own."

She ached for him, his hunched shoulders bunching with muscle in the night.

"That's not what I mean," she said, fighting to keep her balance on her knees as the basket swayed a little. "You lied to me all those years. So many years."

His black eyes widened. "I stole you—"

"You saved me. Even you can't tell that story any other way. You saved my life, most likely. Certainly from anyone who'd carry off a child and do something terrible with it."

"I was the one who carried you off and did something terrible with you. All those years of grubbing, thieving—"

"I had a good time," Bess shrugged one shoulder. "I'd pick it again. But you lied to me so many times, Dan. How can I ever believe what you say again? I need to know why you did that. *Lied.*"

If he said anything but the plain truth, she'd toss him over the edge.

430

He sat back on the basket's floor, clearly astounded by the question. Above them the balloon swayed in the cold night breeze, drifting farther inland, away from the sea. Wisps of clouds had thinned enough for them to see a star or two.

Searching inside himself for the necessary answer, Dan tossed both hands in the air, then let them flop against his knees where he had bent his legs, criss-cross fashion. He was still shirtless. Bess supposed the cold didn't affect him any more.

"It was little boy embarrassment," he finally said, knowing she had to have the answer, clearly humiliated by the simplicity of it. "I knew I'd done something wrong. Something horrible. Not just because the Grand H. was angry. Because I couldn't put you back when I realized I should."

He leaned back against the wicker.

"Big boy embarrassment. I saw everything you had to go through, Bess, *everything*. I tried to make it better but I never could. I should have told you and apologized, but it wasn't big enough for what I'd done. Then grown man regret. A debt I couldn't pay. And knowing..." He stopped himself, but then swallowed, and went on. "Knowing you relied on me and shouldn't trust me like you did."

He let his head rock a little from side to side, and she knew his eyes were on her though she couldn't see them in the dark.

"If I'd told you, and you hated me like you should," he said in nearly a whisper, "I'd know everything everyone else said about me was true."

"You did a right thing—"

"I didn't."

"I killed him. Vellot. He's dead."

Bess didn't know why it came out like that, right then, but Dan surged toward her, swept her into his arms, both of them kneeling in the swaying basket as if the rules of the earth no longer applied to them.

"*Good.*" He made the word solid and sure. His hands cradled her back, her head.

Her relief made her lean into him. She'd never been as worried by what she had to do as that Dan wouldn't like it.

She pressed her cheek against the skin of his chest, bare under his coat. He felt warm even without his coat.

Right things. They were talking about right things. They had years of puzzles to solve.

She asked him, "Why'd they hang Melinda?" She wanted to say something but was still struggling for the words for it.

The strength in his arms shouldn't surprise her, but it was different when it held her to him this way. "Some silver and a tablecloth," he muttered.

Some of the feelings that bubbled around inside her found a way out; some of the confusion found words. "And that's not fair. Lady Winpole can turn out her maid in the middle of nowhere, but the girl can't do anything to her." With a burst of this stuff Dan probably called *shame,* Bess realized she didn't know the girl's name. "None of the rules make sense to me, Dan, and I always trusted you to tell me the right of it. And if I can't trust you..."

"I'm sorry," he whispered against her hair.

"You didn't fail me once. You failed me *every time* I asked where I came from and you lied. You *lied.*"

"I'm sorry, Bess." His gravel-dark voice came deeper, making him sound as old as he was. Older. "You're right. I should have been what I pushed you to be. I should have at least done that."

"And you don't understand." Could she tell him? All of it?

He understood she had more to say.

Silently, he moved back against the wicker, his criss-cross

legs folding again but her in his lap. Let the basket tilt. Pulled the rug up over both of them.

She reached up, pulling his neck closer, and pulled up the collar of his coat. Foolish man who didn't realize how the wicker would scratch him. Perhaps already had.

She slid her arms around his chest and he sucked in his breath, silently, but she sensed it. He must know she would sense it. Something pained him, deeper than scrapes. "What happened to you?"

"Later," he said, holding her against him, letting the balloon rock them in the night. "Tell me whatever you need to say."

CHAPTER THIRTY-FOUR

He'd rather be here than the plushest velvet bed in London.

And Bess was talking to him. "I was so *angry* with you. When you left."

"Fair," he said, hitching her a little closer. She made the little space between them wonderfully warm, and it was all he could have dreamed of in the world.

She could do whatever she liked with him. He'd still remember the way she'd said he *belonged* to her for the rest of his life.

He'd never belonged to anyone, not really.

"Then I was so scared. By Vellot. I thought I knew what he was, but I knew *nothing*, nothing. Then—You didn't really think I took opium willingly, did you?" She punched his ribs.

Dan grunted. At least one of those ribs might be cracked.

"Oh! I'm sorry." Her hand smoothed down over his skin. It was torture, but a much sweeter kind. Then she thumped his chest with her fist. "Honestly, did you?"

"It's not for me to judge you," he gasped out. She had not hit softly.

"But no one else can. And if you don't know me—Of course I didn't know I had opium. He put it in my wine. He —" This time, it was her face that thumped into his chest.

She stayed silent so long, face hidden against him, that Dan worried she'd gone away somewhere, some place in her head where he couldn't follow.

He only breathed again when she said, faintly, "Is it all right if I tell you most of it another time?"

"Any time, or no time," he said, pulling her closer no matter how it hurt. She'd put herself in his arms; it would take an army with crowbars to get her out. He wasn't letting her go.

"He can... he *could* do things. Magnetize people, Agatha said it was called. I don't know what it was or how it worked, but he made me say things. Think things. No, he didn't make me think them, but he... well, he did, a little. It was very confusing. *Confusing* is not a big enough word." She took a deep shuddering breath and let it out. He went on holding her. "Then that night at Road's End I knew who he was, what he was, and he—he could still do it. At least he tried. It spun me around, I couldn't think, I didn't know what was happening. So I ran to you, like a little girl—"

He made a noise of disagreement and squeezed her close again.

Bess just went on. "And you felt like you used to feel. Like you know what the world is, how it works."

"Not much," he admitted softly.

"More than me. You always knew more than me. And I needed that from you, more than anything. Then last night I found out you—I *never* thought you'd lie to me. *Never.* Not like that. Not *about* that."

"I'm so, so sorry." So much time hating himself, and for the *wrong thing.* "I don't know how to make it up to you. I'll never stop trying. Anything you want, Bess. I owe you anything."

He thought she'd ask about the corner where he'd found her, the carriage, whatever he knew.

Instead she said, "Then I need everything you have. All your days, hours, every minute. You gave them all to me before; I want all the rest there are. Give me them all. I know you love me, and I think I love you."

It was not what he expected. He was confused. Of course he'd give her everything. Every coin he had, forever. But she was asking for something else.

She was asking for *him.*

"I'm not what you want, Bess. I'm the man who ruined your life."

"Catching me when I jumped out that window evens the scale a bit."

"Don't forgive me."

"I'd just kicked you through that window, and you caught me. I know that's how you probably strained those ribs."

"It's not enough."

"I didn't say it was. But it adds to the scale." She snuggled closer. He could explain she was rewarding his bad behavior, but it didn't seem smart. "I thought I knew you. Knew everything about you. Then you went away, and that was just the first in a string of bad surprises. It isn't that I want to feel certain. It's that I *do* feel certain. Of you. Make it true, Dan. I'll be the worst kind of fool if you prove me wrong."

"You don't think of yourself that way."

"I spent five years waiting for you to come home. I felt like a fool."

She was asking for the worst possible thing: him. All he'd wanted was not to hurt her more than he had already by stealing her from that street corner. Yet he'd hurt her anyway. With lies and with silence.

How could he escape his nature and avoid hurting her more?

It couldn't be as simple as staying with her and telling her the truth.

But the allure of it was indescribable. He could do that. *He could do that.*

Bess added, "And when you came home, I'd just seen Waresham."

That made Dan shift, and wince. Hopefully, he'd given the man the message to stay away from Bess. "What, in the audience?"

"In the stairwell. Tupping some girl."

Dammit.

"I'm sorry you had to see that." He shifted under her again. He would *not* get hard just from the topic. "Frightening?"

"No, it wasn't. It made some things clear. I wanted that." *Please don't say that again,* Dan thought with desperation. "But not with him. I wasn't ready to tell anyone, but I know now. It was something I'd have died without having, if you never came home."

Please don't. He was all too human, and wounds or no, having Bess in his arms like this was better than he expected of any heaven. The night was quiet; they were floating who-knew-where over the countryside with the Thames a faint ribbon in the distance; and there was no one to stop them, no one to see.

"Tell me you didn't think I'd taken that opium myself."

"We hadn't seen each other in so long. I worried you'd changed." He cupped her cheek, letting his thumb stroke the soft line between her jaw and her ear. "I didn't know what had happened, and that was my clumsy way of asking."

Bess squirmed a little in his arms. "Tell me you still love me even after—"

It was too much. He wasn't made of stone.

He lifted her, hands holding her ribs, and spread her higher across his chest. Her face nested perfectly against the side of his neck.

And he confessed everything.

"From the first second I saw you, you've been all that mattered to me. I had to go away before I did something unthinkable. All those years the Grand H. warned me to watch myself, and there we were, alone in that cellar, and I just thought who's to stop me? And I knew I'd hate myself if I did anything else to trap you there."

"I thought we were better off together."

"I didn't trust how much you might—" He cut himself off.

"You can say it." She nodded against his neck. "It's true. I did love you. I do."

The swearing he tried to keep inside. "I love you, Bess, I swear to God I do, I swear to *you.* I love you more than anything else in this world. You're *all* I've ever loved."

It was a lot to drop at her feet, he realized. She already knew; she'd told him so herself. But here he was hammering on it. He couldn't help it. He'd tried so hard to keep the words from coming out that now they were flying everywhere, free.

"Better than Miss Thorpe?" He could feel her little smile against his skin.

He stroked her hair, first with his hand, then with his chin, hoping the night beard roughness wouldn't scrape her. "You're not serious."

"Good." That pleased her.

"But are you sure? I mean, the *way* you love a grown man. You don't have to give me any particular answer. You don't even have to know." Now he was the one who felt silly, groping for words that wouldn't be too crude. He'd never had refinement, and this was *Bess.*

She was still smiling, and he felt her shift herself, not putting weight on his ribs, sliding around him again the way she had that wonderful, awful night at the hotel. He knew her strength, her abilities; still it astonished him, the way she wrapped her legs around his lean waist, her feet crossed behind his back, resting against the thin wicker that was all that stood between them and the sky.

She pulled the heavy rug up behind her, wrapping them both in it, and tucking it behind him.

Within the cozy shelter she lay against him again, finding the place where her weight against him didn't make him wince, wrapped her body against his even as he wrapped himself around her, the two of them a never-ending ribbon of skin and breath.

"Bess, we can't—"

"Can't we?" When she settled lower, she surely felt the hardness underneath her. Nothing Dan could do to stop that.

"I'm not—"

"Aren't you?" She wiggled lower. "I'm not good at telling right from wrong, Dan, and I don't care. What I know is how we fit together. You're not going to tell me I can find this, feel like *this*, somewhere else, are you? With someone else?"

Her face hovered right there in front of him, her mobile features settled, certain. The delicate pink flush in her skin stood out, a beacon of color in the colorless night. And she looked at him with the only eyes that mattered, those bottomless tourmaline eyes.

"Never," he said, surging below her to wrap her body, her heart in everything he had to give.

* * *

BESS *LOVED* the feel of his body around hers. The muscles that bunched along his arms and legs were hard as stone, but with the soft hot covering of skin. She felt it along the smoothness of his chest, and it felt glorious.

His kisses ran into her blood, more intoxicating than wine, which she doubted she'd ever drink again. It was funny how satisfying they were, rich salty tastes better than anything from a wealthy person's table, yet they left her wanting more.

The two of them curled into a perfect ball of bones and heat.

She tried pushing into him a little more, flattening her feet down and pressing up so the insides of her thighs brushed the sides of his belly. It wasn't enough either. She could barely feel the tickle of the curly black hairs there that led downward.

It would be lovely to do this in a bed. But on the other hand, who else rediscovered their lifelong love in a balloon up in the air, floating among the clouds?

After this—after Dan was *all* hers—there would be no *more* left to want.

She was so happy he'd stopped talking nonsense about what he deserved. This wasn't about deserving. *She* didn't deserve this, but she was going to keep all of it, all of him, for herself.

Finally, they didn't have to talk anymore. Their kisses danced everywhere they could reach; lips hot and brushing against earlobes, jawlines, hairlines, mouths. Bess pushed up so he could reach the spot at the base of her throat, tasting her skin as if about to eat her.

It was more thrilling than sneaking into someone else's house.

The noises he made when she rocked back and forth against the hard core of him fascinated her. He sounded pained, almost angry, and desperate too. There was the hunger she'd seen that she wanted to know better, but more intensely, because this was Dan, and he did not leave things half-done.

He was holding back. She was sure of it. The ache had spread lower in her, made her feel liquid and hot in places she usually didn't, made her feel hungry herself. Sliding back on his thighs, she attacked the buttons of his trousers with both hands.

He grabbed her wrists.

She might have screamed if he'd started the everlasting talking again, but to her great gratitude, he didn't. Nor did he ask her stupid questions about what she wanted. It was clear what she wanted; she was unwrapping it with both hands.

He only held her hands a moment, looking into her eyes, asking and answering all they needed to talk about that way.

Then let her go.

Nimble fingers warmed in the space between them undid his buttons, tucked the fabric back as far as it would go. He lifted his hips a little to help, wincing.

Either his wince or the heat of the hardness that she freed made her pause a moment. Made her wonder if words weren't useless after all. Or perhaps she just wanted a moment to gather herself.

When she closed her hand around him, he groaned deep in his chest, and she knew it didn't hurt.

It was a delightful feeling of power, better than anything she'd felt as Vellot's spy, better than being on stage. It gave her the confidence to keep going. "Have you done this before?"

"Yes," he said, which she liked better than any coy answer he might have given. "Wish I hadn't."

"Why?" She couldn't imagine not wanting this. The pulse she could feel in him was an intense sensation, the smooth, hard, hot skin of him even more so.

"Because it wasn't with you," he managed to get out in his gravelly voice. "Oh, *God.*"

"You can touch me too," she assured him. It would be awkward with him in her hand, but she wasn't letting him go.

"I'm afraid of hurting you."

"Hmm." She didn't have to prove her bravery to him, but she was pretty sure that she could do this. He didn't have to be so dainty about it. "Help me up."

If he really didn't want this, he didn't have to; but if he would...

He did. Bess aligned her knees around him, her legs lying against his wool trousers, and he helped lift her with his incredibly powerful muscles. He winced again, but didn't stop, and neither did she.

Slowly—not too slowly, but without the speed of her usual maneuvering—she lowered herself down on him.

She was right. She knew she was, and it was true. The slickness, the warmth of her had pooled in just the right place. The mechanical workings of it were obvious.

The sensation was not.

She felt some stretching, a slight burn. It was there along with the soul-satisfying feeling of him filling her, touching her exactly where she wanted to be touched, in a way she couldn't do alone.

It was delicious and surprising and even more than she expected. It was dangerous, she knew that. Feelings were involved.

Dan just held her, waiting for her to decide whatever she wanted to decide.

Slowly she rocked against him. He groaned; so did she. It would be difficult to be silent, she could see that.

His hands splayed down her hips, holding her where they joined, steadying her in just the right place.

They stayed that way for a long time, Bess leaning forward to kiss him again, lay herself carefully against his chest, feel his breath mingling with hers.

"Are you all right?" It was Dan's softest whisper, just for her. Like his smile.

"Yes. Are you?"

"I've died and gone to heaven, and I wasn't expecting that."

More soft kisses—it just seemed natural, no, *necessary* to kiss him when they were so wrapped around each other, joined more than two other people could ever be.

"I should've—"

"Shh," said Bess. "Next time."

"For once," he said, breathless, "slow down a little."

The sway of the balloon basket rocked them against each other, so slowly, a motion that was both too small to satisfy and too big to escape. Each little motion moved Dan inside her, and it changed the world again, spinning it around on its axis, but this time it all made sense.

It could have been minutes, but it felt like hours.

The earth slowly turned under them, the sky slowly spun above, and the two of them drew closer and closer, each motion winding and pushing something inside Bess that threatened to push her over a cliff.

She couldn't wait.

When she pushed herself closer, feeling the sensation inside, the feel of Dan's hard heat wrapped around her outside, he tossed back his head for a second, blowing away a lock of his disheveled black hair, and gave her a lopsided grin so sweet that she felt her heart melt.

All it took to sort out her emotions was having him this near.

"Please," he said, oddly hoarse, "I want to touch you."

She just gave him back the same thing he always gave her. "Do what you like."

His hands slid under the gown she'd snatched on the way out of that horrible, fateful, far-behind-them room. Without stays, and made for someone larger, it was loose. The cold around them was nothing. Everything was heat.

The tightness inside her had eased, had grown even slicker, and every tiny motion was pressing full, sensitive places that *wanted* to be pressed, that longed for it. Each tiny rock forward and back made them hungrier, made Bess hungrier. She wanted it to last forever, and if it did, she thought she might die.

Dan's strong hands bunched her petticoat over her thighs, slid over it and up her sides, to brush the undersides of her breasts. The sensation was shockingly strong; she shuddered.

She couldn't understand the things Dan muttered any more. It seemed to be sounds, trying to be words, mostly failing. The way his eyes fluttered closed when she pressed forward, pressing him deeper, said everything she needed to hear.

Then one of his hands slid back under the petticoat, shockingly intimate, finding the spot that she already knew was best.

Waiting for him.

The delicate stroke, then firmer pressure, sliding, circling, just the right place, made Bess buck hard against him, then again, trying not to bump his bruises, eyes flying wide and searching his face.

"I'm fine," he said, curving his neck down to kiss her.

"You're a lia—"

The explosion hit at her center and shot outward, like the sparks from the fireworks, glowing, fiery, shaking her from the inside all the way out.

Dan groaned, holding on to her, and she realized he must be feeling every pulse.

Limp, Bess threw one hand out to her side, bracing on the side of the basket, breathing hard. She knew her mouth had fallen open; she was breathing hard like she'd been running.

She couldn't help herself.

"Now you," she gasped.

"One more time, Bess," Dan said in that roughened voice, pitched only for her.

* * *

DAN WAS CHANGING his opinion about fate.

If he'd waited all his life for this soul-filling feeling, not just of Bess in his arms, but Bess wanting him, *loving* him, it was worth it. Every minute was worth it.

She was so strong, able to lever herself forward and back with tiny movements of the muscles in those dancer's thighs. His own body felt powerful, aches falling away; the conviction that he could do anything for her had carried him through tougher days. This wasn't that. It was bliss.

She looked startled, unaware for the first time in her life that she could go farther, higher. Everything he wanted was to be the one who showed her how.

By the time she reached the second peak, they were flying high enough that the cold mist of the clouds themselves settled on their skin as they let the balloon drive their delicately powerful joining.

She gasped, grabbing at the basket wall again, looking at him with open astonishment.

She must be able to feel him pulse in answer. He was close, so close. But he wanted this to go on forever. After all, one never knew what tomorrow would bring.

"I just want you," panted Bess, which made no sense

because she *had* him. She had him in every possible way that mattered, right now.

He let her breathe for a moment, smoothed the hair back from her face. It was closer to golden again at the edges, above her forehead; he didn't care. The color of her hair didn't matter. That wasn't who Bess was.

Maybe only he knew who she really was, the icy parts and the fiery ones, the lies and the truth, and certainly he was the only one who loved them all.

"You've got me," he reassured her, because that seemed to be what she needed to hear. "Not hurt?"

"Not hurt at all," she said, catching her breath, and looking at him with obvious wonder in her eyes. A bead of sweat chased itself down from the golden edge of her hair; he wiped it away with his thumb. "I can't believe how the second time felt so much *more.*"

"Good," he purred, no animal now but ready to spread his wings and fly. "One more time, Bess."

* * *

"I LOST COUNT." Dan's body was near to giving up in a number of ways, but he wouldn't let it. Muscles screaming to move, screaming for release; he ignored all of it, the bruises, the pain, the pleasure, all had to wait while Bess found the limits of where she could go.

Bess just stared at him. Deeply flushed, the peaks of her nipples sharp through the linen gown, she couldn't lift her arms to brace herself any more. She just let him hold her, let him determine if the basket's sway made a big rocking motion for them or a little one. They'd experimented with swinging the basket harder, just a little, not enough to incur Miss Thorpe's wrath even if she were here. But she wasn't here.

It was only the two of them, locked in a forever spiral of Bess' pleasure and Dan's pleasure in giving it to her.

Truthfully, he was so hard that it was painful. Every escalating silken grip of her body drove him closer and closer to the peak. But she could go over the edge this way, just filled with him, him touching her lightly, whereas he needed more motion. It was keeping him perfectly balanced on edge.

"More?" was all she whispered. She seemed to have few words left. Sounded both hopeful and a little anxious.

"One more?" It wasn't an order; he asked.

Truthfully she was getting closer and closer to a continuous wave, the peaks never coming down, only going higher. The way her body gripped him hadn't stopped, and every tiny motion threatened to push him, too, over the edge.

But then she took a deep breath, and he saw a wave of the determination he knew so well.

"I can if you can," she told him with a determined look that just threw the challenge at his feet.

It was a race. He couldn't hold his own body back forever, and she was hot slippery silk gripping him so tightly that he saw stars he knew weren't in the sky.

Furthermore, she'd learned a few things in the eternity they'd been doing this. She squeezed a little, experimenting, and flowed against him with a liquid motion that made him groan aloud. Copying his motions, she too slid her hands under his coat, in her case brushing a thumb over one of his own brown nipples and then lightly pinching it. He yelped, but the sensation that shot up his spine was *not* pain.

Bellies fit together, chests brushing through and around their clothes, no longer worried about the cold, they tried to beat each other to the finish line, not with their own pleasure, but with the other's.

Dan felt the slow shudder that started in her, right where

they joined, right where he had *her,* and knew he might well win.

It spurred him to lift her slightly with hands around her hips, her own muscles too exhausted to lift her more, his own desperate to stop and rest but his hips driving forward of their own accord, doing what had to be done, for *her.*

He felt it when she bore down on him, the deep swelling pleasure gripping her, shaking her, almost pushing him out but he bore in, to this, to her.

Her scream of final pulsing pleasure, wet, overwhelming, destroying, floated out into the wind, no doubt sounding like a bird of prey to anyone who heard it far below.

Still joined in the circle they formed he let the force of her pleasure carry him over the edge and he fell, not even an inch into her arms, but nonetheless into a hot abyss. The pleasure spiked upwards, radiating out, wiping away any thought, any intention he had left.

There was nothing left of him but the desire to hold her, protect her, love her.

But then, that was all he'd ever been.

CHAPTER THIRTY-FIVE

Cold, also hot, sweating against Dan's skin, drowsy from lack of sleep, and in dire need of a bath, Bess was happier than she'd ever been in her life.

Funny how that feeling wasn't hard to understand at all.

The disentangling could have been awkward, but since they'd spent an eternity entangled, it only felt like a necessary rearranging of limbs.

And separating from him felt temporary.

She rummaged in the hamper woven into the side of the basket. "Miss Thorpe is bloody-minded. Imagine not telling us about the sandwiches." Bess had tucked her knees against one of Dan's thighs, muscles screaming that she had stretched them in new and unprecedented ways. Dan didn't fuss over her language.

She finally investigated the contents of the hamper down to the bottom. The sun was not yet risen, but its faint glow showed, and that helped.

"She was serious about the champagne," Dan observed.

"We drank it." They'd had to. There was nothing else, and escaping via balloon and falling in love at the same time had been thirsty work. There was a crusty little loaf of bread, and a square of creamy cheese; Miss Thorpe was serious about cheese, too. Those hadn't lasted long, and then they'd only been thirstier.

Somewhere in the pre-dawn hours Dan had set himself to picking apart the twine holding the cork in the bottle. It popped, landing they knew not where. Bess still didn't know if Dan had aimed it away from the balloon, or they'd just been lucky.

She felt lucky.

Bess couldn't get over how fast the world could change. It seemed perfectly normal now to be floating high above the ground, featureless dark blobs of trees and the neat shapes of farms below her; perfectly normal to have spent the night woven into a knot of never-ending pleasure with Dan; perfectly normal to escape Road's End and its skimpy table and its guinea pigs and not have the faintest idea where they were going.

"We have nothing to give to the peasants so they don't destroy the balloon."

"To hell with them," Dan said easily. "Let them destroy it. It's paid for."

Just as he said that, Bess found the small pouch in the bottom of the hamper, leather the color of the wicker, barely noticeable even by touch.

She drew it out.

It held a white silk flag, the silk so fine that the entire thing folded up smaller than Bess' palm. A small bone-and-brass pocket knife, the kind where the blade folded into the handle. Oiled linen thread wrapped in a thick bundle, a tin of soft wax, and a wooden case of heavy needles. And fifteen golden coins.

Dan's lurking smile faded as he looked at them heaped in Bess' hand.

"In case of dire straits, I suppose," said Bess. She slid one coin towards Dan.

He didn't take it.

She wasn't ready to worry about everyday things like money. "Let's never land."

He looked down at her, the rosy lightening sky just visible over his head. "I know what you mean," was all he said, softly, pulling her closer again.

* * *

THE NEW BOND FELT DELICATE, not breakable, but raw. Bess felt in a burst of superstition that getting out of the balloon would cut it somehow.

Still, she fussed around Dan as if it were the old days. As if they knew where they'd end up that night.

She tied the corners of the flag together, tucked it under his collar and spread it down the front of him under his coat.

"It doesn't look like a shirt," he observed, smoothing it down.

"They're farmers. I doubt they see much London fashion."

"Are they?" Dan looked over the edge.

The balloon had sunk dangerously low; if they didn't try the release cord soon, they'd be swept into the trees that were approaching in the distance.

Above them the fabric of the balloon itself creaked.

There was no way to know how far they'd gone, or in what direction.

"Hold on to me." Dan didn't need to say anything else; the time had come.

And time, Bess realized, was one thing she couldn't steal more of.

She did hold on to him. Tried to grip around his waist,

where it wouldn't hurt, but he just tucked her against his side, locked her in his steel-hard grip.

For a moment the wind swirled, and the balloon slowed.

Dan took their chance.

Remembering Miss Thorpe's command not to yank, he slowly pulled the cord. He heard something hissing above him and stopped. The balloon dropped.

Not enough. The trees were still some distance off, but getting closer.

"Something we should have practiced, maybe," Dan said grimly, and pulled the cord again.

Longer this time. Their drop was faster, farther. Another gust of wind grabbed the balloon and pushed it *up* for a stomach-churning moment.

Bess looked up and saw Dan's locked jaw, the jut of his chin dusted with black bristles. *Not everything should be given free rein*, she realized in that moment. It wasn't fair for Dan to always have to manage what happened next.

"Be ready," he muttered, completely unnecessarily as Bess' nerves were stretched taut. The dawn light was just breaking, and it was still unseasonably cold; but Bess, bare feet and all, was ready to jump however she needed to jump.

She saw him measure something with his eyes, saw him make a decision. "We're going to hit," he warned her, letting out a gust of whatever magical substance held the balloon aloft.

It did drop, then further, the balloon itself sagging over them even as the basket made a bone-rattling *thump* on the ground. Then the breeze caught it again and the whole thing threatened to lift; it did lift, just a few feet. Pulling the cord, Dan forced the balloon to release all it could. Sinking drunkenly, it tipped, pulling the basket over as well, and dragging them toward the trees.

Then, in the fight between the balloon and Dan, the balloon gave up.

In the tangled mass of their limbs Bess picked herself up off him, still worried for his ribs. Then grabbed his face and kissed him, hard. "You're a wonder," she told him, her honesty brimming over, before she climbed out and turned to help him.

He emerged a little more slowly.

"Look!" She bounced on her toes in the cold turned earth, and pointed.

The balloon had stopped before it became entangled in the trees, sinking down, its stiff fabric flapping with a peculiar clacking noise. It smelled acrid, oily. But it was whole.

"We might want to use it again," Dan told her under his breath.

There was a farmer staring by the edge of the field, sheer astonishment painted all over his face. The donkey next to him looked just as startled.

Dan waved.

Both man and donkey trotted over at Dan's wave.

"I'm terribly sorry," Dan told him. It wasn't Mr. Burton's swooping voice, but it wasn't street Dan, either. He sounded grander than his usual self.

With a pang, Bess realized she was hearing the Grand H.

She took Dan's hand.

He squeezed it, still talking to the farmer. "My wife and I have had a mishap. We'd no intention of disturbing you. If you'd give us the direction of a carriage for hire." He stepped closer to her, blocking her from the cold wind. "And a cobbler who might have a pair of ready shoes for my wife."

No balloon could soar as high as Bess' heart did hearing the word *wife.* It made no sense. It was just a word. Still, it had done something to her.

Words were so dangerous.

"Oh aye," was all the farmer said, his broad face swiveling to stare at her, then at Dan, then at her again.

However lazy his reply, the farmer didn't let grass grow under his feet. He trotted off, the donkey after him like a large dog, and if Bess' experience in the alleyways was any measure, he'd soon be telling everyone he knew, and they'd want to come see. Perhaps they'd have to travel farther than in a London alley, but the gawkers would soon be here.

Like they must have been around the crashed carriage where Dan had rescued her for the first time so long ago.

She was sure. He was everything she ever had needed, everything she ever would need. And so much more.

She took a deep breath. "Do you think—"

"No, I'm not going to ask you now." He turned to look down at her, his straight hair ruffling in the frosty morning breeze. "I think you've had enough of people telling you what to do, and feeling lost. Last night was..." The smile hit them both at the same time, looking into each other's eyes; Dan went on. "Last night could rate as too much persuasion all at once. For anyone. But I will ask you, Bess. When you've had time to think about it. When your feet are under you and you feel safe."

She opened her mouth to argue, but he just shook his head, certain and immovable.

Bess narrowed her eyes.

Her feet were solidly under her, on ground the farmer had turned over with the last of his summer wheat. She knew what she was doing, and she wanted to do it.

But if Dan thought he could decide for both of them, so be it.

He knew perfectly well that she held a grudge.

* * *

THAT NIGHT in the carriage inn, Dan enjoyed every second of pretending Bess was all his to care for.

He helped her up the stairs to the larger room, a happy use of one of the seven-shilling gold pieces.

He told the innkeeper to bring everything he had to eat. It had been so long, years it seemed, since Bess had a proper meal.

Dan could use one too.

His Bess was made of iron, but she'd been through too much. No one knew better than he did how strong she was, how much she could do. No one could see like he did that she was ready to break.

He didn't expect her to order the bath for him, didn't expect it waiting for him once he'd bought passage on the coach the next day for London.

It felt peculiar, in some ways, Bess moving silently around their room, laying out clean linens for him to dry with, the razor and soap he'd purchased. The tailor in town hadn't questioned his sudden need for a shirt and smallclothes. He'd even patched the trousers so the rips barely showed.

It was an easier life when you had money.

The coins had been on his mind when he'd told Bess he had to wait to ask her to marry him. She deserved to be sure, but so did he. Sure he could give her the life she deserved. Sure she didn't want something else.

Sure she'd never regret loving him, because he'd *never* spend another second regretting the way he loved her.

Her quiet movements around their place for the night tugged at his most secret desires even more than the memory of her body around his last night.

This, just this. Having her all to himself, having a home with her. A place to sleep. In a bed. Together.

It would be bliss.

Then he heard words come out of his mouth. "Do you want to sleep somewhere else?"

He didn't know why he'd asked. Habit, perhaps. He hated the question the second he said it. He didn't want her sleeping somewhere else, not ever.

She just looked over her shoulder at the rough wooden bed. "Why, you think we won't both fit?"

The sharp wire wrapped around his heart eased. She wanted to be here, with him. At least for tonight.

"Do you want to send word to the theater?" What was *wrong* with him? Why must he always arrange for her to be able to leave him?

That question too she brushed away like a cloud of gnats. "I thought of sending word to Madame Franck, but she'll have to make do with the message I left. I told Agatha when we switched gowns I might not be back but not to worry, I'd send word when I could."

"You switched gowns with Agatha? Why?" Slowly he stripped off his coat, and the wool waistcoat beneath. He'd scandalized the tailor by traveling without one.

His muscles were stiff with the last day's work, and much activity to which they were no longer accustomed.

"A last effort to make her see that *exciting* doesn't mean *worthy*."

That sounded a little uncomfortably close to home; Dan decided to ignore it. He paused, looking at the shaving soap where Bess had put it out on a clean linen for him.

She motioned with her chin. "Just get in the tub."

"The hairs get all over. A man can't shave in the tub." He sounded peevish, he realized, then wondered how long it had been since he'd eaten himself. His stomach felt hollow.

Bess just picked up a wide porcelain washbasin. "I'll hold it for you. You can shave in the water. Get in. The water will get cold."

He felt shy, and stupid for feeling shy. After the night they'd spent together, it didn't make sense. But those hours had seemed like time out of time, the kind of stepping away from the earth and history that people wished for but never got. He couldn't hold her to anything that happened during that time; he didn't wish to *hold* her at all.

Well, he did, but only as long as it let her be free.

Still, he stripped off his clothes and stepped into the tub. It wasn't huge, but it was big enough, and Bess was right, the water was hot.

Blissfully he sank back, let his head fall against its wooden edge.

Sweeping up his trousers and coat, Bess dropped them outside the door, shut it again.

"Oy!"

"They'll bring them back. Cleaner." She gave him one of Miss Page's sugary smiles, and Dan didn't trust it. But he'd committed now.

When she came back and dipped the dish in the clean water, held it for him so he could scrape the bristles off his face, he felt like *he* was the one magnetized, floating, maybe, in a dream.

This might not last, but at least she clearly enjoyed watching the water lap against his chest. "Tell me when you're done shaving."

He rinsed the blade, gave her a sidelong look. "Why?"

"I want to tell you something and I don't want you to cut yourself."

He laid the razor in the bowl; she set it down. "Since when do you order me about?"

She just rolled her eyes. "Since always. I told you so."

Then she pushed a wooden stool closer to him. It held a vast bowl of stew, buttered bread with plum jam, and a tankard of ale.

He peered at it all. It was despicable he should think it, but he did wonder how he'd tell if it were poisoned.

As if he'd know.

Anyway, if Bess wanted to poison him, that was her prerogative and hers alone.

He picked up the bread. No reason not to eat sweets first. "Why all the bait?"

"No traps. I said, I want to tell you something."

Fear clenched in his gut. Was she leaving? *Now?* "What?"

Hooking her fingers over the edge of the tub, she balanced her chin on them and looked at him. Why she looked so long and hard at him, he didn't know; he knew what he looked like, and it was nothing grand. Still, it made him feel too many things to have her look at him that way.

He felt important. Desired. Special.

And she knew it, too. And she didn't mind. "You always belonged to me, Dan. I don't believe in gods, like Dido and Aeneas did, but I think there's something to fate. We would have found each other somehow. I'm glad you found me first."

The jam soured in his mouth. "I'm not," he said, low, putting the bread down.

She picked it up, put it back in his hand. "I met a girl at Road's End. Well, in the village. One of the Russian girls there since they repaired the Russian fleet."

"Yes?" He didn't like where this was headed, but he'd started these wheels rolling when they were little; it wasn't like he could get off the wagon now.

"She spoke Russian, and it sounded so familiar."

Now the rich butter and bread tasted like dust. Dan put them down again. "Did it?"

"It's fine, Dan. It's all fine." Unexpected as it was for *her* to reassure *him,* it did work, a little. The ratcheting tightness in his gut eased. "I just wondered. The people in the carriage, when you found me." She didn't say *parents*. "If they were Russian. Wouldn't that have made it harder for the Grand H. to find out who they were?"

"Why would they be Russian?"

She shrugged one shoulder, its little curve blocking out the fire for a second, then dropping again. "Why wouldn't they be? I've heard plenty of languages where we used to live, Dan, but not this one. Yet I'd heard it before."

Dan pushed down his rising panic. This was what he'd always wanted. To make amends to Bess, to put her back with her family. The plan to find her a rich husband was always second best, because there was no way to do the first. "When I started working... alone," he said, watching her cock her head to listen, memorizing the turn of her small face, "I started as a thief-taker because I wanted to find out secrets. Wanted to find out how to track people the way hunters do foxes. I looked for your family for years, Bess. There was no one I wanted to find more." Unable to keep himself from touching her, he lifted a finger, dripping with hot water, and traced along the edge of her cheek.

She smiled, wrinkling her nose at him and wiping drops away. "But it might have been harder, if they were Russian. Couldn't it have been?"

"Maybe."

Putting his feelings aside. He was good at that. He tried to think.

He leaned back, letting the water slosh gently around him. It felt so good, easing his muscle aches. Maybe it would ease the pains inside him to know the rest of Bess' story. To give that to her when he'd thought for so long it was impossible.

"I know a man," he said as the thoughts strung themselves together in front of his eyes, one after the other. "He works for a news gazette. It wasn't printing twenty years ago, but...

he might know where to look. We might find news, if they were Russian, and well-off."

"Well-off? Why?"

"They might not have been, but... In a fancy carriage. And you like spun gold."

She gave him the slow, sly smile he loved best. "Shall I let the brown in my hair fade?"

"It's not the hair, Bess." He hoped she knew how he said *Bess* that way because to him it meant *my everlasting beloved.* "The treasure is you."

* * *

DAN'S FRIEND was named Gerry, and he was a grizzled Yorkshireman with eyes that saw everything. Bess didn't like to say so but she was half afraid of him.

He, on the other hand, adored her.

"A girl! Dan, you sly fox. Well, 'at's yer name, innit?" He kept circling Bess in sheer delight. "A real girl!"

"Stop it, Gerry. What did you find?"

"I'm surprised you let her in here," said the journalist, jerking his head toward Bess. Respectable women, of course, did not frequent coffee-houses.

Dan, stretching his legs under the table, just sipped at his cup. "I'd like to see you keep her out."

Around them men gave her curious looks, arguing over news rags, smoking cigars. There were a few maids waiting on them, but it seemed to unnerve them to see a woman sitting at their tables like they did.

Gerry looked closer at Bess, whose golden-brown curls were fading from the walnut-stain and surrounding her face in its starched bonnet.

She blinked innocently at him.

"I feel like I'm bein' had," Gerry muttered. "Awright." He

sat in one of the framework chairs next to Dan. "You've got an accident right at the time you want, if yer innerested."

"I *am* interested."

Hoping her own desperate interest didn't show, Bess leaned closer.

She didn't need a family. She didn't. She had Dan, and that was more than anyone ever needed.

But in the back of her mind she'd always assumed she *had* been bought from the orphanage, because he had. They were two peas in a pod in so many ways; why not like this?

It felt greedy to have something he didn't have, something as special as family.

Once over the shock of his keeping it from her, the most astonishing thing to Bess about her origin was just that it existed. It had nothing to do with her. She had no memory of it. Yet she wanted to know the end of it. The story fascinated her because it was *her* story, yet she didn't know it, and she wanted to know all of it.

She still wanted just that little bit more.

Gerry didn't disappoint. "As it 'appened, t'Ambassador from Russia 'ad friends visitin'. Family, too. Right around the time you said you was interested in. 1793, you said?"

Dan just nodded.

"'E's important, that fella, still is to some I suppose, though not Ambassador any more. Retired years back. 'E's still livin' right here in London. Likes it better'n home, I guess. 'Ad a whole *visitation*—" Gerry carefully enunciated the word, "people visitin' from Russia at th' time."

"Who were they?"

Bess hadn't noticed herself gripping Gerry's arm. Tightly. She let go.

He went on as if she hadn't interrupted. "Noblefolk here t'study the schools, of all things. Big on it at home, you might say. Here's them: Princess Naida Mikhailova, very fancy, an' 'er husband Count Ilya Grishnov." He looked again at his tattered paper of notes, its linen edges showing frays. "Why they don't 'ave the same last name I don't know."

"*Princess?*" Bess hadn't expected anything like that. It knocked her back in her seat. *Princess?* "How can that be?"

"'Ey got princes an' princesses unner every rock over in Russia," Gerry said as calmly as if he'd been there and seen it for himself. "So I'm told. It's a title, innit? Not one crown like we got. Differen' way of doin' it and no better or worse, I guess."

Something inside Bess rose high on a wave of questions. A *mother? And* a father? What had they looked like? Sounded like? What tastes did they have?

Did they like the ballet?

Then the same wave crashed down. She'd never know those answers. Never know what they thought of her. For nearly all the time she'd been alive, they'd already been dead.

Dan reached over the table and took her hand.

Gerry's sharp eyes saw everything, doubtless whatever was written all over Bess' face too. "Did'ya know these people?" he asked quietly, and Bess realized Dan hadn't told him much. Doubtless only what he had to.

Leaving her life up to her.

So many kinds of freedom he gave her.

"No," was all Dan told Gerry when Bess didn't speak, and the older man didn't seem to take it as a personal slight.

"Awright," Gerry said again, and slid his ragged notes toward Dan. "'Ere's the direction of t'old Ambassador, and his daughter. She's young. It's no' far."

Bess didn't even hear him go.

She was finding her way through a wilderness she hadn't even known she was in, and it was all because of Dan.

It was *to Dan.*

He looked more natural here, in a coffee-house among

other boisterous men, his slightly worn black clothes fading into the shadows just like his hair.

No other man would do all the things he'd done to keep her safe, to keep her happy, to keep her whole.

She blinked. "Did you say something?"

"No." He sipped at his cup again, looking at her over it. "Waiting for you."

As he always was.

He asked her, "What would you like to do?" Giving her the choice, the way he always gave her the choice.

She wasn't sure yet.

At least she'd learned to express things like that with words. "I'll think about it. For now, we must meet Madame Franck. She said she'd be back at the players' house today."

CHAPTER THIRTY-SIX

"*S*o clever!"

Agatha turned in the tiny space where Bess slept, touching the veils along the walls, the corner of the cot, the dresses folded and stacked in one corner.

"You're kind," Bess said dryly. "Madame Franck. Why did you let her come?"

"Oh, I wanted to see!" Agatha's big bright eyes took in everything as if it were made of gold. Certainly she'd never seen anything like it.

"I consider it a fine lesson, and Lady Dunsby agreed with me." Madame Franck had lost no time getting back into her usual dress, with scarves floating everywhere, and *two* peacock feathers stuck in the top of her piled-up hair. "If Lady Agatha persists in consorting with bad gentlemen, she should see where she might end up!"

"This isn't terrifying, you know," Agatha scoffed, primly sitting on the edge of the cot.

It rocked forward, nearly dumping her off.

"Well," she said when she recovered her balance. Then

nothing else. It was clear she preferred to pretend she'd intended to do that.

Dan lurked in the corner, and that was the most comfortable thing. Not like the theater; like older times and newer ones. Right where he should be.

He leaned a shoulder against the wall, arms folded in front of him, watching her fondly, indulgently.

Lovingly.

She would never tire of that.

Sitting both Madame Franck and Agatha down on the edge of the cot, Bess told them what she'd discovered about her parents.

Agatha, too excited to keep sitting, leaped up. "You *are* a princess, just like in one of the fairy books! My mother was right, you know. You can tell by how a lady acts."

Bess did not remind her that she was no lady. "I have no idea if their titles make me anything at all. The way Russians do things isn't like here. Apparently she was given the title of princess? Because her friend wanted her to be one? But he was a count." Bess didn't like thinking of her family of *hers* as the kind of useless rich people she'd disdained all her life. But it sounded like the shoe might fit.

At least they'd come here trying to do something with themselves, not just sight-seeing.

"So you're a countess!" Overcome, Agatha sank back to the cot. It tried to dump her forward again; she defeated it by falling backward, hands clasped with excitement.

"I'm not anything," Bess pushed the idea away, confused.

Behind her Dan cleared his throat.

"I'm not a *princess,*" she turned and tossed at him over her shoulder.

"Not to me," and his black-diamond eyes said the things he usually only whispered in the night. *His goddess. His queen.*

"You must go meet these friends of your parents." Madame Franck was already standing again, searching through the folded garb to find something that was not a stage costume and suitable for meeting fine Russian ladies. "An Ambassador might look suspicious, but his daughter is a fine place to start. Surely she can tell you more. You have her direction?"

"Yes, we have it," Bess tossed a hand back toward Dan, then stopped. The *we* was so easy.

Madame Franck did not comment, only smiled a little to herself.

"Oh, I'll come with you!" Agatha had popped upright again.

"I must chaperone you everywhere!" Madame Franck reminded her.

It didn't quell Agatha at all; her hands still clasped in rapture. "We must go now! We can engage a carriage! I'll pay for it myself."

"You must stop paying for things for me," said Bess, and everyone froze.

Three pairs of eyes looking at her.

"All right!" Bess stood herself, brushing down her skirt. "I don't need to take *everything* I want. Madame Franck told me she'd saved my earnings; I ought to have some money of my own." Subsiding a little, she turned to her teacher. "Don't I?"

In answer, Madame Franck left the little room, came back with a worn paper notebook.

She just handed it to Bess.

Bess didn't even bother looking at it, just handed it to Dan. "What?" she said when he gave her a scowl. "I don't like arithmetic."

Dan looked in the little book, then straightened. Looked again. Carefully turned over the pages, none bigger than his palm. "This is every penny I sent."

"Yes, I said so," said Madame Franck, going back to unpacking the things.

Finally Bess realized they were *her* things. The trousseau Lady Dunsby had bought to launch her in London. They were all cut for her, sewn to fit her.

She whirled, wanting to ask Dan if she ought to give them back.

But Dan was still well sunk into the book. Well, holding it at arm's length so he could see it, but peering through it all the same. "*Every* penny."

"I know," Madame Franck said again, imperturbably. "You have a lot of trouble listening for someone who thinks he's clever. Sheer luck for you that the Duke is looking for Mr. Storey, not a secretary who disappeared. Or Lady Agatha's companion," she said with a stern look at Bess.

"It was so romantic." Now Agatha sighed, slowly falling sideways onto the cot. "Everyone assumed Mr. Burton eloped with Miss Page, and they'd never be seen in London society again."

"So they won't," Bess told her with a grin.

"Bess, this is everything I sent you." Dan touched her elbow; she turned to him at once.

It was heaven, having him right there.

But he looked scowly, so Bess shrugged. "Why do you keep saying that?"

"It's everything I could spare for *five years*. I lived on almost nothing. I made fair money. I sent it to you."

"And I saved it," said Madame Franck, with a decided nod of her peacock feathers.

For the first time, Dan looked at her with something like admiration. "I don't suppose you did anything as clever as investing in the five per cents?"

"Heavens no! What do you take me for? A woman like me walking into a banking establishment? I'd be lucky to get out with all my petticoats. It's safely stored with Lock Wally near the Garden."

Dan's grip on the notebook grew white-knuckled. "Who the fuck is Lock Wally?" he said in a slightly louder voice.

"He's the most secure stowage in London, that's who he is. And don't snap at me, young man. You've got five years of disappearance to pay back, and I'm not in love with you!"

That set Dan back a little.

When he looked down at Bess, she knew her cheeks were flushed; they felt warm.

Why should she *blush* because Madame Franck knew she was in love with him? Love might not just be for foolish rich women who couldn't help themselves.

And Dan never took anything for himself. He gave.

"I'm going to talk to Lock Wally. You better come with me," he told Madame grimly.

"And I must come with you to meet your family!" Agatha breathed.

Bess' insides twisted a little. It wouldn't be her family; at best, it would be someone that they knew.

What was a family, anyway?

"I want Madame Franck to go with me," she found herself saying aloud. "You will, won't you? Not that I don't want you, Agatha, it's just—"

"No no, you're quite right! I was transported with the excitement, that's all."

"Agatha." Bess felt an impulse to hug the girl, and as always, obeyed it. "You're too terribly kind. I owe you so much money—"

"—you'll be having candies at Gunter's every day if this Lock Wally is any good," Dan put in from the door, where he already waited.

Bess took Agatha's hands in hers. "I owe you for apples, and carriages, and servants, and—"

Agatha only shook her head. "Before I met you, nothing else ever happened in my *life*." She plopped down again on the cot. "I'll lock myself in and read a play!"

Madame Franck just stood with one of Bess' own petticoats folded over her arm. Looking fondly at Bess. "You don't need me with you, child. You know your own way."

"I want you with me, Madame." It felt awkward, but Bess stepped towards her teacher and hugged her, too. She was so tiny. It startled Bess to think they were nearly the same size. "I owe you too," she whispered, ashamed, a little, of the way her cheek brushed Madame's and she'd never felt that before.

"Well." When Madame Franck turned away, her eyes were suspiciously bright. She dropped Bess' petticoat instantly. "What does one wear to see Russian royalty? I have nothing to wear!"

"Fine, I'll take you," growled Dan, as if he might not have, "then it's Lock Wally. It can't wait."

* * *

THE MOST PECULIAR thing about the visit was that Bess went as herself.

She panicked as they mounted the steps. Fine stone carvings hung over the door, which was polished dark wood. She pushed close to Madame Franck. "Quick, what was your husband's name? The one you liked."

"Graham," whispered Madame Franck, startled, and barely had time to settle her feathers and skirts before the door opened.

"Miss Graham, Madame Franck, and Mr. Fox to see Lady Pembroke," Bess told him, as if it were a well-practiced line.

The butler led the three of them through to a pretty yellow parlor. It had cut leaves in vases and portraits of gentlemen wearing sashes. Bess thought that compared with

Lady Carrollton's portraits of her guinea pigs, they were just fair.

A beautiful young matron with masses of curling dark hair and a plump, smiling face came to greet them. "Do sit. I am so delighted you came to call. Mr. Fox, is it?"

Bess, unused to manners which took men into account first, blinked.

But Dan immediately handed her the lead, as always. "Lady Pembroke. You are too kind, accepting our visit. This is Madame Franck, and this is—"

"Miss Graham," said Bess, curtseying. "In fact, that's exactly what I've come to discuss."

* * *

LADY PEMBROKE SAT aghast behind a vast silver tea service, staring at Bess.

"I thought the second you walked in that you looked so like Princess Mikhailova. I can't believe it. How lucky you've been!"

Not luck, Dan, thought Bess.

"So you think we might be related?" she asked her hostess delicately. "I mean, me and your friend?"

"Think? I am sure!" She had a castle-type London accent, but a Russian flavor to her sentences. "My father told them they should come, I think hoping Naida would convince me to go to Russia. But I have never been there!" The twinkle in her dark eyes drew a little smile from Bess in return. "And who was he to judge? He came here to speak for Russia in 1785 and here he still lives!" She giggled to herself as she poured tea from the silver pot into tiny glasses.

"But you met them. Princess Mikhailova and Count Grishnov." Bess felt like if this connection slipped away, she'd slip to the ground with it.

Why should it matter who they were? She'd never met them.

But no one had ever told her that she looked like anyone else.

"Oh yes! They stayed almost a year, and Naida was a lovely friend. Count Grishnov believed Russia needed better education to make serfs into citizens and princes into leaders. Naida believed it too. They went everywhere together. And they had a charming little girl." Her head cocked as she studied Bess' face. "I was ten. I remember you well."

It felt too strange, suddenly folding her and this mythical little girl into one person.

But Lady Pembroke only nodded to herself. "Yes, you look quite the same. Babies change so much, you know, the year after they were born, but you were already walking. Three, I believe, when they died. Almost four?" She shook her head sadly at the thought. "They told us you died too. I wish I'd known you hadn't!"

Bess didn't know what to say, what to do.

She turned to Madame Franck; the lady always had something to say. But it was Dan's gravelly voice that spoke up. "You wouldn't have an image of them, by any chance?" he asked, drawing Lady Pembroke's attention.

"Oh! That is an excellent question. How silly of me not to think of it. Of course that's what you want! Unless..." She started to rise, settled herself down with a different look at Bess' tasseled day dress, part of Lady Dunsby's gift *trousseau*. "You don't need money?"

"No!" Bess had never answered that question that way in her life. But she didn't care about inheriting the money of dead people she'd never met. She only wanted to understand them a little.

Maybe it would help her understand herself.

"No, of course not!" Lady Pembroke seemed relieved,

reassured. "I'm sure I must be able to locate something among the people who visited then. It was a large tour of Russian nobles who came around that time. I believe I might even be able to draw something, though it has been so long."

An image of her parents? Bess had never imagined such a thing.

She'd imagined jewels and furs and carriages, but never something as rare as seeing parents that were actually hers.

The rest of the visit blurred together. Madame Franck drew their hostess into further conversation, stories of that time. Lady Pembroke had not only an important father, but an aunt who was a princess too, and a very famous woman of letters.

It all went by too fast, and Bess couldn't grasp half of it. It was too insubstantial and too important to put in her pocket.

"I don't understand," she finally said, trying to focus herself with gulps of tea. It was excellent, with tart, sweet spoonfuls of jam in it; blackberry, Bess thought. "I don't understand how all the names are related."

"It's quite a swirl, isn't it?" The merry look on Lady Pembroke's face only brightened more when a tiny version of herself bounced into the room, dark curls flying. "Now you should not be in here, naughty thing," she told the little girl, sweeping her up in her arms.

Bess felt as if she were falling.

The little girl was perhaps a little older than Bess must have been back then, and seeing her gave Bess the courage to ask the question she really wanted to ask, but unaccountably, found difficult.

"What is my name, then?" she forced out the words, trying to sound casual.

"Oh!" Lady Pembroke covered her mouth with one hand. "What a horrible thing for me to fail to see! Of course you don't know! I apologize. Countess Yelizaveta Ilyanova. Your parents called you Leeza, but I called you Bess."

"Did you?" The world was spinning now, harder than it ever had from opium or wine. She reached a hand toward Dan. He was there, standing beside her; he took it.

Lady Pembroke looked puzzled, then pretended not to notice. "My Russian was decent enough, I suppose, but Yelizaveta translates so nicely as Elizabeth, don't you think?"

"Yes, of course it does." Dan's hand, strong and warm, made the world slow down a little.

Then Bess could take a good look at Lady Pembroke's sparkling eyes and dark curls. "I don't remember you," she said.

But she remembered the feeling.

And she must have remembered *Bess.*

Who would have told Dan that was her name, unless it was she herself?

"I must go." She was out of lines for this play. She stood.

Madame Franck stood too.

"I'm so sorry if you must," said Lady Pembroke, standing too, "but I do hope you'll call again. It's rather like being old friends, isn't it?"

"In a way," said Bess, giving the kind woman as genuine a smile as she could, and a curtsey.

* * *

ON THE PAVEMENT OUTSIDE, Dan handed Madame Franck into their waiting cab, then pointed a finger at her. "Stay there," he warned her.

Then he turned to Bess as if the only thing in London right now were her.

"How do you feel?" He blocked out the rest of the world with his shoulders, making her a quiet, *safe* space.

473

She didn't know how she felt.

But Dan deserved better than her floundering. She had to make the effort. He cared about her feelings, after all; and Bess wanted to understand them better herself.

"I feel odd," she said honestly, grateful for the bonnet that blocked out almost everything but him. The rolling carriages and tramping feet around them faded away, and it was just her and Dan, like it had always been. "I must have told you my name was Bess."

"It was the only thing you said I understood." He wore his familiar scowl; she knew he was blaming himself for something. "I suppose the rest was Russian. I thought you couldn't talk right. It must have been Russian, and you had to learn English from us."

"I can't be a countess." It was everything she was *not.*

"Apparently, you already are. But what does it matter? You'll never see Russia." Then he blinked and bent closer. "Unless you want to go. Then, we'll go."

"I don't want to go." It was odd to think there was a whole other country that had roots for her. Perhaps cousins? She didn't know. It was too much all at once. "She never questioned who I was."

"She recognized you."

"No one ever knows who I really am."

"I *always* know," he reminded her, and the world stopped tilting for a while.

* * *

LOCK WALLY HAD FOUR DOORS, each with a collection of devices securing them shut he did not divulge, and which were not in evidence by the time they passed through his door.

It might have suited the toothless old man to live in a

stone burrow in the ancient part of London, and Dan assumed it did. He didn't blame the fellow. Bess looked more comfortable here than in Lady Pembroke's yellow parlor.

Where, Dan suspected, Bess hadn't noticed one thing she wanted to steal.

She was still shocked silent, lost in a world of wonderings he couldn't imagine. What kind of life might she have had if he hadn't taken her? What kind of life might she still lead?

Lady Pembroke would likely be happy to introduce her to other Russian diplomats. She might well find her way to her parents' home. She'd be one of the sparkling people.

Well, she always had been.

"Yep, 'at's me mark," Lock Wally said laconically when Madame Franck presented her notebook. As if he waited upon tiny dark-skinned women in peacock feathers every day.

He started to pull a stone out of the wall behind him.

"Stop, stop!" Dan lurched forward just in time to keep the wall intact. "Is that really the amount you have stored here?"

Lock Wally had a bent back, but thick fingers, and he drew himself up to full height, glaring at Dan from a few inches below him. "You questionin' my figures?"

"No! Just..." Dan looked around the stone cellar. He'd seen so many like it. "Just your truthfulness. If you lie to me now, I'll take you out in pieces."

"You can eat shit an' roll into yer grave, young man," Lock Wally said with all the dignity of a king's guard. "I never been accused o' bein' a penny short, not once, and you won't accuse me either."

It was incredible.

Dan had never, not once, expected that money hadn't been spent. By his figuring it should have been enough to keep Bess and Madame Franck comfortable in rooms of their own somewhere, perhaps even a townhouse, with servants.

He'd tried to give Bess exactly the life she deserved.

By keeping away from her, never seeing her or the teacher, he'd nearly got himself killed to make her... about as much money as she already had.

There was hating himself, and there was making a truly catastrophic mistake.

"Bess..." He couldn't tell her.

He had to tell her. No more secrets. He'd hurt her with secrets before and he never would again.

"Bess, you've got more than enough here to dower yourself. If you want to marry yourself a lord." He swallowed. "What did you think of that Lord Harman?"

"Boring," she said. She wasn't taking it seriously. She loved sparkly things, he realized, but didn't have any deep concept of a budget. "You actually intended to give me money so I could marry someone else?"

Dan was not feeling any smarter.

"Originally," he rasped, looking away.

"Oh."

He looked back her way. She stood on one leg, the other knee bent, finger tapping on her chin as she seemed to contemplate him over folded arms. "It's so kind of you," she said in Miss Page's overly-sweet voice. "I should have applied myself better to assessing the gentlemen. The fellow you mention was very kind, but for sheer beauty Lord Zach—"

He bent over and grasped her around her poplin-clad thighs, not to lift her, but to toss her over his shoulder.

He carried her out to cobblestones, leaving Madame Franck sputtering in her cave with Lock Wally.

Dumped her on her feet.

"I made a mistake, all right?"

Just like that, his Bess was all spit-fire again. "Five years without one note is not *one* mistake!"

"I didn't trust myself around you!"

"You didn't trust *me*, that's who you didn't trust."

"You needed a chance to find your own life."

"My life is *you*, you clod-head! I could have made that choice at eighteen just as easily. You could have *asked*, you could have—"

He caught her up in his arms. She only went quiet because she decided to kiss him back.

"I had all the responsibility for you for fifteen years," he breathed, when she let him go again. Slowly she slid down to the stones, her tip-toes keeping her higher and plastered against him. In this part of town, no one would care. "It would have been too much. I couldn't just take you because you were there. I couldn't live with that. And you didn't deserve that. You deserved better."

"There *is* no one better, idiot," she said, and kissed him again. She pulled him down by his neck with her strong hands, trusting him to hold her up, keep her balanced, never let her fall.

"I'm sorry." It was getting easier to say. He rubbed his nose along the edge of her ear; it made her shiver, and he loved that. "I love you so much, Bess. I always have. I'll never leave you again. Will you marry me and let me spend the rest of my life apologizing to you however you'd like?"

"Wait." She leaned back; he let her go. She put up one gloved finger, as if making a point in a lecture. "Is this just to get my money?"

"No. In fact, I'll soon be paid." He had the ledger on him right now; he always did, wrapped in oiled cloth against his spine. "The second I hand it over, you'll be doubly rich."

"That's very kind of you." She studied him from head to toe, and Dan was conscious of the worn edges of his black coat. "I'll consider it."

"*Bess.*" He didn't know whether to laugh, growl at her, or carry her back to his room. They'd been staying there quite comfortably waiting for Madame Franck to return, waiting for space and time to separate the disappearing Mr. Burton and Miss Page from the reappearance of the ledger. "I'm serious. I want to marry you."

"Thank you." She curtsied to him. *Him.* "I won't answer now. But one of these days, when you feel more certain about things, I'll give you an answer."

Fuck. Bess did love a grudge. "Bess, dammit, I love you more than life itself and all I want is to spend my life with you. All we've had and all we will have. Marry me."

"Because now you have the funds?" She made a *tch, tch, tch* sound. "I'd rather a man marry me for love, even if he were poor."

"Well forget it, because I'm not going back to being poor and neither are you."

"I suppose if that's what marriage is all about..." She turned away from him, started back into the little tunnel that led down to Lock Wally's warren.

He touched her elbow. She spun to face him.

"Come back to my room," he said in a voice that felt and sounded like crushed stone. She couldn't be doing this. "I'll show you what marriage is all about."

"Ah!" Gasping, she fell back a step, the most affronted young innocent on stage. "I see your true aims now! I'll never fall for them again!"

"*Bess!*" If he yelled any louder, neighbors would start coming to see the fuss. They always did, in places like this. "I mean it! I love you, dammit!"

She turned and looked back over her shoulder at him. "I love you too, Dan, more than anything. I always have, and I always will." She blew him a kiss. "But you should have asked me in the farmers' field, when I wanted you to."

It was all ballet-loving London could talk about.
The Tourmaline was back on stage.

For the third evening in a row, Dan threw his copy of
Bridle's Gazette down on the dining table. He was often a few
numbers behind; the paper didn't print every day, and he
didn't always read them when they came. If something
happened to him or Bess, he'd know. Everything else could
wait.

"You can't keep dancing on stage," he said for the
hundredth time. "Someone will recognize you."

"Recognize who? The Tourmaline? I think they do." As
always, Bess applied herself to putting food on his plate. It
was a habit that had begun to fascinate her, and Dan didn't
care why; she enjoyed it, so he enjoyed it.

Tonight their table held a modest spread of one remove,
six whole dishes Bess decided they should eat together.

Following some whim about which he wasn't yet entirely
informed, on a visit to the Temple of Books, Bess had chosen
a book in two volumes called *The Housekeeper's Domestic
Library*, which promised to teach "The Whole Art of Cook-

ery" including baking, roasting, boiling, broiling, hashing, frying and five other things.

They'd engaged an excellent cook, but Bess was determined to make some of these things. It baffled her that moving as fast as possible to the end of the prescription and beyond did not always result in edible dishes.

Tonight she had partridges on the table, tiny roasted birds that smelled divine, as well as bacon, mushrooms, greens, soft buns, and strawberry cream. It was not the season for strawberries other than in jam; he wondered where she'd got them.

Presumably, she'd paid for them.

"I mean *you*, Queen Difficult."

"Oh, they won't recognize me," Bess scoffed as she always did, spreading butter thickly on a bun.

Dan knew she put her store in her disguises. On and off the stage, she always did look very different.

As long as no one peered too closely at her eyes.

He picked up the paper again, pushed his spectacles higher on his nose. These were clear, and more suited to his work in the Exchange. He didn't spend so many late nights reading ledgers by candlelight; and they could always come off before a fight.

She took up a silver knife to slice a piece of bacon into pieces small enough for one bite.

"You don't have to do that." It always made him feel awkward.

"No, I don't." She paused, silver held in the air. Like a statue made of precious things. Like a goddess. She gave him a meaningful look. "How many times did you cut food for me?"

"That's hardly the same."

Still, he didn't fight when she stood out of her seat and kissed him.

"Open your mouth," she said against his lips, always bringing all of him straight to attention. *Always.*

When he did as she asked without fighting it... she laid a bite of bacon on his tongue.

It was delicious—he suspected someone else had cooked it—but that wasn't what he really wanted.

"I sent word to the bishop again today."

"Oh?" All mock innocence. "What about?"

"A special license, as you know damn well." There were some unique barriers to their wedding.

Designed as it was for rich people to share their money with other rich people, weddings required the reading of banns by a vicar who knew them. The whole point was for people to recognize them as two people joined into one; they didn't have to show baptism papers or whatever it was sparkly people had, but they had to be *recognized.*

That was the one thing they didn't want.

The Archbishop could give them a special license, affirming that *he* at least knew them; but Dan didn't know the Archbishop.

The one bishop he'd met didn't seem inclined to give the Arch one a good word.

"The Archbishop might be interested in the Tourmaline's wedding, but hardly a broker in the Exchange," said Bess, giving him a wide-eyed look before taking a delicate bite of partridge.

"You think he admires ballet?" Dan gave Bess a pointed, searching look. "Do you *know* he admires ballet?"

"Mercy Bennett, I can't imagine," said Bess with a tiny shrug. "Certainly if he did, I'd never dream of using that to my advantage."

"Dammit, Bess, let's get married!" To hell with his plate.

Bess had another bite of partridge, thoughtfully chewed, and swallowed, before raising her glass. It held ale, never wine. "I think the proper time for a proposal—I'm sorry, did you want to give a toast?"

"Fuck King and country," said Dan succinctly. "There, that's my toast. When's the proper time for a proposal?"

"*I* think the proper time for a proposal is right after a gentleman has deflowered the young lady he supposedly loves, and has her dizzy with pleasure under a dawn sky, alone."

That did sound pretty good.

"I didn't want to be one more man trying to tell you what to do." He leaned back in the chair. Bess would do whatever she wanted to do; she always had.

In fact, that was her point. Fuck everything.

"You didn't *ask,* Dan, at some point you'll learn to *ask,*" she said in a musical way, spooning up a bit of the strawberry cream.

"I've been asking." He didn't want to growl. He just wanted to get this right. "It'll be the new year soon. How many times am I supposed to ask?"

"I suppose," she said with a dainty lick of the spoon, "as many times as I like."

He didn't really mind. Weddings were a rich person's game. Where they'd grown up, a woman or man often just picked up their things and moved in with their spouse. People with any means married in churches, all legal-like; but other people did not.

But the idea had taken on a kind of glow, for Dan. He finally had given Bess the house she deserved, the comfort, the freedom he'd always wanted for her. Maybe it wasn't right to entangle her in marriage; but he wanted it just the same.

He had the place he'd fought and scraped to get, and it suited him. It didn't matter how rough or polished his customers were; he found them, and arranged their buying and selling, and the more he did, the more profit he made. It was lucrative, and it was honest.

The news from the Continent was hopeful. Napoleon was shrinking back into his former boundaries, sad, diminishing. Maybe Europe had had enough of emperors. Maybe of titles altogether.

Maybe the new Europe would belong to the people who lived in it rather than the crowns.

The colonies in America had certainly cut a path in that direction. And their business was growing in his marketplace —not shooting up like one of the Jacks' rockets, but slowly, steadily, the kind of growing that, unchecked, outgrew everything else.

He ought to look more closely into their trading.

Madame Franck bustled in. "Oh good. I'm starving." She sat at the plate they always left for her, helping herself to the things on the table. "You should never eat before a performance," she told Bess, pointing her fork, after swallowing her first bite.

"Not at all," Bess agreed, adding mushrooms and greens to her own bite of partridge.

"I should retire from the stage," Madame Franck said, sighing heavily. It was a new performance, and still in its early stages. Dan, given Bess' explanation, thought of it as *number seven*, the heavily-burdened grandmother.

At the rate things were going, she might well be in a grandmother's role before this wedding came about.

Dan didn't want that. He didn't want people calling any child of his *bastard*, and that was about him and his past, not the child's; that was true. But he also just preferred to keep to the right side of the law whenever possible, and he found that extended to having children.

It wasn't an argument he'd tried; he knew Bess didn't care.

Maybe she was just waiting for something else to happen with the license. That was likely it. If she said yes now, they still had no smooth way of being married.

For better or worse, they did not attend church.

"Oh! I must dress." One glance at the etched-face clock on the sideboard and Bess leaped from her chair.

And caught his eyes.

This house, the warmth of the fire, food on the table. It all seemed so simple, and they both knew how rich they were.

She loved it, he could see it in her face. And she loved him.

And he loved her back, fiercely, with all he was and everything he had.

"We can't leave anyway till Jack and Jackie get here!" he reminded her as she disappeared out the door, blue dress flying.

"I would never!" she called back to him.

"She would," Madame Franck told him, which he already knew. "But not to the ballet. Not this close to Christmas."

* * *

People bought each other admission to the ballet as gifts this time of year.

So the theater held not only its regular subscribers, glittering in their boxes by the light of the crystal chandeliers and watching each other's comings and goings.

It held groundlings, crowding their benches, and an exploding number of people like Dan, the kind crowding the city, bringing their work, their ideas, and their families to see what London could do for them.

There were too many, but Bess loved it. The more people there were, the less chance anyone would really know the Tourmaline.

That was how she preferred it.

As always, she let Jack and Jackie walk through first, checking to make sure neither Waresham nor Lady Winpole were in attendance.

Waresham she knew about. He'd returned to London weeks ago, his reputation already delightfully in tatters. Lady Dunsby and Agatha seldom were in company, so no one could blame them for the story about his sheer effrontery, greeting Lady Agatha by her first name as if they were still children, expecting her to stay alone with him in places where she absolutely would not go.

Such stories usually turned against the young lady in question, but funnily enough, this one always stayed accounted to him.

There were darker rumors too, that he had failed to pay gambling debts, that he smoked opium in dens with sailors, that he'd tried to set a press-gang on Lord Harman—*Lord Harman!*, whom everyone knew—nearly getting him shipped off to the ends of the earth.

No one was sure that last was true, but no one saw him in public with Lord Harman anymore either.

In fact, it was not true, but Bess enjoyed the opportunity to lie without consequence. Honestly, it could be considered a public service, given that Waresham was no longer accepted into houses where ladies could be importuned and despoiled at his will.

She only had reports of Lady Winpole, who was apparently wintering in Bristol. Her card games no longer ventured into London.

Declaring herself sorry for the quality of her playing, Lady Dunsby desisted from cards now, even on those occasions where she and her daughter did venture into public.

Lady Carrollton had come with her back to London. She claimed the bitter cold was unbearable at Road's End, but she still wanted Lord Carrollton, so busy in Parliament, to have his peace.

So she left him to his peace, and his mistress, and his townhouse, and stayed at Dunsby House with her guinea pigs, where Bess had seen her... from a distance. She had gained some much-needed weight.

Lord Zachary's pretty golden head never appeared at the opera house. Bess assumed he was drawing somewhere.

"Go on in," Jackie stuck his silver hair into the carriage window.

Dan stepped out and handed down the lady with him. Mrs. Fox, as Bess liked to think of this role, tended toward black, as he did; likely because it contrasted in a stunning fashion with the deep red of her hair.

Slowly she walked at his side, to all appearances simply leisurely in her motion. The reality was that her shoes were four inches tall, and required she walk carefully, as if a carnival player on stilts.

The two of them moved, a striking couple, toward the stairs where Mr. Fox had subscription tickets. He did not take those stairs, but walked down the gallery with her, towards the back door where she could slip out and across the cobblestone yard to the rear of the stage.

There in the gallery, a large hulking man stood near the orchestra, hands behind his back, watching the curtain.

Something about him warned the hairs on the back of Bess' neck. She tried to slip back out into the audience. It would attract attention for a languid red-haired woman in black to pick her way through the shallow-pocketed people on the benches, but she'd rather that than come to his notice.

Before she could, he turned.

The Duke of Gravenshire still had that high-sailing look, the bulk of him up and ready to push forward, a warship under sail.

He saw her, and she knew by the look on his face that he recognized her. Not just Dan on her arm; her.

"I beg your pardon," she said brazenly, preparing to move past him as she'd originally intended.

He didn't move; just looked her over again. "I don't believe we've met," he lied to her face.

That she hadn't expected.

"I would certainly remember if I had the pleasure." Bess could play any scene he liked. She felt Dan brace beside her.

"I was looking for a young lady I heard a rumor was here. In the audience," he clarified, which made no sense unless he knew Bess was heading for her place on stage.

"There are any number of young ladies in the audience; you may take your choice, sir." When would he step aside?

He didn't. He said, "There's a lady's companion I'm looking for who might have found a certain ring."

That damnable ring. Her heart started beating again.

The Duke went on, "I think she meant to return it, but hasn't yet. Perhaps you'll tell her the young lady is still looking for it. In fact, she'll be at Lady Gadsbury's Christmas masquerade."

"If I see any such lady's companion, I'll tell her so," said Bess, knowing that only made sense if she knew exactly who had the ring.

Which she did.

With another measuring look, the Duke only added, "And thank you."

Then marched down the gallery, clearing the way.

"What fucking ring?" Dan whispered as he whisked her out the door and into the cobblestone yard.

"You said you wanted to curse less often."

"You still have that damn sapphire ring?"

"I like it." Pouting was not attractive, onstage or off, but

Bess felt it coming on; it was a rare feeling, but she could name almost all of them now. "It's pretty."

"I'll buy you sapphires."

"Where's the challenge in that?"

The cold was raw tonight, wet, like it had been that night at the theater when nature itself had staged her performance with thunder and lightning and snow all at once. When Dan had come back.

"At least you must admit," grumbled Dan, holding her elbow so she didn't fall off the tall shoes hidden under her skirt, "it's too dangerous for you to keep coming here. He knows. Someone else will notice."

Once back inside, he helped her between the ropes behind the scenery, back to the closet that was only hers.

Her fears of her audience, she told the other players, had only gotten worse when one had approached her after a performance, claiming he was mad with love for her, and tried to throw her over his shoulder and carry her off.

She loved that story.

Dan had built the little closet behind the scenery so she could hang up her red wig in private, like she did now, slip out of her gown, and put on the bright spangled costume of the Tourmaline.

Tonight's piece was a silly little thing, something about a fairy. She did it anyway, just because she knew Lady Dunsby would like the sound of it; she hoped the lady would see it before it closed.

Now that mail arrived more often from Europe, there were rumors of a ballet of Cinderella from Vienna, and something French about a woman named Nina driven mad by love. Both sounded appealing.

She dabbed at Madame Franck's specially compounded face paint, making the bones of her face ethereal, glowing with crushed pearl.

At the last minute, Dan leaned forward and kissed her. Not a quick kiss; the kind that settled the world around her, holding down the ground so she could fly.

* * *

THE DAY AFTER CHRISTMAS, a paper invitation arrived at their door.

Dan took it up to Bess.

Her maid Ellen had just finished dressing her for the evening. This dress hadn't come from Lady Dunsby. Dan had paid for it himself.

The dress was red, a color young unmarried girls didn't wear. The kind that looked luscious next to her skin.

The kind she wore for him.

"Thank you, Millicent," she said, making the girl smile and curtsey before she left. Dan didn't know why Bess called the maid Millicent; Millicent wasn't her name.

If he asked questions about every little thing, he'd have no time to work.

"We've been invited to Talbourne House," he told her right in her ear, handing her the paper.

Carefully she read it, looking, as he did, for any stray symbols that might tell them anything they needed to know other than that the Duke and Duchess of Talbourne requested their presence.

"There's no reason for the Duke and Duchess to invite us to Talbourne House," said Dan, still under his breath, and laid the paper in the coal grate to let it catch fire.

Bess watched it burn, nearly singing her increasingly golden hair as she leaned close to sweep scraps out as they floated to the bricks, and burn them again.

"They want the ledger," she murmured.

"I want to be rid of it." He couldn't risk leaving it

anywhere, and it had become a heavy burden. It bumped him as he slept at night; it jabbed him first thing in the morning.

He just wanted to get married—Bess still wouldn't say yes—and get on with the rest of his life.

"Then we'd better go." It was afternoon, and soon it would be dark, and Talbourne House, they knew at least by rumor, was a long way away.

* * *

WHEN THEY ARRIVED, the butler gestured them into the grand hall. Its marble floors led to a sweeping staircase that seemed to go all the way to the sky, no doubt to impress visitors.

Bess smiled. She'd visited the sky.

"Mr. and Mrs. Fox," she told the butler, making Dan start. The butler just bowed, waved them into a room off the foyer full of delicate porcelains, and withdrew.

"I don't like using the name without the paper," he muttered, still staying close by Bess as she strolled through the room.

"You're too fond of rules."

A completely different man came for them, and Bess realized the other had only been a footman. How many servants must this place have? It was vast, stretching what seemed like miles in its surroundings of green.

She wondered how easy it would be to pretend to be a maid here.

The actual butler led them up the stairs and on a long winding tour that both of them could have easily retraced.

At the end of it he announced them, as Mr. and Mrs. Fox, in a small library containing a vast desk, and the Duke and Duchess of Talbourne.

The room full of books could have felt intimate; it didn't. The little sections of wall that didn't already bear books were papered in hand-printed Eastern patterns, with dark wood in between; the inkwell on the desk sat on a silver tray, and the paper knife beside it had a richly enameled handle. The carpet below their feet was chased with color all over like a melting jewel. Everything was opulent, including the green gown edged with a red pattern along its hem worn by the Duchess. Bess realized suddenly that it was made entirely of imported Cashmere shawls.

The Duchess was pretty. Bess didn't know why that startled her so, but she was, and only a few years older than Bess. Dan's age.

And she was blind.

"Thank you for your visit," Her Grace said, and Bess curtsied, feeling a little foolish as the lady couldn't see it. Beside her, Dan sketched a short bow.

"Please sit." The Duke was older, with silver streaks in his hair that looked like embellishments to his plain but expensive suit. He was powerfully built. Bess didn't like being closeted with him in such a small room.

But when she took a step back, there was Dan, just behind her, and she felt her muscles relax.

While his tightened.

A section of the books swung in, and from the hidden passage in stepped a tall man in a fine blue coat.

"F—" Dan cut off his own curse. "Fitz," he said instead.

The suddenly appearing man came straight for Bess.

"I am Lord Henry Fitzwilliam," he said, bending over her hand; Bess didn't remember offering it. It was hard to hold her position when he so cheerfully charged right into the space around her. He had a genial grin. "Allow me to introduce myself, as you are the only person here with whom I'm not previously acquainted. My apologies for the unusual invitation. It came from me."

Dan wasn't swearing, but he wasn't happy either. "You are all friends?" he asked the room in general.

"I'm everyone's friend!" insisted the genial newcomer. "Please. His Grace asked you to sit. So will I."

Awkwardly, they found places in the too-close settees and chairs grouped on one side. Her Grace's gown made no sound as she settled into place. Bess made a note to investigate Cashmere more closely.

There was a tense moment when it looked like His Grace intended to remain standing beside his wife, and Dan, never willing to be put at a disadvantage, drew next to Bess and remained standing too.

They must have exchanged looks; Bess ignored them, and eventually everyone sat.

She thought His Grace would do the talking. But it was the Duchess instead.

"An awkward meeting in awkward circumstances," said Her Grace. She had the fresh prettiness of a natural beauty her age, and was clearly entirely comfortable in her rich surroundings. A duchess indeed. Bess studied her pose, in case she ever needed to reproduce it on stage. "We are all interested in justice for Lady Winpole, and to that end we thought it necessary to meet."

"You want the ledger? Take it." Leaning into Bess, Dan reached into his own coat. Unabashedly he scrabbled under his waistcoat, untucking the back of his shirt, and drew the thing out. "I'm dying to be rid of it." He tossed it into Fitz' lap.

"Thank you." Fitz didn't look so genial as his long fingers closed around the oilcloth-wrapped book. "You've been paid, of course."

"You paid him before the delivery?" Her Grace sounded interested.

"I trust him," said Fitz.

"He's a sap," said Dan.

The Duchess wasn't flustered at all. "I'm glad you are such good friends. I hope that helps with what I have to say. The trial will have to wait."

"What?" Dan shot up to his feet.

Lounged in his chair, an expression flicked over Fitz' face that Bess would have called *murderous.*

"This is how it works. One law for them, another for us. Let's go." Dan reached down for Bess' hand. His felt hot.

"I quite agree with you." The first full sentence from the Duke. Bess was surprised to hear how beautiful his voice was. He could have been on stage, with a voice like that.

Or snagged himself a pretty blind wife despite his unremarkable looks.

Not that he needed it; he was a duke. Bess thought Dan was right to be wary. "Then we'd like to see a trial," she spoke both their minds. "Preferably one as quick as poor thieves get."

She expected him to wave her down, or frown; instead, he only nodded his solemn agreement.

The Duchess said, "We want nothing less. But in a trial of a peer, one must convince the convictors. That would be people like us." She didn't try to shy away from her title, only included herself with her husband, possibly Fitz. "And what's more, there must be a judge. We... have not found one."

Bess did not ask how she expected to be able to select the judge. "So that means, no justice?"

She shook her head, *no.* "There will be justice. Just a bit more slowly. She can't have corrupted every judge in London. We do not intend the case to come to trial until we can be sure the judge will at least be fair."

Fitz didn't look in the mood for niceties. "Bribe a judge our way," he said, the hard glint still in his eye. "If she can do it, we can."

"That is not how justice works," said the Duke, with a kind of tone he must have learned in the cradle. It had its effect; even Bess found herself disinclined to argue with him.

"Moreover," said the Duchess with an urgency that spoke of disposing of all bad news at once, "we may have to ensure *multiple* trials. You see," she said over Fitz' and Dan's noises of disgust, "a peer may claim the right of privilege at their first conviction, and so escape punishment. It's medieval, but still true."

"So she could shoot the King and still walk away?" Dan was beyond disgusted; he was furious.

Bess let him be. He knew she was here, right here with him, all the way.

"No." The Duchess was firm on that. "For treason or murder, there is no privilege."

"But she has done murder! Look." Jumping up, Dan snatched the ledger from Fitz' hands, turned the pages. "See, here. And here. Payments for murder."

For the first time, Fitz studied the writing. "I can't read this." His puzzlement showed in his tone and on his face.

"It's diver's cant. Language from people like *us*," he clarified for all their benefit. "A written kind. For people who can't write words. Look." He pointed to the page. "This is a kill. And this one. This one. Over and over again."

Fitz peered at the book, baffled, his anger growing.

The Duke, interestingly enough, just watched his Duchess.

She seemed to think it through. Her hands rested on the arms of the chair; one of them rubbed her fingers together.

"Very well," she finally said, and all eyes turned to her. "Let us take the slowness of the court and turn it to our advantage. We must investigate these crimes and find more evidence. More witnesses."

"This was all for nothing?" Dan's voice was rising.

Bess reached for him. He came back and stood beside her, still not sitting. She slipped her hand into his.

"This was everything," said the Duchess with a decisiveness that echoed her husband. Bess wondered how long they had been married. "It is the map we needed, Mr. Fox. We know the crimes, and likely something of the dates and payments, do we not?"

"True," Dan admitted, his shoulders un-hunching a bit.

"If you'll forgive the metaphor," and a girlish smile played around the corner of the Duchess' mouth, "we have been searching blind. Now we know where to look. It is a long game, Mr. Fox, but now we approach the end, thanks to you."

Bess felt rather than saw Dan twitch, and wondered what had startled him in her words.

He sat down next to Bess, still holding her hand.

"Like treason, murder has no privilege." Now the Duchess' back was straight. "It would be best if we could prove she'd committed a murder herself."

"Surely we can," muttered Fitz. His fingers locked around the ledger, bending it nearly in half. "She claims Storey shot Lord Vellot, but I bet it was her."

Dan settled back into the settee, his arm draped behind Bess. It looked casual, calm.

Bess knew he was ready to fight his way out of this room.

"Was Lord Vellot shot?" Bess could play any character she liked; *innocent lady's companion* was something she'd practiced long enough.

"Yes, the Duke of Gravenshire himself confirmed it."

"You know him?"

"Fairly well," admitted Fitz, still distracted, "he's my father-in-law."

"There you go, then," said Dan, "convict her for that."

"No witnesses but her and this Storey fellow," said Fitz,

"and they're not likely to be believable testifying against each other."

"What if there were another witness?" Bess leaned forward.

"Like?"

"Like me."

Dan shot to his feet again, and Fitz' surprised sound was echoed by the Duchess, who took control of the conversation immediately. "You've done enough, Mrs. Fox. And you, sir. Truly, we could not justify putting you in danger again."

"You have a life you deserve to live," said Dan, blocking out the world with his body, tense at the mere suggestion that she associate herself with the crime or Lady Winpole.

She looked up at him, knowing he could always see the love in her eyes. "So do you," she told him softly.

His wife's ruling was enough for the Duke. "It's out of the question," he pronounced, then added, "Her Grace is correct. You've done everything, Mr. Fox. Let us do more investigating now."

"That is the best approach." Her Grace spoke as if it were all settled. "Yes, this will give us time to find an honest judge, and perhaps gauge how the case will appear in trial. We don't wish to bribe or sway the peers who will judge her; I'd like to *know* they can be fair."

"That's more than I can help with," Dan said, with obvious relief.

Fitz stood, and after a moment's pause, handed the ledger to the Duke, who stood as well. "I'm off," he said without further ado, clearly agitated, and departed through the bookcase where he'd entered.

"Mr. Fox, you've come all this way, and we've given you so little entertainment. Do you play games at all?"

When the Duchess stood, Dan did too, and he let her

reach around the table and find his arm because it seemed rude to brush her away.

A successful ploy for a blind woman, Bess thought.

"Do let me show you our gaming tables. We don't play cards often, but the people who come of an evening love it so."

Dan looked ready to dig in and stay by Bess, but she told him with her eyes to go, and added the words. "I'll be just behind you."

His own eyes flicked between her, and the Duke, then back to her.

"Just in a minute."

He let the Duchess take his arm and led her out slowly. He'd only leave Bess alone for a few seconds, that was clear enough.

Already Bess felt the tie between them stretch, but it would never break.

Quickly she turned to the Duke. He had already done something with the ledger; it was gone. Bess wondered fleetingly if there were a lock safe in this room, or if it was on the shelves with the rest of the books. "How grateful do you feel, Your Grace?"

"Very." A man of few words, he leaned a hip back on his desk and folded his arms over his black coat, looking at her as he would an adversary. Oddly, Bess found it cheering. It was encouraging, being considered a threat by a duke.

"Mr. Fox would like a very specific favor in return."

"Which is?"

"A special license to marry from the Archbishop," she told him smoothly.

He didn't blink.

He was a bit unnerving, Bess thought, capable of holding very still and being very silent.

Finally, "In whose names?" was all he said.

"I assume you can keep a secret."

"Madam," he said as if she were as titled as he, "you have no idea how closemouthed I can be."

"The names are Mr. Dan Fox and Miss Elizabeth Graham."

"You're aware it's peculiar, as you call yourself his wife."

"I, sir," she said with a little curtsey and a girlish smile she'd just learned, "can do anything I like."

He blinked. As if he half-recognized the smile, and it upset him to see it on someone other than his Duchess.

"Done," as if they'd struck a contract, and he went to the library door that was drifting shut, and opened it wide.

Delighted, Bess didn't curtsey again. She suspected she'd see him again, and she supposed dukes must have their due, but she'd extended herself far enough in that direction.

It would be a slightly late Christmas present, but Dan would love it.

EPILOGUE I

The fog that evening as they drove the long way back to London proper was excessive, creeping between the trees around Talbourne House, drifting over the grass, nearly hiding the road.

"You all right?" Dan called up to the driver, who called back "Right enough!"

So they snuggled together in the warm carriage, and Bess felt the tension drain from him the further and further they got from the grand ducal palace.

It was luxurious to travel in the coach's warmth, its glassine windows closing out the worst of the cold air if not the creeping gray of the fog.

"I want to be on your lap," said Bess, and without hesitation Dan lifted her there.

A lap robe made them a comfortable shelter, so much like their night in the balloon that Bess wanted to tell him about the special license. It would be hard to keep a secret, at least from Dan.

But so worth it when the time was right.

She put her arms around his neck, nestled into his rock-hard chest. *This spot was hers*, she thought with deep satisfaction. No one else had it; it belonged to her. *He* belonged to her.

"Would you like to love me in a carriage?" she whispered into his ear, feeling his heartbeat jump under her skin.

"A carriage? Pheh." He looked around dismissively even as his arms tightened around her. The velvet of the red dress might crush, she knew; but she'd find a way to fix it.

Or he would. Dan was so good at arranging things.

"Too big for us," he went on, even as he lifted her effortlessly in his arms so he could say it against her throat. She shivered. She couldn't help it.

"Also too warm," he went on, sliding his hands up her ribs to trace the shape of her breasts through the velvet. He made them feel warmer, and full, and desperate for more.

"No champagne," he pointed out, even as he slid his hands up over the gown toward her throat, framing her face in his powerful fingers, holding her more delicately than if she were cut glass, turning her so they could kiss.

"But I am a bit hungry," she said, breathless, once he set her lips free.

"I apologize. Their Graces should have sent us home with a picnic, shouldn't they? It's really too bad of them." He shook his head as if the world was nothing but a source of regret.

"You do know," she said, sliding around a little to feel his growing hardness under her, "that if you don't give me what I want, I'll just take it."

"Never say so!" His mock gasp was huge. "I thought you had morals now."

"Not really," she said, reaching for his hand and sliding it along one of her so-proper lady's stockings. Finer ladies, she had discovered, wore a tremendous amount of clothing under their gowns.

It was warmer than she used to dress, but it was also in the way.

Not that Dan found it so. Sliding his hand for himself up over her garter and along the smooth top of her thigh, he pressed his hand against the achiest part of her, making Bess sigh.

"I want to keep an eye on this fog," he told her in his low, serious voice. "But that doesn't mean I can't indulge you. As many times as you like, all the journey home."

"I think I want more," she admitted, squirming in his arms a little.

"As I should have been telling you all along," he murmured into the edge of her hair, sliding his kiss around to light ever so gently on her lashes before tracing down toward her mouth, "if you could have a little patience, you might find it rewarded."

* * *

A flushed, warm, slightly disheveled Bess stepped down from the carriage at their own door.

It was late, and the lower windows held no light.

Dan looked at the house with suspicion. "Stay by the door," he told her, closing it behind her. "Let me fetch a lamp."

Never believing she'd be fine on her own.

Well, she wouldn't be, not without him.

As Bess stood waiting for him in the dark just inside their front door, a small tap on the door's wood from outside made the hair on the back of her neck stand on end.

Not waiting for Dan, she swung it open. If there were anything coming for him *or* her, she'd deal with it.

It was the carriage's driver. Their vehicle still stood in the street, fog drifting closer around it; she couldn't see past the horse.

"A word," said the driver, stepping up the last step and pushing his way in.

He was tall.

He didn't push farther. Bess measured him with her eyes. One side of his cloak was tossed back, and below it Bess saw a far finer one, a lord's cloak, of blue velvet. Even in the dark she could see its sheen.

"What word do you want?"

"Don't kill Lady Winpole," he said, shocking her down to her bones. "She might not get justice in court, but if anyone gets to repair that, it will be me."

"What makes you think I'd kill Lady Winpole?"

She couldn't see his eyes in the shadow under his old-fashioned tricorn hat, not with two hoods bunched around his neck. "I hear things," was all he said. "Remember."

He turned to descend the steps.

"If that time comes," Bess called down quietly, not wanting anyone to hear, seized with the sort of urge that sent her flying through windows, "you and I can flip a coin for it."

He paused and half-turned back. She couldn't see his face, but something about the way he turned his body made Bess think he was amused.

He didn't answer, just swept down the stairs, leaping up to the seat of the coach, and in another moment both he and it disappeared into the fog.

Dan returned down the hall, a shining circle of light all around him. *As it should be,* she thought to herself with a mind addled from too much passion.

It was much her favorite drug.

"Do you know what the Caped Count looks like?" she asked him as he pulled her back from the open door.

"Just what Fitz writes in *Bridle's Gazette.* No one really

sees him. Tall, and a cape. Not much you can do with that." He looked over her shoulder at the gray paving stones and foggy street. "Why, did you see something that made you think of him?"

"I'm not sure," she said, utterly truthfully, and let him bar the door behind her, sealing them both in.

She had far more appealing things to think about.

EPILOGUE II

Lady Winpole did not care for Bristol.

The whole city had a brashness to it she did not like. It reeked of fish and the slave trade it had carried on for decades in its port, banished only a few years since.

Not that she minded the slave trade itself; she'd dabbled in it from time to time, when it would pay. She minded the evidence of it, the traces it left. It left unpolished marks.

Bristol society was of an inferior sort, and so were its cakes.

"Pandora," she told her doll, rearranging it in a new dress on the walnut dressing table in her room, "this is an appalling situation."

She hadn't worked her way into a position shipping goods around the world to be chased back *here,* back to where Lord Winpole tried to banish her in the first place.

She had hope, because no guardsmen had knocked on her door. She had not been escorted to London's Tower. She was still free, such as she could be, in Bristol.

So perhaps Mr. Storey's faith in his coded writings had not been entirely without merit.

But he had not been found. She'd expected him to be found and hung or, more conveniently, shot. Instead, the damnable man insisted on staying hidden, failing once again to perform his function adequately.

The whole situation was untenable.

She didn't have the means to kill him herself. She didn't relish going to that much effort, and it was dangerous to travel. The fogs had been replaced with relentless snow.

Unless he presented himself here, which she wished he would do. It would only be decent of him, after all the trouble he'd caused.

The more weeks she spent walled up in her house, the more brutal the winter cold, the more she blamed him for her troubles. Not that stupid companion or the secretary. Storey.

He was the one she'd trusted with her secrets; he was the one who'd failed her.

She couldn't shed her worries that something about her connection to Lord Vellot would still come to light. Vellot was dead, true, but she didn't have faith he'd left no trace of her involvement. As long as his plot to overthrow the British King went to the grave with him, she was safe.

They might find a judge willing to try her; there were plenty not in her pocket. Though few who couldn't be frightened.

But they'd never find a jury of her peers to convict her of murder or treason, and anything else she could escape.

She turned to the doll again.

"We don't need *more*," she told it in a burst of philosophy. "We need something *different*."

* * *

Want a little more of Bess and Dan's story? Be a guest at their wedding; get your bonus chapter now.

Turn the page for a sneak peek at The Castaway Countess *and the author's historical notes. Because as Dan and Bess and you will discover,*
Lady Diane was not lost at sea after all...

THE CASTAWAY COUNTESS, FORTHCOMING

BOOK 3 OF CLOAKS AND COUNTESSES

**A year in the wilderness has changed her.
Now she's just the sham wife he needs.**

* * *

Surviving a shipwreck showed Lady Diane the faults of a life in London. She wants no part of it any more, and that includes her vast inheritance.

For Aloysius Dusseau, she is the perfect bride. Rich and suspected to be no longer chaste. No other London heiress would overlook how the Revolution stripped him of his title.

When a villain's treachery destroys Diane's dreams of a whole new life, she charges after revenge, trailing her feigned husband. The more she learns why he wants her money, the more she is charmed by the man he hides inside. Until she'll have to choose between revenge and making her marriage real.

* * *

Subscribe to Judith's newsletter at judithlynne.com for news when it breaks about Cloaks and Countesses and all Judith Lynne books!

The *Cloaks and Countesses* books draw many details from history; if you enjoy learning how those bits and pieces got pulled together to make Bess and Dan's tale, read on. If you prefer the magic of mystery, just know that, like real life, nothing comes from nothing, and many fragments of real history were knit together in the making of this tale.

Melinda Mapson was a real person who lived until she was hung by the neck until dead, on a gallows outside Newgate prison, on a Wednesday, June 13th, 1810. Accused of stealing silver and linens from the house in which she'd only worked for one day, she claimed that her husband had come and forced her to let him inside and done the stealing himself. Of course, there's no appeal beyond an execution. She was not the last woman executed in the United Kingdom, and in the United States, there are fifty women sentenced to death now.

Franz Mesmer, a German physician, called his ability to affect another person through mental force *magnétisme animal,* drawing parallels with recent discoveries in "mineral magnetism" and "planetary magnetism." His methods traveled via his students more than from him, and drew much consternation from authorities. The French government appointed two commissions to investigate an unscrupulous practitioner in Paris, both concluding there was no scientific basis to this business of animal magnetism, and decrying, not Mesmer or his methods, but the activity of his students who pursued them for unscrupulous purposes of showmanship.

One of those commissions included Benjamin Franklin himself, a highly respected scientist throughout Europe at the time even though the word was not yet in use.

In Paris, Benjamin Franklin also met Princess Yekaterina Romanovna Dashkova on her travels outside Russia while on the outs with her former best friend, Catherine the Great. Franklin and the Princess met only once but became lifelong correspondents; he eventually invited her to become an honorary member of the American Philosophical Society.

Princess Dashkova spent a great deal of time touring all the parts of the United Kingdom, where her brother, Semyon Vorontsov, had been appointed ambassador in 1785. He stayed there, as we know, but she returned to Russia and Catherine the Great's good graces; the Empress appointed her head of the Petersburg Academy of Arts and Sciences. Later she founded and served as the first President of the Russian Academy, and invited her friend Franklin to be its first American member.

Count Vorontsov served Britain as well as Russia during his time there, contributing more than perhaps anyone else to a Russian impression that Britain was a civilized country worth emulating to a Russian court packed with lovers of French language, history, and style. Woronzow Road, named in his honor, still exists in the City of Westminster, along with a plaque commemorating his later gift to build almshouses for the poor. His son Mikhail served as a lifelong

Russian soldier and general; his daughter Lady Pembroke stayed in England and had many children.

This book inspired far more research into the history of the aristocracy in Russia than anyone should try to do in a short time, and any mistakes are entirely mine.

The *Charlière* hydrogen balloon was named for Jacques Charles, who launched his first flight in 1783. On its first flight, it flew 21 kilometers and landed in a village where obviously, no one had ever seen anything like it descend out of the sky before. They destroyed the balloon, launching a tradition of giving champagne to one's unwilling hosts wherever a balloon lands, because regrettably, balloons are still nearly impossible to steer.

I've learned as my research progresses that there are gaps right where I don't want them. Twenty years of war between France and Britain made travel difficult and sapped money from everyone's pockets, in a way that might feel very familiar to us today.

As in research on the United States, where one finds significant gaps around the Civil War in all kinds of mundane records, in Britain we find things created in the 1790s like fine art of a particularly picturesque spot, then nothing until the 1820s.

So I'm particularly grateful for the Allen engraving of Gravesend dated 1820, displayed by Michael Finney Antique Books and Prints, which along with many other art references for Gravesend over the years, gave me my particular view of the town at a time as close to this book's setting as I could get. I'm also grateful for all the records of the actual Falcon Hotel, and my representation of it is entirely fictional, except to borrow from its actual façade for the layout of the windows and boardwalk.

The 1793 edition of the *Royal Toast-Master's Guide* is

available digitally, copyright-free due to its age, and available to everyone for all their toast-giving needs.

Opium could be bought at any chemist's well into the 20th century, and while its addictive qualities were well known, so were its medicinal ones. It was considered a defect of character to succumb to addiction, a flaw of lower orders of people, as we all too often still hear people say today.

During this book's creation, the beautiful daughter of a dear friend of mine succumbed to her own addiction, and died.

While the plot had already been written, the pain was far more clear. If I shy away from the difficulties of addiction in this book, it is solely my own failure to represent so insidious a thief, one that robs young people of their lives and our country of its future. While even tiny doses have an effect, our character of Bess was lucky to escape its grip when she did, because in fiction, anyone can be lucky.

ACKNOWLEDGMENTS

I always pictured this book as the dark middle movie in a trilogy, the one where everything goes wrong… but we know there will be more.

I'm more grateful than I can say to you, the reader, who came along with me for this second installment of a series I worried no one would read. The idea for *Cloaks and Countesses* came to me as silly fun, but like the comic books that inspired it, it can take dark and emotional turns, and I thank you for coming with me on this ride.

My tremendous thanks and admiration go to the Ohio library system, from the Columbus Metropolitan Library (especially the delightful staff of the Canal Winchester branch!) to the wonderful collaborative members of OhioLINK.

I want to express my tremendous gratitude to the Oklahoma Romance Writers' Guild for awarding *No Titled Lady* their best Steamy Romance of 2022 and giving me faith to go on.

Love is real… and it takes faith.

Thanks to Tamara for listening, and Holly as always for explaining my own writing brain to me.

As always, I also am grateful to my own inspiration, my rock and my wings, my husband.

ABOUT THE AUTHOR

Judith Lynne writes rule-breaking romances with love around every corner. Her characters tend to have deep convictions, electric pleasures, and, sometimes, weaponry.

She loves to write stories where characters are shaken by life, shaken down to their core, put out their hand…and love is there.

A history nerd with too many degrees, Judith Lynne lives in that other paradise, Ohio, with a truly adorable spouse, an apartment-sized domestic jungle, and a misgendered turtle. A past writer of SF and screenplays, she pens Regency romances of love you can believe in, with a rich sense of place and time.

If you enjoyed this book, help keep them coming - share a review at your favorite bookstore, Bookbub, or Goodreads!

Sign up for the author's newsletter, including exclusive book news and sneak peeks,
at judithlynne.com.

ALSO BY JUDITH LYNNE

Lords and Undefeated Ladies

Not Like a Lady

The Countess Invention

What a Duchess Does

Crown of Hearts

He Stole the Lady

No Titled Lady *Series prequel*

Maids Done Waiting

The Lord Trap

The Lady Escape *Forthcoming*

Cloaks and Countesses

The Caped Countess

The Clandestine Countess

The Castaway Countess *Forthcoming*

Ladies' Own Bakery

Ladies' Own Bakery Season One: The Collected Episodes

Ladies' Own Bakery Season Two: The Collected Episodes